Love and
Student Loans
and Other
Big Problems

A Novel

ISBN: 1497405076
ISBN 13: 9781497405073
Library of Congress Control Number: 2014905864
CreateSpace Independent Publishing Platform
North Charleston, South Carolina

Published in the United States by Melissa Stacy.

Cover design by Beth McMacken, Athena Communications.

Ebook design by 52 Novels.

To all of the people
      who take care of their families
      nursing, cooking, scrubbing, and loving
      making ends meet
      keeping faith, keeping hope.

And to all of the people
      who donate money to schools
      so that kids who grow up in poverty
      have a shot at a dream.

This book is for you.

CONTENTS

Title Page   i
Copyright   ii
Dedication   iii

1 Change of Plans   1
2 The Cowboy   11
3 A Horse Named King   21
4 Property Tax   29
5 The Fathead Situation   37
6 Tangential at Best   49
7 My GPA Sucks   61
8 The Dead Woman from Idaho   67
9 Candy Man Cadillac   75
10 Happy Garden   87
11 Toothache   97
12 The Taliban   105
13 Carver Greyson   117
14 Mark Twain   127
15 Real Culture   135
16 You Two Boys   151
17 The Grizz   161
18 The Rules of the Game   171

19 Dancing   179

20 Hole-in-the-Wall   193

21 Purple Is a Religion   203

22 Baseball   215

23 That Other Him   225

24 Expectations   233

25 Dark, Secret Places   247

26 Grace   261

27 Twenty-five Cents   269

28 Aw, Chuckwagon!   281

29 Love   295

30 Battle   307

31 Wildfire   313

32 The Human Condition   323

33 Waves in a Storm   331

34 The Wrong Question   339

35 Split Open   349

36 Flying   359

37 Splits-Ville   367

38 Silence and Magic   379

39 An Act of Precision   387

40 Heroes and Risk   401

41 Skin Deep   411

42 The Thing About Babies   423

43 Resistance Poetry   437

44 A New Dream   447

45 Abigail's Ring   457

46 Nine Weeks in Nairobi   463

47 Bad Luck   475

48 Special Agent Ghorbani   489

49 Wins and Losses   499

50 A Parade of Pure Noise   505

51 Madness   517

52 My Gremlins   531

53 Getting There   541

54 Dreaming Again   553

Acknowledgments   561

About the Author   565

CHANGE OF PLANS

I hoped having a diploma printed in Latin would make me feel better about being broke, but I only wished I knew Latin. A speedy end to this graduation ceremony would also be nice. But the final speaker today was in love with his voice, and he droned along like a turboprop passing by overhead. I glanced at my diploma again.

It was a pretty certificate, printed on heavy cream cardstock in a small matte leather case, custom-made for my university in a nice shade of red. I touched the signatures at the bottom and read the words *Artium Baccalaurreatum*. Bachelor of Arts.

Above that was my name: *Mary Jane Logan*. History major now in need of a job.

When the speech finally ended, I threw my cap with the others and did my best to look happy, but I wished I could turn back the clock and be a freshman again.

Whenever I'd imagined this day, I had always looked joyful. Triumphant. My best friend and I posed in pictures together, pigged out on cookies and sandwiches, and hugged our professors goodbye.

In reality, I didn't even attend the reception. I had no family here to take pictures, and I couldn't bear to think about how much I missed Hanna.

Hanna. My Hanna. Who should have been here beside me, with her own diploma in hand.

So I left as I'd come, too lonely and empty to keep faking a smile. I took off my gown and walked back to my room. I kept trying to find a way to overcome grief: with gratitude, with acceptance, with internal peace. But those tactics were failing me this time around. In five months of grappling my sense of loss over Hanna, I had lost every battle, and today was no different.

Before she died, Hanna told me, *Don't cry, Mary Jane. I hate seeing you cry.* She wasn't just my best friend. She'd been my inspiration, my safe harbor, my rock in the storm. All of my Big Dreams for my life had been wrapped up with her.

I wanted to film documentaries, and Hanna wanted to act, and we both wanted to learn more about African history. So we'd come up with a film project called *Brighter Than Stars*. We had planned to film people in Africa talking about their countries and the journeys they've taken from imperialism to independence, and overlay those narratives with a history lesson on each place. It would be like a Ken Burns film or Fred Hampton's *Eyes on the Prize*. I loved the hell out of Ken Burns and *Eyes on the Prize*. I wished I could spend my whole life on history projects like that.

But Hanna's cancer and death had changed all my plans, and I had other priorities now.

I tossed my gown in a trash can, entered my building and climbed the stairs to my dorm. I signed the paperwork on the desk that said I was leaving my room in good order. No damage to the furniture, no marks on the walls. Floor swept, window shut, lights off.

Then I took my diploma, my backpack of clothes and all three of my quarters, and this time, I walked to the main road out of campus. I was glad it was May, and the weather was warm. I would get home to the kids faster if the sunshine held out. I had sent them the last of my money six days ago—along with a promise to see them right after I had my diploma. But I was in Pennsylvania, and they were in Colorado, and it would take me at least three days to get home.

I placed my bag at my feet and stuck out my thumb.

I have been warned at least three thousand times not to hitchhike. People liked to remind me I'd end up raped by a psycho and carved into pieces. But I followed two important rules when I bummed for rides:

1. I *never* thumbed on interstates or highways that gave me the willies, and

2. I carried a gun.

Not a big gun. It was a nickel-plated .22 Magnum, with six rounds in the cylinder and a wood grip. When I was sixteen years old, I fell in love with a boy who gave me a diamond ring and a handgun, and while I gave him the ring back, the pistol I kept.

I taught myself how to shoot in the usual way, with a bunch of aluminum cans and a fence post. I propped an empty can on the fence and stepped three feet away, aimed and fired. It's hard to miss anything from that distance. The next can I shot from four feet away, and then five feet, and then six, all the way back until the point where I couldn't hit the target anymore. When I take aim at anything now, I mentally pull the object closer to me, like when I learned how to shoot, and I can hit any mark.

I have never needed this gun in all the years I've been hitch-hiking, which meant I had a few lucky stars. I called my .22 Ravi, after the Sanskrit word for the sun, since learning to shoot was a bright spot in my life. I wished I could have kept that boy's ring as well as his pistol, but I had a few lucky stars, not a ton.

I also wished I wasn't hitchhiking home. And not just because thumbing for rides was Pure Suck. I really wanted to be moving off to a city and finding a job. I wanted to drive my own car and have the money for lattes, and some free time at night to try to follow my dreams. That's why I'd gone out and earned this diploma. I thought I could escape the Place with No Hope.

But my twelve-year-old brother had called me last month in tears, and Ethan never called me when he was crying. Mom's unemployment was gone and she was hiding in the basement again, which was Mom's way of dealing with life when life got too hard.

Sometimes it was great when Mom hid in the basement, since she was a superstar in the ranting and raving department. When she was down in the basement, no one had to listen to her. But it could also be scary when Mom went into hiding and there wasn't a parent around. And since my rageaholic brother, Landon, had moved home last month, and decided to camp out in the living room with his rageaholic girlfriend, things were crazy.

I was the middle child of seven, with three above me, three below. I'd been the runt of the litter before the second trio was born, which meant my three older half-brothers had made me a scrapper. Spitting and fighting were the backbone of my childhood. After my father died and Mom remarried, my older brothers mellowed out. They were too obsessed with drugs and alcohol by then to care much that Mom had three more kids after me. Mom didn't care too much, either. She was sick of being pregnant by then, and had her tubes tied. She called that operation the happiest day of her life. But that was a lie. The happiest days of her life all happened before she had kids. Once the babies came along, her whole world fell apart, which was why she was such a superstar in the ranting and raving department.

Landon was the oldest, four years older than me, and he never laid a hand on the others when I was around. But while I'd been in college, he'd gotten worse with his rages. That was why Ethan had called me in tears. And that was why I was on my way home.

I knew what I'd find at the house: a big mess. And five days of hitchhiking didn't help matters much. By the time I arrived home, I hadn't eaten anything in two days but what I could bum from my rides, which had been a bag of pork rinds, some licorice, and a can of smoked salmon. The kitchen cupboards were empty. I'd landed smack at the bottom of what was my life, though at least I still had those three quarters. There was always some hope if I had coins in my pocket.

My younger brothers and sister were as hungry as I was— except my two younger brothers were old enough now to have jobs. They worked bussing tables at The Sambino Café, which meant they had at least eaten lunch, lucky dogs.

"All right," I said, "hand over your money." I thought we'd at least scrape up enough to buy a package of rice or maybe a sack of potatoes. But my brothers had already spent their tip money on candy. Go figure.

I rubbed my hands together and tried to think. Who did I know who could feed us? Someone who'd be home at seven o'clock at night and wouldn't mind missing groceries, which was not the easiest combination to come up with.

"Let's go over to Beth's," I said, and the four of us headed off on foot across town.

My family lived in the San Juan Mountains, a range of the Rockies in southwest Colorado. Our home was in Goldking, which was actually a really great town, outside of the fact that the climate was Arctic Tundra and there was no economy in the winter. The mainstay of survival in Goldking was that old standby, vodka, because no one knew how to live through freezing conditions and poverty better than Russians.

Hard as it was here in the winter, the San Juan Mountains were beautiful. They surrounded the valley of Goldking like the peaks of a crown, tall and magnificent and breathtaking. This time of year, they were still capped in snow, and the aspen were budding spring leaves. I loved Colorado, and I really loved the San Juans. I always felt my spirits lift when the mountains filled the sky like old friends. I didn't even mind being hungry so much, when I could take in the view. We lived above nine thousand feet, and the summits around us were close to fourteen. The only way out of this town was up.

Goldking had four hundred people who lived here year-round, but a whole nation of folks who came to visit each summer. Tourists rode the narrow gauge railroad or drove their RVs from Texas, snapping pictures of wildflowers and tooling around on old mining roads. But when the train stopped running after the first of November, Goldking went back to looking like a ghost town again, with our Main Street boarded up and plywood nailed over the windows, nothing but eight feet of snow and bottles of vodka, and occasionally some reject hippies from Aspen who came to ski and smoke pot. Those were the folks my mom liked the best, the hippies with pot. It wasn't for nothing she named me Mary Jane.

Beth Brighton was a pretty nice lady, in her late sixties and retired from teaching. I knew she'd have a sack of rice in her cupboard and some giant cans of baked beans, because Beth was a Mormon and always prepared for the Rapture. This meant she kept food stockpiled in her basement the way rednecks stashed guns. One of the biggest benefits of the LDS Church was being taught to plan ahead for when the shit hit the fan, which, let's face it, you can pretty much count on in life.

I took an alley to Beth's house and the kids followed in silence, so I asked Richard, the oldest, how school had been going.

"I'm learning nuclear physics," he said, which sounded impressive for eighth grade. I might have been excited to hear this, except I knew this was not schoolwork. This was just Richard reading a book about nuclear physics. He did jack in the classroom, which I was aware of because his teachers called me long distance to complain. They never called Mom because she'd just yell, "*Fascists!*" and hang up. Mom thought school-teachers were all Supreme Fascists, and referred to civilization as the Ultimate Buzzkill. It was not the healthiest outlook on life, to be sure.

"How about you, Mia?" I asked my sister. "How's school?"

"I hate it," she said, which was not news to me. Mia had always loathed school. If I tried to tell her about kids in other countries who were forced into slave labor, or selectively starved to death because they were female, appealing to logic to convince her how lucky she was, Mia would remind me that school was a prison and that I could shut up. She was in the sixth grade and therefore smarter than everyone, and to top it off her best friend was shallow and catty, though Mia's choice of phrase right now was to call her an ass-munch.

"Enough with the language," I said, reminding her she couldn't talk like that around Beth.

I turned to Ethan and asked, "How's track?"

Ethan was the only one who did his homework and played sports—track and basketball—and he kept a box of candy, mostly Airheads and jawbreakers, stashed under his bed in a shoebox. Ethan knew how to plan ahead, which was a rare skill in our family.

"Track is good," he said, and then he asked me if I was done with college.

"I've even got this to prove it," I said, and I stopped to take my diploma out of my pack. Richard and Ethan tried to read it, looking puzzled, but Mia only raised an eyebrow.

"What does that say?" she asked.

"It says I owe money," I told her, so Mia nodded sagely and said, "Figures."

Ethan thrust the diploma back into my hands. "Did you bring us presents?"

"Hmmm…" I said, stalling for time, and then I remembered the three quarters in my pocket. "Actually, I did."

I told them to close their eyes, and then I handed each of them a quarter.

"Is this one of those investment lectures again?" Richard asked.

"Oh my *God!*" Mia shouted. "I do *not* want to hear about *compound interest right now!*"

"Chill," I said. "We're paying the water bill tomorrow, that's all." I'd seen the red notice taped to our door. We owed ninety-three fifty or the pipes would be shut off, and having seventy-five cents was a good way to start.

"We are *always* paying that *stupid* water bill," Mia said. "We should just dig a well and tell the city to fuck off."

"Language," I sighed, and Mia rolled her eyes one more time. "And Goldking's a *town*, not a city," I added, "So we would have to tell the *town* to F-off." Mia shot me a look, but then cracked a smile. She put her head in my armpit, so I'd have to keep walking with my arm on her shoulders.

As long as we were together, I thought that we'd be okay. Because my family lived within one law of the universe: Entropy Happens. Things break down, fall apart, crumble into disorder. We'd never really been a functioning system, but our general decline was speeding up lately.

Not that I needed any more guilt trips about leaving my family and going to college. I lived with that guilt every day. And it sucked. But no one earned a diploma without some kind of sacrifice, and mine had been spending time away from the kids.

I'd still done a lot for my family, even while I'd been at school. All of my student loan money had gone to pay the property tax, utility bills, and other essentials in Goldking. I'd always known there were more important things in life than driving a car and spending money on lattes, and the kids meant more to me than chasing after a dream.

But I was still wracked by the idea that I was a failure. Because after four years in college, I was back at Square One.

No money, no job, no prospects.

And now I needed to pay back my loans. And keep the kids out of foster care. And keep reminding myself that this wasn't—this *couldn't*—be the end of my road. I still had my dreams, and

9

I wanted to follow them. But that one little word—*failure*—was killing something inside me. And the more I dwelled on my life, the more I felt myself dying.

I was at the most dangerous place I had come to so far. This was the scariest Square One I had landed on yet.

But I couldn't tell the kids that. I lived in a delicate balance between grit and denial, which had always been my two home-boys of survival. Grit and denial hadn't let me down yet. But I supposed there was a first time for everything.

2

THE COWBOY

When the kids and I arrived at Beth's house, she was not exactly happy to see us. Not that I blamed her. She knew we were only coming over to deplete her stockpile of food, but she still let me make a pot of rice and a dish of baked beans. I grilled up the onions and peppers and hamburger she had in her fridge. Beth watched me the whole time, scowling, while the kids washed their hands and set the table.

"Did you actually get a diploma?" Beth asked, and I motioned to Richard to take it out of my pack. He handed the diploma to Beth.

"Well, look-it this," she said. "And here I thought you'd never finish."

"Me neither," I joked, though that was a lie. I had always seen myself graduating. On the same day as Hanna.

"And your black friend, she died?" Beth asked. I cringed at the term *black friend*. Even though Beth had met Hanna—numerous times—I didn't try to correct her anymore and make her use Hanna's name. Beth let my family come over and eat up her food, and I had accepted by now that I couldn't change her.

"Yeah, Hanna died," I said. "Christmas morning."

Beth seemed surprised. "I thought you missed school." She put a lilt to her voice that made it sound like a question.

I tried to tell her, "I did," but choked on the words. I almost started to cry, right into the beans I was stirring. Then I took a deep breath and pulled it together.

I'd missed a lot of class this past winter and fall, while Hanna received her final round of chemo. Both her parents had died a long time ago, so she'd stayed with her aunt in Cincinnati for treatment, and that was where she'd been when she learned the cancer was terminal.

But I couldn't talk about any of this. Not out loud. I'd start weeping. Beth didn't care, anyway, about my best friend or my life. She was only asking me questions to do right by the Lord, and that meant looking out for all God's heathen children. Beth liked that phrase. Since I've worshipped in temples, mosques, synagogues, stupas, and churches, I really was a heathen, so I didn't mind the moniker.

"Tell me how things have been," I said, changing the subject, and allowed Beth to talk. She shared the latest gossip in Goldking, and then she talked about her health problems, and she talked about a stray cat she'd taken in that was hiding upstairs. She sat down to eat with us and talked straight through dinner, and then she talked while I washed the dishes and Richard wiped down the table, and when we finally headed out the back door, Beth was still talking. She was so happy we'd listened the whole time that she invited us all over for supper tomorrow, because she was addicted to talking now and just wanted to keep doing it. So I told her sure, we'd come over, and then I walked home with the kids in silence.

It was dark now, and cold, and Richard wanted to go into a canyon and shoot Ravi in the moonlight.

"No," I said. "You have school in the morning. And we've got to pay the water bill before I waste all my ammo."

I sensed by this point that the kids were really hating my guts. Not only had I made them put up with Beth Brighton for three hours, but I was going to force them to go to school in the morning. I could feel their glares on my skin like a bombardment of pebbles. I was sympathetic to their plight and wished things could be better, but then I thought of how much I missed Hanna, and why she wasn't here with me now, walking home with my family and cracking a joke. She'd have said to let Richard shoot my gun and let the kids skip tomorrow, and I suddenly felt so exhausted, it was all I could do not to lie down in the alley and sleep in the dirt.

"Mom's awake," Ethan said, and I glanced up at the house. Sure enough, the basement light was on. Mom smoked pot in the basement so the cops wouldn't catch her. She taped construction paper over the two cellar windows, but when the light was on, the windowpanes had a faint glow.

Outside of her brief dating spells, Mom liked being alone. She'd decorated the basement with white furniture and pink pillows, and the ceramic fairies she found at yard sales. The cellar was her safe haven, where she insisted that threats like al-Qaeda terrorists, collection agencies, and Sarah Palin couldn't reach her.

I loved my mom. God, how I loved her. But she was a force of the universe, not unlike radiation. Taken in small doses, she was no more harmful than the atmosphere or an x-ray. But she also had the power to fry my self-esteem like a warhead. Given how lowly I felt at the moment, I hoped she stayed in the basement tonight.

The kids knew they could appeal to our mother to get out of school, or anything else that required alarm clocks. When I wasn't home, the kids went to school when they felt like it, which amounted to either rarely or sometime after ten. As school actually started at eight, they knew I was planning to wake them up after seven.

I heard Richard take a breath, probably to tell me they could sleep in, so I dug deep and said, "Give me a couple of days, and I'll buy us an Xbox."

"Fine," Richard said.

I didn't have the money for an Xbox, of course. I'd make the boys save up their tip money and paychecks to buy one. But I couldn't tell them that. That wasn't how this game worked. If you wanted to live with denial, you had to follow the rules, and since denial was my homeboy, I always made it past go.

When we trooped up the back stairs and walked into the kitchen, I discovered that Landon was home. He was in the living room, probably drinking Jack with his girlfriend.

Landon was the meanest of all my half-brothers. Technically, Richard and Ethan and Mia were my half-siblings as well, but I never thought of them that way. Landon was different though, because he was an asshole. Plus, his girlfriend hated my guts. She called me a loser and tried to shove me sometimes, because I had too much pluck for her liking. I was not in the mood to see them tonight.

I avoided opening the door of the living room for this reason, and sent the kids upstairs. I washed the dishes piled in the sink for ten minutes, and then went to check that the kids had crawled into bed. They must've been feeling sorry for me, because Mia was already sleeping, and Richard and Ethan weren't far off.

I went back downstairs and finished the dishes. I opened a tub of Folgers coffee but found it was empty. Landon's girlfriend, Janine, walked into the kitchen.

"Fuck," she laughed when she saw me. Then to Landon, she called, "Your fucking *sister* is home."

Janine's eyes turned to slits while she smoked. She flicked ash into a can on the table and grinned at Landon when he came into the kitchen.

"How'd you get here?" he asked.

"Airline ticket," I said. "Special deal."

"Seen Tom yet?" he asked.

Tom was the neighbor who lived across the hill from our house. He was seventy-five and a complete letch. Of course I wouldn't go over and see him. But Tom had promised Landon he'd pay for a new truck if Landon helped him hook up with me. The whole situation was gross.

I took one of the jackets off the hat rack and said, "Later," and then I hurried outside and walked down the alley. Landon and Janine wouldn't follow me, and I couldn't sleep in the house with them there. Janine would try to pour pee on me, or some other prank, and then I would blow her head off and be sentenced to prison. So I left.

I walked across town to the Cowboy's house. I passed a few ramshackle places, and then a couple of well-kept homes owned by people who were not alcoholics. When I reached the bridge, I watched the river a minute. Then I kept walking and found myself at the Cowboy's place, and I slipped in the back door without knocking.

The Cowboy still lived with his parents, but only because Goldking was expensive. Lots here now ran half a million dollars or more, even if the property on them was condemned. The Cowboy's parents had bought a second place in Riverdale ten years ago, so they were hardly ever around. As soon as I walked in the house, I smelled blood, and when I rounded the corner to enter the workroom, I found the Cowboy butchering a deer.

"MJ!" he said when he saw me, and he ran toward me a moment, and then jumped to the sink to wash the blood off his hands. "When'd you get home?"

"Tonight," I said. "Landon was there."

The Cowboy scowled. "That asshole," he said. "His father kick him out again?"

I shrugged to let him know that was my guess. Landon was twenty-six and usually lived in a trailer with his father, a man named Duck McAffie. I had no idea why anyone would name a child Duck, but that guy was a hard-ass and drank like a miner. Whenever he lost his temper and threw Landon out, my brother went to stay with Mom.

My other two older brothers kept their distance. Their dad was in Louisiana somewhere, though he mailed Jeff and William money sometimes. William lived with his girlfriend, and Jeff was single and gay. They were both here in Goldking, but their crowd didn't put up with straight-edgers like me. Having fun meant drunk driving and herpes, and anyone who didn't see it that way was stuck up. So I had one friend in town my own age for this reason, and when he'd finished washing his hands, he tore off his wet apron and hugged me. Under the stronger scent of the blood, the Cowboy smelled like cedar smoke and wood chips, same as always.

"Did you eat yet?" he asked, and I told him of course. He walked to the kitchen and passed me a can of Mountain Dew from a six-pack. The Cowboy drank caffeine and did not go to church, which was enough for his relatives to call him a Jack Mormon. His real name was David Kimball, but he was the Cowboy to me. He'd known me since my father moved to Goldking eight years ago.

I had moved around a lot as a kid, though I'd mostly grown up in Alabama and South Carolina. I'd gone to high school in Illinois. When I was fourteen, Dad tried to save me and the kids from life with Mom. He'd brought us all to Goldking that summer, to give us a Real Home and keep us from living like gypsies. I worked bussing tables, and when I met the Cowboy, it was love at first sight.

But Dad died three months later, and I'd moved the kids to Illinois and rejoined our mom. Each time I came back to Goldking to visit, I spent time with the Cowboy, and when my mother relocated here four years ago, he'd been ecstatic. He wanted to marry me, but as I've already said, I gave the ring back.

The Cowboy ached for a family. He wanted a wife, and he wanted young children to bounce on his knee, and I'd known before I'd met him that I was too wild and too broken for that. My childhood had been consumed with motherhood duties, and the last thing I wanted was to repeat the whole process. Another woman would love him and give the Cowboy a family. I'd made my peace with him years ago over that.

We were both twenty-two, which felt unspeakably old, as I thought I would know something by now. I thought I wouldn't feel like a failure. But I'd never felt farther from all of my dreams.

We went to the back porch and sat on the step. I stared up at the stars and the peak of Kubla Khan, with the snow past the tree line glowing blue in the moonlight.

"How was her funeral?" the Cowboy asked.

"Terrible," I said. "Worst funeral ever."

My Hanna had died in small pieces. First her fingers and toes, and then both arms and legs. The rest of her body had shut down in stages. Her mind went dark, and her heart kept on beating. That organ did not yield to death lightly.

Don't cry, Mary Jane.

But I still started to cry. I wiped my eyes though, and kept my voice steady.

"Her aunt buried her," I said. "In Ohio."

"Thought she wanted cremation," said the Cowboy.

"She did. But her aunt, you know." I took a deep breath. "That's how it goes."

The Cowboy swigged his Mountain Dew. "That's how it goes."

He took my hand in his and followed my gaze to Kubla Khan's peak. I could see my breath in the air, pale silver and white. "So who hit the deer?" I asked.

"Guy from Riverdale," he said. "Jim called me to come get it." Jim was Jim Kimball, the Cowboy's brother. He was one of the two police officers in town.

"I want to be cremated," I said. "If my mom buries me, come find me and fix it."

"All right," said the Cowboy, and I knew that he would. He'd do anything I asked because he loved me that much.

From the front of the house, I heard a vehicle pull up. Pop music blared on the radio.

"*David!*" a girl squealed, and the front door was thrown open. "You in here??"

The Cowboy jumped up and called, "B! I got a deer back here!" But then I heard the girl scream, which meant she'd arrived in the workroom. The Cowboy tried to head her off, but she reached the back porch to find me.

Her name was Bree Taylor, and I was as surprised to see her as she was to see me. Bree had been cruel to the Cowboy when they'd been in high school. He'd told me the stories. And now she was showing up at his house, probably trying to date him.

"Hi, Bree," I said. "You look good."

She wore a pair of dark jeans with sequins, and enough makeup to resemble a layer of tree bark.

"What are you doing here?" Bree asked. "Aren't you in *college?*"

"I finished," I said.

"Where's that girl you hang out with?" Bree charged. "You know who I mean."

I handed the Cowboy my can of Mountain Dew. "I gotta get going," I said. He took the soda from me, looking devastated, so I slapped him once on the shoulder. He knew I couldn't stand here and talk about Hanna with Bree Taylor, so he didn't try to stop me from leaving. "Take care, Bree," I added, and then I crossed the backyard and finished walking through town.

I arrived at the river again and stood on the bank, watching the snowmelt rush by, and then I headed to the pasture where Don Doonan kept the horses.

I needed to go break some rules.

3

A HORSE NAMED KING

Don Doonan had lived in Goldking all his life, and he owned some nice pasture near town. Don was also the caretaker for five horses that belonged to a man named Will Powers. Will used the horses for hunting every fall, and he'd given me permission to ride them whenever. Will was a really good guy. Don, however, was a curmudgeon. He'd forbidden me to ride Will's horses, not because he worried I'd hurt them (cause I wouldn't), but simply because he was a control freak. Don was just all-round ridiculous. Those horses loved running free, and so did I. We were buddies that way.

Will had even given me a legal document to prove I had permission to use his horses. But Don always claimed I was breaking the law, and he thought yelling at me would make me stop riding them.

I still rode Will's horses though, and Don could call me a horse thief all he wanted.

When I arrived at the pasture, I climbed through the fence and heard hoof beats approaching, so I tore off toward the creek that ran through the field.

Ever since I was little, I've loved messing with horses. Not just riding them, but squirreling around. If I'd been smarter about it, I'd have been a trick rider, and then I might have a job for myself now and some kind of future. As it was, I simply had King coming after me, a Quarter Horse roan named after the town. I knew King could smell me, and he definitely smelled the two carrots from Beth's house I had stashed in my pocket.

King pounded along at my heels with a lope like a thunderclap, and I jumped the creek and raced up the hillside away from him.

"King!" I yelled, laughing. "Go away!" But of course I wanted him to keep chasing me, and he did. We went all over the pasture, while the other four horses continued to stand around, snorting. They weren't as keen on carrots as King was. But King always chased me, even when I didn't have produce.

When I'd had enough running, I stopped and King slid to a halt. I hopped on his back and we rode to the gate. I used to be able to jump the fence with him, but Don had raised it too high for safe jumping at night. So I had to open the gate and let us out.

"Let's ride to the mill!" I said, as if I could really control him. King went where he wanted without reins and a bridle. Sometimes I pressed my hands on his neck to direct him, but mostly I accepted his sense of adventure. Tonight, he listened to me and we headed off to the mill, which was a half-mile up the side of Kubla Khan.

I loved to sit a horse in a gallop, and at sixteen hands, King had some speed. He hadn't been run in a while, so he shot toward the old mine road like a race had begun. King had been raised to cut cattle, but it was all derby blood that ran through his veins.

There were several old mills you could see from Goldking's town limits, but the Caroline Mill was the nicest. It hadn't shut down until 1947, and it was so sheltered from avalanche by pine trees that it almost looked the way it had in the forties. The windowpanes were gone, and the interior was full of dust and old boards coming loose, but I could walk through the ore chute to access both floors. I had a favorite window I perched in when I wanted to sit by myself, and since King would crash through the beams, I gave him both carrots and told him to go home.

"Go home, King," I said, but he ignored me and grazed. I left him there and climbed up to my window.

The last time Hanna had come with me to Goldking, I'd bought us both Old West sheriff's badges with our names in gold plastic. In the end, Hanna had taken the badge with my name and told her aunt to bury her with it. Then Hanna had snapped hers apart and told me, *I want you to forget me. I want you to live.* She said I should go film *Brighter Than Stars* without her. She wanted me to find a new partner. *Don't you let me and this cancer stand in your way. I'm not scared to die. So throw that busted thing in the garbage, Mary Jane. It's trash now. You have to start over.*

I still had the pieces of her badge though, and I took them out.

I couldn't read her name in the darkness, but I felt the letters. The pin had broken loose when she'd snapped it, and I hadn't saved that section. I kept most of the star though, with its tiny spheres at the points, and I liked to assemble it and hold it in my left hand. Hanna had been left-handed. One of the ten thousand things I had loved about her.

I didn't think it was at all fair she was gone. I missed her so much that my whole body hurt. I felt like I'd been hit in the chest point-blank with a shotgun, but somehow kept moving without my lungs or my heart. There was a reason Butch Cassidy and Sundance had died together in Bolivia. Butch had been the dreamer and Sundance the gun, and there was no life for either man without the other beside him. But my best friend was gone, and I wasn't allowed to go with her. All I wanted to do was just sit here and cry.

I had pushed myself so hard all my life. Neither one of my parents had finished high school, but I had. With honors. I'd always been placed in the advanced classes, with students who talked about going to college—so I decided to copy them. I saved every penny to take the SAT and apply to six different schools, and I made it. I was accepted to college, and finished. But now I felt more desperate than I had back in high school. I wanted so badly to break out of poverty. To rescue my family, to make sure the kids finished high school. I'd always made sure they had food, running water, blankets and beds. But now the cupboards were empty, the utility bills weren't being paid, and I couldn't take out more student loans. I needed money, and I needed it badly. I'd have to find a job here in Goldking. Washing dishes, waiting tables, cleaning hotel rooms… those were the jobs that existed in this town.

I felt so ashamed of myself. To have a college degree, and be faced with those facts. The word *failure* pounded through my brain like a drumbeat. I started to cry like I had at the Cowboy's, but this time, I couldn't stifle my tears. I clutched Hanna's broken badge in my fist until I heard a piece crack.

I wished Hanna had not died of cancer. I wished the one person I needed was still here.

It took me a long time, sitting there, to find my backbone again. Between grit and denial, grit was the harder to come by these days. Since Hanna had died, I struggled to keep up my steel. I had to dig deeper and deeper to find it.

I told myself I'd survive this. Whatever it took, I'd make it somehow. Hanna would've said the same thing, if she'd been here. Her childhood had mirrored mine in so many ways. She'd known what it meant when your parents couldn't hold down a job, when your family sometimes lived in a car because they couldn't pay rent. The kids had never been homeless, and I wanted to keep it that way. There were some memories that haunted you no matter how hard you tried to escape them, and living in a car with Mom and my three older brothers had terrified me as a child. It wasn't until Mom had met the kids' dad, a man named Dole Preston, that we stopped living in that old Chevy. But the year we spent in a car had almost ruined my family, had almost broken us up forever. It was also the reason my three older brothers had dropped out of school, and why I was so worried that Richard, Ethan and Mia might end up the same way.

I didn't want the kids to end up like Landon. Unemployed. Lost. Full of rage. Landon had given up on himself. So had Mom. And everyone else in our family. The kids were reaching that crossroads right now. Richard was almost finished with middle school, but he had arrived at the point where dropping out of school sounded like a good plan. He'd started mouthing off to his teachers about it. *I don't have to do what they say—I'll just drop out and do nothing.* That was the Anthem of Losers, right there. All over America, kids were singing that song. Most of them ended up trapped, struggling in every way people could struggle in life.

I knew that if Richard dropped out of school, Ethan and Mia would do the same. It was why the word *failure* pounded so loud in my head. Because not only had *I* not escaped the Place with No Hope, but the kids might not, either.

And that hurt worse than anything. I'd never wanted that for those kids. I had spent so many hours with bottles and diapers and burping and thumb-sucking… watched first steps and first words and spent hours potty training… taught them to read in kindergarten, to ride bikes… And I was going to fuck-all kill myself if they turned out just like Landon. I had wasted my entire life if that happened.

I wasn't sure I could force the kids to finish high school and get their diplomas.

But I damn sure planned to try.

I dried my face with my coat sleeve, and then I dozed for a while. When I opened my eyes, the eastern sky was deep green, and King was still grazing nearby. The valley was beautiful, a dark shade of blue. I returned Hanna's badge to my pocket, and then I walked down the ore chute and stood next to King. I leaned my face on his neck.

I was so grateful King was here. It was such a relief he had stayed at the mill, even though I'd sent him away. He was one of those lucky stars in my life.

"I need some coffee," I said, and he snorted. King pawed the earth as if to say, *Coffee's for wimps*. He wanted to run.

So I climbed on his back and we started down the mountain. I felt pretty groggy but King was a bundle of energy, and once we were on flat ground again, he took off at a gallop through the streets of Goldking.

King loved dusty dirt roads, and this town had plenty. We passed by the trailer where Landon's dad lived, and we passed several old shacks where some hippies grew pot, and then we cut through an alley where a bunch of Presbyterians lived. Mom attended the Baptist Church in town when she wanted religion, and she didn't care much for the Presbyterians in Goldking. The Poindexter Pinheads, she called them. I liked the Presbyterians though, mostly because they had potlucks on Sundays. I loved a good potluck.

The hardware store was open, so I knew it was at least five in the morning. The security light was still on at the grocer's. I didn't see either of the police in their Cherokees. King took us outside of town again, to the other end of the valley, where the Visitor's Center and Mining Museum were located. King cut across the main road, making a sound like gunfire when his hooves struck the asphalt, and then he ran along through the ditch by the highway.

There weren't any cars for him to race at this hour, but I could tell he was happy just running. The *Welcome to Goldking* sign was still lit. We get a lot of hitchhikers through town on their way south to Riverdale, and I noticed some hobo had fallen asleep on a turnout. Then I saw something move near his body, like a marmot. I had King slow up and hopped down. Small animals near a body could mean this hobo was dead, or near dead, so I thought I should check on him.

The man heard King's hoof beats and raised his head off the ground, and I realized the animal hiding under the willow was simply a dog. His fur was colored like a marmot's though, a dark reddish-brown with gold highlights.

"Hey, fella," I said to the dog, and I knelt on the gravel as he made his way toward me. His fur was matted, but still soft in places. He licked my hand with enthusiasm.

"Nice dog," I said, and the man frowned and sat up. His eyes were bloodshot and he hadn't shaved in a while. Even ten feet away, I could smell whiskey on him.

"Ain't my dog," he said fiercely. "Guy in a pickup left him with me."

"Guy live here?" I asked.

"How in the hell should I know?" the man snapped. He rubbed the side of his head, winced, and then swore a few times.

"What's his name?" I asked.

"I don't fucking know!" the man bellowed. "Do I look like I have a dog?"

I chose not to answer this, and jumped back on King. "Well, good luck to you," I said, and nudged King with my heels. He started to trot, but I tugged on his mane and said, "King, *walk*," so he walked.

The dog followed us, wagging his tail. King turned and sniffed at his muzzle. The hitchhiker moaned and went back to sleep on the turnout.

I didn't have any food for a dog, but I didn't want to stop him from following us. King and I had to be better company than that old drunk he'd been left with.

"I need some coffee," I said. King whinnied and nodded his head a few times, and then he carried me over to God Save Me Liquors.

4

PROPERTY TAX

God Save Me Liquors was the only booze store in town, and it was owned by a man named Fred Murray. Fred had been involved with my mother two years ago. He'd even lived in our house for three months, though my sister had told me he'd mostly stayed in the basement.

Fred would give me some coffee, I bet. When I knocked on the door in back of the liquor store, where he had a small bedroom, Fred growled from inside, and then he opened the door to find King being nosey, trying to look in his house. Fred turned from the horse to the dog, and then me.

"It's a damn three-ring circus out here!" Fred shouted. He checked his watch, and I knew by the light in the sky it must be six. That was better than five, anyway.

"Hey, Fred. How are you?"

"Sleeping!" Fred said. "I was sleeping!"

"Yeah, well, I need a job," I said. "Water bill's due. I was hoping you could give me some coffee."

Fred disappeared, and when he returned, he shoved a tub of Maxwell House at me.

"Now get out of here!" and he slammed the door.

"Thanks, Fred!" I called, and then I started down the street toward home. King plodded along at my side, as well as the dog. He wagged his tail when I looked at him, and I wondered what I should name him. If I called him Gandhi, I could force Richard, Ethan, and Mia to read about Mohandas Gandhi and learn who he was. I could also make them watch the film from the library.

"Gandhi?" I tried, and the dog ambled toward me. I knelt and petted his head a few times. "Gandhi," I said, "that's going to be your new name."

Having settled the issue, I headed down the street again and, ten minutes later, I was home. King started to graze in the yard, and Gandhi followed me into the house. I walked into the kitchen and started the coffee pot. Then I turned on the radio to KTUR Rock, which was playing the Stones. I peeked into the living room, and saw Landon and Janine passed out on the couch. Janine was getting a beer gut. Her stomach bulged out over the top of her jeans, and she'd unzipped her pants before falling asleep. Landon was snoring. I tiptoed through the room and found a bag of potato chips, a sack of beef jerky, and pretzels. Gandhi watched from the doorway, and licked my pant leg when I returned to the kitchen. He followed me upstairs to wake Richard, Ethan and Mia.

"Hey, look who I found!" I told them. Each of them glanced at the dog and shut their eyes again, tight. They hated going to school.

Annoyed, I said, "Don't make me change my mind about that Xbox," which put life into Richard. Ethan muttered something, and Richard shook Mia until she lifted her head.

I left them alone and went back to the kitchen. I picked up a dishtowel and started cleaning the counters, scrubbing off the layers of food that covered everything. I checked the refrigerator again for a carton of eggs, but the shelves were still empty, except for a bottle of ketchup. There was also a squishy brown head of lettuce in the crisper, but I threw that away.

Mom appeared in the kitchen when the coffee was ready. Sometimes she slept in the den rather than down in the basement, which meant the aroma of coffee had woken her. She poured a mug for herself and took a seat at the table. She wore a pair of pink jeans, white pumps, and a sparkling purple t-shirt with fairies all over it. She'd tied a blue ribbon through her hair, and fluffed out her bangs. Dad had once said Mom had the black hair of a gypsy, but Landon's father thought she was Black Irish. She'd been born in West Virginia, left as a teenager and never looked back. She was a beautiful woman, as sleek as a dancer with a smile that still sparkled. All of her children had her dark hair.

"When'd *you* get home?" she asked.

"I came in last night," I said. "Took the kids out to dinner."

Mom sipped her coffee and tapped her nails on the mug. "Bring me anything?"

"Just what's on the table," I said, gesturing toward the jerky and chips from the living room. Landon would be pissed that I'd stolen his food, but he was such an incorrigible freeloader that I didn't feel guilty.

Mom picked through a bag on the table and selected a chip. "Why'd you chop off your hair?" she asked. "You look like a dyke."

I ran a hand through my hair, which covered the tops of my ears rather than the back of my neck. After Hanna had died, I'd been too depressed to keep my hair long, and I'd cut it short as a boy's in a fit of depression. It had grown out since then, like a strange jungle plant, so instead of a pixie cut, I now had a bob. Richard called it my Final Fantasy haircut. It didn't really look that bad. Mom just liked to rag on me.

"God gave you that face," she said, "and what do you do with it? Nothing. What a waste."

Mom had this idea that I should copy her lifestyle, and use the looks I'd inherited to win favors from men. She resented that she'd passed on her figure, her smile, and her silky black hair to a daughter who never took advantage of them.

I also had my father's smoky blue eyes and his height of five-ten, which had stretched me thin as Popeye's girlfriend and earned me the jeers of my classmates growing up. After someone's father called me "about as ugly as Olive Oyl" at a banquet for honor roll students in junior high, I finally realized that it didn't much matter that I had a bright smile or a face that landed some girls on magazine covers. I received the message from my peers and their parents loud and clear: pretty girls don't amount to much when they're poor. Especially when they sat with three toddlers at an eighth-grade awards banquet, without a parent in sight.

Being beautiful, in my life, was not a self-esteem builder. It only brought out the worst in the people around me—jealousy, animosity, constant bullying. And my mother's warped insistence that a girl's looks were her only valuable asset never made me feel any better. According to Mom, if I'd been born ugly, then maybe having a brain would have mattered. Maybe being a good athlete would have meant something.

Because pretty girls were supposed to flirt. And talk to boys. And be loved.

But being pretty had never brought me any of those things.

My brain and my prowess though—those had brought me respect, and dignity, and a sense of self-worth. Those were things that I valued. Whereas, being beautiful was a drag. I'd grown up a pariah, which was just life being mean. A cruel joke. Kind of like women like my mom having babies.

"I see the water bill's due," I said.

Mom's expression turned stony. "Vultures," she said, which was what she called everyone who worked for the government. The Vultures of Goldking were worse than the Fascists and Pinheads, because they demanded money from Mom, especially property tax.

We hadn't paid property tax for two years, which meant that our house was listed in *The Goldking Gazette*. With the accumulated interest, I thought we probably owed at least five thousand dollars. Maybe six.

My mother had never been good with money, which she blamed on her hatred of math, so saving up to buy real estate had never been possible. Her great-uncle had died four years ago and left Mom this house, and she'd already tried to mortgage it twice, mostly so she'd have money for pot. She also liked fixing martinis. Thank God a few moneylenders had decided she was too much of a credit risk and rejected her mortgage application, or we'd have been in real trouble.

I'd used half of my student loan money to pay the property tax during my first two years of college. But once the banks had run into trouble, I hadn't been able to borrow enough to keep up, and I worried that we might lose the house. In Colorado, someone could put a tax lien on the property, pay the taxes for three years, and then get the deed to the house. And since we were already two years behind with our payments, our time was running out.

"You know who's been paying the back taxes, don't you?" Mom asked. I shook my head no and poured a cup of coffee. "Tom Morbun," she said, and I felt my heart seize in horror.

Tom Morbun was the seventy-five-year-old neighbor who wanted to sleep with me. Sometimes he showed up at the doorstep with bouquets of pink roses, when I came home for Christmas or spent a summer in Goldking. The idea of paying off the back taxes to *him* left me feeling like I'd jumped in a snake pit.

I started chugging my coffee. I didn't have enough caffeine in my system to tackle this news.

"I'm sure he'd write off the money if you… *you* know," Mom said, and at the mention of sex with Tom Morbun, I poured another cup. The coffee burned my throat raw, and I coughed.

"No!" I gasped. "No *way!*"

The doorbell rang, and I glanced down the hall toward the door. I saw a bouquet of pink roses framed in the window.

I dashed up the back stairwell to hide. I refused to see or speak with Tom Morbun right now. If Mom wanted to answer the door, that was her problem. When I arrived in the main bedroom, Gandhi paced over to lick my hand.

"Who rang the bell?" Mia asked.

"Tom," I said. "With roses."

Mia made a horrified little sound, and then stifled it.

"Gross," Ethan muttered.

Richard said, "I see King in the yard."

I gazed out the window. "Yeah. We went to the Caroline Mill. Then we found Gandhi," and I patted the dog.

"Who was Gandhi, anyway?" Ethan asked. "I mean, I know he was on that money you gave me."

"The rupee," I said, and Ethan repeated the word *rupee* to himself. I had smuggled some rupees home from India after a semester abroad junior year, and handed them out to the kids last summer as presents. Ethan kept his in his shoebox. "Gandhi was a resistance leader. He took down the Raj."

"The nonviolence dude," Richard said, and I smiled. All the kids had good memories, even if they tried to deny it sometimes.

I said, "I thought we'd learn more about him."

Mia groaned in dismay. "Oh my God, not more *compound interest*—"

"Gandhi was a lawyer," I said, and Mia sighed in relief. "But he probably calculated interest in some of his court cases."

Mom appeared in the bedroom doorway and placed her hands on her hips. She tapped the toe of one shoe on the floor and cast me a pissed-off expression. "Tom would like to know if he can take you to breakfast."

I kept my voice neutral. "Why don't you go?" I suggested. "I've already eaten."

Mom's eyes flashed as she said, "You are a *mean* little *pill*. And that *horse* is out there in the yard again." She pointed at the window for emphasis.

"King's taking Mia to school," I said.

Mom left the room in a huff, and I listened to her heels clack-clack down the stairs.

"She is the only person who wears high heels in Goldking," Mia said.

I thought for a second. "Lots of girls here wear heels."

"I mean, around the house," Mia said.

Our mother was Prime Time, all right. She liked high heels and highballs and anything pink and sparkly. And marijuana, of course. Mom couldn't function anymore without hash.

It was too bad Tom Morbun didn't like to smoke weed. He had plenty of money to feed an addiction and sit around with Mom in the basement all day. But Tom abhorred drugs, alcoholics, poor people, and everyone in my family but me, and if we didn't get caught up with our taxes, Tom could end up with our house, which meant he had a powerful hold over me to get me to sleep with him. For a straight-laced Republican, he was one dirty bastard. Some rich men were ingenious at turning girls into prostitutes, but I was not going to end up as Tom's shady lady. He could promise Landon a truck and make insinuations to Mom all he wanted—Landon and Mom couldn't hold down a job, but I sure as hell could. And I would just cough up the money.

Of course, that was easier said than done. I'd need multiple jobs to get myself out of this mess. Good thing I had some caffeine in my system. Crawling my way off Square One was hard enough as it was.

5

THE FATHEAD SITUATION

I sent Richard downstairs to retrieve breakfast. Mia ate a few pretzels, while Ethan and Richard polished off the bag of jerky. By the time Tom Morbun left the house, the kids had fifteen minutes to walk to school. I carried an old nylon dog leash outside, and when I looped it around King's neck, he lowered his ears and bared his teeth at my arm. King hated halters, bridles, and saddles, but I wasn't scared King would bite me. He just liked to frighten people with those long teeth of his.

Once I had the leash around his neck and yelled, "Cut that out!" King shut his mouth, and I could toss Mia up on his back and walk to school with the kids. Gandhi came with us, of course.

"He seems like a really nice dog, for someone to just dump him," Mia said, watching him trot along beside King.

"I can't even remember the last time we had a dog," Richard said. "I think Burt died three years ago."

Burt had been a mutt Mia had found. He'd been hit by a car east of town, by some tourist in a Jeep gunning it out to his campsite. Even the memory of this upset Mia so much that I changed the subject.

"I'll probably get a job at The Caroline," I said, which was a restaurant in town named after the gold mine. Most restaurants in town were named after mines. The Caroline served the best burgers, and the heater never broke down. Tourists were always freezing when they stepped off the train, and finding a place with good burgers and heat made The Caroline popular.

I told the kids to come meet me for lunch, since all the students in Goldking were dismissed for lunch. The public school here was simply too small for a cafeteria.

After I dropped the kids off, I started toward Main Street and ran into Bree Taylor. She stood with a group of her old high school friends, smoking cigarettes. While the boys sported coats, the girls wore spaghetti-strap tank tops to look sexy and tough, as it was only about forty degrees. With the clouds coming in and the temperature dropping, I thought it would snow.

I waved to them, but they looked at me warily, so I decided to walk up with Gandhi and King and ask where they were working. It would be good to know who in town was still hiring. A lot of the grunt work could be done by illegals, but May was still the best time in Goldking to pick up a job.

A guy named Stoner Joe offered me a cigarette, which I took and pretended to smoke. I wasn't a smoker, but knowing how to fake smoke was a good skill to have. It was the one sure-fire thing I could do that always helped me—to the extent that I ever could—fit in.

I thanked Joe for the smoke and asked for the word around town. Joe told me The Caroline needed a dishwasher. Big Belle Blue also needed a waitress. Then I asked about Gandhi, if anyone in town owned the dog, but they all said no. They thought he belonged to the hobo asleep at the turnout.

"That guy is an asshole," I said. "It wasn't his dog."

I waited until the cigarette was gone and snubbed the butt in my fingers.

"Hey, MJ," Joe said. "Weren't you going to some Ivy League school?"

I smiled and said, "Sounds way too fancy for me." I hadn't attended an Ivy League school. I'd been to what people called a Little Ivy, but since Joe wouldn't know what that meant, I didn't see the point in acting conceited. Bree was shooting me daggers as it was.

"I'll see ya," I said, and I started on my way to The Caroline. I didn't know why the young adults in this town spent so much time near the school smoking cigarettes. I supposed they were too broke to get Wi-Fi, though they texted each other nonstop. There was another group of smokers who kept a turf near town hall, and they constantly texted the crowd by the school, mostly with updates from Main Street. This information might include who was driving by in a vehicle that second, where the two police Cherokees were at the moment, and where the next woodsie would be. Goldking was just full of excitement.

I didn't have time to ride King back to his pasture, so I walked him to The Caroline with me. I figured he'd stand around and graze in the side lot, which had two rusted old trucks and a broken-down ore cart. Don Doonan would probably have a shit-show when he found Will's horse at The Caroline, but I had bigger problems right now. And then there was Gandhi. He followed me inside, so as soon as Ellie saw me, she started yelling.

"Do *not* bring that *dog in here!*" Ellie shouted. "Get that animal *out!*" Her voice carried across the whole room, until even the tin ceiling shook. People eating eggs and hash browns at the bar cast me looks of annoyance. Ellie Miller was normally a fairly nice person, but then, I'd just let a dog follow me into the building.

"Now, Ellie," I said, trying to get her calmed down. "This old pup will only be here a minute. He was out with that hobo this morning."

"What hobo?" Ellie snapped. "You mean the guy at the turnout?"

"Yeah, that was him," I said. "This wasn't even his dog, so I took him in."

"I thought you were in school," Ellie said.

"I was, and I'm finished now. Joe told me you needed a dishwasher."

Ellie eyed the dog and glanced up at my face again. "I'd rather have you wait tables," which was her way of saying I was too pretty to waste in the kitchen.

I shrugged. I didn't feel up to waitressing. "Dishwashing's fine. Gandhi here can lay low in the alley." I thought it might be too cold to keep the kitchen door open, but I didn't know if Gandhi had the brains to hang out by the dish drain. If he was like most dogs, he'd want to wander around, and the Health Department didn't take kindly to finding dogs in the kitchen. So I figured he could sit in the alley, and I could toss him scraps on occasion. I couldn't leave him at home with Landon, of course, because Landon would kick him. Landon hated dogs.

Placated now, Ellie hired me, and then she introduced me to her other summer employees. There was a girl who was my age named Justice Garcia. Justice had graduated Colorado Plateau in April, which was the college in Riverdale. She'd gone to high school in California, some little town outside Sacramento, and was spending the summer in Goldking with her boyfriend.

"Congratulations," I told her when she said she had graduated. "What'd you major in?"

"Environmental studies," she said. "Psychology minor."

"Are you doing some work with land reclamation?" I asked.
I thought she might've studied mine clean-up in college.

"I don't know what I'll do," Justice said. "My boyfriend
wanted to live here, so I thought I'd ski this winter. Maybe get a
place in Ingot-Ville next year."

Goldking did not have a ski resort, but nearby Ingot-Ville
did. An ingot was a block of metal, like a bar of solid silver or
gold. When the mines in southwest Colorado had been oper-
ating, the bars of gold and silver they'd produced had been
shipped to the mint in Denver, which had led to all sorts of
stagecoach robberies and train heists and other shenanigans.
Everything that kept the Wild West so wild and interesting.

While Ingot-Ville had originally been just another mining
town in the San Juans, that community had recently developed
into a heartland of liberalism and condominiums, a place that
sold Starbucks coffee and boasted celebrity homes. A lot of
people in Goldking hated Ingot-Ville's pretentious McMansion
guts, and preferred the unpainted shacks and rampant alcohol-
ism that Goldking maintained. There were still plenty of poor
people in Goldking, and they were proud of that fact. The old
miners' war of who had more gold had become a philosophical
battle over pure authenticity. According to popular theory, if
the mines around here ever opened again, the men and women
of Goldking would pick up their hardhats and hustle to work,
whereas the California transplants of Ingot-Ville would simply
buy more electronics and jewelry and join the Sierra Club.

So it was anyone's guess how long Justice would last in this
town. Being a Californian and partial to Ingot-Ville, I decided

her chances weren't good. She might dump her boyfriend before the summer was over. Justice was kind-hearted and sweet, which was a red flag to me that she was too soft for this town. She'd either have to toughen up and get smart, or hit the road.

After meeting the cooks and telling Ellie's husband hello, I made my way to the kitchen. I put on an apron and began scrubbing pots. When I noticed Justice was crying at lunchtime, I assumed one of the locals had said something.

I tossed some bacon to Gandhi and asked her, "What is it?"

"Nothing," she said. She dried her eyes and left the pickup stand with two platters of burgers and fries. I glanced into the restaurant and saw a group of three men in her section who were yucking it up. By their oversized hats and belt buckles, I guessed they were Texans.

I hate it when people treat their waitress like crap. And I had a hunch that's what these guys were up to.

I took off my wet apron and walked toward them. Ellie shot me a look from the register, but went back to counting out change. Whatever was going on with these yahoos, she was already aware of it. And they must have pissed Ellie off, or she'd have said something to stop me.

One of the men whistled as I stepped toward their table. "Look at this *tall* drink of water!" he crooned. "You live here, sweetheart?"

"Sure do," I said.

"Year-round?" he asked.

Game for the accent, I said, "Reckon so." I could pull off Texas twang if I wanted to.

"Well what in the *hell* do you do in the *winter?*" he laughed. "How in God's name do you people survive?"

That was a popular question in Goldking. One most locals answered at some point. I glanced over at Justice, to gauge what the problem was, but she was crying again by the Coke machine.

"Where you all from?" I asked.

"Not *California!*" another man roared, which inspired more laughter.

In the San Juan Mountains, we had three groups of transplants: the people who came from back East, the people who fled tax and tax California, and then we had the hordes known as our summertime Texans. With so many liberals and hicks and Rust Belt deserters in one tiny place, people were bound to butt heads.

"What's wrong with California?" I asked.

"Nothing, unless you have to live there!" the man cried, slapping his hand on the table while his companions kept laughing. These guys were a regular comedy tour.

"You mind telling me, fellas, why your waitress is crying?"

"Could be she's got the brains of a *hamster*," one said.

"Could be she went to college to major in *waitressing!*" another chortled. "Guess she needed a four-year degree to learn how to write the word *cheeseburger!*"

"Or refill my beer!" laughed his buddy.

"Well, beer's a popular pastime in Goldking," I said, which made them yuck it up even more. "You boys come with me, and I'll show you what else is popular." I gestured for them to follow me, but only two of them stood. "Come on," I told the one in his chair. "You'll miss the surprise."

I could smile and wink at a man like a belle at cotillion, so after I sent that third bozo my *aren't-you-handsome!* grin, he lurched to his feet and followed his friends. I led them through the front door and onto the sidewalk. Then I stepped back inside and locked them out. I picked up the dry-erase board that Ellie used for the specials, and wrote *GET BENT, FATHEADS!!*

I slapped the sign against the front window, where they could all read it, and when they started raising hell and pounding the door with their fists, I yelled, "Hey, King!" through the window. King rounded the corner, snorting and pawing the sidewalk like he might bring the apocalypse, baring his teeth at the men with those wild eyes of his, and all three of them took off down the street.

King didn't like bullies, either. Another reason why we were buddies.

I unlocked the door and patted his neck a few times, and then I put the dry-erase board away. King trotted back to the side lot, and I crossed the room toward the kitchen. Ellie was grinning, and I slapped my hands like I'd thrown out the garbage. Justice came over and hugged me, and I said, "Just tell them you're still working on your degree when they ask. Then you don't have to deal with that stuff. Helps with tips, too."

"All right," she said. "Guess you can tell I've never done this before."

I shrugged to say it didn't matter. She'd been doing fine before the bozos showed up. "Just don't let them get to you," I said. "You can't pay attention to those Big City morons. They don't know what it means to live here," and I patted her shoulder and started back toward the kitchen.

"You grow up in the South?" someone asked. I stopped and glanced down at a table. I saw two men, both wearing khakis and dress shirts, which meant they weren't locals.

I turned to the one who had spoken. His skin carried a tan, the sort of uneven coloring that only came from the sun.

Stubble surrounded his jaw line, though I bet he had shaved since he woke up this morning. His pale silver eyes made me think of a leopard. He had a grin like the devil when the devil played poker.

"I lived in Alabama some," I said. "South Carolina. Indiana, Illinois… and here." I didn't mention Pennsylvania, where I'd gone to college. The guy might be a rust-belter, and I didn't want to stand here and talk about industry.

"We're from Texas," he said, motioning toward his companion, so I glanced once at his friend. But he didn't have silver eyes or a grin that was trouble, so my gaze shifted back to the speaker.

I had never seen a man who had so much muscle. Not slick like a bodybuilder, but layered for size. His shoulders were massive, like a wide slab of granite, and each of his arms had the girth of a cannon. I could see the swell of bone in his wrists, and the great knuckles in his hands, which he'd folded together while he leaned on the table. His mop of brown hair needed combed, not to mention a date with some scissors. I thought he was built like a bear, all meaty and thick and uncivilized. His smile and his eyes had the bright glow of mischief, and I had the strangest desire to take a step toward him.

"I, um…" I stammered, but then I fell quiet. I didn't know what to say. I wished he would speak again, because I liked the sound of his voice, but after a moment, it was clear he was waiting on me. I remembered the temperature had been dropping this morning, so I told him, "Stay warm." Then I went back to the kitchen.

Ellie's husband came up to me while I put on my apron. He was a bald little man, with a loud, booming voice. His real name was Chuck, but we all called him Warren. "Who are those two?" he asked.

I pushed my bangs from my eyes and turned on the sprayer. "I don't know. Just some Texans."

Warren crossed his arms like he didn't believe me, and he stared at the diners like he might guess their names. I glanced through the window and saw those two men were leaving.

"That big one looks familiar," Warren muttered. "I think he's been on TV."

"Really?" I said, though I wasn't paying attention. I was picturing that Texan's face again, and I blushed. Why hadn't I asked who he was? I acted so stupid sometimes. He would've told me his name, I felt sure of that. But instead I'd just stood there and gawked.

Warren snapped up a ticket, and then he turned to the grill and started fixing two Ruebens. He shouted something to me about baseball and football, and I thought I heard the word *basketball* once. He'd decided that the bear-man was an athlete, and that was why his face seemed familiar. Only Warren didn't even know which sport he might play, much less what team he was on. As I barely managed to watch the Super Bowl or the NBA playoffs, and I usually missed the first game of the World Series each year, I thought Warren's shouting about sports sounded nuts.

That bear-man had been handsome though, really handsome. It was rare for a man to land on my radar like that, because all growing up, I'd believed that if I fooled around, I'd end up just like my mother: birthing a whole pack of kids and hating the world. I thought I'd never escape the Place with No Hope if I was nursing a baby. The Cowboy knew that more than anyone.

So it was lucky for me that the bear-man was a tourist, and I wouldn't see him again, because I kept thinking about him, and picturing that grin. I loved that he'd guessed I'd grown up in the South. And the way he had smiled at me made my heart glow.

Sometimes I still hoped my life would turn out like a Disney movie, and Prince Charming would show up with a white horse and carriage. Only in *my* movie, the kids climbed into the white carriage with me, and we all rode off into the sunset together.

Any single woman with babies can tell you how likely that ending is. Good thing denial was my homeboy. I knew I was not Cinderella. I was the Old Woman Who Lived in a Shoe, only without the *whipped her children all soundly before she put them to bed* part. I didn't believe in whipping kids. At all.

Besides, my mother had been married four times, and not one of those men had been a Prince Charming. They'd been much closer to Bluebeards than anything Disney came up with. My childhood memories included Duck once hitting my mother so severely that his handprint stayed on her face for two weeks, and all of the times Jeff and William's father came home from work to start screaming obscenities. The kids' dad, Dole Preston, had liked to wake Mom up at four in the morning by kicking the wall near the floor where she slept, yelling, *Wake up, woman! I want breakfast!*

Even my own father ran out on our family when I was young, and several years passed before I saw him again. That was why Mom kept going back to her first two ex-husbands, begging them to take care of us, and why I still had nightmares about living with those men. Since Mom swore that Duck and the others had all been "extremely nice fellows" before tying the knot, getting married seemed as dangerous as playing Russian roulette. It was easy to believe in Prince Charming in the world of cartoons and fairy tales. Far more difficult to find him in the world of real men.

At twelve-thirty, Richard, Ethan, and Mia came through the back door. "Hey, MJ!" they yelled. They seemed pretty cheerful for a school day.

I had Warren make them grilled cheeses and french fries, and then I asked him to advance me a hundred bucks, so Richard could go pay the water bill. When the kids were done eating, they walked back to school, and Gandhi started to follow them down the alley. Then he trotted back to the door and crawled under a box. The snow had arrived, wet and pelting, so Warren took pity and let Gandhi come sit at my feet by the drain pipe. I heard the steam engine blow, which meant the train had arrived.

I walked outside and saw King was still in the side yard, standing under an awning beside the old ore cart. Some tourists were taking his picture. I heard one woman say, "I guess this really *is* a one-horse town! And that's him right there!"

I knew King could have gone back to his pasture. But he loved the idea of aggravating Don Doonan. Someone had surely called Don, and told him Will's horse was hanging around unattended in town. King was the orneriest trickster I'd ever met. And he was sure going to land me in big trouble with Don.

6

TANGENTIAL AT BEST

I left work around three and rode King to his pasture, and by the time I walked home with Gandhi, Mom was in the basement again. I'd brought back some cookies, which I let the kids eat, and then I opened a kitchen cupboard and started sifting through bills.

I discovered we were in the hole for six thousand dollars, and that the town was charging thirteen-percent interest on the unpaid property tax. The house was assessed at $402,000.00, which was slightly comical considering it had been built in 1894 for less than a thousand. Inflation was such a fearsome, relentless beast. It made my head hurt.

I took the latest bill into the living room, where Landon and Janine were playing Call of Duty. Landon owned a Play Station, but he'd beat the tar out of the kids if they touched it. That's why they wanted an Xbox so bad. They were desperate for video games, but if they bought a PlayStation, Landon could fly off the handle one night and thump them, claiming they were stealing his games.

I held up the tax bill and said, "We need six thousand dollars."

Landon glanced at me once and went back to his game. "You ain't gotta pay that."

"I'm not having sex with Tom Morbun," I said. "So you can forget that plan."

Landon paused the game to scowl at me. "Why you gotta be such a *bitch?*"

Janine smirked and flicked her cigarette ash at my feet. I'd have turned her into a pillar of salt if I could.

"Like I said, we need six thousand dollars."

"Ah, fuck *you*," Landon said, and he unpaused the game. Under his breath, he added, "*Fucking cunt.*"

"You know," I said, "for someone who doesn't even put out, you sure like to call me a *fucking cunt* all the time."

I went back to the kitchen, sat down at the table and ran my hands through my hair.

"Can we still buy an Xbox?" Richard asked.

"Course," I said, but I was feeling a bit shaky. I'd started to suffer panic attacks, when everything hit me at once, and that property tax bill had me rattled.

"Come on, get your homework done," I told Richard and Mia. Ethan was already working on his. "We're going to Beth's for supper again."

The kids weren't happy about this, but that was tough. I made myself a cup of coffee and tried to stop thinking, but I could feel one of my attacks coming on.

***

After supper at Beth's house that night, I tried to help her teach the kids how to play pinochle. Beth loved pinochle and anyone who knew how to play it, but the game only frustrated Mia. Richard and Ethan weren't fans, either. So we gave up on pinochle and ate pie instead, and Beth passed the time occupied with her second-favorite activity to pinochle, which was talking. She chatted about the corns on her feet and the Sheriff's Blotter in Goldking. Mia's eyes glazed over after fifteen minutes.

Walking home later, I told the kids we could leave town on Saturday and shoot Ravi. This cheered them up after all the forced socializing.

I'd have to borrow a vehicle to pick up an Xbox, as Riverdale was more than an hour away. The thought of that city reminded me of Justice Garcia, who'd attended college there, and sometimes I wished I'd stayed closer to home and gone to Colorado Plateau. I might've been able to pay the property tax last year if I had done that. But the Plateau was a fourth-tier university, and I was a college snob. The people of Goldking lumped college snobs in with everything Ingot-Ville stood for, and as I didn't want to be lynched, I kept all that fourth-tier university stuff to myself. Not to mention, I would've never met Hanna in Riverdale. So while my private university had been insanely expensive and located on the other side of the country, I was loyal to my school. That campus had given me Hanna, even if God had later decided to take her away.

At the house, I made the kids go to bed. Gandhi went upstairs with them, and slept under Mia's bed. I washed the dishes Mom had left in the sink, and then I put my feet up and studied the tax bill. Six thousand dollars. With the interest accrual, this would take a while to pay off. I reached into my pack and took out an envelope, the one that held my student loan papers. I had borrowed fifteen thousand dollars in the last four years, all of it to take care of my family while I went to school.

I felt my hands shake, and put away my student loan papers. Debt was such a frightening thing.

By September, I'd have to find work in Riverdale. Summers in Goldking were a short-lived cash cow, and I needed steady employment to make my student loan payments and get the taxes caught up, or Mom would lose the house. She liked living here, and so did the kids.

Mom had some other bills in the cupboard. I flipped through them quickly. The power company was planning to shut off our electricity this Friday. Visa had given Mom's name to a collection service. We owed seven hundred dollars to Goldking Propane. And the hardware store wanted payment for a fan and a hammer that had been purchased on credit.

I sorted through all the bills, and then I went upstairs. I didn't have anywhere to sleep, as Landon had caught my futon on fire last winter with his cigarette ash. He'd almost burned the house down, but Mia had smelled the smoke, run upstairs, and had the good sense to push the futon out the window.

So Landon owed me a bed for the night. He and Janine were spending their nights in the living room, anyway.

Landon kept a lock on his old bedroom door, but I picked it. I had to open the windows to diffuse the smell of his cigarettes, and then I latched the deadbolt and dropped onto the bed. I didn't sleep long. I woke after midnight, short of breath. I sat up for a moment, and then flipped on the light. I tried to take deeper breaths, but couldn't pull the air into my lungs. My heart started racing. I felt a pain in my chest, like all of my muscles had seized and then started burning. Sweat rose on my skin until I was drenched, and I thought that if I didn't escape this room, I would die. I stumbled onto my feet and ran into the hallway. I almost fell down the stairs trying to get out the front door.

The wind felt like ice and cut right through my shirt, while I staggered through the yard and struggled to breathe. I felt the snow on my feet, and then I dropped to my knees. Ten minutes passed, with my chest burning and seizing, until finally I felt something change and I pulled in some air. I lurched to my feet and walked in a circle, because when I made an effort to move, my heartbeat slowed down. I started breathing again.

I had never suffered these attacks before in my life. The first one had come last month, after I'd ditched the GRE, the Graduate Record Exam. My college advisor had signed me up for that test. He'd been certain my future was in graduate school, especially once I stopped talking about my documentary project. He called me the best student he'd ever had in a class. He wanted me to pick up a doctorate in history and join academia. He paid the $160.00 testing fee for me.

But when the April exam date arrived, Ethan had already called me in tears, begging me to come home. So instead of taking the GRE, I'd walked to a park and sat under a tree. I didn't think about anything all morning, I just stared off into space. I felt like a horse with two broken legs, one that someone ought to take pity on with a bullet. Asleep in my dorm room that night, I'd woken up feeling like I was having a heart attack. I ran out of the building and returned soaked in sweat. I didn't tell anyone because it scared me so much. I had another panic attack the night before I graduated. I was starting to worry I might be losing my mind.

By the time I returned to the house after my trip through the yard, my teeth were beginning to chatter, so I pulled on a coat and went to the kitchen. I filled a pan with water and set it to boil. I would have made tea, but the pantry was empty, and I didn't want to drink coffee at this hour. Mom came upstairs from the basement. She tottered around on her dusty white pumps, and her voice had that dreamy quality that meant she was in a good mood. She smiled when she saw me.

"You know, I was thinking we might buy a donkey," she said. "I've always liked burros. They're such cute little animals." She took a seat at the table and removed a joint from her pocket. "If we had a donkey, we could make him our mascot."

The water started to boil and Mom lit her joint. I poured a mug for myself and wrapped my fingers around it, listening to my mother expound on her latest idea. Mom always had a lot of ideas.

"It's like this country and sports teams," Mom said. "Everyone wants to cheer. Rah-rah-rah! Have some fun. Get some fresh air. Go win, yay! Be happy! So we should have a mascot."

Mom smoked her pot daintily, and then frowned. She pointed the cherry toward the far wall and stabbed at the air, talking to no one. "You know, mules built this town. Mules and donkeys. Those miners beat the hell out of those animals. Bashed their heads in with shovels. Poor little things. Hauling ore... pianos, stoves... Mules went blind in those mines... hoisted down, left to die in those shafts…"

Mom liked to shift gears and ramble like this. She went on about mules and mining for a while, and when she realized I was sitting next to her, she asked, "Why are you wearing a coat?"

I took a sip of hot water. "I was cold."

"Is that coffee?" she asked.

"Just water," I said. "Want some?"

Mom frowned again, and I could tell by her eyes that her mind was shifting again, switching gears. "You are such a spoil-sport," she fussed. "You never want to have any fun. Never want to go anywhere. Like, hi, Mom, how are you? Like, hi, Mom, let's go out to dinner. Let's go buy a steak dinner. Let's go out for a beer."

"I don't feel good," I said.

"You never feel good," Mom snapped, raising her voice. "You just want to sit around here all day, doing nothing. Everybody wants to do nothing. Except, here *I* am! Here's Gilly! She wants to get a donkey. She wants to have a mascot. And what's wrong with that? Nothing. But then all these people in town. Oh no, Gilly, you can't have a mascot! You can't have any fun! When we could all have a picnic, and go pick some flowers, and everyone could have nice little things. No! I get Vultures. I get all these Vultures around me. Because no one wants to have any fun."

"I have fun," I said.

"You don't know how to have fun!" Mom said. "You just sit there. Wearing a coat in the house. You don't even drink beer! You don't know anything! Me, I'm trying. Don't you think I'm trying?"

I left the table and crossed the room for the phone. I dialed the Cowboy's home number.

Mom stood and started pacing, almost shouting. "Who takes care of Gilly?" she asked. "Who bought the diapers, who cooked all the food? All those babies I raised. And now I can't even have a mascot. Now I've got nothing. Nothing but *screw you, Gilly*. Go to hell, Gilly. Give us your money!"

Mom had slipped into Full-On Unreasonable, which happened a few times a week. Her attachment to reality was tangential at best, though she did a fairly good job of medicating herself these days. She didn't turn violent anymore. That was a plus.

When I had been little, Mom wasn't the only one who suffered abuse. Mom used to beat the hell out of me and my three older brothers. Especially Landon. It always seemed worse than the slaps Mom took from Duck and the others, because Mom didn't just hit us. She picked up objects to use on our bodies, things that broke skin and left even worse bruises. The men in the house never hit children, but Mom could be watching TV, suddenly get a wild look in her eye, and then grab me and beat me until spit foamed from her mouth.

I couldn't understand why she did that, until one time I was sitting in the yard, and I watched a drug-dealer neighbor we had beating his dog with a crowbar. Every night, this man beat his dog. I could hear the pup yelping and crying the same way I screamed and cried when Mom knocked me around, and I thought: that man should not be laying into that dog. *There was no reason for it,* which meant that guy was crazy. That was how I figured out Mom was crazy. A couple weeks after that, our neighbor beat his dog clean to death, but Mom never went that far with her children, and for that, I have always been grateful.

She had once gotten so irrational in a grocery store that the State of Alabama had locked her up in a psych ward, right after Mia was born. Mom had spent two weeks on medication in a little white room. That hadn't gone over so well. Dealing with her after that had been worse than before she'd gone in. There was just no fixing Mom. She didn't believe there was anything wrong with her, and she'd try to put the hurt on a person for even suggesting it.

I wasn't scared of Mom any more, and hadn't been since I outgrew her, but I was too worn down tonight to listen to one of her episodes. So I was calling the Cowboy to rescue me.

He picked up after six rings. His voice sounded groggy. "Hello?"

"Hey," I said, "you want to go for a drive?"

"Now…?" he sighed.

"Yeah. Come pick me up?"

I ended the call and put on my shoes. I found a thermos under the sink and filled it with the rest of my hot water. Mom's mind had slipped into what I called The Abyss, when she started to rage about that most dead-end of all subjects: The Past.

"Where is he, *huh?*" she shouted. "Your worthless father? Dead! That's where he is. Dead! And Richard and Ethan and Mia, where's their father? Huh? Is he here buying groceries? Is he fixing the toilet? I didn't want to divorce him! He stole your money. He burned down Macy's shed. And now he's in prison. But I didn't want to divorce him! I didn't want to hurt those poor kids!"

She was still talking when the Cowboy pulled up. I called, "Bye, Mom!" and walked out to the truck. My teeth started to chatter as soon as the wind hit me. I smiled at the Cowboy as I pulled the door shut.

"Why are you shivering?" he asked, and he cranked the heat in the cab.

"I went outside tonight," I said. "Without a coat on."

He put the truck into gear and studied my face. He had that worried expression, the serious one.

"I'm all right," I said. "Thanks for coming to get me."

He drove onto Main Street, still looking severe, so I said, "Let's listen to music," and I turned on the radio. KTUR Rock was on station break, but I found a pop station that played Katy Perry and One Republic, and then I found an old Hank Williams song and settled on country. The Cowboy could listen to anything except rap, so he was a nice partner to have on a drive.

We left town and headed east, onto the long unpaved roads that led into ghost towns. Sometimes the headlights picked up the remains of a mill or a tram, but mostly we drifted through the shadow of trees. We couldn't go four-wheeling, as the high roads weren't plowed yet and still covered with snow, but we could drive all night in the valleys and be completely alone.

I found a Mountain Dew in the glove box, cracked it open, and passed the can to the Cowboy.

"Are you dating Bree Taylor?" I asked.

"No," he said. I could tell he was worked up over me catching Bree at his house.

"I wouldn't mind, if you are."

"I'm not dating Bree Taylor," he said.

I placed my hand on his shoulder, and he caught my gaze for a moment. He muttered, "I can't get any woman to date me."

"Well, you're shaving now," I said, noting a few nicks on his chin. The Cowboy looked a lot younger without his beard. "Won't be long, you'll have a parade at your door."

"Men don't get parades," he said.

I took a sip from my thermos. "In Goldking, they do. Law of supply and demand."

The Cowboy gave a deep sigh, like Jesus at Gethsemane contemplating his suffering. "I don't want a parade."

I patted his hand on the shifter to show him some sympathy. "I need a ride to Riverdale soon. For an Xbox."

"Just say when," he said. The Cowboy worked construction in town, and he did a lot of odd jobs for his father. He was usually free in the evenings.

"The kids have to save up," I said. "I'm not sure how much they cost."

"About three hundred," he said. The Cowboy didn't play video games, but he did build electronic gadgets in his basement. The rest of his free time he spent hunting and shooting, or hiking the valleys in search of cliffs to rappel. Every time I had asked him, he'd ridden on horseback with me. It never mattered to him where we went.

"I love you," I said. He let out his breath, and then his frustration dissolved, and he smiled at me, almost laughed.

I didn't mention Bree Taylor again, but the Cowboy knew what I meant. I was so lonely and scared I didn't know what to do with myself, but I hadn't come back to Goldking to wreck his life. I was glad he was trying to date other girls. Our breakup four years ago had ripped him apart, and if he was moving on, that meant he was healing. I wanted him to follow his dreams, and find love, and have a family. I wanted the Cowboy to be happy.

I gazed out at the mountains while he told me his stories, which were far more interesting than anything Beth had to say. We drove the back roads until sunrise. When we arrived in Goldking again, the truck started coughing and almost ran out of gas.

"We're down to the fumes," said the Cowboy.

He made me stay in the cab while he filled up the tank. When he took me home to wake the kids up for school, Tom Morbun was standing at the front door again, holding another dozen pink roses and wearing a suit.

"What is *this?*" asked the Cowboy, but before I could answer, he stomped on the brake and jumped out.

Tom Morbun took off.

"Cowboy!" I called, but there was no stopping him. Tom gave a high little squeal and fled the yard with his roses, and the Cowboy ran after him, chasing him up the hill to his property.

"No is *no*, you old perv!" the Cowboy yelled.

I hopped out of the truck and saw Don Doonan arrive in his Jeep. I guessed he'd come to rip me a new one for riding King yesterday. I watched Don slam the door of his Jeep and stalk toward me. His face had turned a deep shade of crimson, and his neck had flushed purple. He looked like an eggplant.

7

MY GPA SUCKS

"**N**ow you *listen here*, Mary Jane!" Don yelled. "I'm not putting up with this crap! Riding those horses! Leaving them out around town! I'm calling the cops the next time I catch you!"

"Morning, Don," I said. "Why don't you come in for some coffee?"

"I'm going to padlock that *gate!*" Don screamed. "I'll build a *barn* for those horses and *board them* at night!"

I nodded my head, like this was all reasonable. Don seemed ready to pop a blood vessel.

"I can help with your barn," said the Cowboy, walking over to join us. He tipped his hat to Don Doonan like the man wasn't screaming. The Cowboy had been around my mother enough to know when people were in the realm of the lunatic. He kept his cool.

"You're *nothing* in this town, Mary Jane!" Don shouted. "The Sheriff ought to *run you out!*"

"That ain't gonna happen," said the Cowboy.

"Hundred years ago, we'd have hung you for *stealing!*" Don shrieked. "Taken you *right up to the gallows!*"

I started laughing because Don was so nuts. Then I got hold of myself, and said, "Don, you calm yourself down. You know I'm not stealing those horses. And if you keep yelling at me, you're going to end up with a heart attack. So I want you to come inside with me now and I'll make you some coffee."

Don glowered and crossed his arms, heaving, but he followed me with a "*Humf!*"

I gave the Cowboy a peck on the cheek. "Don't forget what I said," I told him. He waved me off and climbed into his truck.

Inside the kitchen, I made a pot of coffee and woke up the kids, and then I asked Don how his winter had been. I poured some of Landon's pretzels in a bowl and listened to Don. He talked about his own issues in Goldking, which revolved around hauling feed for the horses and a mine claim he had in Mad Violet Gulch. I served him the pretzels and a cup of black coffee, and when he asked me for sugar, I gave him some packets I'd swiped from The Caroline. The kids ate the last of Landon's potato chips and went on to school, and I told Don he could drive me to work.

"I'm washing dishes for Ellie," I said.

"Well, that's decent," he muttered. Don was such a nasty curmudgeon, but at least he had a soft side. I thought he had a crush on my mother.

"Gilly's still sleeping," I said. "But I'll have you over for dinner some night."

"Thank you kindly," he said, and then he drove me to work. Gandhi rode with us. The Caroline was only four blocks away and I didn't need Don to drive me, but men liked to do things for women, no matter how small.

"Bye, Don," I told him, and I patted his arm. "You have a good one today."

"All right," he grumbled, and tore off in his Jeep.

I made Gandhi sit down in the alley again, and when I walked into The Caroline, Warren shouted, "MJ! Get over here!"

He stood by the staff table next to the kitchen, sifting through a mountain of papers. I joined him and saw dozens of pictures of football players, probably printed up from his computer last night.

"*This one*," Warren said, shoving a paper in my face. "That's him, isn't it?"

I held the picture where I could see it, and studied the face for a moment. This man sort of looked like the bear-man, only he had green eyes and some blond in his hair. "Not the same guy," I told Warren.

"*Damn*," Warren said. "I thought for sure he played for the Cowboys. I already told everyone I had an NFL player in here for lunch."

I glanced at the paper again. "If you want to say—*Marshall Bramson*—was in here eating a cheeseburger, I won't tell anyone different."

Warren grinned and then asked, "You had breakfast yet?" which was his way of offering to cook me something.

"Eggs and toast," I said, and picked up an apron.

***

By my third day at The Caroline, Ellie made me start waiting tables. I preferred to stay in the kitchen, where I didn't have to act cute, but I couldn't argue that the money was better out on the floor. Don Doonan started to come in for lunch every day.

He always tipped me two or three dollars. Tom Morbun came in as well. Of course he sat down in my section.

"I want to see that *diploma!*" he crowed. Tom still had all his hair, which was fluffy and white, and his dentures were always impeccable. He smiled a lot when he stared at my breasts. "My daughter went to UPenn," he said. "Did I ever tell you that?"

Tom had mentioned this to me only four hundred times. He loved to brag on his kids, especially as they'd all attended Ivy League schools. He'd lived in New Jersey before he retired and moved here, and his daughter was a mechanical engineer, just like he'd been. I smiled and said, "You must be so proud of her."

"Graduated *summa cum laude*," Tom gushed. "What about you? What was your GPA?"

The last thing I wanted to do was admit my miserable grade point average to someone like Tom. I'd tried hard in college. I'd even carried a 3.96 until senior year. But when Hanna fell ill, that was it. We were supposed to have studied abroad in Vienna last fall. Hanna had convinced me to go to Austria with her. But I spent most of that semester in Cincinnati instead, watching her die. If I'd had any dreams of graduating *summa cum laude*, they'd been replaced by prayers that I'd graduate at all. If my professors hadn't loved me, I'd have been kicked out of school. I should have flunked every class I had senior year, but love made you do crazy things. My professors had conspired together to make sure I walked, and I had a diploma because of it.

So rather than answer Tom's question, I asked if he wanted more Coke.

"Sure, thank you," he said. I picked up his glass and walked toward the machine.

Justice was wearing her hair in a ponytail. She hung up a ticket and asked, "Is that man *flirting* with you?"

I said, "He's old. They all flirt."

She snickered a little and refilled a lemonade. "Hey, what was that NFL player's name again? The guy at the bar wants to know."

"Marshall Bramson," I said. I glanced over and saw Fred from the liquor store.

"Hey, Fred!" I called. "I owe you some coffee."

"Oh, *shut up*," he snarled, in one of his moods. I went over and poured him a beer.

"Was there really an NFL player here?" he asked, and I noticed his hands were trembling. Fred loved football. It was his whole *raison d'être*, especially after his wife left him.

"I don't know, Fred. Warren didn't get a good look at him."

"Well, would you check for me?" Fred asked, and he held up his phone. He'd loaded the screen full of head shots of football players.

I didn't have time to search through every NFL player right now, but I picked up the phone and said, "Sure." I breezed through the pictures in less than a minute. "Nope," I announced, and then I lowered my voice. "But don't tell anyone else, okay? Bad for business."

Fred took a deep breath and smiled. "Oh, thank *God*," he said. "I felt my DTs coming on." Like a lot of people in town, Fred was an alcoholic, and his delirium tremens would start if he was too stressed to drink.

"Well, Warren wasn't even sure he played football," I said. "The guy could've been in the Majors, for all he knew." Warren was far less familiar with baseball players. In the summer and fall, he listened to games on the radio, because he burned every-one's food when he had a TV in the kitchen.

"I like baseball," Fred said.

I cocked an eyebrow. "Who doesn't like baseball?"

"My old lady," Fred chuckled.

I kept my mouth shut, as it went against sense to bash on ex-wives. A lot of men still loved their dames, even after the lawyers. "You order yet?"

Fred pointed at Justice. "That girl there took my order. She smarter than you, college girl?"

I winked at Fred and said, "Everyone's smarter than me, you old coot."

8

THE DEAD WOMAN FROM IDAHO

For the next month and a half, I made Richard and Ethan save their money in the empty Folgers tub, so they could buy a few games as well as the Xbox. After the school year ended, Mia started babysitting to earn income for clothes and a copy of *Gladiator*. Mia loved that movie. She called Landon *Commodus*, after the bad guy in that film. I think she hoped Russell Crowe would show up in the living room one night and kick Landon's ass. But that was about as likely as Prince Charming showing up with a white horse and carriage.

Money in Goldking was good in the summer. With all the tourists to wait on, I could make a hundred dollars in tips every shift, sometimes more. With two shifts a day, I did pretty well, as long as the trains were on time and people were hungry.

We still couldn't purchase the Xbox until July, after the pantry was stocked and I had the propane paid off. I also kept the electricity on and took care of that bill at the hardware store. My student loans were in a six-month grace period, so I would write my first check for those in December. I gave Tom Morbun nine hundred dollars to start paying the back taxes down, and he tried to kiss me, but I turned my face aside and he only managed to get his tongue in my ear. I wasn't kissing that man, no matter how pearly his dentures were. I carried the pink roses he left on my doorstep to Justice's boyfriend and said, "Here. Tell your girl that you love her," since Justice had said they'd been fighting a lot.

I worked at the Big Belle Blue on my nights off from The Caroline, and I painted Beth's shed for her for an extra twenty bucks. I mowed a few lawns between shifts. On the day the Cowboy gave me a ride down to Riverdale, there was a highway fatality that shut down Gunner Pass for an hour. The kids were all in the truck with us, Mia up front and Richard and Ethan in back.

Mia was upset about losing her shopping time. "When are these people ever gonna learn to *slow down?*" she asked.

"Remember that when you're a teenager," I said. Mia blew me a raspberry, which blasted some spit in my face, but then she said, "Sorry," and dried it up with her sleeve.

Riverdale held the station house for the narrow gauge railroad, so it was as much of a tourist town as Goldking. It also had Colorado Plateau University and a community college, not to mention thirty-eight thousand more people, so there were plenty of bars and thrift stores, even a mall. It was a tiny mall, with not much more than a Sears and a J.C. Penney, but there was a Spencer's there, so the kids wanted to visit and read all the fart jokes. The Cowboy obliged them while I slept in the truck. I felt exhausted all the time, since I often woke up in the night to suffer through a panic attack. Panic attacks reduced me to tears and left me feeling hopeless, which was about the least helpful thing I had in my life at the moment.

After we'd been to Spencer's and Walmart and an hour in Albertson's buying groceries, our evening in Riverdale had come to an end. We started for home. The kids fell asleep and I talked to the Cowboy.

"Dean Licks has a car I can buy," I said. "A '91 Regal. Five hundred dollars." Dean Licks ran a repair service in Goldking. He was also one of my mother's ex-boyfriends.

"You have enough?" asked the Cowboy.

"Sure," I said. I didn't have the money right now, but I would in two weeks.

"You looking for work here in Riverdale?" he asked.

"I talked to the paper," I said. "*The Riverdale Times* will let me write o-bits. That's actually something that needs a degree."

The Cowboy frowned. "What does that pay?"

I laughed. "Not much. Fifteen dollars a write-up, if that."

"What else have you got?"

"It's grim," I said. "Teacher's aides, bus drivers, hotel work, and daycare."

The Cowboy thought for a moment. "Bus driving is easy. Go for that."

"Not enough hours," I said. "And I can't work a second or third job with a split shift like that."

"The highest anything pays here is nine dollars an hour," he said.

"More like eight," I sighed. "With one full-time job, I'll only clear about nine hundred a month. Obituaries would bring in a hundred, maybe two. With a second job on the weekends, I'd earn about three hundred more."

"That's after taxes?" he asked.

"Of course." I gazed through the window a minute, at the moonlit valley below. The Cowboy downshifted again as we started up Gunner Pass.

"Less than fifteen-hundred a month," I said quietly. "And the high school in Goldking is closing. So Richard is coming with me. Mom thinks they all should."

"Your mom hates those teachers," said the Cowboy. "The best ones were fired, years ago. Over politics."

The Cowboy liked to make comments that included the word *politics*. He did that to get philosophical with me. It was his way of flirting.

"What's going on with Bree Taylor?" I asked.

"Nothing," he said. "Like I told you a month ago."

"Someone else then?" I pressed.

The Cowboy glanced at me, hard. "There *is* no one else."

"Not yet," I said. Mia had curled up with her head in my lap, and I combed my fingers through her hair. I wasn't sure what else to say, as I rarely heard the Cowboy turn bitter. "You mad?" I asked.

"Not at you," he said.

"Good," I sighed. "I can't handle anything right now without someone else in my corner."

"I'll always be in your corner," he said. That made me smile, so I reached over and skewed his hat to one side.

***

The Cowboy pulled up to the house before midnight, and he carried Mia inside while I woke Richard and Ethan. Then we hauled in the groceries. The Cowboy left around one in the morning, but he called the house less than five hours later.

"What is it?" I asked.

"Woman from Idaho had a heart attack," he said. "Up Primrose, past the turnoff."

"You collecting the body?"

"Leaving now," he said.

"You want company?"

I could hear the smile in his voice. "You bet."

I was sleeping in the upstairs hallway, on an Army cot I'd picked up for five bucks. I made up the blankets and headed down to the kitchen. I started a pot of coffee, and then hurried upstairs again to dress and tell Mia and the boys I was leaving.

A few minutes later, Mom came into the kitchen, wearing a purple robe with her heels. "Where *you* going?" she asked.

"Cowboy has a body to fetch," I said. "Some woman from Idaho."

"His dad's still the coroner?" Mom asked.

"No, Bob Mandell's the coroner," I said. "But he's busy this week."

"Why does David have to go get her?" Mom asked.

"Cause he's the Cowboy," I said.

I filled a thermos with coffee and put on my coat. I tossed a jar of peanut butter and a loaf of bread in my pack, and headed out to the truck. Gandhi padded along at my feet.

"Can he come?" I asked.

"Sure," said the Cowboy, rolling his window back up. So I let Gandhi hop in, and I climbed in beside him, and the three of us left town for the high country. I hadn't been Jeeping in ages. It felt like a gift.

"It's like we're having a party!" I said. Even Gandhi kept wagging his tail. When the Cowboy shifted into four-wheel-drive low, he took a break and let me drive for a while. I loved Jeeping almost as much as I loved riding King.

We watched the sunrise at twelve thousand feet, and then we climbed higher to arrive at the campsite. The woman from Idaho had been up here alone on a backpacking trip. Jim Kimball had already been by in a Cherokee, to check that it wasn't a homicide. He thought the woman had died of a heart attack, since there weren't any wounds or signs of a struggle. The people who'd found her had stayed with her body all night. They'd built a big campfire and stood around talking.

The Cowboy walked over to the body and removed the blanket on top of her. He zipped her into a bag, and then he and another man carried the body to the truck. The campers were friendly, as most people are, and offered us hot chocolate and graham crackers. So we joined them for breakfast and stood watching the mountains.

"This is truly God's country," a man said. "If you're going to live and die anywhere, this is it."

The man who'd helped with the body asked the Cowboy, "How many times have you done this?"

"Enough, I suppose."

"Lot of people die in these parts?" asked the first man.

The Cowboy smiled at the fire. I knew what he wanted to say: *It ain't Disneyland here.* So I cut in and said, "Falling, drowning, freezing, avalanche—no shortage of ways to die here."

"Especially for children," the man quipped. Then we fell silent, and I knew everyone was thinking about what had happened four days ago: a toddler had drowned in the river in town. His parents had stopped to take pictures, turned away from their baby an instant, and into the water he went. Rivers take life the way a dog plays with a chew toy, hiding it for a while and then bringing it back like a gift, all mangled.

"There's tragedy here, and beauty," said the Cowboy. "Like anywhere else."

I had to smile at this comment. The Cowboy had never been anywhere except Colorado and Utah, a fact he was proud of and wore like a badge. I'd been far more places and I still felt the way he did—that there was no place so beautiful as right here.

"Thank you kindly for breakfast," the Cowboy said to the campers. "MJ and I need to get on to work."

"God bless and Godspeed," a man said. "Maybe we'll see you in town later on."

"You should come into The Caroline," I told them, and they promised they would.

Gandhi and I took our seats in the cab, and the Cowboy palmed the wheel starting down. I thought of an old routine that we had, one we'd made up together after my father had died.

"Why are the mountains so beautiful?" I asked.

"Read me the names of your dead," said the Cowboy, "and I'll tell you why."

"I don't remember their names," I replied.

"Not one?"

"Not one."

"Then you don't need their names, to know why."

I smiled at the Cowboy and asked, "When was the last time we did that?"

"When Hanna was here," he said. I hadn't forgotten, of course. The Cowboy knew that, which was why he'd spoken her name. Hanna had called this our Death and Beauty Routine. She'd told me I was obsessed with war and thought about it too much. She might've been right. Hazard of being a history major.

"I saw the Buick last night," the Cowboy said, which meant he'd driven past the repair shop on his way home. "Licks ought to just give you that thing."

"He's got a girlfriend," I reasoned. "He must need the money."

"That car's a piece of crap," said the Cowboy. "It won't even get you halfway up Gunner Pass."

"Beggars and choosers," I mused. "Dean wouldn't sell me a lemon."

"Dean *is* a lemon," he groused.

9

CANDY MAN CADILLAC

Five hundred dollars doesn't buy much of a car, and the '91 Buick Regal I procured from Dean Licks had seen better days. The car had been repoed from drug dealers, who'd driven it through several barbed-wire fences and into a canyon. There were two bullet holes in the trunk that Dean had covered with duct tape. From what was left of the paint, I guessed the car had originally been maroon, though there were several patches of teal and black spray paint on the passenger doors. I'd have to sew some new seat covers, as the drug traffickers had ripped up the chairs to hold bags of meth.

"Engine's still good," Dean said. "Get you about twenty miles to the gallon." We stood outside the repair shop on a hot day in July, out in the back lot where Dean kept his wrecks.

"How about the brakes?" I asked.

"Pedal goes to the floor, but it stops," Dean said. "I put some tires on for you."

I had seen that already. These tires weren't new, but they weren't missing all of their tread. "Thanks for that," I said.

I gave him the money and drove the car home. Mom came outside when she saw me pull up.

"What in the hell is *that?*" she shouted. "This fucking thing belongs in a junkyard!"

"It's my candy man Cadillac," I said. I stepped out of the vehicle and patted the hood of the car. "Don't bash on him too hard, he'll get his feelings all hurt."

Mom wore a pink dress today, with a white lacy sweater. "You should've bought a donkey instead," she fussed. "This house needs a mascot."

"Yeah, sorry about that," I told her. "But I can't get to Riverdale with the kids on a burro." I went inside to change clothes for my night shift, and Mom followed me. I glanced again at her dress. "You have a date?"

"Michael Bean," she said. "He's taking me out." By the way she was smiling, I knew this was a big deal. Michael Bean ran the grocery store.

"Didn't Michael cheat on his last wife?" I asked.

"Spoilsport," Mom said. "He already bought me this," and she held up a necklace she was wearing, a small golden kitten on a thin metal chain.

"That's pretty," I said, and Mom smiled again. She'd curled her long hair, and I could smell Vanilla Fields perfume.

"I was thinking about getting a kitten," she said. She tucked the necklace away. "You want a mint julep? I made some ice cubes this morning."

I wiped the sweat from my brow and said, "Why not?" Mom busied herself with the cocktail, and I went upstairs to change.

When I returned to the kitchen, Mom said, "You know, you'd probably get a fella if you didn't work all the time. Just your hair is so ugly. How old are you, anyway?"

"Twenty-two," I said.

Mom startled at this. "Already?"

I nodded. "Since May fourth." Mom's birthday was April nineteenth, which was why she never remembered mine. Aging was not something Mom enjoyed one bit, so she spent a few weeks after her birthday each year remembering her life as a teenager, and wishing she could go back to that time. Mom was forty-six. She'd borne seven children and survived four different husbands, and she still wanted to imagine herself as she'd been at sixteen. I didn't get it, except to say that Mom liked having boyfriends much more than husbands.

She finished the mint julep and passed me a glass. "Didn't you have a couple boyfriends in college?" she asked. "Why didn't you ever bring one of them home?"

I hadn't dated in college, but if I told her that, Mom would start in on me about being a loser, so I said, "Well, none of them really worked out."

Mom nodded and patted my shoulder. "You get your heart broken?" she asked.

I took a sip of my drink and gazed out the window. I'd never liked telling Mom anything personal, because she always used it against me in one of her fits. Right now she was fine, but she was like the weather that way.

"Yeah, my heart is broken," I said.

Mom beamed at me and held up a finger. "I'll make you another cocktail!" she said, and she hurried to cut some more spearmint. Mom kept a tiny herb garden on a shelf in the kitchen, so her martinis and cocktails were usually perfect.

"Isn't Michael coming over?" I asked. I didn't want to drink anymore, as I was working tonight and couldn't be sauced, but Mom was so happy, I hated to ruin it.

"I can make another for him," Mom said. She looked hurt.

"Okay, sure," I said, and I accepted the second drink from her hands. "Except I have to leave now, or I'll be late."

"All right!" Mom said brightly, and she waved me goodbye. I carried the glass out of the house with me, and dumped the second mint julep in the alley. Then I caught sight of Mia walking home.

"Is that our new car?" she called out down the street, pointing to the front of the house.

"It's a Cadillac!" I said.

"You fat liar!" Mia yelled, and I laughed.

***

The public school in Goldking had always been small. From preschool through high school, the students all met in one tiny building in town, which was located two blocks down the street from the old miner's hospital. While the days of having twenty students per grade level were long gone, enrollment in Goldking had dropped to less than five students per class. The number of educators had also been dwindling, until the last high school teacher had been fired in March.

There was one important thing people never discussed when they talked about student learning, and that was the impact a principal had on a school. Teachers worked on a ship, and the students were passengers onboard a vessel, but the principal was the captain, and he directed the whole program. No one ever remembered that when they started screaming about No Child Left Behind. But who was in charge of hiring the best teachers, and who was in charge of getting rid of the bad ones? The hardest thing on this earth was to be a good leader, so it was no wonder to me that so many school systems suffered.

Bunker Wilson had been principal of Goldking Public School for the last twenty years, and he had captained his ship right into the rocks. The School Board thought he was a Rock Star, and I thought that was true, but not in the way that they meant it. Bunker had fired all of his good teachers because they made him look bad, and he'd replaced them with bad ones because they made him look good. The School Board responded by saying, "Oh, Bunker! You are the most wonderful, magnificent administrator! What would Goldking ever do without you?" After several families left town, appalled that their children weren't learning, the Board said, "Don't worry, Bunker! It's just this economy! You can't expect people to stay here when there's a recession!"

Bunker had also tried pretty hard to get himself fired. He'd totaled one of the school's Suburbans four years ago. He'd had two affairs with married women in town, both of whom had children in grade school. He'd even been caught abusing the school's credit card. But Bunker Wilson had a sixty-watt smile and a ten-gallon hat, and he swaggered around and told jokes and people loved him for that. He was the Prodigal Son who had single-handedly destroyed the high school in town, and as Richard was moving into ninth grade this September, I was feeling the effects of Every Principal Left Behind. Bunker made seventy-six thousand dollars a year, and he was as useful as a condom in a roomful of eunuchs.

When he came into The Caroline for dinner Thursday night, Bunker smiled and winked at me and I felt my skin crawl. He sat at the bar and ordered a beer, and then he asked me, "Why don't you come work at the school, Mary Jane? I bet you'd make a mighty fine teacher." He winked again and stared at my breasts for a moment, and there was no doubt in my mind as to what Bunker wanted. "You're sure awful pretty," he added.

I placed his mug of beer on the counter and said, "I'm moving to Riverdale. I just bought a car."

"Teachers start at twenty-eight thousand," he said to entice me. "Only goes down to twenty, after taxes," and he waggled his eyebrows.

Twenty thousand dollars, and sex with Bunker Wilson. Gosh, he made it sound so appealing.

"Richard wants to take physics," I said. "There's a freshman class in Riverdale he's all set to sign up for."

"Well, you might change your mind," Bunker said, and he slurped at his beer.

***

I did not change my mind. I found an apartment in Riverdale in August. It came fully furnished and was only five hundred dollars a month, which was a complete steal in a rent-crazed college town. It was the first time my diploma had done something useful, as the woman who owned the place let me sign the lease as soon as she heard where I'd gone. After I coughed up two months' rent and the security deposit, I was allowed to move in on the last day of August.

School had already started by then, which meant I commuted to Riverdale every day with the kids until we could move. As I'd expected, Ethan and Mia decided to enroll in Shooting Star Middle School, which meant they were going to spend the school year with me.

After the first day of classes, Richard asked me if his best friend from Goldking, Gus Heldon, could join us. Gus Heldon was fifteen years old, red-headed and freckled, and so shy he barely spoke. He'd been terribly abused as a child, which was why he couldn't talk around strangers. He had even been held back in kindergarten, on account of his then-total muteness and inability to communicate. Lack of public speaking skills put Gus on the geek-end of the social spectrum, which meant he read a lot of books, and collected baseball cards and Spider-Man toys from garage sales.

Gus never invited Richard or anyone else to his house, since his mother had some paranoia issues and made people uncomfortable. She had already lost most of her teeth to meth mouth, and I'd heard she smoked opium now. Someone was growing poppies not far outside town, so product was cheap and addicts were happy. Another benefit of life at high altitude.

But what was good for his mother was not good for Gus. He didn't know what to do now that the Goldking High School had closed and his mother couldn't afford to relocate. So I told Richard that if Gus wanted to sleep on a cot and go to high school in Riverdale, that would be fine with me. When Gus heard the news, he broke down and cried so hard, I felt bad I hadn't offered to let him live with us sooner. Gus was a good kid, and he wanted to earn a diploma, so I hoped some of his attitude would rub off on Richard.

The apartment I rented had two bedrooms. Richard, Ethan, and Gus slept in the larger one, and Mia and I shared the other. Richard and Ethan shared a bed, and Gus slept on my Army cot. Mia and I shared a bed, too. The furniture looked new, if a few decades outdated. The interior reminded me of an old woman I'd known in Alabama, who'd taken me to church with her several times. She'd been a Methodist and had always smelled like wild onions, and her house had looked a lot like this place. My new apartment smelled like juniper though, as I'd managed to buy a few candles.

The nicest thing about the apartment in Riverdale was that I didn't have to put up with Landon and Janine anymore. They stayed in Goldking with Mom, though I wondered what would happen when they ran out of propane. Unless Landon got a job, they could not afford heat.

"Xbox goes off at ten," I told the kids and Gus the first night. "Unless you want me to pawn it."

Richard looked horrified. "Ten o'*clock??*" he yelled. "That's *bullshit!*" The boys had been playing video games until one or two every morning, sometimes all night if they didn't have to bus tables the next day. But that summertime schedule was over.

"I'm not keeping you here if you flunk out of school," I said. "Sleep-deprived kids fail their classes."

Richard hung his head in his hands.

"Ha-*hah!*" Mia laughed. "Suck it, Richard!" He tried to throw something at her, but I grabbed it in time. I opened my hand and saw a quarter.

"This isn't the end of the world," I told Richard. I patted his back and took a seat next to him, but he wrenched away from me and ran into his room.

Gus remained on the couch and stared at the wall. "Ten o'clock will be good," he said softly. His voice sounded so faint and whispery, it was hard to understand him sometimes. But his comment cheered me immensely.

"All right, Gus!" I said, and I made him give me a high-five. "Let's have tacos for dinner."

"I *love* tacos!" Mia squealed, and she ran into the kitchen. It was a tiny kitchen, only big enough for two people to stand in, but I could hear her pulling out my cutting board and opening the fridge door. I had stopped by a thrift store in town for my culinary supplies, like mixing bowls and measuring spoons, so at least Mia was happy.

"Hey, there's no cheese!" she cried.

"Too expensive," I said. "We're having tacos sans cheese."

From his bedroom, Richard yelled, "Why don't we just eat more *rice and beans??*" His mood had shifted from nasty to heinous. Xbox restrictions threatened his whole sense of self.

From his position sprawled out on the living room floor, Ethan groaned. He called out to Richard, "Knock it off. You knew there'd be rules."

"*Fuck you!*" Richard shouted, so we left him alone. When he came out of his room later, after all the tacos were gone, he said he was sorry, and then he went back to bed.

When the dishes were finished, I picked up my purse and took out my wallet, and I opened it to study what was inside. Nothing but a fifty-cent piece and two dimes in the billfold. For the second time in three months, I was almost totally broke.

"Oh, Blue Magic Wallet," I said. "Fill up with money again, so I can buy us a phone line." I'd picked up a cordless telephone from the thrift store today. I didn't want to buy a cell phone, in the event someone dropped it in the toilet. That was likely.

"Stop praying to your wallet," Mia said.

"I'm not praying to my wallet," I said. "I'm praying to God."

"Is that what Mormons do?" Mia asked.

I laughed. "That's what most people do."

Later that night, after the kids went to bed, I took the coins from my wallet and jiggled them around in my hand. As long as I had a few coins in my pocket, I had hope. I tried to remember that.

But keeping everyone in school was going to be hard. Really hard. Financially, I wasn't quite sure I could do it. If I could register myself as their legal guardian, I'd sign us up for assistance, like food stamps or Medicaid. But Mom would register the kids as her dependents so she wouldn't have to pay taxes, and I didn't know what would happen if the IRS found out I was claiming dependents I shouldn't have. Would the police get involved? Would I have to pay a huge fine? Or what if the red tape discovered that Mom was incapable of taking care of herself, and the State ruled that the kids should all be in foster care?

The idea made me shudder. No matter what, the kids weren't going to foster care. Richard would never make it through school if that happened. He'd mouth off to his foster parents, fail every class, and drop out. Unacceptable.

And nothing sent a jolt of fear through my body than getting tangled up in a court battle with the IRS. Mom would never let me claim the kids, which meant I was on my own with my bills. Signing them up for free lunch at their new school was the best I could do.

Three months out of college, and I wasn't making much progress moving away from Square One.

I stared down at the coins in my hand, and then I took out Hanna's badge and traced her name for a while. Her death had broken something vital inside me. Something far worse than when my father had died. The more days that passed since Hanna breathed her last breath, the more shattered pieces I felt in my heart. Grief didn't soften with time. It only took a new shape, found new ways to hurt. Sharp and cutting, like the broken ends of this badge. All the pain I held now.

✳✳✳

The next morning, I woke the kids up at six, so they could eat and ride the bus to school, and then I climbed into the Buick to report for my first day of work. Out of all the wonderful jobs available in Riverdale, I'd gone with the only position that required a college degree: teacher's aide at a kindergarten and daycare called Happy Garden. I did not want to work at a daycare, but this was the only job that would allow me to be home at night, to make sure the kids did their homework and went to sleep before ten. So I was off to make eight dollars an hour, and I silently prayed that this first day would go well.

10

HAPPY GARDEN

It took me thirty minutes to drive to Happy Garden. The woman who'd originally opened the facility had called the place Kiddie Academy, but the new owner had changed the name two years ago. According to the glossy parent brochure, Happy Garden was a place where "children can marvel at the wonder of nature, while developing their own intelligence without harmful constrictions." I wondered what sort of harmful constrictions could possibly exist at a daycare. Obsessive song-singing? Forced playground time? Imaginary-friend denial? What were modern childcare professionals doing, that a phrase like *harmful constrictions* ended up on a brochure? I hoped these people weren't whacko.

Happy Garden had been built as an addition to a farm-house. The house sat fifteen miles outside Riverdale, in a pictur-esque valley next to a tributary, a horse pasture, and a large farm of peacocks. As soon as I stepped out of the Buick, I heard the peacocks screaming. The birds did not seem to like Happy Garden, or anyone associated with it.

There were no children in sight yet, as the facility didn't open until seven-thirty, so I crossed the empty parking lot and walked to the front door. When no one answered the bell, I went to the main structure in back, where I waited for the owner to unlock the door. She'd asked me to arrive at seven today. Her first veteran worker didn't appear until seven-fifteen. This girl was in her twenties, maybe a couple of years older than me. Her clothes were covered in patches, and her blonde and purple dreadlocks reached her waist. She looked like the Rastafarian version of Raggedy Ann. She held a basket of laundry on her hip, a travel mug of coffee in her hand, and her eyes lit up when she saw me.

"*Oh, hellooooh!*" she exclaimed. "Oh my *God, so divine!* You must be here to replace Keira!"

"That's right," I said with a big smile. "MJ."

"Izzy!" she said. "Ooo—all right! Let me show you the door!" So my first piece of business involved learning how to unlock the door, which was a heap of rusted iron that belonged in ancient Babylon.

Once inside, Izzy showed me how to put the laundry away, how to prep the sign-in board for the day's arrivals, and told me that the opener always made the first pot of coffee. This involved grinding beans, boiling water, and setting up the french press. At Happy Garden, everything was organic and whole-some, from the roast beans the staff used in their coffee, to the Veggie Booty and rice cakes the children ate at snack time.

Children started arriving at 7:25, and Izzy introduced me to their parents. Happy Garden staff were required to memo-rize everything important about the children we cared for as well as their parents, including first and last names, occupations, hobbies, vacation preferences, food allergies, sports affiliations, living situations, current ex-spouses, custody battles, shopping habits, interior decorators… and somewhere at the end of the list was the emotional and psychological development of each child.

So meeting all of these parents and children took serious motivation. Izzy peppered her dialogue with phrases like, "*So* wonderful!" and "Abso*lutely!*" until she felt confident I could manage the *oh-my-God-I'm-so-happy!* lingo by myself. Happy Garden had a main room for the three-to-five-year-olds, and a smaller room with a rocking chair for the one- and two-year-olds. As I was new to Happy Garden, I was assigned to the older children.

Our charges all arrived before nine, and along with learning family trivia and bursting with enthusiasm for my new job, I was in charge of stopping squabbles and overseeing unstructured play-time. There were forty-three children with us today, so two more women arrived before eight-thirty. One was a grey-haired hippie named Linda, and the other a reserved young woman named Grace. Grace had my favorite kind of hair—brown crazy curls—so I liked her immediately, though I soon discovered that Grace was uncomfortable around adults, including me. She only came to life when she interacted with children. She told me she wanted to marry and have three little girls, and name them Cheshire, Misha, and Nobu. I thought those were interesting names.

The older woman, Linda, arrived with a sack of fresh goat meat, and she carried another bag with seven boxes of almond milk. Linda was relieved to see me in the building.

"Yay!" she cheered, placing the supplies in the kitchen. "The cavalry is here!"

The kitchen had originally been a small causeway between the two daycare rooms, so it was as tiny and crowded as my kitchen at home. The refrigerator and stove were lime green and black, and looked to have been built around 1972. The cabinets were flaking, chipped, and overall disgusting. Linda hurried to put the food away.

"Where's the meat from?" I asked, eyeing the Ziploc bags.

"From my farm," Linda said. "My husband and I have a place in Benson." Benson was another thirty minutes away, or about an hour from Riverdale.

"How many goats do you have?" I asked.

"About a hundred," Linda said. "But most of the money we make comes from our produce. We keep a huge garden."

"Sounds great," I said. I didn't exaggerate my expressions with Linda, as I only had one cranky three-year-old on my hip and no other adults were around. I was at liberty to speak like a normal person.

"How long have you worked here?" I asked.

"Ten years," Linda said. "I love children, so I can't imagine doing anything else." Then she disappeared into the room with the rocking chair to start watching the younger set, and I returned to monitoring the big space with the rambunctious kindergarteners and preschoolers. The cranky three-year-old followed me around the whole day, though that was his choice.

Happy Garden was owned by a woman named Stella McLaughlin. Stella did not appear in the daycare until nine o'clock, though I later learned that Stella did indeed come into the kitchen each morning, as she was the one who drank the pots of coffee we made. Her appearances before nine every morning were simply stealth visits, to slip in and fill her coffee cup and occasionally spy on her staff. Then she retreated back into her home, which was connected by a door through her laundry room.

The fact that this woman had told me to show up at Happy Garden at seven, when her regular employees did not arrive until quarter-past, and when she herself did not start work until nine, told me two things about Stella McLaughlin:

1. This woman was a slob, and
2. Working here would be unpleasant.

Female slobs running businesses were a dangerous breed. If male slobs wanted sex and subservience from their peons, then female slobs were all just insane. They were like being around adult monkeys, who could attack and bite even the most beloved person in their lives for no perceivable reason. So the staff tiptoed around Stella and praised her constantly, whether she was in hearing distance or not. I picked up on all this after about thirty seconds, as I've had a lot of experience being around crazy women.

"Oh, good *morning!*" Stella said to me when she finally arrived in the daycare. Her eyes were spread wide from all the caffeine she'd been drinking. She had a beer belly like Janine's, though Stella's was much more substantial, and she also had something like jowls that hung loose when she smiled. She had flushed, meaty skin and thick arms. There were wrinkles in her face from all the time she'd spent scowling, since not even manic happiness can mask that kind of anger—though Stella certainly tried. She was around thirty years old.

In a giddy voice, she asked me excitedly, "Are you getting the *hang of things?*"

"I think so!" I gushed. "Izzy's been *wonderful.*"

"Oh my God, *yes!*" Stella said. "Izzy's *fantastic.* Are you *loving* these *children??*"

"Definitely!" I agreed. "I am *loving* these *children!*"

"And Linda?" Stella asked. "Did you meet *Linda?*"

91

"Absolutely!" I said. "Linda's been a *huge* help! *So* wonderful! You have *such* a great program here!"

Stella continued to beam at me, so I added, "It's *really* impressive! The parents all *love* Happy Garden!" I added a few more compliments, and then Stella started to interact with some of the older children, talking to them in the same high-pitched tone that puppies adore, and then she rounded up the five- and six-year-olds and took them outside.

"Where are they going?" I asked Izzy. Izzy worked in the kindergarten/preschool room with me.

"Drum practice!" Izzy called, tossing her dreadlocks over her shoulder. "They go around the side of the house to Stella's living room. Then Stella teaches them *African drumming*. Isn't that *awesome??*"

"Awesome!" I said.

"She's an *amazing* teacher!" Izzy said. "She was a kindergarten teacher for a year before she started this business!"

I knew that Stella hadn't started this business, but I couldn't point that out or I would sound negative. So I said, "*Awesome!*" again.

We served the kids scrambled eggs and rice crackers for morning snack, and grilled cheese with steamed peas for lunch. We poured glasses of almond milk or apple juice if they didn't want water. For afternoon snack, we popped popcorn in an air-popper and coated it with special sauce, which was code for Bragg's Liquid Aminos soy sauce.

Happy Garden staff were expected to know how to cook the correct amount of food for the children present each day. Izzy told me that Stella blew a gasket if her uber-expensive organic food went to waste. Everything she bought came from either Whole Foods, Linda's farm, or in trade with other local families, which meant Stella spent as much money on food as she did on her staff.

Whoever was assigned cooking duty that day was also the person who managed the "troubled children," or the ones who'd turned violent or sullen. This meant perching the problem child on the counter next to the fridge while you worked. Sometimes other problem children were added to the small kitchen space. They would be given a toy to play with and kept underfoot of the cook. This was to keep them from throwing things at people, or otherwise causing a scene. Children were all desperate for one-on-one attention, so bad behavior was guarded against by using the kitchen as a quarantine space.

As the children at Happy Garden flocked to me like I was secretly handing out crack, and since I had a knack for keeping "problem children" out of the kitchen, Izzy decided I was her new best friend. She was on cooking duty today, to show me the ropes, and it was my mission to make this as unstressful as possible for her.

"Oh my *God*, you're like, *amazing* at this!" Izzy cried. "I bet you can't *wait* to have your *own* babies! Oh my *God!* You're like, a natural!"

"Well, I've had some practice," I said, trying to show a little boy how to catch a beach ball. "Do you have children?"

"A little girl," Izzy said, glowing with pride. "She's in first grade."

This surprised me so much, I asked, "How old are you?"

"Twenty-nine," she said happily. "I live in Riverdale. Near the college?"

"Sounds great," I said.

"Mmm-hmmm," Izzy murmured, flipping the grilled cheese for lunch. "My little girl *loves* horses. She's taking riding lessons at the Pink Angel." Pink Angel was a riding school not far from Happy Garden.

"Does she like it there?" I asked.

"Oh, she *loves* it," Izzy said. "I'll bring her with me one day, so you can meet her."

I smiled and fielded a rubber ball to a three-year-old. "That would be great."

We spent a lot of time that day with the children outside. There was a maypole down by the river, and we had the children run with us over the field to touch the pole, and then back to the farmhouse. I walked them to the horse pasture and called the horses over. While the children were petting them, Izzy said, "I've never seen these horses come to greet the children before. There must be a calming spirit in the air today. Positive forces must be emanating from the earth."

I said, "I love days like that."

There was a large wooden playground near the pasture, with swings and two slides, and this was where we played after petting the horses. We didn't walk over to see the peacocks, as those birds screamed even louder at the sight of the children, not to mention there was a collapsed shed in the field between the two properties. Old boards and rusted nails were scattered everywhere. I reasoned that rusty nails might be one of the harmful constrictions the Happy Garden brochure had alluded to.

As I'd been an opener with Izzy, we were both supposed to leave at five o'clock. But when five o'clock arrived and there were still too many children present to allow more than one staff member to leave, I volunteered to stay so Izzy could pick up her daughter.

"Oh, *thank you!*" she cried, and she gave me a hug. I continued to monitor the older children outside until 5:45 that evening, when Stella came into the yard to announce I could go. She was scowling at first, but she quickly put on a big smile.

"How *was it?*" she asked, beaming at me like I might've just won the lotto. There was something frightening about Stella when she tried looking that happy.

"Fantastic!" I gushed. "I had a *ball!* These kids are just *awesome!*"

"So we'll see you at eight o'clock tomorrow?" Stella asked.

"Definitely!" I said. "Thank you so much! This is such a great place to work!"

I had parked the Buick between two willow trees across the road, and as I walked to my car, I thought I'd hidden the vehicle pretty well. I'd been worried the Happy Garden parents would see my car and assume I was a drug dealer, so the trees came in handy. I felt exhausted as I took a seat behind the wheel. It was the first time I'd been off my feet since seven that morning. I was dying for a drink of water and maybe some coffee, as I'd never managed to finagle a cup from the kitchen all day. Stella drank most of the pots we made in her little french press, and I had the impression she resented providing anyone with free coffee, and that's why she drank so much of it herself.

I was also incredibly hungry, since Happy Garden staff did not receive breaks. Even our time in the bathroom was limited. We were allowed sixty seconds every three hours to pee, and we had to notify our coworkers when we chose to use up our toilet minute, as this left the children understaffed. Stella was very strict about this. Docking pay for bathroom abuses had been alluded to more than once. And the noise of the children had been a nonstop assault on my brain, even when naptime arrived, as half the kids never slept. There was something about the incessant screeching and yowling of dozens of toddlers that left me feeling diminished.

So when I arrived home that night to find Richard and Mia fighting over a videogame, the yelling and shouting hit my ears like a jackhammer.

11

TOOTHACHE

"He started it!" Mia screamed, and she hurled the video game controller at Richard. The hand console struck the side of his head with a crack.

"Knock it off!" I roared. I pointed to the small bedroom, to tell Mia to leave, and she glared at me before she stalked off.

"Turn off the TV," I said to Ethan, and he did. "Go to your room," I told Richard, and he slunk away.

It was going on seven and no one had made dinner. I walked to the kitchen and put on water to boil for some pasta. Then I poured jars of tomato sauce in a pan and started the oven to toast garlic bread.

I left the kitchen again, and called, "I want to see you all in here at the table!" It was time for homework.

The kids slumped to the dining area with their backpacks and sat down. All of their school supplies had gone on my MasterCard, and they took them out now, pissing and moaning all the way.

"I don't want to do homework!" Mia whined.

"Fuck this fucking shit," Richard said.

"Oh my God," Ethan mumbled.

Only Gus worked in silence.

I walked around the table occasionally, checking over their work. Gandhi padded around at my heels. We ate dinner before eight, and then Richard had to finish his math problems. I refused to turn the television back on, as I didn't want to hear any more noise than I had to, so the kids bellyached even more, and by ten o'clock, they had all gone to bed.

I put the dishes away, and then I went through my bills at the table. I still wasn't sure if I could afford a telephone line, so I sat crunching numbers a while. I couldn't write obituaries if I didn't buy a phone line, but the phone was just too expensive. I scribbled out my sums and put the bills in a drawer. Then I turned out the lights and took Hanna's broken badge from my pocket. I sat in the dark and held the pieces together.

If Hanna had been here with me, we would have had two incomes, and I could have purchased the phone line. She would have said, "Keep your chin up, Mary Jane. This'll all work out fine." I wished I could believe that.

***

Monday through Friday, I worked at Happy Garden. My schedule changed daily, depending upon whether I was an opener or a closer. Closers stayed until the last child was gone, which was usually sometime after six p.m. When parents were late, Stella yelled at the closers rather than the late parents, because if she yelled at the parents, they would yell back. Happy Garden was already the most expensive daycare facility in Riverdale, so Stella never wanted to charge late pick-up fees. And she wouldn't pay us past six o'clock, since she claimed that she couldn't afford it. So when parents were late, not only was Stella plunged into one of her moods, but closers were mandated by law to stay with unsupervised children, whether we got paid or not. Go figure.

Since being a closer was the absolute worst, and since I was the newest employee, I was assigned as the closer a lot. This meant I didn't arrive home until after seven most nights. As a result, supper was always served late, and the nightly homework battle with the kids was high-stress. But at least I was there to make sure they ate something and went to bed by nine-thirty or ten. That wouldn't have happened had I worked a night shift.

There was nothing I dreaded so much as homework time. Forcing the kids to finish their assignments practically gave me an ulcer. I felt numb with exhaustion most nights, and the kids turned obnoxious and surly over writing a few stupid spelling words or solving math problems. It pushed my temper up near the boiling point. My siblings saw nothing positive about education, and since I was not really a poster child for college increasing your earnings, I managed to hold my tongue most evenings. The kids could almost flunk out of high school and still work the jobs that I did, and this made our homework battles a war of attrition. Whatever energy I had left at the end of each day, I burned up fighting with the kids over school. Family time resembled the Long March through China, circa 1934. My role, of course, was that of Mao Zedong. Talk about suck.

On the weekends, I took a job as a bellhop for a ritzy hotel and condominium business called The Summit Exclusive. The Summit was located outside of Riverdale, close to a ski resort called Riverdale Mountain, and even during the recession, there weren't any condos for sale on the property. Hotel rooms at The Summit ran from one-fifty to four-ninety a night, so I was hired on at ten dollars an hour, plus tips. Not only was the pay a lot better than Happy Garden's, but the work was easier. My duties included escorting guests to their rooms, hauling luggage, and occasionally shoveling snow, but most of my time was spent driving the airport shuttle.

The airport shuttle was my kind of gig. I drove a van big enough to seat fifteen passengers, and I traveled all over the grounds of The Summit to pick people up or drop them off at their condos, vacation homes, or hotel rooms. So not only did I get to see the extravagant interiors of these huge condos and houses, but I was allowed to spend time sitting down, simply driving the van. The airport was an hour away from The Summit, and after spending a week chasing young children and never finding two seconds to even drink water, the time spent driving the shuttle felt like a day at the spa. I loved this job. I worked Friday and Saturday nights until eleven or midnight, and then each Sunday morning, from seven a.m. until three p.m. That gave me time Sunday night to have a few hours' rest before the dinner-and-homework-battle routine, so Sundays were easily my favorite day of the week.

Before the ski season started and the shuttle service picked up, I did maintenance work at The Summit. I enjoyed my time with my coworkers, who were mostly retired cops from Delaware. They told stories about shoot-outs and crime scenes they'd been in, and they used the word *ignoramus* a lot, especially when discussing a criminal. They'd come to Riverdale to retire, and then discovered they couldn't afford to live here on a pension. So they worked at The Summit, making ten bucks an hour like me. We wore matching uniforms: black slacks, oversized collared shirts, and hideous fuzzy vests with The Summit's logo on the left side of the zipper. When I dressed for work, I looked like a forest-green Yeti.

"How come you're not married?" the Delaware cops liked to ask me.

"Why, you offering?" was my standard reply. All of the cops were married and loved their wives, so this response shut them right up.

"Where'd you go to college?" was another popular question. Sometimes I used a southern drawl when I spoke, sometimes I sounded Midwestern, and sometimes I mimicked the clipped diction the rust-belter cops liked to use.

"Who said anything about college?" I asked.

"You went to college, no fooling," they said. But I'd never admit to having a diploma around them. It shamed me too much. I didn't have a boyfriend, and I didn't have a career. If I'd only wanted to get married and have babies, I wouldn't be single right now. But that was almost as shameful to admit as having a college diploma. I didn't want to be perceived as an idiot, and I also didn't want to hear that "healthy women" wanted children. Whenever I admitted I didn't want to have babies, people always started in on their *What is the matter with you?* speech. *What kind of human being doesn't want to have kids?*

Me. I didn't. But I was still a human being. And I didn't think there was anything wrong with me.

But the Delaware cops would have told me as much, so I kept my life private. I'd raised my babies already, and those men would never understand that, no matter what I said.

***

By the first of December, I was starting to wonder what I would do about Christmas. I'd bought the kids and Gus passes to the community center, so they could spend a few hours after school each day swimming or rock climbing, and I'd paid for Ethan's sports physical and other expenses so he could play basketball. With the money set aside for the Goldking property tax, and two hundred dollars set aside for my first student loan payment, I was skating by as it was and sliding into the red. We ate a lot of rice and beans, and I knew I didn't have the money for a holiday feast. But if we volunteered at the homeless shelter Christmas morning, we'd receive a free turkey dinner with potatoes and gravy. I hated not being able to cook at home on the holidays, but I hated eating rice and beans for Christmas dinner even more. The thought of it was pushing me toward despair, so I told the kids and Gus that we'd work at the food kitchen and eat the free turkey.

December fifth was Ethan's birthday, so I bought an extra box of bullets for Ravi and drove us all outside town, and we spent two hours shooting at Coke cans. Richard had gathered our targets from a Riverdale recycling tub, as we only drank water at home.

Before I went into work at The Summit that night, Mom showed up at the door. She wore a blue evening dress and a pair of black snow boots, and I guessed that her relationship with Michael Bean hadn't worked out. She stood clasping her white high heels in one hand, and a small vintage suitcase with the other.

My heart sank to my knees. I wished I could tell her to leave, but I couldn't summon a sufficient level of meanness to pull off such a thing. Letting her in here would bring nothing but trouble and hardship. But how could I slam the door in her face?

"Hi, Mom," I said.

"Something sure smells good!" she called, strolling in.

"Rice and beans in the crock pot," Richard said.

Mom asked, "Can I have some?"

I said, "Help yourself."

I went into the bedroom to change for work. When I came out a few minutes later, dressed in my fuzzy green vest, Mom frowned and asked, "Where are you going in *that?*"

"Lumberjacking," I said. "These vests are all the rave now." Mom rolled her eyes and I smiled when I razzed her, but then I felt a sharp pain in my mouth. I placed a hand on my jaw.

"Got a toothache?" Mom asked. "It's your own fault if you do. You eat too much candy."

I didn't eat candy, and I wasn't sure why my mouth hurt. My teeth were white and straight, and I knew I didn't have any cavities. I flexed my jaw and hoped the pain went away.

I asked Mom, "Gonna stay the night?"

"It's warm here," she said.

I'd reasoned as much. Without the money for propane, she was probably freezing in Goldking. "I've got extra pillows and blankets in the closet," I told her.

"They better not have come from the *thrift* store," Mom said. "I'm not ending up with some disease. Or lice."

"They're not from the thrift store," I lied. I put on my coat and headed to work.

Over the course of my shift at The Summit, the pain in my jaw grew progressively worse. I'd brought a peanut butter sandwich for dinner, and it almost hurt too much to chew. The Delaware cops were concerned.

"You'd better see a dentist," they said. "That's nothing to mess around with."

My breathing turned fainter at the thought of a dentist. Where would I come up with the money for that? Whatever was wrong with me, I couldn't afford it.

When my shift ended at eleven, I drove home to find Mom asleep in bed with Mia. So I took the extra blanket and pillow from the closet and slept on the couch. I woke up before five and had a panic attack, and my jaw hurt so bad, I couldn't open my mouth more than a fraction. It felt like my teeth had been wired together.

By the time I could breathe again, I was sobbing. I went outside and cried on the steps of the apartment complex, so I wouldn't wake up the kids or freak out poor Gus. I kept trying to open my mouth more than half an inch, but my entire head was on fire with pain. There was nothing to do but return inside for the phone book and flip through the yellow pages. I prayed to God I'd find a dentist who wasn't a quack.

12

THE TALIBAN

There weren't any dentists who could see me on Sunday, so I swallowed four aspirin and worked my shift at The Summit. I could still open my mouth enough to speak clearly, though I couldn't eat solid food. For breakfast, I mixed two raw eggs with water, and drank that down. For lunch, I drank peanut butter and water. My mouth hurt so much I couldn't taste anything, which was fortunate, because peanut butter in water was slimy and gross.

On Monday morning, I drove to work at Happy Garden one hour early. I needed to use the phone in the kitchen to call a few dentists, and since I was closing, I could make the calls before my shift started. The pain in my jaw had increased in two days, and my peripheral vision was white with pain. I was running a fever.

The earliest any dentist could see me was Thursday. I worked at Happy Garden all week, since Stella would fire me for missing a day. On Thursday, I left work early and drove into Riverdale. After waiting an hour and a half for this overbooked dentist, I took a seat in his office. When he discovered I could not even open my mouth, he told me I needed to clear up the infection I had before he could find out what was wrong with me. He wrote out an antibiotic prescription, annoyed with me for wasting his time on something as dumb as an infection. I had to wait another hour in line again to pay one hundred dollars for the visit (which went on my MasterCard), and then I scheduled my next appointment.

After that, I walked outside to my car and started to sob. I was in so much pain, and I had to face the reality that it was not going away any time soon. Working at Happy Garden all week had been so hard, and instead of ending my misery, I would simply have to face more.

I drove to the pharmacy and charged the fifty-five dollars for the antibiotic. Faced with yet another bill I couldn't pay, I felt impudent and pathetic, and when I arrived home that night, I didn't even have the strength to make the kids do their home-work. I lay on the floor in the living room and stared at the ceiling. I forced myself not to cry. Gus sat down beside me and patted my hand, and then he drew me a big heart on a piece of paper. I propped it on top of my chest and stared at the ceiling again. Gandhi laid his head on my stomach, but I didn't have the energy to pet him.

"Oh, big *deal*," Mom said. "So you can't open your mouth all the way. What does that matter? I broke my collarbone once. In a head-on collision! I had a concussion. I spent two nights in the hospital. Now, that's what really hurts. Broken bones."

"Teeth are bones," Richard said.

"Yeah, but they're little," Mom said. "A collarbone is much bigger, not to mention your skull. You kids have never broken your bones. You wouldn't know."

"Landon broke his leg," Mia said. This had happened three years ago, in a dirt biking accident.

"Well, Landon has a *passion* in life," Mom said. "Unlike *some* people I know!" I could tell by her voice that she was speaking to me, even if I couldn't see her face at the moment.

"Almost time for bed," I told the kids in a dull, lifeless voice. "Get your book bags ready." I always made the kids prep their book bags at night.

As no one had done any homework this evening, Mia said cheerfully, "They're ready!" Then she asked, "Can we play Monopoly?"

"No," I said. "It's ten o'clock. Go to bed."

"Mom says we don't have to," Mia sassed.

At this, I sat up and lurched to my feet. I must have had the wild, evil look of a dragon from hell, because Mia said, "We're going!" and the kids fled the room. I heard them brushing their teeth and changing for bed, so I settled down on the couch next to Mom and resumed my dead stare, this time at the wall.

"Why don't you go out to a *party?*" Mom said. "When I was your age, I used to party! Even after Landon was born. How are you ever going to meet a man and start a family, if you never go out?"

She stopped talking a minute and fussed with her hair. I could hear it swishing around beside me. "All the men your age are being snatched up," she went on. "And what are you doing? Finding a husband who can give you some babies? No! You're just lying around here on the floor! So what your heart has been broken. You go to a party. You don't act like a slob and give up!"

I noticed the bedroom lights were still on, so I called, "Lights out!" to the kids, and the hallway went dark.

Mom flipped on the TV, but I reached over and switched it off. She sniffed at me, vexed she couldn't watch CBS. "You think men want to have *babies* with some ugly old broad? You think you can turn forty, and still find a young stud? Huh?"

I left the couch and walked into the kitchen. I made a glass of water and peanut butter, stirred it mightily, and drank it down. The antibiotic didn't help the amount of pain in my jaw, and aspirin wasn't enough to put me out of my misery. I wanted to just whimper and die.

"At least you're *skinny!*" Mom cried. I wished she'd be quiet. I started washing the dishes from dinner, to drown out her voice, but I could still hear her comments over the sound of the water. "If you hadn't cut all your *hair* off, you wouldn't look like a *dyke!* Then maybe you'd have a boy with you here, instead of that mangy old dog! You'd have some *fun!* Maybe go out for a steak dinner once in a while! Or you could buy some egg rolls, and not eat rice and beans all the time! You'd go find a party!"

Mom finally ran me down enough that I leaned my arms on the counter and started to cry. Not because I wanted some egg rolls or a steak dinner. That wasn't enough to turn on my waterworks. Love though—someone to love me—it burned me up sometimes, how much I wanted a man in my life. A man who wouldn't ask me for babies. Who'd love me in spite of all that. That kind of longing hurt worse than anything.

I might be the Old Woman Who Lived in a Shoe, but I knew I still wanted to be Cinderella. Grit and denial might help me survive, but underneath that, I was just as mushy and lonely as any girl on the earth.

✳✳✳

I went back to the dentist a week later. It turned out I had a wisdom tooth growing in, and the infection in my jaw had been caused by a tiny split in my gum, where the tooth was trying to push out. My x-ray showed I only had three wisdom teeth, and the dentist said that the one growing in would definitely have to be pulled.

"You don't have enough room in your mouth for another tooth," he said. "I charge eleven hundred dollars for an extraction. I'll only charge you four hundred more for the other two, if you pull them together. You should really get rid of them all, and save some money up front. If you do them all separately, I'll charge eleven hundred each time."

"So, fifteen-hundred?" I asked wearily.

"Plus an extra hundred for anesthetic," he said. "I have to cut through the gum and grind into the bone. Sometimes I have to split the teeth apart to remove them. You'll probably want to be under for that."

"Yes," I agreed. I didn't want to witness my teeth being broken. "I think you should pull all three."

I felt my lower lip quiver, ready to cry again at the thought of how much this would cost. I hurried to leave his office and queue in the waiting room line to make the appointment for surgery.

The receptionist had me fill out some papers, and then she said, "We can't sign you up unless you have someone to drive you home. You can't operate a vehicle for twenty-four hours after this anesthesia."

"I'll find someone to drive," I said. So she told me to return at eight o'clock tomorrow morning.

***

I struggled to find someone to drive me. Gus didn't yet have a permit, and all of my neighbors had to work the next day, which meant only Mom had a license and the time off to drive me.

"Sure I can drive you!" she said when I asked her that night. "And while you're with the dentist, I can catch up on my reading!" She meant the magazines like *Woman's Day* and *Good Housekeeping* that were kept in the waiting room.

"I have to be there at seven," I said. I'd learned to cushion appointment times by an hour, to avoid being late. Mom thought fixing her hair was far more important than being on time.

"I'll be ready!" Mom said.

So I woke before five the next morning, showered, and made the kids eat some breakfast. They boarded the bus while Mom groused and complained about missing her beauty sleep. Seven o'clock rolled by, and then it was eight and we still weren't in the car. Mom was having a conniption over her earrings.

"I'm leaving without you!" I yelled, and I walked down to the car. Mom hurried after me and jumped in the passenger seat.

"You make a big deal out of *nothing*," she said. "These doctors don't have anything better to do with their time than to—"

"Buckle your seatbelt," I said, and I stepped on the gas. My apartment was on the north side of Riverdale, and I gunned it to the dentist, but there was no way I could get there before eight-twenty now.

When we arrived at the building, the receptionist gave me the evil eye about being late, and she chastised me twice. "Sorry," I said. "I overslept."

I had to fill out more papers, and I had to hand over my MasterCard so she could pre-charge the bill. Apparently, people tried paying for dental work with terminated credit cards quite a lot. Well, mine had a balance of one thousand dollars, which had all been unforeseen school expenses for the kids and Gus (but mostly for Gus, who'd ended up needing eyeglasses). But since my credit limit was ten times the amount of my current balance, the charge for today's surgery went through just fine. Satisfied I wasn't a bum, the receptionist led me to the room where I'd be anesthetized.

She was cheerful now, smiling and chatting about the procedure, but I'd stopped listening to her. I'd decided that she was annoying and not a very nice person. I heard her say, "*Blah-blah-blah*, and then the dentist will *blah-blah-blah*, and we'll take you into room *blah-blah-blah* for the *blah-blah-blah* and *blah-blah*."

I said, "Sounds fine, thanks," and took a seat. I was trying to calculate how long it would take me to pay off this bill. I had eight-percent interest on my MasterCard. If I made good tips at The Summit, I might have the bulk of this tooth extraction paid off by March. My palms started sweating though, I was so anxious about it. What if I didn't make decent tips? What if one of the kids developed a cavity and I was back in here next month?

The dentist came in to see me. I must have looked stressed. "Oh, don't worry," he said, trying to bolster my spirits. "I promise you won't feel a thing. You'll be completely unconscious for the next hour."

"Okay, thanks," I said. I wasn't actually worried about having the teeth pulled. I'd been in so much pain that I hated those wisdom teeth. In fact, I wanted the teeth back after he pulled them, so I could shoot them to smithereens with my gun. I'd drop a nuclear bomb on those teeth if I could. The faster they were out of my mouth, the better.

***

I woke up after surgery around eleven o'clock. I heard a sound like fifty bees buzzing around in my skull, and my mouth was packed in gauze. I tasted blood. I started moving my tongue, and felt dried blood on my teeth, on the gauze, and in the back of my throat. I tried to sit up, but the whole world was spinning.

"Hey!" Mom said. "You're awake!" I blinked my eyes a few times and saw she was sitting beside me.

A woman came in and checked on me, and after my vision stopped spinning, she told me I had three huge holes in my mouth (duh), and that I'd need to clean out these holes frequently until they'd healed over. She handed me a small plastic bottle with a screw-top lid for this purpose. The bottle had been built with a nozzle for spraying. She said the swelling in my cheeks and my jaw would go down in a couple of days. She gave me a prescription for painkiller.

I asked, "Can I have my teeth?" but due to all of the gauze in my mouth, the words sounded like, "Goorroo llemm nee beef?"

She left the room and returned with a tiny bag holding my three wisdom teeth. "Here you go."

I took the bag and hobbled out of the room. Mom followed me to the car.

"Well, these people seem nice," she said. "They had *Woman's Day* in the lobby."

"Super," I said, which sounded like, "Zooober." I decided not to speak for a while.

I wrote down the name of the pharmacy I used, so Mom would know where to go. When she parked in front of the One Stop Drug Shop, I went inside and had my prescription filled. The painkiller cost me another thirty-five dollars, which went on my MasterCard. As I was leaving, I noticed four men who lived in my apartment complex standing around in the parking lot, smoking cigarettes. They were all dressed in blue scrubs and white tennis shoes. I waved to be friendly.

"Good morning!" one called. I pointed to my swollen face and waved again, to leave without speaking, but the man broke away from his friends and jogged over.

"You are feeling well, Miss Logan?" he asked. "Your dentist did a good job?"

"Yes," I said, which sounded like, "Bress." I tried to remember where he had said his parents were from. Iran, I thought. I was pretty sure he'd told me he and his friends were all Persian.

I'd taken a seat in the car, and when I glanced at Mom, I saw she looked frightened. She obviously thought this man was a terrorist. I told him, "Zriss hizz nie nnrrom."

"Hello, Mrs. Logan!" the man said happily. He reached over the passenger seat and shook her hand. "Very nice to meet your acquaintance."

Mom stopped shaking his hand, looking miffed. She was not Mrs. Logan. She was Mrs. Preston, after the meth dealer in prison. She hadn't been Mrs. Logan for more than sixteen years.

As I didn't want to sit here and explain my mother's marital status, I struggled to ask the man where he worked. "Bear blu youl bork?" I pointed to his scrubs since my words were so garbled.

"Tucky Hilson's," he said, pointing to a building across the street. Tucky Hilson's was the name of Riverdale's largest home for the elderly. "Wonderful place," the man added. "Everyone is so kind."

I nodded and tried to smile. I gestured toward my swollen cheeks again, and the man understood. "Get well very soon, Miss Logan!" he said, stepping away from the door.

As Mom left the parking lot, she kept studying the man through the rearview mirror.

"Who are those people?" she asked tensely.

"Zershans," I said.

"They look like the Taliban," Mom said. "What does the Taliban want with the old people here?"

I wrote on my paper sack: *They are NOT Taliban!!* and held it up where she could read it when she stopped at a red light. Those men didn't even have beards.

"Yeah, *right*," she said. "Not Taliban my ass. They're probably collecting dynamite! They probably want to blow up the water plant here!"

I leaned back in my seat, too tired for this. I must have been more exhausted then I realized, because I went to sleep for a minute, and Mom slammed the car into a streetlight. My forehead smacked the dashboard as I was thrown forward on impact. Waking up to a car accident scared me half to pieces.

"Goddamn it!" Mom yelled. "Goddamn it to hell!"

When I had my bearings again, I stepped out of the car to hear an evil hissing noise. I saw she'd smashed in the radiator, and permanently damaged the streetlight. Mom was still yelling. "Goddamn it! Goddamn these people! You try to drive down the road, and they just put shit in your way! All this shit in the road like it's not hard enough! How are you supposed to get anywhere with all this shit in the road?" I thought she must've been trying to light a cigarette, and not paying attention when the car veered off course.

I glanced around at the traffic. I knew I was supposed to wait for police and file a report. But I walked around to the driver's side and told Mom to get in, and I drove the car to a repair shop in town. I took the back roads, as my vision was swimming again.

While I was parking out front, the old men who worked in the shop looked appalled, probably because my Buick seemed like a drug-dealer's ride more than ever. Mom stayed in the car to rant to herself, and I went to speak to a man about fixing the radiator. I had to write down my questions on a piece of paper, and after he inspected the damage, he gave me a quote of four hundred dollars.

Okay, I scribbled. *Please fix it.*

"I should have it ready for you in a week, maybe two," he said.

I shook his hand, gathered my things from the car, and motioned to my mother we were leaving. We walked back to the highway and I put out my thumb. Fifteen minutes later, a guy in a pickup pulled over. He gave us a lift the four miles to my place. He went out of his way to deliver us, which made me turn weepy with gratitude. I blamed the anesthetic, which was still wearing off.

Mom told the driver about the accident. "I tell you, *where* do they put up these *streetlights?* On the side of the road where they *should* be? No! They build them right in the highway! Right where you can hit them!" She even pointed out the one she'd slammed into, as we were driving by in the truck. "There, you see that?" Mom yelled. "It's right in the road!"

"I see that, ma'am," the man said politely. "That sure is a shame about your vehicle."

"Tell me about it!" Mom said. "I almost broke my nose on the steering wheel!"

13

CARVER GREYSON

After the guy in the pickup dropped us off, I went into my apartment and passed out on my bed. I didn't wake up until the kids came home from school. They were cheering and laughing in the living room, and I thought they were just excited it was Friday and they could stay up past ten. I glanced at the clock and realized I needed to head down to my night shift at The Summit.

I sat up gingerly, swallowed another pain pill, and changed for work. I walked into the living room to find a sea of balloons.

Huge helium balloons.

Pink, green, yellow, and blue, every color of the rainbow flooded the room. It was like walking through a shiny, sparkling cave. The kids were slapping the bright strings, making the balloons wiggle across the ceiling. Gandhi was hiding under the dining table. Mom was singing a Bob Dylan song mixed with "Can't Buy Me Love." She was dancing in her heels.

"Surprise!" she yelled when she saw me. "Happy Birthday!"

I sank into an armchair. I'd removed the gauze from my mouth, so I could speak clearly. "It's not my birthday," I said.

"Yeah, well, I missed your last birthday," Mom said. "So here you go!" I knew it was her way of telling me she was sorry for wrecking the car. I appreciated the gesture, but—

"Where did you get the money for this?" I asked. Mom went to her pocketbook and held up my MasterCard.

"The charge went through, no problem!" she said happily. I rose as calmly as I could and took the MasterCard from her hand.

"Mom, I don't want you to use this," I said.

"But I needed to get you something for your *birthday*," she said. "How else could I do that?"

"Mom," I said. "Don't take my credit card again."

"Well, you'll be happy to know that I had these *delivered*," she huffed, as if that would cheer me up. "And the guy gave me a *bargain*."

Mom used the word *bargain* to try to butter me up, but I couldn't have lost my temper if I'd wanted to. I felt beat.

"You going to work?" Richard asked.

"Yeah," I said. "Listen, the car's at the repair shop for a week or two." To Ethan, I added, "I can't drive you into school for your game tomorrow, so we'll have to get up early and walk."

"Okay," he said. "I can go by myself."

"We'll see," I said. I was actually going to try to thumb a ride into town, but I couldn't say that in front of Mom. She'd think I was trying to teach the children bad habits.

I checked the fridge to make sure they had something for dinner. "There's a carton of eggs here, and a sack of potatoes. You can make breakfast for dinner tonight."

From his seat at the table, Gus smiled at me and made a light panting sound, which meant he was happy and excited. Gus loved breakfast for dinner. Especially pancakes—even if I couldn't afford syrup, and he had to sprinkle his pancakes with sugar.

"I'll cook!" Mom volunteered.

I gazed steadily at the kids until Ethan finally said, "It's okay, Mom. I'll cook."

"All right," Mom said. Her shoulders slumped, and I heard the catch in her voice.

"Mom, how about you cut potatoes," I said. "You can make a big bowl for the hash browns."

"Okay!" she said brightly, and she hurried into the kitchen.

"All right, I'm off," I said. I pulled on my coat and left the apartment, and then I strolled out to the highway. I walked about a mile before someone picked me up in the dark, and drove me the fifteen miles to The Summit.

After I clocked in, the Delaware cops whistled at the sight of my face. My cheeks and jaw had swelled considerably since that morning.

"That looks totally painful," they said. "Hope they gave you some painkiller."

"They did," I said. Then I used the phone at the desk and called my MasterCard number. I discovered Mom's balloon purchase had come to $198.00, a sum large enough to almost make me turn weepy again. That was only two dollars shy of a student loan payment, and my next one was due on January sixth. God, did I hate being broke.

At least it was busy at work. Guests kept checking in, and I hustled with the luggage cart. I also shuttled several guests out to their condos, even though I wasn't supposed to be driving. My vision wasn't swimming anymore, and I really felt fine. If I had the strength and wherewithal to haul trunks and suitcases, I could certainly steer the van.

I only made thirty dollars in tips. If I'd been a man, I might have made more, but female bellhops made people uncomfortable, so they often tipped less. My only equalizing power with men was my smile, and with my face like it was, that wasn't going over so well. So I decided to make an extra ten bucks on the clock and work until midnight. I was watching the front desk for the night auditor when someone walked into the lobby.

I glanced up to see a man in a dark woolen trench coat, with a black cotton scarf and expensive black boots. He stood maybe six-three or six-four, with long massive arms and shoulders so broad they put my dining room table to shame. He didn't wear gloves, and his hands were muscled and huge. As he walked up to the desk, I recognized the bear-man who'd had lunch in The Caroline. The one Warren had thought was an NFL player.

I felt such a jolt to suddenly see him again, that I smiled more than I had all night. "Good evening," I said. "How can I help you?"

The bear-man had been smiling at first, exactly the way I remembered, with that mischievous grin, but as he approached the front desk, his expression turned to one of alarm.

"What happened to you?" he asked, and I knew he meant my red, swollen face.

I spotted Steve, the night auditor, returning to his place at the desk, so I said, "I got smacked with a shovel. Steve hit me," and I pointed at Steve.

"I didn't hit her with a shovel!" Steve said, and he glowered at me as he walked toward his chair. Steve was a geeky, pimple-faced boy with messy blond hair. He was twenty years old and he loved to play chess. We got along swell. "MJ just likes messing around," he snarled, and he shot me another look. "She had three teeth pulled today."

I was still kind of laughing at Steve, but I managed to ask the man, "Are you here to check in?"

He eased his big hands into his coat pockets and said, "No. I think I came in for some dinner." The Summit had a four-star restaurant located on the second floor.

"I'm sorry," Steve said, all manners now. "The dining room closed at nine. We have vending machines down the hall, or you can drive into Riverdale. There are several fast food restaurants still open at this hour."

The bear-man seemed abashed. He glanced down at the floor, and then he looked up again and said, "Well, thank you. Good night," and he strolled out the door.

I wished he'd stayed longer. I liked the look of that man, especially his bright silver eyes. His jaw line was also pretty thrilling. Empires were made and destroyed by men with nice jaws.

But I couldn't blame him for leaving. I was dressed like a Yeti and my head resembled a basketball. Talk about suck.

Steve organized a few room keys. "You wanna play chess?" he asked. Steve kept a travel game under the counter. We weren't supposed to play chess on the clock, but most people hated the management here, including Steve. I thought The Summit was heaven compared to Happy Garden, so if I played a few surreptitious games of chess with Steve on occasion, it was simply because I liked talking to Steve, not because of any animosity toward my boss.

But I was too tired. It was after midnight, and I had to hitchhike home. It was snowing outside. "It's late," I told Steve, and he looked disappointed.

"See you tomorrow then," he said, and I left to clock out. I put on my coat and hurried outside. I switched on my flashlight and walked down the hill toward the main road, turned right at the stop sign and headed up to the highway. The Summit had a tollhouse at the highway turnoff, but no one ever manned the booth. I passed the main gate, crossed the highway, and prayed someone would drive by soon. I also prayed they wouldn't run me over in the snow.

I hadn't gone very far when a Lincoln Navigator arrived. As the vehicle pulled up beside me, the passenger window went down, and I saw the bear-man at the wheel. The light reflecting on the snow brightened the inside of the cab, and I could tell he looked happy to see me.

"Hey!" I said, beaming. It was freezing out here. "You mind giving me a ride?"

"Of course not," he said. I loved the sound of his voice. He had a smooth baritone, almost deep as a bass, and it suited him. I hopped into his Lincoln and buckled up.

"I thought you'd be on your mustang," he said.

"My wha—?" I had to think for a moment. "You mean King?" and I laughed. "He belongs to a friend." I realized suddenly that this man *remembered* me. From six months ago. *Six months ago!* The idea made me feel almost giddy.

"My boss at The Caroline told everyone you were an NFL player," I said, and the bear-man laughed.

"Which one?" he asked.

"Marshall Bramson," I said, and the bear-man found this funnier still.

I asked, "What's your name, anyway?"

"Carver Greyson," he said.

"I'm Mary Jane," I said, and I reached over to shake his hand. He had a warm, friendly grip, and I wished I didn't have to let go. "You keep a place at The Summit?"

"My sister does." He paused for a moment, and then added, "I bring my boys here each December to ski." I noticed he wasn't wearing a wedding ring. Boys and no ring. Something was up.

"How many kids do you have?" I asked.

"Three," he said. "Seven, eight, and nine."

"Those are cute ages," I said.

Carver grinned to let me know he agreed. He had some grey in his hair, which still looked like it needed a good combing and at least two inches trimmed off. Most of his hair was light and dark brown, so the grey wasn't that noticeable, but he didn't look old enough for grey hair. Carver was still in his twenties, I felt sure of it. Some men started losing their hair as teenagers, but that wasn't his problem. Carver had plenty of hair, which made the contrast between his youth and his coloring all the more interesting.

"You seem pretty young to have a nine-year-old," I said.

Carver looked slightly surprised, slightly amused by this comment. "I was twenty when Jack was born." He smiled again and added, "Three of the best days of my life were the days my children were born. I didn't plan having a family so soon, but I'd do anything for those monkeys. Christmas vacation is my favorite time of year. Except my boys are playing with their cousins tonight, and don't need their old dad."

I smiled at this, glad I'd been right about his age, and that he was a man who loved his children so much. I also knew now why he'd seemed kind of lost when he'd walked into the lobby tonight. He'd been looking forward to spending time with his boys, but they had other plans.

I glanced through the windshield and said, "I live just north of town. Another five miles, on the left."

"Why aren't you at home?" he asked. "If you had three teeth pulled today?"

"Oh, I have to go in to work so I can give Steve a hard time. You know how it is." I smiled to myself, and then out of nowhere, I added, "Ty Cobb once had his tonsils removed without anesthesia. But he still played a ballgame that day." It was a bit of trivia from a Ken Burns documentary, which meant I was in a particularly good mood.

Carver glanced at my face and returned his gaze to the road. He was smiling again.

"Not that I want to be like Ty Cobb," I said quickly. "He was so mean and racist. I don't ever want to be an unbearable cuss."

"He does go down in history as the biggest S.O.B. in baseball," Carver said.

This made me grin. I really liked men who knew about baseball. It was my favorite sport, even if I didn't follow it much. Playing softball in high school had helped me get into college, but I could play softball without spending hours watching baseball games. I was never a girl with a lot of time on my hands.

"So, are you a Rangers fan?" I asked, since I knew he was from Texas. "Or do you pull for the Astros?"

"Right now, Saint Louis," he said. "But as a kid, my heart belonged to the Tigers. That was my grandfather's team."

"How about your dad?" I asked. "Did he cheer for Detroit?"

"He was a Braves man all the way," Carver said.

"I like the Braves," I said. "I saw them play once." At a school I'd attended in Alabama, if students made the honor roll in seventh grade, they were invited on a field trip to see the Braves play in Georgia. That had been a fun day.

"Did you grow up with the Braves?" Carver asked.

"My dad loved the Phillies," I said, "and if heaven is a base-ball diamond, then that's where he's at. He'd play second base." I stopped talking a moment, aware I was being unusually chatty. I wished I knew why this man wasn't wearing a wedding ring. "I went to a high school in Illinois," I added, "mostly redbird fan country, where I was. But there were a lot of people who loved the Cubs, too. So I'm partial to both those teams."

"Did you follow the Cardinals this year?" he asked.

"No," I said, blushing now. "I don't know… It's hard to find the time to sit down for a game."

"Cause you're out riding horses?" he asked.

"Oh!" I laughed. "I wish." I retrieved the bottle of pain pills from my pack and swallowed another one, because my jaw was hurting again.

"So, you ski?" I asked.

"No," Carver said. "Not for me."

"You're missing out," I said, smiling again. "Not as fun as horseback riding, but it's close," and I kept grinning at him. I didn't know what I was thinking. The man was probably married. That damn jaw line of his had me all out of sorts.

I pointed ahead to the road he needed to take and said, "That's my turn." Then I fell silent a minute, while Carver slowed down and turned off the highway. He coasted over the road and I showed him which building I lived in.

"That's me," I said. "Thanks a lot for the ride."

I unbuckled the seatbelt and Carver said, "Wait." So I dropped my hand from the door handle to see what he wanted. He jumped out of the vehicle and jogged around to the pas-senger's side.

He stood by my door for a moment, grinning down at me through the glass. The snow was falling between us, and the light from the headlights cast a glow on his face. I could see his eyes dancing. Then he opened my door and held out his hand to help me down.

"What a sweet gent," I said, and I held his hand for a second as I hopped to the ground. "You better be careful. You're gonna melt someone's heart."

Carver laughed again and slapped his hands once. Then he shut the passenger door and stood in the snow, watching me as I walked up to my building. I turned and waved him goodbye.

14

MARK TWAIN

Inside the apartment, I found Mom and the kids still awake. Gus had fallen asleep in one of the armchairs, with Gandhi curled up in his lap. Richard and Ethan were playing a video game, while Mia was fixing something to eat in the kitchen.

Mom was in Cleaning Mode.

Mom's idea of cleaning house was to wear a pair of ski goggles, a shower cap, and rubber gloves, and squirt ammonia water on everything: furniture, walls, and even the dog. That was what she was doing when I came home. She was dressed in her cleaning gear and she was squirting the living room. When she blasted Gandhi, he made a little whimpering sound. The helium balloons still covered the ceiling, and Mom started squirting those, too.

"Hi, everyone," I said.

"Hey, MJ," Richard said, and the others all echoed him.

I walked over to Mom and took the spray bottle. She clasped her hands together and said, "I found some germs. Those things are dangerous."

"Yeah," I said, and I planted a kiss on her forehead. I always gave her a kiss when she stopped her cleaning sprees peaceably. Mom smiled, and I carried the spray bottle to the kitchen and stashed it under the sink. Then I returned to the living room and said, "Ethan, you ought to be in bed."

Ethan sighed and left the room to brush his teeth. I placed my pack on the dining table and stripped off my coat. Then I counted my tip money again. I set out four dollars for Ethan, so he could eat at McDonald's tomorrow with his basketball team. That left me twenty-six dollars to buy a few groceries. I wanted bananas, potatoes, eggs, and more rice.

"Hey, Richard," I said.

"Yeah?"

"You wanna come with me and Ethan tomorrow? Help me bring back some groceries?"

"I guess," Richard sighed.

Mia said, "I wanna go."

I said, "Well, if you go, then Gus'll wanna go,"

"Gus likes the grocery store," Mia pointed out.

"Gus likes everything," Richard said.

With that settled, I herded them all off to bed. I caught Mom trying to start another cleaning spree, so I took the spray bottle again. I also made her hand over the goggles and gloves.

Since Mom wouldn't give up her place on the bed next to Mia, I'd purchased another Army cot at the thrift store this week. When I stretched out on my skinny mattress that night, I didn't want to sleep. I wanted to think about Carver, and picture his face again, smiling at me. So that's what I did. I swallowed another pain pill, and I thought about Carver Greyson: his silver eyes, his tanned skin, and the way that he smiled. I bet he would be fun to kiss.

***

I woke the kids up at seven the next morning and we all trooped into town. Ethan climbed aboard the school bus with his basketball team, and the rest of us walked to the grocery store. We put our supplies in two burlap sacks, which Richard and Gus carried home.

At one o'clock, I changed for my Saturday shift at The Summit, and I made sure Mia was set to make dinner. Then I went to the highway to thumb a ride up the mountain, but I ended up walking seven of the fifteen miles to the resort that afternoon. Pure Suck.

I was almost late to work. Steve was on shift again, and I could tell as soon as I saw him that he was unhappy. As Steve was unhappy a lot lately, this didn't faze me too much.

"Hey, Steve," I said.

"Hey, MJ," he mumbled.

I walked over and put my face close to his, to tease him. He tried to bat me away. "Stop it," he said.

I clocked in and prepped the van for an airport run, and then I drove out and collected several people from their condos. By the time I dropped them off at the airport and returned to The Summit, Steve's mood was decidedly grim.

"Seriously, are you okay?" I asked.

"I'm fine," he sighed.

We had several hotel guests arrive then, so I hustled a lot. I kept a lookout for Carver but I didn't see him at all. I hoped he might stop by around midnight again. I ended up dealing with several problems that evening, including a broken door lock, a woman who'd slipped on some ice outside her condo and needed an ambulance, and another guy who ran his car off the road. By the time I arrived in the lobby again, it was time to clock out. I caught Steve crying in the staff room, but he acted so embarrassed I'd seen him, I didn't say anything.

I was hoping I might catch a ride home with him, but then some guests arrived late, and they had luggage for me to bring in, so I stayed an extra twenty minutes. Steve left without me, and I hitchhiked home again. This time, an old man in a Bronco picked me up and dropped me off north of town.

At home, I asked Ethan how his game had gone. The kids were all awake watching *Gladiator*.

"We won," Ethan said. "JV and varsity."

"All right!" I cheered, and I walked into the kitchen to eat dinner. I broke open two eggs and dropped them into a glass, stirred them up with some water and drank it down. Technically, I was supposed to be drinking milkshakes and feasting on Jell-O while those holes in my gums closed over, but there wasn't any protein in Jell-O, and I didn't have the money to buy milk for a shake. I did worry a little about salmonella, but I was too hungry to care.

I wrapped myself in a blanket and curled up on the couch. "So tell me about the game," I said to Ethan, and he did.

***

It took an extreme amount of effort to wake up early on Sunday. My jaw was throbbing in agony and my eyes did not want to open. I had to tumble out of my cot and lay on the floor for a minute, before I could force myself to go take a shower. I drank some peanut butter with water for breakfast and hurried to work.

I had an airport run at seven-fifteen, and another at ten. At noon, I asked Steve if he'd seen the man who'd come in at midnight on Friday. I was hoping maybe Carver had been there while I was gone.

"That big guy?" he said. "No, haven't seen him."

Then Steve went into the staff room and returned with an elaborate chess set. The game pieces were carved in purple and gold marble, and the board had opal inlays. He handed it to me.

"Mary Jane, I would like you to have this," he said. "You're a nice person and all, so I want to give you this chess set. It's an early Christmas present."

I looked at the chess set in my hands, and then studied the sad expression on his face. I happened to know that this particular chess set was Steve's most prized possession… and he was trying to give it away. Not a good sign.

I said, "Steve, why don't you come sit by the fire."

"Okay," he mumbled, and I led him into the Glacier Room, which was next to the lobby. The Glacier Room had a huge electric fireplace and windows that looked out over The Summit's golf course, which was currently buried in snow.

"Sit down, Steve," I said, and he dropped onto one of the leather couches. I placed the chess set on the coffee table, careful not to jiggle the pieces. I sat down in front of him, gazed at his crumpled face for a moment, and asked, "Are you thinking about killing yourself?"

"Yes," he said. I'd guessed he'd say that. People in that state of mind didn't pull any punches, so it was always best just to ask them. I'd learned that in college.

"And how were you planning to do this?" I asked.

Steve rubbed his hands on his knees. "Laudanum," he said. "I calculated how many pills I needed to take. Then I added five more. I lined them up on my kitchen table. They're waiting for me when I get home."

"Are you planning to do this because you're crazy, or are you depressed?"

"I don't know!" he cried, and he started to sob.

I moved to sit beside him and put an arm around his shoulders. "Why do you want to kill yourself?"

"Willow left," he cried. "She dumped me two weeks ago." Willow was Steve's girlfriend. I think they'd lived together for the past three months.

"Well, that's a bummer," I said. "But I don't think it's worth a whole bottle of laudanum."

"Yes, it is!" Steve sobbed. "I'm dead without Willow!"

"Sounds pretty bad," I said.

"It is!" he cried. "She was supposed to meet my family for Christmas! I bought her a ring!"

I let him cry for a minute, and then I said, "How about I trade you this chess set for that ring? I'd rather have an engagement ring anyway. And you can come over and stay with me a few days."

Steve didn't respond. He cried and cried, so I sat there and rubbed his back. Someone came into the lobby, and I heard one of the Delaware cops step out of a back room to address whoever it was. I heard a woman start complaining that someone had parked in her space.

After a while, I asked Steve, "You like playing Xbox?"

"No," he sniveled. "Only chess."

"Well, Gus might play with you," I said, and I told Steve about Gus and the kids. He knew I lived with my family, but not many details. I also shared a few things about my mother and Gandhi.

"I'm not supposed to have more than four people living in that apartment," I said. "But I've already broken that rule, so one more person won't matter. I'm not going to let you go poison yourself. You'll have to come back with me and sleep on my couch. And when we're both sure you're not going to off yourself, you can go home again."

"There's nothing wrong with suicide!" he shouted.

"I didn't say there was anything wrong with it," I said. "I'm just saying you're not going to kill yourself, that's all."

Steve started sobbing again. "Mark Twain tried to kill himself."

"Yeah," I said. "And where would the world be if he had? No Tom Sawyer. No Huck Finn. The only person who ever should've killed himself was Hitler, and he took way too long doing it."

I left the room and found a box of tissues. I brought them to Steve. "You wanna clock out?" I asked. "And just rest in here for a while?"

"Sure," he said, reaching up for the tissues.

I gave him a stern look. "If you take off and drive home," I warned, "and go pop those pills, I swear to God I will hurt you, Steve. Is that understood?"

Steve blew his nose and nodded. "Understood."

I held out my pinky. "Pinky-swear me right now. Then I'll go find you something to eat."

Steve and I shook pinkies, and I returned to the front desk. I clocked Steve out, and I told the Delaware cops what was up, so they could cover the desk. Then I went to the second floor and scored a free bowl of soup from the restaurant. Summit employees were forbidden free food from the restaurant, but I convinced the chef that this was an emergency. I carried the soup down to the Glacier Room, along with some bread and a cloth napkin.

"Here, eat this," I told Steve, and I sat on the couch for a minute, to make sure he tucked into it. Then I spotted some guests walking in, and I was off to be a bellhop again.

***

I left work at three p.m. and took Steve with me. He owned a mint green Camry, and he didn't argue at all when I told him I was driving. Once we arrived at my place, I made him carry his chess set into my apartment. I introduced him to everyone, and then I told Gus that Steve was going to teach him how to play chess.

"You'll love this game," I assured Gus. "Steve's a really good teacher. Huh, Steve?"

"I guess so," Steve mumbled.

I made them sit at the dining table together, and I boiled water for hot chocolate. I wasn't normally a thief, but I'd stolen a tub of hot chocolate mix from the restaurant tonight. I'd slipped in the back door after the lunch shift had finished, and nabbed a canister from the pantry. I figured if there was ever a night we needed some hot chocolate in the house, this was it.

Mom was especially happy to drink something other than water. She kept asking for marshmallows and refilling her mug. Gus and Steve played chess, Mia read a book for class, and Ethan napped. I helped Richard with algebra. Mom flitted around and tried to bother people, mostly by bopping them on the head with balloons. All in all, it was a very good Sunday, and I thought it would have been perfect if I'd only seen Carver again. I wished with my whole heart I'd laid eyes on that man.

15

REAL CULTURE

On Monday morning, I made Steve stay home with Mom. It was his day off from work anyway, and if he was still doubting whether or not he was sane, then one day with Mom would probably cure him of that. I told him to watch out for her cleaning sprees, and to make sure she didn't offer to cook him something. Mom would cook everything in the kitchen once she got started, and then I'd be out of groceries. She also burned the food when she cooked, the bulk of which usually ended up in the garbage.

So Steve remained in the apartment, and I drove his Camry to Happy Garden. The children were all excited for Christmas, which was only five days away. Stella arrived in the kitchen early that morning, to tell us she was flying to Nigeria on Thursday, to study African drumming for two weeks and absorb some "real culture." She was ecstatic.

"It's going to be like, *so amazing!*" Stella said. "I can't *wait!*"

Taciturn Grace, of the brown crazy curls and deep love of small children, appeared at the door. She asked Stella, "Aren't you sad you'll miss Christmas? I mean, with your family?"

Stella's expression changed from openly joyful to openly hateful. She leveled her gaze on Grace with an intensity that would roast a post-apocalypse cockroach. In a calm, careful voice, she asked, "What do you mean, I'll miss Christmas…?"

"Being in Nigeria," Grace said, much more timidly. She saw the look Stella was giving her, and it was making her tremble.

There was only one subject that the African drum-loving Stella did not ever want to discuss, and that was the topic of Christianity. Stella thought of Christians as a horde of barbarians, torturing and killing the masses on behalf of their dogma, and destroying the cultural diversity that made the world beautiful. Sorry episodes throughout the past two thousand years, like the Crusades, the Inquisition, and Church officials purposefully infecting Native American children with smallpox, fueled Stella's disgust with the entire religion. She believed Christianity was the Great Disease of the Earth, and anyone who worshipped that disease was an abomination. Mark Twain had said similar things, especially as an old man.

After four months of working with Stella, I'd overheard quite a few of her nastiest comments. But since Grace didn't like to interact with adults, she hadn't picked up on all of Stella's opinions. For one thing, everyone who worked at Happy Garden knew Stella had been raised as a Christian, and that her two loving parents had given her the money to buy this daycare facility. And she was only thirty-two, after all, which seemed a young age to have developed such bitterness.

I understood it like this: in some psychological space that I will call Stella's mind, she believed that denouncing Christianity made her more intelligent, more beautiful, and therefore more worthy of love. (My mom did the same thing, only with Civilization as the root of all evil.) But when a person hated something in order to prove they were worthy of love, this created all sorts of problems. So Grace's innocent comment about missing Christmas had questioned Stella's internal logic, and Stella was about to go off on her. I saw it in her eyes when she looked at Grace. Stella's pupils started to glow, the same way a dog's eyes will light up when an enemy approaches.

"Stella," I said cheerfully, and I stepped in front of her to block her view of Grace. "Tell me about this class in Nigeria you'll be taking. It sounds so *fascinating!*"

Stella stood and blinked at me a few times, as if in a daze, and slowly that hateful look left her face and she turned happy again.

"Oh, the *drumming* class—*yes!*" she gushed. "Well! My teacher is a *tribal* leader who's been a *drummer* all his life, and I'm going to stay in his *village* and learn a traditional *beat*. It's something outsiders are usually *never* taught, but since I have a *friend* who personally *knows* him, he was willing to make a *special exception* for me…"

I proceeded to spend the next hour listening to Stella discuss her trip, as well as aspects of what she called learning "real culture" and "true heritage," while Grace disappeared to spend her morning with the toddlers. She avoided Stella for the rest of the day.

***

On Monday night after work, I drove Steve to his house so he could pick up some clothes. I went inside with him, so I could flush all the laudanum and his suicide note. I also asked him to find that engagement ring he'd purchased for Willow. He hadn't kept the receipt, so I suggested he pawn it for another chess set. Steve chose one made of carved cherry wood, which meant that we could have two games of chess in the house. Steve was pretty excited about that.

***

Happy Garden closed three days before Christmas, as every child at the daycare lived with a family who celebrated this holiday. Stella flew to Nigeria, and I picked up extra shifts at The Summit. On Christmas morning, I woke early, dressed, and went outside in the dark. I walked alone for two hours, down the streets of Riverdale and along the river.

Hanna's heart had stopped beating at eight o'clock Christmas morning, exactly one year ago, and at 8:03 a.m. she'd been pronounced dead. Sometimes I felt like my heart had been cut out in that hospital and gone in the coffin with her. And sometimes I still wished I was already dead, just so I could be with her again. Maybe that feeling was supposed to diminish. Maybe a year meant I was supposed to feel better by now. But not even grit and denial could help me stop hurting and missing my Hanna.

So I cried while I walked, and I stared up at the stars fading out with the dawn. God wanted me to keep living. So I had to keep living. God was such an asshole sometimes. Not letting us pick when we lived and we died. That was a pretty raw deal.

But the stars sure were pretty. Hard to stay mad at God too long, when the universe was right there, reminding me that the world was a far more magical place then I'd ever understand.

And I knew Hanna would say, *Geez, Mary Jane. Get a grip*, if she could see me right now. So I finally stopped with the sniveling, and returned to the house.

I made a big pancake breakfast, and then I woke the kids, Gus, Mom, and Steve and had everyone dress and eat breakfast together.

"Where's our presents?" Mia asked. I knew she was only joking around.

I held up the bottle of syrup. "Maple syrup!" I said. "Merry Christmas, everyone!"

"And *balloons!*" Mom added. "The balloons really liven the place up, don't you think? It looks so festive in here!"

We gazed around at the balloons for a moment, and Richard said, "Yeah, it does look pretty Christmassy, come to think of it. You did good, Mom."

I had to agree these were great balloons. They'd been up for a week and were still floating strong.

Ten minutes later, we left the apartment and piled into Steve's Camry. I drove us all to the homeless shelter/halfway house, where we spent the entire morning cooking. Mashed potatoes, green beans, baked turkey loaf, pumpkin pie—we loaded and unloaded ovens, and we prepped the hot trays for the metal buffet cart. The people who worked at the halfway house were excited and happy, and they gave us hats with green tinsel to wear. They especially loved Mom because she acted so quirky. She even added some bobbles to her hat, which she borrowed from the Christmas tree in the corner, and the bobbles chimed together as she moved.

When the doors opened at eleven a.m., the buffet was ready. We served everyone who arrived for the feast between eleven and three o'clock that afternoon. The kids were a big hit with the adults who came in, and Mom had a ball, as she took regular breaks to sit at various tables and chat. At one point, she started a long conversation with a fragile old man, and later she brought him over to meet me. He clutched a bowler hat in his hands and wore a three-piece suit.

"MJ, this is *Harold*," she said with excitement. "You won't believe what this man has to say! It's incredible!"

"All right," I said, still serving up mashed potatoes to the people in line. "What's the news?"

"Harold knows the true story behind FDR's death!" Mom shouted. She turned to Harold before she went on, studying his face while she repeated what he'd told her. "He says that FDR didn't die of natural causes. He says the secret service men actually grabbed his wheelchair, and pushed him off a cliff!" Mom latched onto my upper right arm and shook it. "Can you believe that's been covered up all this time? They pushed that old man off a cliff! Right out of his wheelchair!"

I pulled my arm free, took hold of Mom and directed her toward an empty chair at a table. Then I sat down beside her.

"Mom, that doesn't sound right," I said. "FDR wasn't pushed off a cliff."

She was still breathing hard, and her eyes seemed wild. "But Harold says he was there! He saw it happen!"

"If the Secret Service was pushing presidents off cliffs, our country would kill them."

"No!" Mom gasped. "It's a cover-up, MJ! It's all a cover-up! Harold was an eyewitness! You have to believe him!"

I glanced up at Harold and said, "Sir, why don't you take a seat here, and tell me the whole story." I gestured to the chair next to me.

Harold shuffled over, placed his hat on the table, and recited everything Mom had already said. Only Harold added details about FDR's agonized screams as he plummeted through the air, and something about a fake body being put in his coffin, so no one would see his numerous broken bones, and learn the truth. I didn't know what hurt my heart more, listening to this terrible nonsense about one of my personal heroes, or the sight of this lost old man in his moth-eaten suit. I wondered if he'd actually seen someone pushed off a cliff, and that was the kernel of truth for this story.

When Harold had finished, I said, "Thank you, sir, for sharing that with me. I'm glad I know what really happened." I stood and shook his hand, and after that, Harold shuffled off.

Mom breathed a sigh of relief. "You see? You see the truth?"

I patted her shoulder. "Hey Mom, how about you help me serve potatoes a while? My feet are tired."

"All right," she said, and she went off to find an apron.

***

After our work at the homeless shelter, I drove everyone home and we polished off the last of the hot chocolate. I refused to turn on the television, so the kids sat around the dining table and played chess with Steve. Mom resumed her tactics with the balloons, which meant she bopped us all on the head in the hopes of getting a rise out of someone. But the only one of us who ever reacted was Gandhi, who crept under the table and whimpered whenever she tried to bonk him. And sometimes Richard growled at Mom and said, "Quit it!" But that was about it.

I cooked pinto beans and cornbread for dinner, and turned on the radio. I found an AM station playing old Christmas music, which made Mom turn nostalgic and whop our heads even more. I considered popping those stupid balloons, I found her behavior so annoying, but I just sat and listened to the music and let it go.

I took Hanna's badge from my pocket and assembled the pieces, and I sent her a prayer up in Heaven to help God and the angels and maybe a few bodhisattvas try to look out for me and my family. I needed three hundred dollars in tips before New Year's Day, or I was not going to make rent. As it was, I didn't even have enough to buy groceries tomorrow. So I told Hanna, "You had better send me some high rollers with lots of luggage to carry, or I'm going to lose this apartment."

Then I said a prayer for Harold and all of those other folks who'd come in to eat dinner at the homeless shelter today. As anxious as I was about making my rent, at least I had a roof over my head. I'd promised myself to keep the kids in school and make sure they had a home to sleep in each night, and so far, I'd been keeping that promise. I didn't have a lot I felt proud of right now, but as long as I kept my apartment, I was not a complete failure. That word still rattled around in my brain though, as intent as ever on killing something inside me.

***

Steve and I woke early for our shifts at The Summit the next morning. We arrived on time, about a quarter to seven, and when I was given the job of picking up a man and his wife at the private airport, I thought my prayer to Hanna last night had worked. The private airport meant this couple owned their own plane, and when I arrived for the pick-up, I was instructed to drive the van right onto the tarmac. It wasn't a huge plane, maybe big enough to seat twelve, an older model than some of the others I'd seen. I thought it could do with a fresh coat of paint.

When the plane's stairs were lowered and the couple walked out, I saw they were two baby boomers. The woman wore a fur coat and jewels, and her husband sported a trench coat that probably cost twenty grand. I opened the passenger doors for them and helped them into the van, and then I unloaded everything off the plane. They'd brought several suitcases with them, as well as a dozen wooden crates holding oil paintings and some boxes with antique lamps. I knew these were decorations for their ski lodge/vacation home, and I squared everything away in the van so nothing would tip over. Then I climbed in and drove to The Summit.

The couple sat on the bench seat behind me, and I could tell right away that they did not want to talk. So I entertained them a while, and told them about wild animals I'd seen in the area and the happenings in Riverdale and Goldking, and soon they were both smiling and asking me questions, and they told me how much they looked forward to skiing. Then they started on about their kids and how great their grandchildren were, and I agreed that they probably had the best grandkids in the world. They said they'd bought their airplane ten years ago, and how it was so much more convenient than flying commercial. They told me which airports were their favorites.

When I arrived at their house, it was one of the stand-alone homes, built of stone. I unloaded all of their luggage and paintings and boxes, and then the man called me over to where his Range Rover was parked. The vehicle was underneath a wooden carport, but the battery had died and the man needed a jump. So I pulled out my cables and gave the Range Rover a jump, and the man chatted a while longer about his family.

I put the cables away and the man came toward me holding some money in his hand, which I took and said, "Thank you." Then he turned on his heel and walked into his house, dismissing me with a flick of his wrist. I hoped that meant he had tipped me a twenty. I thought of my prayer to Hanna, and wondered if he'd been a high roller and maybe given me fifty. That would be really great. If I made enough to cover my rent, I wanted to buy the kids a pizza from Papa Murphy's, one with pepperoni and sausage and olives, and maybe I'd have enough for two pizzas, and that made me really excited, because I was to the point where I could eat solid food again. So if I had enough for two pizzas, then I could have some—

I backed the van out of the drive and started off toward the lobby, and that's when I saw what the man had given me.

I opened my hand and found a dollar.

The most tattered, faded dollar bill I'd ever seen in my life. It wasn't even a whole bill… about a quarter of it had been ripped away, maybe by a vending machine somewhere. Only frayed cotton fibers were still holding this greenback together, the color of which was a bleached, grayish-white. It seemed ready to disintegrate in my palm. I could only barely make out that it was even money.

I realized that four hours of my shift today had been spent helping that man and his wife. From driving an hour and twenty minutes one way to pick them up at the private airport, to loading and unloading all of that extra luggage, to the drive back to The Summit, to helping the man jump his Range Rover. Four hours. One dollar.

And then I realized the most horrible thing… I wasn't going to make rent next month. I was going to lose my apartment. And if I lost my apartment, and ended up back in Goldking, with the high school closed—

My breathing changed and grew fainter, and I had to park the van and get out. I walked into the snow of the golf course, trying to tell myself not to worry, that I'd make the money. I'd make better tips. I'd work harder. But it hit me regardless, and not even walking outside in the open helped ward it off.

This panic attack was as strong as any other, and I had that terrible sense I couldn't breathe, that my heart would explode, that all of my muscles had burst into flames. I stumbled around for ten minutes in agony, waiting for my body to keel over and die. And when this attack ended, I sat in the snow and cried. I couldn't understand how I'd been so nice to those people, how I'd done everything I was supposed to, and more, and that man hadn't even said thank you. He'd never once said that. And he'd given me this tattered old George who was missing his face, this bill that didn't even look like a dollar, when that man had his own airplane and vacation homes and a Range Rover and his kids had gone to Yale and his wife wore fur coats. And I would've taken a thank you over this measly dollar. I would've rather had nothing than this.

When I realized I was still holding that tattered bill in my hand, I did the only thing I could think of to save my sanity. I walked back to the van, pushed in the knob for the cigarette lighter, waited until it popped out, and then I lit that dollar on fire. I felt the relief flood through me as it burned. I left all of the ash on the side of road, careful not to let any of it touch me. I didn't want any particle of what was left of that bill in contact with my body, not even my shoes.

After the dollar was gone, I pulled myself together. I scrubbed my face clean with a few handfuls of snow, and then I drove to the airport again. I had to pick up the next round of hotel guests. This time, it was a family with two kids still in college, and a group of single guys who were having a male-bonding ski trip. At the sight of the men, I was glad that my face was no longer swollen and lopsided, as I relied on my smile to handle such crowds. After I had everyone loaded, I drove the van to the hotel lobby, and those men tipped me *thirty-five dollars.* When I saw how much money they were handing me, I almost started to cry. I barely managed to tell them all thank you, I felt so choked up about it. They didn't even let me carry their bags, not their suitcases or their skis. The man with the two kids in college even gave me five dollars, simply for being the driver and picking them up.

I was left feeling wrung-out for the rest of the day. If someone handed me a five or a ten, just for carrying their luggage or giving them a ride to the mountain to ski, I had to struggle to stay cool and professional. Sometimes gratitude can be overwhelming, and make me want to cry more than anything. Especially when people are so full of kindness after someone else has been cruel.

I ended up working a double, from seven a.m. until eleven that night, and I cleared almost two hundred dollars in tips. Steve had left The Summit at three o'clock that afternoon, but he drove back in his Camry to pick me up before midnight.

In the car, I counted all the money I'd made and Steve joked that he should be a bellhop instead of working front desk.

"I'd leave Happy Garden in a second, if I could," I said. "But I can't make enough with one job, and I can't work nights on the weekdays. Thank God the holidays are here and people are out on vacation."

Steve waited a few moments, and then said, "I'm feeling a lot better. I think I might be ready to go home soon."

I reached over and gripped his shoulder, and then shook him a little. "I'm glad to hear it," I said. "I'm glad to see you smiling again."

Steve grinned for a minute, and then laughed. "No offense, but your mom's really weird."

"Yeah," I agreed. "Did you try to teach her how to play chess?"

"Every time I sit down with her, she just makes up her own bizarre game with the pieces," Steve said. "It's actually kind of funny. I mean, don't take this the wrong way, but I think something's wrong with her. Like she needs medication."

"Well," I sighed, "Mom does the same thing with her meds that I did with your laudanum. And that's never going to change."

"She wants me to buy her pot," Steve said.

I laughed. "If you want to smoke pot with Mom, that's your choice. It's your money. But you can't smoke in the house, and neither can she."

"Fair enough," Steve said. "By the way, I saw that guy again. That big one you asked about last week."

"Yeah?" I asked. My heart skipped several beats.

"I saw him drive by the hotel when I left. He was in a black SUV and a bunch of people were with him."

"He has three kids," I pointed out.

"A woman was with him," Steve said. "In the passenger seat," and I felt deflated again. I didn't want to have a crush on a married man.

"She might've been his sister," I said, more to give myself hope than anything else.

"Yeah, they weren't kissing or anything," Steve said, which cheered me back up.

***

By New Year's Day, I'd picked up so many extra shifts at The Summit that I made five hundred dollars in tips, which meant I had saved the apartment and paid another electric bill. When my paycheck arrived, I even had enough left over for my student loan payment. I celebrated by buying some extra ammunition and taking the kids and Gus out shooting. I let them blow apart my wisdom teeth for me, which they found especially exciting. Shooting teeth off an old post was a lot more challenging than shooting at cans.

"We *killed* those teeth!" Mia shouted after the last one had been blasted. She and Ethan turned to each other and high-fived.

"This has been an excellent day," I said. I even gave Ravi a kiss on his barrel. I was so proud of my gun for blowing up those damn teeth.

Happy Garden remained closed for the holidays until January sixth, and on my last holiday shift at The Summit, I felt sad that I'd be back at the daycare on Monday. It was so much easier to be a bellhop, mostly because I didn't have to listen to screeching toddlers all day. The high-decibel screaming of young children was something my nerves could never completely adjust to, and I dreaded the weariness that set in after ten straight hours of listening to it.

Late Saturday morning, I was assigned an airport shuttle run, so I left the hotel in the van for a lodge pick-up. I prayed and prayed that I wasn't picking up the two baby boomers who owned their own plane. I thought I might have another panic attack if that happened.

But when I pulled up in front of the ski cottage, it was not the same house. This house had also been built of stone, but instead of a carport, there was a two-door garage. As I parked in the drive, I saw only one person waiting for me on the doorstep. And that was Carver Greyson.

16

YOU TWO BOYS

"**H**ello, Mary Jane," he said when I stepped out of the van.

"Hi," I said. That was all I could manage. I felt speechless again, partly because he was so alarmingly handsome, and partly because he might have a wife. I didn't want to be too friendly with him if that was the case.

He wore his black trench coat again. Dark slacks, black boots. He seemed so dashing and assured, whereas I was dressed like Sasquatch.

I opened the back door for his suitcase, but he said, "I just have this one bag. I'll put it up by my feet."

"Okay," I said, and I shut the door. We climbed in.

"I have three more people to pick up," I said. It had started to snow, and I flipped the wipers back on as I drove down the road. "Where are you headed today?" I assumed his vacation was over, if he was taking a shuttle ride.

"Saint Louis," he said. "I've got some things to take care of."

"Are your boys staying here?"

"No," and he smiled. "My sister wanted to take them to California, to her home in San Diego, and they all left yesterday. She has four children, and two of them are finally old enough to start going to theme parks, so they voted on Disneyland. I'll meet up with them later, when this is done."

"You have to go back to work?"

"I promised a friend of mine we'd get together," Carver said. "Some work, some just cutting loose."

I glanced at his face again, pondering the age difference between us. Seven years. He really wasn't that much older than me. I wondered which college he'd gone to. I was about to ask, but his question came first.

"Did you get your car back?" he asked. I felt a bit surprised by the question, since I couldn't remember telling him anything about my car.

"Not yet," I said. "How did you know I have a car?"

He looked amused. "Lucky guess." His tone implied *logical conclusion*, since I lived fifteen miles from The Summit, and there wasn't any public transportation that far north of town. I guess I didn't seem like a regular hitchhiker. Win. "What's wrong with your vehicle?"

"The radiator," I said. "And some belts and some hoses. Nothing too bad."

I was almost to my next pick-up location, and I was slowing down for a turn, when I spotted an old woman who'd run her car off the road. Her little white Chevy was plowed into the ditch. So I pulled over and stopped. "I'm gonna see if I can give her a hand," I said. "This'll just take a minute."

The woman opened her car door and stepped out. Her whole body trembled when she spoke. "I don't know what happened," she said. "This snow is so *slick*."

I walked over where she could hold onto my arm. She looked to be about ninety-five, wearing pants so pink they made my eyes hurt.

"Yeah, it's not much more than ice on this road," I said. "You have any cables? Or chains for your tires?"

"Oh no," she said, trembling. "Nothing like that."

Carver came out and helped the old woman into the van. He turned up the heater. I had a small shovel in the back and took it out. I dug through the snow to some gravel and tossed it under her tires. Carver said, "I bet I can rock it loose."

I stopped tossing gravel and gazed at those massive shoulders of his. Then I put down the shovel and slid behind the wheel of the old woman's car. I straightened the tires, shifted into reverse and eased down on the gas. Carver pushed the front end of the car, and the Chevy leapt out of the ditch and landed back on the road.

"Oh my, that was fast!" the old woman cried. When I stepped out of the car, she hobbled over to tell me, "Thank you, sonny! You two boys have been a big help!"

I almost fell over. Normally, it didn't bother me much when people with failing eyesight mistook me for a man. Tall, thin, and dressed like a bellhop, it was an easy assumption to make. But as Carver was walking toward us, I wanted to die.

"Mary Jane's a girl, ma'am," Carver said, and I could tell by the light in his eyes that he was laughing. "Happy we got your car out."

The woman peered at me carefully, and murmured, "Girl, huh? I don't really see the resemblance…"

Carver crossed his arms and turned away, and I could see that his body was shaking. Har, har. Glad somebody thought this was funny.

I asked the woman, "Where are you headed?" and when she named a condo that was on our way to my next pick-up, Carver volunteered to finish driving her there.

"You should buy some cables," I told her as she sat down in the passenger seat. "Or trade this thing in for a Subaru." Then I closed the door for her and followed them out.

Once we had the old woman home again, Carver helped her inside, and then he climbed back into the van.

"Hey, sonny," he said.

I muttered, "Oh my God."

He kept grinning at me. "Sure is awful nice to have such a pretty boy to drive me around. I could almost swear you were female."

My face turned a bright shade of carmine. I stared out through the windshield and wished I could evaporate. Then I thought, wait—did he just call me *pretty?*

I decided not to postpone my curiosity any longer. Since I couldn't possibly feel any more embarrassed than I did at this moment, asking him a personal question was well within reason.

"Are you married?"

Carver stopped chuckling. His voice became quiet. "I was married," he said. "I'm not anymore." Then he thought for a moment, and smiled at me. "Why are you asking me that?"

"Huh?" I said, staring out the window a moment to avoid looking at him. "I didn't say anything."

"All right, sonny," he said, "whatever you say," and I wanted to die all over again. But this time, my embarrassment was cut through with a sharp twist of happiness—because he *had* called me pretty. And I was relieved to hear he wasn't married.

I picked up my three other passengers, two men and one woman. More baby boomers who wore preppy clothes. They had a lot of luggage, and Carver came to the back of the van and helped me load it.

"Don't do that," I said. I tried to push him away. "I've got this." If he helped me like that, then I wouldn't earn any tips. I had too many bills to pay to deal with machismo.

Carver smiled, but he wouldn't give up. He loaded the bags with me and let me close the back doors, and then he returned to the front seat. He introduced himself to the three other people as Carver, and he told them my name was Mary Jane. Then he said, "I'm starved for some lunch. How about we stop at Wendy's for burgers?"

I cocked an eyebrow at this. The airport shuttle did not make pit stops. These people had a flight to catch.

"There's nothing to eat at the airport," Carver said, which was true. The Riverdale airport served microwavable sandwiches, and not much else. "So let's hit the drive-through." He pulled a couple of twenties from his pocket, glanced at the people behind us and added, "On me."

The woman in the orange and teal jacket sniffed. "Well, I do like their chicken sandwiches," she said. "I guess that's all right."

Carver waited for the others to speak. One man gave a grunt of ascension, and the other muttered, "I'm not opposed."

"Now we're talking," Carver cheered, and put his money in a cup holder.

"So, where are you all from?" he asked the three people, and I half-listened to them say they were from Tampa, and how they loved winters there and dreaded the summers, and blah-blah-blah they went on about Florida until I drove into Riverdale and stopped at the Wendy's.

Carver took everyone's order, but when he asked me what I wanted, I said, "I'm not hungry, thanks," because I'd rather have the four dollars cash in a tip than a burger from Wendy's. Not that I didn't like Wendy's burgers. But if my choices were eating fast food or paying my bills, then it wasn't really a choice. I'd take the money.

Carver bought me a cheeseburger anyway. I didn't dare eat and drive on the clock, but everyone else ate on our way to the airport. Carver inhaled his food the way big men often do, which meant he was finished and stuffing away the trash in about sixty seconds.

The people from Tampa returned to discussing their favorite topic, the weather. They talked about the weather in Colorado, the weather in Tampa (again), and the weather in Arizona. Then they discussed the weather in Wyoming and the weather in California and the weather in Washington, D.C. Carver listened attentively and made appropriate comments, but I was sick of hearing about the weather. I felt completely distraught with this shuttle ride. On the one hand, I had to listen to all this boring crap about the weather, but on the other, once we arrived at the airport and the weather-loving Tampa people got out, Carver would also be leaving. I decided this trip was just hell.

When we arrived at the airport, I parked outside the front doors and hurried to unload the bags. Thankfully, Carver did not try to help. The Tampa people tipped me three dollars and disappeared inside. I peered around the van and saw Carver standing with his airline ticket and his carry-on bag.

"Well, sonny," he said, "I guess this is it." He held out his hand, and I gazed up at his face for a moment, wishing with all my heart he would ask for my number. I knew it was stupid. I didn't even have a telephone.

So I reached out and clasped his hand, and we shook goodbye.

"Thanks for the ride," he said, and he turned away and strolled into the airport.

I watched the glass doors close behind him, and then I climbed into the passenger seat and leaned back. I thought about how I was sitting where Carver had been, and that made me happy. Parking security was lax at this airport, so no one would mind if I sat here and daydreamed for a minute. I could smell Carver's cologne, a soft, sweet smell like white pine and amber. My whole body felt warmer just thinking about him, and wishing he was still here with me. I closed my eyes and pictured him smiling at me. Crazy, how much I liked Carver. I never felt this swoony around men.

Maybe I was just hungry. I opened my eyes and picked up the sack with my burger. Then I noticed Carver had left money in the cup holder. There were several bills stuffed together, and I unfolded them to find two tens, two twenties, and several—

I made a strange little shriek and my hand jerked in shock, and the money went skittering to the floor.

I leaned forward to scoop up the money.

They were hundred dollar bills. He'd left *hundreds* in the van. He must have made a mistake! I pushed open the door, planning to run it inside to him, but then I spotted Carver walking out of the airport.

"You left all your cash in the van!" and I hopped out of the vehicle to hand it to him. Of course he'd come back for his money.

"Mary Jane, I, um—" he was saying, and then he glanced down. "Oh," and he covered my hand with both of his. His skin felt so warm against mine, that my heart hammered a bit when he touched me. He wrapped my fingers around the bills. "No, that's yours. To get your car from the shop. I came to see if you could give me a ride back."

"I can't take all this money," I said. But he wouldn't accept the bills back. I glanced at the people walking into the airport, since he ought to be taking his cash and running to join them. "Why aren't you leaving?"

"My plans changed," he said.

I cut him a look. In the last five minutes, his plans had changed. Was I supposed to believe this? I looked down at the ticket sticking out of his coat pocket. People often bought plane tickets and then chose not to get on the plane. Sure they did.

"I decided to stay," he said, and he followed my gaze and pulled out the ticket sheet. He folded the paper, to prove he had no intention to use it. "St. Louis is miserable this time of year." He glanced up at the sky, which had stopped spitting snow and allowed a bit of sun to break through. "There's nothing I have to do that won't wait a week, when I'm home with my boys." He tucked the paper into his pocket again and shrugged. "So I'd rather spend some extra time here, and fly to San Diego next weekend to pick up my kids."

"What about your friend?" The one he was bailing on in St. Louis.

"Oh, he's all right," Carver said. "I'll see him before long, anyway."

This still felt too strange. "Won't you lose your job?"

Carver laughed. "No. That's the least of my worries."

I couldn't picture a job being the least of my worries. Must be nice.

I tried to hand him the money again, but he shook his head no. "That's for your radiator. I'm not taking that back."

God, this was a weird situation. Why didn't he just get on his plane, and leave me alone to daydream about him again? I was more comfortable with that.

I stood for a moment, wondering what he was planning to do in Riverdale for another week. Probably hang out at the ski resort, talking to people, and spend nights in town. Riverdale was chock-full of nice restaurants and bars, and women with time on their hands and choice lingerie. If Carver was lonely and single, and didn't have his kids a few days, this was definitely a place where he could be entertained.

"All right," I said. "Let's get going then."

Carver was grinning as he took back his seat, and as I climbed in beside him, he said, "I was hoping you'd have a drink with me. If you don't have to work tonight."

That really knocked the wind out of me. I couldn't answer right away. I said, "You want to have a drink… with *me?*"

"Yeah," he smiled. When I didn't respond, he asked, "Is that really so strange?"

I gave him another sharp look. He had ditched his flight home, and now he was asking me out? Strange didn't begin to cut it.

"I like you, Mary Jane. I like being around you."

I had to laugh. "You don't even *know* me."

He shrugged in a way that meant, *What does that matter?* "We should go on a… you know, when two people get together, and they go out for a drink, and then they go dancing or something… what are those called? I can't quite remember."

When I spoke, I sounded skeptical. Sarcastic. Men didn't ask Yetis on dates. Snow bunnies: yes. Sasquatch: not so much. My tone implied he was nuts. "You want to go dancing."

"I'd love to," Carver said, and he kept smiling at me. "Thanks for asking."

17

THE GRIZZ

I shook my head to let him know I thought he was crazy, started the van and drove away from the airport. I realized I still had all that money in my hand, so I stuffed the bills in my vest pocket. Then I glanced over at Carver and asked, "What do you do, anyway? You live in St. Louis?"

"Right now I do," he said. "I have an office there. I travel a lot. I take my kids with me sometimes, especially in the summers. When they're home without me, my parents take care of them. I try not to make them miss school."

"Sounds like a good arrangement," I said.

Carver grinned. "Yeah, they love Grandma and Grandpa. And Aunt Clarissa and their cousins. They come to visit a lot. My boys go back to school next Wednesday."

"My brothers and sister go back this Monday," I said. "And Gus. He's in ninth grade with Richard."

"You live with your family?" he asked.

The correct way to phrase that was: *They live with me*. But I just nodded yes. "My mom moved in last month. We have a place in Goldking, an old Victorian house, but the high school there closed. I think Mom got lonely and missed everyone. So she joined us in Riverdale. And my friend Steve from work. He was having some trouble, so I let him come over and sleep on my couch. It's not a… I mean, with Steve—it's nothing romantic. Just until he gets back on his feet."

Carver pondered this for a moment. I hoped he didn't think I was lying about Steve. Men were weird about things like that.

"You brought your brothers and sister to Riverdale to keep them in school?" Carver asked.

I nodded again. "Richard is… Well, he's the one I'm most worried about. Staying in school. The others are all pretty good."

Carver seemed to consider me for a moment, like he had many more questions to ask. I hoped he wouldn't. I glanced away from him, out the side window, to let him know he should drop it.

"High school is tough," he said.

"Yeah," I sighed, and felt my smile disappear. I didn't know Carver well enough to share any more about my personal life.

"How are his grades?" Carver asked.

I shrugged. "Not awful." Richard currently had As and Bs. He did well in school, when he just did his homework. The thought of homework battles made me tired though. I'd enjoyed Christmas break, probably more than the kids had. But they'd be back in school in two days, and I did not want to dwell on it.

Carver must have picked up on my reluctance to discuss this topic anymore, because he changed the subject. "So, where should we go dancing tonight?"

"Yeah, about that…" I said.

He looked at me curiously, like he wanted to guess what I'd say, but couldn't quite pull it off.

I wanted to tell him a number of things, like *Surely you can do better than me*, but Carver said, "There's a blues place on Fifth, and Vivienne's on Second has a nice dance floor."

See? He knew the Riverdale scene. Of course he did. Plenty of people with money, plenty of skiers, and plenty of women who wanted nothing better than for a man like Carver Greyson to walk into a bar and buy them a drink. He certainly didn't need to be asking me out. If Carver wanted to run away from his life for a week, he wouldn't want for some company. Not in this town.

"How do you feel about country?" he asked, and I felt myself tucking my head in my shell, like the turtle I wished I could be. These vacation-home people I drove in the shuttle—I helped them out when I could and I lived on their tips, but we did not interact outside of work. Why would we?

"Muldoon's is nice," Carver said. "My sister likes to drag me in there. Cowboy two-step, West Coast Swing—she's into all that. But if you just want to have a drink somewhere, that's fine with me."

Oh my God, no. I needed to put a stop to this. Now. "Carver, I really appreciate the gesture and all, and the money for my car, but… This isn't my scene."

"You don't like Muldoon's?" he asked.

"I don't take car-repair money from men and then go to the bar."

"Well, I *am* worried you might sic your horse on me," Carver said. "But I'll take my chances."

"I'm not desperate," I said. "And neither are you."

Carver raised his eyebrows. "You obviously don't know my sister, or you'd never say such a thing. Desperate is my middle name."

"Exactly why I'm not going out with you."

Carver only laughed. "Mary Jane, it's one drink. What's the worst that can happen?"

"I find out you're a serial killer," I said. "That's the worst that can happen."

"Oh my God," Carver laughed. "Desperate: yes. Serial killer, I promise you: no."

I quirked an eyebrow at him. "That's what every psychopath says."

Carver leaned his head back, like he wanted to burst into laughter. "Have there been some murders at The Summit I haven't heard about yet?"

"Several," I lied. "Body parts everywhere. It was all over the news."

He propped his chin in one hand, and then sighed. "Mary Jane, would you please just come have a drink with me—one drink? I promise I'll bring you home safe."

I thought about this for a minute. He did sound extremely sincere, and I had the night off. I normally put the kids to bed around ten, but since this was their last night to stay up late for a while, I was going to wait until midnight. I could have a drink with Carver and be back by then. "You remember where I live?"

Carver nodded. "I do."

"Then come over at eight, and we'll go to Muldoon's."

Carver dropped his hands to the seat, like he'd stand if he could. But we were still in the van, passing through Riverdale. He gave me that devil-grin, the one that seemed to brush up against me like I did not have a shirt on. How could a man who smiled like that ever be desperate? Not possible.

"I'm glad you came around, Mary Jane. I was starting to worry."

"I own a gun," I said. "You probably ought to stay worried."
He chuckled again. "Consider me warned."

***

Back at The Summit, I dropped Carver off at the ski cottage,
and then I spent the rest of my shift inside the hotel. I went
home with Steve in his Camry, and told him about my date.

"Why dancing?" Steve asked. "Why not just a movie?"

"Steve," I said, "if you don't know how to dance yet, then
you should come with us and learn."

"No way," Steve said. "I hate dancing. I've got eighteen left
feet and as much rhythm as a piece of lead pipe."

"Anybody can two-step," I laughed. "Next time I've got a
minute, I'm going to force you to learn."

"You can save the two-stepping for this Carver guy," Steve
said. "I want nothing to do with it."

Once we were home, I went into my bedroom and opened
the closet. I had one dress to my name, a white eyelet sundress
that was more suited to summertime. The fabric was clean but
wrinkled, so I took out the ironing board.

"What are you doing?" Mia asked, walking into the bedroom.

"I'm going dancing tonight," I said, and I told her about
Carver. Mia returned to the living room and let everyone else
know what was happening.

After I had my dress ironed, I tried it on. Sadly, it didn't
fit anymore. I had lost so much weight since college, especially
since my teeth had been pulled, which meant this sundress hung
loose in places that were highly unattractive. So I opened the
bottom drawer in the bathroom and found a small jar of safety
pins.

I spent an hour pinning my sundress until it seemed like it fit me. Then I stripped, hopped in the shower, and said a prayer to Jesus to please not make my hair look too stupid tonight. My short bob from that summer had grown into a long bob, almost reaching down to my shoulders, but I didn't own any hair products to whip my mop into shape. I hoped it wouldn't do its strange jungle-plant routine, when pieces of it stuck up every which way. That would suck.

I did have some mascara, however, and lip gloss. I applied them both liberally, trying to compensate for the lack of hair gel. I studied my reflection in the mirror for a while. My heather blue eyes seemed prettier with mascara, and my hair was not acting psychotic, which was good. And no matter how scrawny I was, I always had nice cheekbones, a slim nose, perfect eyebrows, a big smile. God had cut me some slack with my face. My one saving grace.

Carver rang the doorbell a few minutes before eight, and I was so wound up that I didn't know what to do. I wanted to hide in the bathroom. But then I yelled, "I'll get it!" and ran to the door. There was Carver, in dark jeans and boots. Pearl snap buttons on his deep red shirt. He took off his hat before he came in, a black felt Stetson with a dark woven band.

"Hi, Mary Jane," he said.

"Hi, Carver." I waited for him to step inside, and shut the door.

"I brought you these," and he held up a bouquet of roses and lilies.

"Those are lovely," I said, and smiled as I took the bouquet. I waved around at my family, who were all in the living room. "Well, this is everyone. Everyone, this is Carver Greyson. He lives in St. Louis." I led him over to Mom. "Carver, this is my mother, Gilly Preston."

Carver shook Mom's hand. "Very nice to meet you, Miss Preston," he said. I had asked him in the van earlier to call Mom a miss.

Mom smiled with approval. "You look like you know how to party."

Carver grinned and said, "I sure hope so."

Then I introduced him to Richard and Ethan and Mia, and then Gus and Steve. I could tell Carver recognized Steve from that night in The Summit, though he didn't say anything more than, "Hi, Steve. Nice to meet you." Gandhi came last, and Carver knelt to pet him.

I noticed Gus had started making that strange panting sound which meant he was excited, and then he tore off into the boys' bedroom.

I called, "Gus, you okay?" from the living room. I didn't want him to be too weirded out by this situation. Carver was so big he had to duck his head around the balloons on the ceiling. The size of him made the entire apartment feel like it was six sizes too small.

I walked to the bedroom door and said, "Gus?" He was digging through an old cardboard box that had once held a food processor. "You okay, Gus? Are you worried about something?"

"No," Gus whispered. He said something else, but his voice was so faint, I couldn't make out the words.

I took a seat on the bed. "You'll have to repeat that," I said.

Gus pulled something out of his food processor box, and I saw one of the smaller boxes that my checks were mailed in. Gus always asked me for those boxes, so I let him keep them. He opened one, and removed a stack of baseball cards he had stored in a sandwich bag. Some of the cards looked brand new, but most were old and tattered.

Gus thumbed through the cards until he found one he wanted, and he handed it to me. The man pictured on the card wore an Atlanta Braves uniform, number 52. Before I even read the name on the card, I recognized a young Carver Greyson. He was nineteen in this picture. The card called him the Grizz. Even with my limited exposure to baseball, I'd heard of this player before. He was the slugger they always compared to Babe Ruth.

"This is Grizz Greyson," I said, almost too stunned to breathe. I'd never known his first name was Carver. He was always called the Grizz during ballgames—but Gus just nodded happily and made that strange panting sound. "Go show him this," I said, and handed the card back to Gus. He jumped up and ran to the living room.

I peeked around the doorway to watch. Carver smiled when he saw the card, and then he tousled Gus's hair. Gus was so tickled that he laughed out loud.

"Looks like you found me out, Gus," Carver said, and he shook his hand again, more of an arm-embrace with a hug than a handshake this time. "How long have you had this?"

Gus held up five fingers, indicating five years, and Carver said, "Sounds like we ought to go throw a ball around then. Maybe tomorrow afternoon, if that'll work."

Richard was on his feet, watching this exchange. He asked Gus, "Can I see that?" and Gus passed him the card. After Richard glanced at the picture, he yelled, "Holy *shit!*" and his eyes grew to the size of semi-truck tires. He looked up at Carver. "You're *Grizz Greyson??*"

Carver was still holding his hat in one hand, and he covered his heart with it before bowing slightly to Richard.

"Oh my *God!*" Richard yelled. "You play for *the Majors! You're a Major League Baseball player!*"

Richard went into shock. He placed both his hands on his head, gripped his hair, and started to run back and forth through the room. He seemed ready to hyperventilate. Richard could get as keyed up as Gus did over things, which was why they got along so well. Ethan caught up with Richard and pried the base- ball card from his hand. He studied the picture a moment, and then glanced up at Carver.

"Wow," Ethan said. "You're in one of our video games." He handed the card to Mia so she could see it.

"Cool!" Mia giggled.

Mom said, "I wanna look!" and Mia passed her the card. I went over and grabbed Richard and made him lie down in his bedroom. If he didn't take it easy, he was going to pass out. And I needed a place to sit and process this, too. Richard wasn't the only one who was more than a little freaked out.

18

THE RULES OF THE GAME

In the living room, the kids and Steve all started bombarding Carver with questions, and he answered them with ease and good humor. They asked him how many years he had played (ten), how old he was (he had just turned twenty-nine), and how many teams he had played on (four: the Braves, the Yankees, the Tigers, and the Cardinals). They asked how many homeruns he had hit (quite a few) and if he liked playing for the Cardinals (yes, very much) and who his favorite baseball player was (Jackie Robinson, first and foremost, with Honus Wagner and Christy Mathewson tied for second).

While all of this was going on, I sat on the bed and stroked Richard's hair, because his breathing still sounded erratic. Carver's answers about those baseball players surprised me. Not only had all three of those men been terrific athletes, they'd also been tremendous human beings—which was a much harder feat to accomplish.

Then Mia asked Carver some questions about his family, like how many children he had (three), if he was married (not right now), and what kind of food he ate (pretty much anything). Once the subject was no longer baseball, Richard returned to normal, and he hopped back to the living room to rejoin the party.

I remained on the bed though and stared at the wall. I thought, what in the hell am I doing with a ballplayer? The only games I ever watched were the World Series. That was the only reason I'd even heard of Grizz Greyson. He'd played in two of them that I could remember, and I'd listened to those on the radio.

He had been a phenomenon, I remembered that much. The announcers had always been excited when he stepped up to bat, had cheered every time he hit a homerun, or whenever he made a great play. And then something had happened to him, and the Grizz had dropped off the map. He must have been in his prime when he'd played for the Yankees, because I couldn't remember him playing for the Tigers, and I certainly had no idea he now played for the Cardinals.

If he was twenty-nine, he probably had at least five, six, maybe seven more years to play in the majors. Most men retired between thirty-five and forty, if injuries didn't stop their careers sooner. Or lack of performance. If Carver was no longer the phenom he'd been, he was probably lucky he was still playing ball. Pro sports were ruthless when it came time for cuts. He'd said he wasn't worried about losing his job though, so he must have a contract to play through the next season.

Carver had called himself desperate, and now I thought, maybe he was. I knew the stories of baseball players, and how lonely they were. Ballplayers traveled constantly for at least half the year, and I realized that by the end of next month, Carver would be playing again, when spring training would start.

Give a young man a hot body, a lot of money, and force him to travel from city to city for six or seven months straight—it was no wonder so many ballplayers were regulars at strip clubs, and had affairs with multiple women each year.

Which made me a bit panicky, realizing how easy it was for Carver to pick up a woman. He only had to smile, maybe at the hotel where his team was staying—and what woman wouldn't follow him up to his room for the night? Hello, goodbye. Thanks for the quickie. Here's a diamond necklace for your time.

I shuddered. Was this what Carver had in mind? Go have a drink, hook up for the night... and leave a piece of jewelry on the nightstand, before he walked out the door? And did he always bring flowers beforehand? And what about that *wad of cash* he'd put in the cup holder today? Was that standard procedure?

Oh my God. It was probably no wonder Carver wasn't married anymore, if he'd been caught cheating on his wife. What had I gotten myself into?

I rubbed my face with my hands, trying to reason this out and calm down. He was taking me dancing tonight, not asking me to visit his hotel room. And that money he'd left me was for my car—not thanks for a lap dance. There weren't even strip clubs in Riverdale.

And if he'd really been picking me up like a... like a baseball player who wanted distraction... then wouldn't he have at least told me he played ball? Why keep that a secret, if we all knew the rules of this game?

I dropped my hands and took a deep breath. He'd said that he liked me. And I... well, I definitely liked him. Knowing he was a ballplayer didn't change that.

So I could still go dancing with him, and not feel like a hooker.

But one-night stands and jewelry? That wasn't my scene. If Carver wanted someone to keep his bed warm tonight... well, there were plenty of other women in the bar who could oblige him. I wasn't waking up tomorrow to find a necklace and cold sheets. Just the idea of it made me feel... sad and cheap. My life was hard enough without bringing that on myself.

With that settled, I stepped out of the bedroom to find everyone standing in a cluster around Carver, so I said, "Why don't we all sit down," and gestured toward the dining table. I had several plastic folding chairs, but I made sure Carver picked one of the seats made of wood, on account that he was so huge he might break the others. I took out a bowl of hardboiled eggs from the fridge, and I told Richard to wash his hands. Then I had him give everyone a paper towel, and I followed him around the table and handed everyone an egg. I placed the salt and pepper on the table, as well as the bowl with the rest of the eggs, and sat down to join them. Then I remembered we needed drinks, so I rose again to pour everyone glasses of water.

While this was going on, Carver entertained us with stories. The kids leaned toward him like plants toward the sun, their mouths gaping open while they listened. He directed his attention toward them, and didn't put any pressure on me to chime in, and this helped me relax and adjust to this strange revelation: that not only was Carver Greyson a ballplayer, but that he'd avoided telling me. I wondered if maybe he just never needed to, when he picked women up. Maybe the other women he asked out already knew what he did. Or maybe Carver was so sexy that nothing else mattered: one smile and a wink, and they climbed into bed with him.

Or maybe he told them a story, like he was telling the kids a story, and the sound of his voice was what did women in... because Carver had a voice made for seduction, warm and rough and as rich as a secret. I felt his words trip through my body and tickle my skin. He could recite stock market numbers or the periodic table of elements, and I knew I'd still shiver with pleasure and think about peeling his shirt off. Between his smile and his voice, I wasn't sure which was more dangerous.

And these were goofy, kid-friendly stories he was sharing. God help the woman he decided to whisper sweet-nothings to.

In the next baseball story he told, he'd been running a fever. "I was playing for the Yankees that season, and this game was in Baltimore. The sun beat down hot enough to melt the concrete in the stadium, and I was playing third base. I could hear some guys in the stands chanting, *Booger, booger, booger,* which is what they call Beau Rieson, our pitcher that year. I kept closing my eyes and falling asleep, I was so dazed by the heat and my fever. The next batter up hit the ball toward me, and after I caught it, I started to run off the field. I thought the inning had ended. Then I realized no one else was moving, which meant *I'd lost track of the outs*, and I had to turn around and run back. I even forgot I was holding the ball. The second basemen had to holler at me to throw it in."

He had the kids giggling at this. So was Mom.

"That was extremely embarrassing," he said. "Coach had to tell everyone later I had the flu, which was more embarrassing still."

I noticed Steve had bought some pretzels, so I opened one of his bags. I asked Richard to give everyone a handful, which he did, and Carver told another story about a game in Detroit when he'd hit four homeruns. "I was stepping into the batter's box that last time, and someone threw something at me. The umpire picked it up, and it turned out to be a Cabbage Patch doll, wearing a jersey that someone had stitched my name and number onto."

"A *Cabbage Patch* doll?" Richard snorted. "Ballplayers don't play with *dolls*."

"I still have it," Carver said. "My oldest boy keeps it on a shelf in his room." It had taken Carver a long time to pull all of the shell off his egg, and once it was picked clean, he passed it over to Gus with a wink. Gus popped the whole thing in his mouth and beamed at him.

"You hit a slump though," Richard said.

"I did hit a slump," Carver said.

"How come you don't slam the ball anymore?" Richard asked. "You haven't hit homers in like, years."

"That's baseball," Carver said. "Lot of things can go wrong when a lot of things start going right."

"That sounds like life," Mom said.

Carver nodded. "Yes, ma'am."

"Hey, you wanna play some baseball tonight?" Richard asked. "There's a field here in Riverdale. I could brush the snow off the baselines."

"Enough light to see the ball?" Carver asked. His voice made it clear that if the answer was yes, he would do this. He'd go play some ball with the kids, out in the snow.

Richard remembered it was evening. "Oh," he sighed. "No, it's not lit. Guess not."

"Sun'll be back tomorrow," Carver said.

"MJ has to work until three," Richard said glumly.

I felt myself flush. "I'll get off early," I promised. "Unless there's a shuttle, I'll leave work at noon."

The boys were excited by this. Even Mia seemed thrilled to go play. They started to speculate on the number of people we had for a game, and who should play which positions. Ethan and Richard had several clashing ideas, and even Gus tried to pipe in. Finally, Richard took over. "I'm shortstop," he said. "MJ can play first, Ethan on second. Gus can pitch, and Mia can catch. Mom and Steve can play Carver's team."

Of course, no one wanted to agree with this plan, and there was a long discussion as to various skill levels and aptitudes, and Richard kept trying to convince everyone he was right. Gandhi wandered over and put his head on my knee, so I scratched behind his ears and gazed at Carver a while. Even with the streaks of grey in his hair, he was one beautiful man.

I went to the bedroom and retrieved the bouquet of flowers, and then I arranged them in a plastic pitcher and set them on an end table in the living room.

When the raging debate at the table settled down, I told the kids that Carver and I were going out to Muldoon's for a while, and that I wanted them in bed by midnight.

"I'm going to come home and check on you," I said. "So don't blow it."

"Yeah, yeah," Richard grumbled, and he started to pick up the paper towels from the table. "Go on then, and stop bugging us."

We all left the table, but Gus and Steve quickly returned with the chess set. Ethan and Mia jumped in front of the TV. I put on my nice jacket and walked toward the door. Carver glanced down at my feet, grinning again, and I realized I was about to leave the house barefoot. I hurried down the hall, pulled on a clean pair of socks, and stepped into my black cowboy boots.

"All right, I'm ready," I said.

Mom stood and held out a balloon to Carver. It was one of the sparkly pink ones, with a neon green string. "Here, you take this one," she said. "I want you to have it."

Carver took the string from her fingers and tipped his hat. "Thank you, Miss Preston." Then he opened the door for me, and we left the apartment. Carver walked beside me with that big pink balloon.

At the bottom of the stairs, I stopped at a door where a little girl lived, knocked twice, and when the girl's mother answered, I gave her the balloon. Then Carver and I were on our way to his Navigator.

"You told me you worked in an office," I said.

I heard him laugh softly. "Office, cathedral, battlefield, morgue..." he said. "Diamonds are all of those things."

"Why didn't you just tell me you played ball?"

"Why don't you just kiss me?" he replied. I shot him a look that meant *In your dreams*, though my body went a bit haywire at the idea of kissing him. I *did* want to kiss him—and more, I just didn't want to deal with the empty-bed aftermath. He'd picked the wrong girl, if this was his standard Casanova routine.

He opened the passenger door for me, and waited until I hopped inside.

"I like your dress," he said with a grin.

"Uh-huh," I said. "Get in and drive." His shoulders shook with his laughter as he walked around to the driver's seat.

19

DANCING

The Muldoon Saloon was in downtown Riverdale, not far from the train depot. Carver parked his Navigator near the tracks, and we walked to the bar. He kept opening and closing doors for me, and when we arrived inside, he helped me take off my coat. Proof positive that he was from Texas.

We found seats at the bar and Carver ordered a beer, but I needed something stronger and asked for a rum and Coke. There was a good crowd in Muldoon's tonight, mostly people in their forties and fifties, which was typical. A lot of the women wore colorful dresses or blue jeans with print shirts and big hats. Most of the men wore bolo ties and vests. Belt buckles flashed. The bar's sound system played Garth Brooks while we waited for the band to set up. A few people were already dancing.

I finished my drink and ordered another. I was feeling nervous already, wondering if my safety pins would hold up, and hoping my hair looked okay in the yellow haze by the bar. Carver kept smiling at me, so that helped. I was glad he had hung up his hat, and I could see the light in his eyes.

"When was the last time you took someone dancing?" I asked. "I mean, someone who isn't your sister."

"Long time," he said.

"Have you ever tried swing dance? Spinning girls on your arm and what-not?"

He sipped his beer and raised an eyebrow. "You want me to spin you on my arm?"

"No!" I said. "I just wanted to know."

He laughed and sipped his beer again. "Come on, let's warm up," and he pushed his bottle away and stood. He held out his hand to take mine, and I let him lead me onto the dance floor. The boards were dusty and worn, and the band was still checking equipment.

Carver placed his right hand on my back, below my shoulder, so I rested my left hand on his arm. Our other two hands were clasped together, and I felt my heart beating so hard, my whole body was thick with nerves. There was a Travis Tritt song playing, a fast one. I took a deep breath and we tried to start moving, but I had my quick-quick and slow-slows all messed up with Carver's, and it was a total disaster. I started to laugh, as we obviously looked ridiculous.

Carver was undaunted. "Come on, sonny," he said, "we'll figure it out," and we kept moving and turning and trying to get into sync with each other, but it took nearly the whole song before I felt even a glimmer of hope we were making some kind of progress. For a man who was so big he'd been named after a bear, Carver was light on his feet, and he could shift directions so fast that maybe a cheetah could keep up.

He cheered when we finally managed to quick-quick and slow-slow together, but then we fumbled a spin and looked like fools again. The band leader even said into the microphone,

"Check out these newbies! Cutting a rug!" Carver lifted his chin toward the man and smiled, and we kept right on dancing, since Carver was determined we'd get this and refused to give up. We kept changing our steps, trying to find our rhythm together, this time to a Tim McGraw song, but it wasn't until the band started playing, kicking off with "T-R-O-U-B-L-E" that we finally started to match up our steps.

"Now we're moving!" Carver laughed, and I had to laugh, too. We were in a sea of people all dancing in a circular pattern around the floor. I could smell perfume everywhere, and the music hummed through my body.

We danced for three more songs before we stopped and went to order more drinks. I was so happy, I could've started pulling my hair and running around like Richard. I ordered a glass of water, and a few minutes later, Carver was tugging my hand to start dancing again. I stopped watching the clock at the bar, and I didn't remember I needed to leave at midnight until it was already quarter-past.

Carver left some money in the band's tip jar, found our coats, and opened the door for me when we left. The cold air felt nice after the heat in Muldoon's.

"Thanks for dancing," I said, and I was laughing again, I felt so giddy.

"Thanks for joining me," Carver said.

He drove us back to my apartment, but I asked him to wait for me outside. I hadn't felt this happy in so long, I didn't want it to end. I clicked with Carver, clicked in a way that was different than enjoying his looks. I liked talking to him, and just being around him, and I didn't want to part with his company. "I'll come right back, okay?" I asked. "You don't want to go to sleep yet, do you?"

He laughed and said, "I'll wait."

So I ran up the stairs and went inside. The kids were in bed, already asleep. I slipped out of my dress and changed into jeans and a t-shirt. Then I jumped into my winter boots and took the blanket off my Army cot. Mom sat up in bed, where she'd fallen asleep next to Mia, and asked, "Where you going?"

"Hole-in-the-Wall," I said, and Mom lay back down. I put on my coat again and went outside to meet Carver. He opened the passenger door for me, and I hopped into the front seat with my blanket. I waited for him to climb in again.

"Do you have a snow shovel?" I asked.

"At the house, I do."

"Good," and I buckled my seatbelt. "That's on our way." We started off for The Summit, and because I was taking him to Hole-in-the-Wall, I began to tell him about Hanna.

"When I was in high school, I played softball and basketball, and when I made it into college, I joined the basketball team. I met this point guard named Hanna, and she was a freshman like me, and I was going to make a documentary with her and help her become a movie star. She was so pretty and smart, I knew she could pull it off."

I smiled over at Carver, hoping I wasn't talking too much, but he seemed game for this story, so I went on. "We only played basketball for two years, and then Hanna convinced me to study abroad in India with her, so we left for a semester our junior year, and we hiked in the Himalayas and we saw the Taj Mahal, and Hanna decided then that we should film our documentary in Africa. We came to Goldking that summer and planned it all out, and that's where we're going tonight. I made us a hideout in the mountains, like a couple of gunslingers. Butch Cassidy and the Sundance Kid had that place in Wyoming, so I named mine Hole-in-the-Wall, after them."

"So why do we need a snow shovel?" Carver asked.

"It's up in the canyon, you'll see," I said. Goldking was only an hour away. "About fifteen minutes past town."

Carver laughed. "I thought you had to work tomorrow."

I shrugged, too excited to care about this. "We'll be back before seven," which was when my shift started.

When we arrived at The Summit and parked in front of the house, Carver asked, "You want to come in?" and I nodded and followed him. I liked seeing the inside of these vacation homes. The interior of this one was lovely, with antique furniture and oversized couches, and there was a whole room with kids' toys and two Pack 'n Plays. The living room had an old record player with a shelf full of records, and I could see covers for the Rolling Stones and Janis Joplin and George Strait.

"Your sister did a nice job with this place," I said, and Carver smiled.

"She loans it out to her friends most of the year," he said. "It sure weathers a lot of abuse."

I followed him into the kitchen, and he opened the fridge and set out a few water bottles, and then he stuffed some granola bars in his coat pockets. I said, "Let's take some beer," and he reached for a six-pack of Heineken. I spotted some candles and a box of matches in the pantry, so I took those, too. We walked outside again and Carver grabbed a snow shovel from the garage. A few minutes later, we were on the highway to Goldking.

"So when are you going to make this documentary?" Carver asked.

I opened my mouth to say something, but then I fell silent. I tried several times to speak, but the words never came. I kept thinking of Hanna, when she'd asked me the same thing. I'd had no words then, either. And two weeks later, her heart had stopped beating. I wished I knew what to say, but I didn't.

Carver finally said, "I first came to Colorado when I was nineteen, to play the Rockies."

I found my voice again, relieved he'd changed the subject. "Really?"

"Yeah," he said. "I asked my sister to come out and drive around, see what was here, and she found Riverdale and asked me to buy her that place at The Summit, so I did. She signs her children up for ski school each year, and decided I had to do the same with mine. I never imagined I'd have three boys who knew how to ski. That seems so foreign to me."

A man buying a house for his sister seemed foreign to me. I couldn't really fathom the kind of money Carver must have. I'd read an article once about how a lot of professional athletes were big spenders, and burned through their huge incomes so fast that they were broke within one or two years after their careers ended. I wondered if Carver was better with money than that. He didn't seem like a man who was addicted to bling and big parties, or making bad business bets… but I could be wrong.

"What did your dad do?" I asked, since I was assuming Carver's father retired when his son made the Yankees.

"Worked on an oil rig," Carver said. "We never saw much of him at home. My mother sold makeup."

"How'd you get into baseball?"

"I played in the neighborhood," Carver said. "And when I was five, my kid brother decided we should play t-ball. He had someone in preschool with him who was playing, and Ben loved baseball. We already had a group of boys we played with after school. Clarissa was seven that year, and she even came and played with us sometimes. She liked standing on third and taunting the batters. Anyway, Ben cried and whined enough about playing t-ball, that our mother signed both of us up."

I liked the idea of Carver playing ball with his brother and sister, although it was hard to imagine him ever being that small. By nineteen, he'd been six-two and weighed two hundred pounds. That was a good size for a rookie in the majors.

"How big are you?" I asked.

Carver laughed and looked a little abashed. "Five years ago, I was six-four, two-forty-one. Now I'm two-fifteen." He was still so big it was hard to think of him with twenty-six extra pounds. As to asking why he'd lost weight—that seemed like a sensitive topic. Professional athletes often agonized over gaining muscle weight the same way anorexics agonized over losing it. Probably best to change the subject again.

"Guess which position I played," I said.

He caught my gaze with a grin, and said, "Shortstop."

"No way, first base," I laughed. But I knew he'd just handed me a compliment, and I felt my whole body flush. "Except softball is sort of… you know, not baseball. And the metal bats weren't my favorite. That pinging sound. I like watching bats blow apart when someone hits a ball. I think that's one of the best parts of the game."

"Your coach wouldn't let you use wooden bats?"

"Only if we bought them ourselves," I said. "But sometimes I'd talk a girl into buying one and letting me share it."

"Were you good?" he asked.

"Good enough," I said. "But I think I was better at basketball. I'll tell you something unpleasant."

"What's that?"

"The girls on my high school teams… A lot of them were gay, and on my softball team, they tried to recruit me to join them. Sometimes it led to actual fistfights. I pretty much hated them. I quit the team seven times, and every time, the coach came and convinced me not to. She kept telling me I couldn't let everyone down, and how I just had to ignore them and play ball. So my memories of softball are kind of… tainted by that."

"I'd say," Carver said. "In all my years playing baseball, none of my teammates ever tried to hustle me for sex. That sounds like hell."

"Yeah, it was," I said. "Are you really going to stay the whole week?"

"Sure," and he smiled. "I'll fly out to see my boys again on Sunday. Being at Disneyland for three days, and staying at my sister's house with their cousins, they won't miss me too much."

"Does she live right on the beach?" I asked.

"She does," Carver said. I wondered if he had bought her that house as well. The idea that he *could* have was still… really shocking. I also wondered if his sister was grateful she had a brother like Carver—someone who was not only self-sufficient, but could afford extravagant gifts for his family. My three older brothers would never do something like that, even if they weren't rageaholics.

As to Carver staying all week, I wished I didn't have to work, but other than that, I was happy. I hoped he'd want to spend more time with me.

I asked him if he'd liked playing t-ball (definitely), and then I asked how old he'd been when he'd hit his first homer (thirteen), and if he'd gone to college at all (he was admitted, but drafted out after high school to play for the Braves).

"I'd like to go back to school one day," he added. "After I retire, I want to coach, so I'll need my degree."

"It's wild how people love baseball so much," I said. "Or any sport."

"I've loved baseball since I was old enough to pick up a bat," Carver said. "I think I was two. I broke a vase."

I laughed. "How about your brother? Did he play pro ball?"

"Not Ben," Carver said. "He turned himself into an agent—my agent. He was the reason I made the big leagues."

"Was he the one you were with that day in Goldking?" I asked. "In The Caroline?"

"No, that was an old friend of mine. His father died in June, and his funeral was held in Peatlyn." Peatlyn was a town north of Goldking. "We flew into Riverdale, and passed through Goldking on our way to the service."

Since we were almost to the top of Gunner Pass, I decided to point out an avalanche run. "That's a slide zone called Midway," I said. "Forty years ago, a woman died there, and people say sometimes you can see her ghost late at night. She prowls around looking for cars to get into."

I was grinning as I said this, so Carver asked, "Is that true?"

"No," I laughed, "but the slide is called Midway. I wasn't kidding about that part."

There were actually two mountain passes between Riverdale and Goldking, both of them equally frightening to most flat-lander motorists. Carver didn't seem to have any problem with heights though.

"Can I have one of those granola bars?" I asked, and he reached into his coat pocket and handed me two. "Thanks."

I decided I wanted to eat a granola bar and just look at him a while. I loved that stubbly skin on his face and his bright silver eyes. I couldn't imagine playing professional ball like he did. How much self-control did you have to have, to swing at a ball in a stadium where thousands of people were screaming? I didn't even like batting in front of high school crowds. Striking out just sucked too much ass. And I mostly hit grounders and line drives. No one expected me to slam the damn thing, although I'd managed to do that on occasion. But the pressure to hit a homerun? No way. I got on base, or I brought someone in, and that was the extent of what the coach ever wanted from me. I played sports for only one reason in high school: I needed the self-esteem. Because sports operated differently from every other facet of life. You could be unwashed, dirt poor, and illiterate, and still be a hero. It was one of the most magical parts about civilization.

I opened the second granola bar and passed it to Carver. He hesitated a moment, and then smiled and reached for it. His fingers felt warm against mine.

"Do you ever get scared?" I asked. "At bat?"

"I didn't used to," he said. "I didn't used to think at all."

I knew what he meant by that comment, and I knew how painful it was. To lose the ability to stay in the zone, to perform without hesitating—the result was to be self-conscious. Thinking, in this sense, meant fear. The opposite of slamming the ball… was to stand in the batter's box, worrying about striking out.

I thought of my own life for a moment. All those panic attacks. The college degree I wasn't using. The bills I couldn't pay.

I knew what fear was. I knew the power the word *failure* held over me.

Take away the exterior, and I bet Carver and I were the same person inside. Trapped in our minds. Not doing, but thinking. It was not a good place to be.

But I wondered if Carver really wanted to discuss this with me. He didn't seem uncomfortable talking about his at bats… but maybe he was just better at hiding it. I decided to keep the conversation upbeat.

"I'll tell you a story," I said. "When my softball team went to state."

Carver grinned. "Sounds like a good one."

"Especially looking back," I said. "When I don't have to relive it." So I told him the innings the way I remembered them, including every stupid mistake I had made, every stupid mistake my teammates all made, and how we arrived at the bottom of the seventh, at the end of the game, down by three runs. Then we started to hit and loaded the bases. Two outs. My turn at bat.

"It was the game made in hell," I said. "It's the stuff night-mares are made of. Especially my nightmares."

Carver kept grinning at all this. I had him hooked on this story.

"This girl who was pitching, she was so mean and nasty. I mean, absolutely disgusting. A total slob. She chewed tobacco and tried to spit it on me, like a camel. I was ready to clock her. And now we're facing each other down and she's giving me the evil eye and calling me dead cheese and guacamole puke, and I kept think-ing, screw you and your tobacco juice, you dumb hamster-head. I really hated that girl. I could see the chew in her lip and the way she was smirking at me, and she did her big wind-up and gave me the fastest pitch that she had, low and inside—"

Carver glanced at me, waiting. "And you slammed it?"

"No," I said. "Strike one."

He laughed.

"You should have seen this girl's face," I said. "She called me every sick stupid thing she could think of. And then she spit more of that chew and dusted her hat on her leg, and my hands were so slick with sweat I dropped the bat. I picked it up, and then I dropped it again. Three times, this happened."

Carver kept chuckling.

"That crowd was chanting my doom. They had my number, I'll tell you. My coach couldn't even watch the game anymore. She had her face in her hand in the dugout. And I kept thinking, I'm going to die in this ballgame, and that hamster-head pitcher is going to come over here and spit on my corpse. All I could see were my teammates waiting on the bases. I needed one line drive or one grounder past center—those were my hits, but I wasn't hitting for beans. None of us had been hitting until the last inning. It was awful."

I decided it was time to drag out this story, so I asked, "Can I have another granola bar?" and Carver reached into his coat pocket and passed me two more. I took my time peeling them open.

"So I had nothing to do but stand in the box, and the pitcher called me a few other choice phrases, and she did her idiotic tobacco-spit pitch, and I watched that ball coming down, and I swung so hard—"

Carver caught my gaze. "And you slammed it?"

"Hell no, I didn't slam it," I said. "Strike two. You think this story has a happy ending or something? No way. Softball sucks as much ass as baseball does. Probably more."

I passed Carver another granola bar, and he held it loose in his fingers, laughing again.

"The catcher called time and walked up to the mound, and I stood there just wishing and wishing I didn't have to get back in that box. I wanted to puke, and the crowd wanted blood. They were all in a frenzy behind me, shaking that hurricane fence, and the catcher came back from the mound and told me I was done for, that this game was dusted up and *finito*, and I thought, well, I'll show you done for."

I paused for a moment and glanced over at Carver. He was just eating this story up, I could tell.

"My coach was still hiding her face, and the pitcher called me dead cheese one more time, and then she made her big spit-juice wind-up dumb pitch, and I saw the ball coming down, and I swung that bat harder than I ever had in my life—"

Carver was beaming at this point, the biggest smile I'd seen on his face. "And you slammed it?"

"Of course I slammed it," I said. "That game helped put me in college. Well, that game and an SAT score." My athleticism and my grades had been a winning combination.

"How old were you?" he asked.

"Sixteen," I said. "Junior year." I polished off the granola bar, and I gazed at Carver's face for a while and just enjoyed myself, because when you find someone beautiful you simply want to stare at them like an idiot, and if they don't mind this eccentric behavior, then you know they might like you back. Carver did not seem to mind.

✳✳✳

We arrived in Goldking, and I had him drive through the town, and then onto the gravel road that led into the canyon. The plowed snow on either side of us looked like mounds of blue ice.

Fifteen minutes outside of town, I told him where to pull over. I had him park where people wouldn't notice the car, in case someone passed by at this hour. This was *my* secret hideout, and it needed to stay that way.

I zipped up my jacket and hopped out. Carver came to my side, shovel in hand.

"So, which way?" he asked, and I pointed past the place we had parked. We had a distance of thirty feet to the mountain base, with waist-deep snow to get through.

"Oh, man," Carver laughed, and he started to shovel.

20

HOLE-IN-THE-WALL

Halfway to the mountainside, Carver stopped shoveling and stripped off his coat. I reached out to hold it for him. For a Texan, the boy could seriously throw some snow. If there was an Olympics for this, Carver would have taken the gold.

When we landed at the rock face, he turned and tried to look at me in the moonlight, but I pointed to the stone and said, "Can you see it?"

"A door?" he asked.

"That's right," I said. "It's right there."

Carver tried to find a handle or some way into the rock wall of the mountain, but then he said, "Mary Jane, come show me," so I did. I took his hand and led his fingers under a lip in the stone, and when he pulled, the door opened.

Hot, humid air swelled out of the cave and steamed around us, and I gave him my flashlight and said, "Don't bump your head," as I nudged him inside. I walked in behind him and pulled the door closed.

Carver gazed around at the rock walls, taking in the dimensions of the vapor cave. Past the low door, the ceiling in here was almost nine feet high, the walls ten feet wide and twelve feet deep. It was the size of a room in a house.

"This is my Hole-in-the-Wall," I said, and I knelt to light the candles I'd taken from Carver's place. "I made it myself. Me and the Monkey."

There was a stream of hot water that ran through one side of the floor, and Carver knelt and put his fingers in it. "Who's the Monkey?"

"The Monkey is Charlie McCree, and he's got a claim in Mad Violet Gulch. Him and Don Doonan. The Monkey loves Prell, so that's where his nickname comes from. He's like an old powder-monkey."

"Prell's an explosive?" Carver asked.

"A blasting agent," I said with a smile. "It's just the trade name for ANFO, ammonium nitrate and fuel oil. The Monkey uses diesel fuel in his mix, like a lot of miners do. I found the hot springs seep outside, and asked him to blast it for me."

Carver stood and gazed up at the ceiling again. "If I wasn't in here with you right now, I'd never believe it."

"Here's the best part," I said, and I took the flashlight from him and lit the bottom left corner of the cave. There was an opening here, only three feet wide and two-and-a-half feet tall. I had Carver kneel down so he could see inside of it. "There's a whole room in there," I said, and I shone my light on the floor. Half of that floor was covered in rock, the other half in water. "That room has a hot springs. The little pool's about three and a half feet deep. The water's always one-hundred-six."

"Wild," Carver said.

"That's a natural cave," I said. "But just sitting in this big room is nice. The vapor will make you sweat though. It's really better to come here in a swimsuit, but this is okay." I spread the blanket out on the floor, where it wouldn't be soaked in the stream, and switched off the flashlight. The candlelight made the rock appear deep orange and red. "The iron and manganese turn the rock that color," I said. "There's no sulfur in this hot spring, which is why it doesn't smell. I like sulfur springs though, so I would've liked to have found one like that."

I took a seat on the blanket and Carver sat down beside me. I'd carried in two bottles of beer, and Carver popped them open.

"I made this last summer, so Hanna and I could be the Hole-in-the-Wall gang. We'd come out here and soak and talk about going to Africa." So strange how my whole life had changed so quickly. In one semester of college, I'd lost my best friend, my dreams, all of my plans after school… I'd never gone to Vienna, or played basketball again, or signed up for grad school… When I thought about it now, it was probably no wonder I'd started having panic attacks. The skinny girl I saw in the mirror every morning was only a shell of the person I'd been in college.

But there didn't seem much I could do about fate. If there'd been another path for me to follow, I certainly never found it. Which was why grit and denial were my homeboys.

Carver draped his coat against the rock behind him, leaned back and sipped his beer. He studied my face for a moment, and I wondered how I looked to him. My cheeks were probably still red from being out in the cold. I hoped my hair wasn't being dumb, but I felt too self-conscious to run my hands through it and check. The way Carver was gazing at me made me glance down at my knees.

In a soft voice, he asked, "Mary Jane, where's your boyfriend?"

"I've had only one boyfriend," I said quietly, without looking at him, "and that was the Cowboy. I thought he was dating Bree Taylor this fall, but it turns out he's with a girl named Abigail Turner. She's a really nice person. She likes painting pictures of birds, and hunting elk, and wearing her hair in a braid. I heard a rumor that she and the Cowboy had gotten engaged, and I hope that they are."

"Why do you hope they're engaged?" Carver asked.

"Because I'm not going to marry him, and he's known that a long time."

Carver reached over and took my hand, and when his skin touched mine, I felt my heart skip until it was hard to think clearly. "What happened to Hanna?" he asked.

The memory of watching Hanna die was suddenly upon me, so raw and unwelcome, so painful to me, that I wondered if I should answer.

But then I took a deep breath and said, "Hanna is gone. Gone to the one place I can't follow." I paused, and then added, "Not yet."

Carver sat without speaking a while, not even drinking his beer, and he seemed very somber. The kind of sorrowfulness that fills the air up with sympathy. Sometimes that means more than hearing someone say they are sorry, when you know how they feel without words. I wondered who Carver had lost in his life. I was about to ask, but then he smiled and tried to lighten the mood.

"I know how to read palms," he said brightly, and he turned my hand over and spread out my fingers. He traced the lines in my skin, but I knew he was faking it. He wasn't doing any of the things people did in the movies.

"You don't know how to read palms," I said, and he laughed. He studied my face again, and I watched the candlelight flickering against his skin. Then he glanced down, lifted my hand and planted a kiss on my palm. The feel of his lips on my skin sent a burst of butterflies through my stomach, and I felt the stubble on his jaw like sandstone on my fingers. But when Carver met my gaze again, his eyes looked so different. They were colored a much deeper grey, all murky and troubled.

I had answered his questions, and now I had one for him—a question that I was so nervous to put to him, my words were almost a whisper. "Why aren't you still married?"

Carver tried to hide his expression by smiling, but it was too late. I'd seen what was there inside of him. It turned out Carver Greyson was aching inside, and he couldn't make the pain stop.

"Audrey," he said, and he turned toward the wall. "She died in a car accident." The expression on his face was so gentle it would break a wild horse.

He bowed his head for a time, and then he stretched out on his side and laid his cheek on my leg. He moved like a panther, massive and graceful, and the sudden contact with his body made my heart pound.

I placed my hand on his shoulder, and then I ran my fingers through his hair, the same way I did for the kids. His hair was so thick, it almost felt rough, and I kept expecting to find tangles, but it was actually combed.

"You should cut this," I said, and he chuckled.

"I do cut it," he said. "It always looks this way. I could shave it all off tomorrow, and it would grow back by nightfall."

"Maybe you're a vampire," I said.

"Maybe I am," he sighed.

I placed my hand on his forehead. "You don't feel cold enough to convince me."

"It's heating up in here," he said.

"Vapor caves tend to do that," I grinned. "I was thinking just now, about the kids, and there's an area inside the community center where we can play ball tomorrow—inside the track. No one ever runs there on Sundays." I waited a moment, and then added, "But we don't have any equipment."

"I'll bring mine," Carver said, which was the kind of comment that made my heart skip a beat. He was so practical about things, I thought he oozed romance.

"So what do you think of my hideout?" I asked. "Feel like a gunslinger yet?"

"All I need is a six-shooter," he said.

I reached for his arm then and picked up his wrist. I checked the time on his watch, and saw it was half-past four. Carver caught my hand and pressed it over his face. I could feel the curve of his cheeks, his five o'clock shadow, his lips, and I shivered. I liked touching him, but it frightened me, too.

"Time to go yet?" he asked.

"Almost," I said. His breath on my fingertips tickled. "Since we rode all the way up here, I wanted to stop and say hi to King."

"The mustang?" he mused.

I laughed. "King is a Quarter Horse."

"Looked pretty wild to me," Carver said.

I was still so surprised he remembered this from last summer that I fell quiet. He rolled onto his back so he could gaze up at my face, and I glanced at his hips while he moved. Carver had a beautiful body, all laced up with muscle.

"How did your brother get you into the Majors?" I asked.

"Ben and I played ball together through high school," Carver said. "He was our relief pitcher. But he also loved scheming and finding ways to make money. Ben ran for student council, joined political organizations. He knew all the county commissioners and the mayor and everyone who sat on the city council. He had such a knack for people and how to butter them up and figure out what they could give him. He wanted to be rich one day and run for political office. Sometimes he talked about becoming a Senator. That's where his mind was, all the time, even when we were young. Ben's two great loves in life were baseball and politics, and I think he usually thought of them as one and the same."

I ran my fingers through Carver's hair again, enjoying this story and the sound of his voice.

"So once Ben figured out that I could hit the ball hard enough to play pro, that was it. He turned all of his talent for scheming into making me an athlete. He convinced me to bulk up and keep putting on muscle, and while I lifted weights, Ben started writing letters and emails and making phone calls. He found ways to meet people. Coaches, sportswriters, scouts. He figured out how to make people listen to him, and what he was selling was me. It was even his idea for me to sign up for college, all part of his plan to drive a hard bargain. He had so much charisma and talent, it was like watching a cyclone. He had that much energy. You felt it when you stood next to him."

"He was smaller than you?" I asked.

"Smaller physically," Carver said. "Mentally, a titan."

I dropped my voice and asked, "What happened to him?"

"Ben and Audrey were driving back from one of my games, when I played for the Yankees," Carver said. His voice sounded neutral, with an emotionless quality that meant he expended some effort to keep it that way. "The game ran ten innings, New York won. They were on their way to the house. A man in a semi crossed the center line and hit them head on. Audrey died instantly. Ben made it to the hospital and died a few minutes later. July twenty-second. Four and a half years ago."

My fingers in Carver's hair went still. I said, "Oh, Carver. I'm so sorry," and he was quiet a while. Then he pressed on with his story.

"When my contract ran out with the Yankees, they let me go. Detroit picked me up, and a year later, they traded me off to Saint Louis. Despite everything else, I know Ben would've been proud. He always had a soft spot for the Cardinals. My youngest son is even named after their old manager, Branch Rickey, in tribute to Ben's deep admiration for that man."

Carver smiled at this last. I knew that Branch Rickey had gone on to be president and general manager of the Brooklyn Dodgers, and had been the man who'd signed on baseball's first black player in the Majors: Jackie Robinson. 1947. Carver had named his first son Jack, after the same Jack Robinson who'd broken the color line and been his all-time favorite athlete. I often thought that racism was truly the war that love fought. Love might not conquer all, but athletes could sure use it to move mountains sometimes. People said the outpouring of love for Jackie Robinson had paved the way for Martin Luther King, Junior, and I believed them.

Carver fell quiet a moment, and then he chuckled, and I guessed he was remembering something about his family. He'd been wistful throughout this whole story, but I could feel something change. A tension came out of his body, like he wanted to tell me something else, but whatever it was made him anxious. A few moments later, I felt the sensation pass, and I knew he'd decided to end his story there. He rolled onto his stomach and propped himself on his elbow.

"Did you give up on it?" he asked. "The documentary?"

It was such an abrupt change of subject that I had to think for a minute. "I don't know if I gave up on it, or if it gave up on me. Maybe in a couple of years, I can figure something out. Without a high school in Goldking, I'm not sure what else to do." I realized I was scared to talk about *Brighter Than Stars* any more, since I normally kept everything about who I'd been at college locked up in myself. And here I'd only just met this man, and look what I'd done? Brought him here to my hide-out, and told him things—secret things. When a gorgeous pro athlete was definitely the *last* man I should've brought to my Hole-in-the-Wall. Everything important to me could only be a passing amusement to him, a tiny diversion between his seasons of ballgames—and I suddenly wished I hadn't shared so much of myself. I already knew I didn't want to be one of his stadium girls. And friendship with a man who was only in town for one week was not realistic.

So I checked the watch on Carver's wrist again, and announced we should leave.

21

PURPLE IS A RELIGION

Carver sat up, and we folded the blanket and put on our coats. I blew out the candles and switched on my flashlight, and once we were outside, I pushed the door shut. Carver picked up the shovel and I followed him to the Lincoln. The air was so cold it almost felt hard to breathe. So I decided I'd visit King another day, and we headed toward town.

"You okay to drive home?" I asked. "Not too tired?"

"I'm not tired at all," Carver said, and sent me a smile. "You know, Mary Jane… the first time I saw you… when you threw those men out and called up your horse…" I nodded, and Carver reached over and clasped my hand. "I thought you were the most beautiful woman I'd ever seen in my life. You had such an impact on me, Mary Jane. I can't quite describe it. I've never had someone give me a first impression like that."

I stopped looking at Carver, too nervous to speak.

"I held my breath when I saw you. And not just because you were beautiful, but because you struck me as… just so powerful—and *free*. Free to do what you want, free to speak your own mind. Not many people have power like that, Mary Jane."

Hearing him say such things made me breathless. Of what I recalled of that day in The Caroline... it had not been a good day in my life. I'd just finished hitchhiking home, Tom Morbun had come knocking on the door, Landon had been acting like his usual asshole self, and I'd just gotten a job washing dishes for ten bucks an hour.

And yet, Carver hadn't seen a girl who was miserable. Carver had said I'd looked *powerful* and *free*, and I couldn't reconcile those two things in my head: the miserable me, and the person Carver had seen. They were like two halves of a locket that would not clip together.

The cab had grown quiet, so I finally said, "The snow looks really pretty tonight."

Carver agreed. "It sure does."

"You're pretty, too," I said. "I mean, handsome. Men are handsome. You're very handsome, Carver. Very."

Which had to be the most ridiculous compliment he had ever received. Great. He tells me I'm *powerful* and *free*, and I respond with *you're pretty*.

I felt myself blush, and I couldn't seem to calm my nerves, which made me even more anxious. So I pulled my hand away from Carver's and sent him my *well, that was awkward* smile. I glanced out the windshield and added, "Watch out for this turn—it's really icy tonight."

Carver quirked an eyebrow and sent me a puzzled expression, and I worried he was going to say something about my genius fumble of a compliment. So I said, "I'm glad we're already on our way back—I'll miss my ride in to work with Steve if I'm late."

Carver remained pensive a moment, and I tried to think of something I hadn't asked him about baseball… except all I wanted to know was if he'd like to see me again. But if I asked him that now, he'd probably think I meant sex. And I didn't want him to think that. So I kept struggling to come up with a good baseball question.

We passed through Goldking, reached the highway to Riverdale, and started up Capital, which was the section of highway that led out of town. The heater was blasting, so Carver slowed down and stripped off his coat. I watched as he did this, imagining how he looked in his baseball uniform, and the thought made me smile.

"Where were you born, Mary Jane?"

"Raleigh, North Carolina," I said. "You?"

"Port Arthur, Texas," he said. "Where I grew up."

"You miss it there?" I asked.

"Sometimes," he said. "But I'm happier where it's cold. I deal with heat when I have to, but I'd have gotten along better in Alaska than Texas."

"You must love it here then," I said, and Carver smiled.

"I think this part of Colorado is a piece of heaven on earth," he said, which was exactly how I felt.

"Of all the places I've lived, this one is my favorite," I said. "Except for being at college. My first three years in college were the best time of my life."

Carver caught my gaze for a moment, and I realized—too late—that I'd said too much. I shouldn't have brought up college again. I should've left that subject behind us, back in the vapor cave.

"I saw your diploma," Carver said, and I felt my heart quicken. "In that little glass cupboard, down in the corner. When you were putting on your coat before we went out, I noticed it there."

The cab felt stifling all of a sudden, like the air was too thick to breathe. I knew what was coming. I knew it like watching a car accident the split second before the vehicles come screaming together. I knew it like the day Hanna said, "Mary Jane, I don't feel good..." and I looked into her eyes and knew that something was wrong.

And I knew it right now. That I had made a mistake inviting Carver to pick me up at my house. And I had made an even bigger mistake to forget about my diploma.

"My friend Matt wants his own son and daughter to go to Swarthmore one day," Carver said. "He met a financial advisor who'd gone there who just blew him away. So Matt's always saying kids who come out of that school are brilliant. And now that I've met *you*, I'm convinced that he's right." Carver smiled warmly and placed a hand on my shoulder, and I was too horrified by what was coming to shift away. I wanted to jump out of the vehicle, just to spare myself what I knew he would say. But of course it was coming. Like cancer, like death, like all the pain in the world, it was coming. Some things you just can't run away from.

"Why aren't you using your degree, Mary Jane? Why is the smartest, most beautiful woman I've ever met in my life— hauling luggage for people at a ski resort? Why are you driving a shuttle and living on tips, when you ought to be going to Africa and making movies?"

A rushing sound filled my ears, like I stood next to a waterfall. My vision turned speckled and grey, like all that white noise in my head. Whatever Carver said now only came through in pieces, like a radio signal that kept flickering out. "Where's your father...

Mary Jane... Don't you have... isn't there... someone to help you... Why are you... taking care of... when your mother is... You're so... a degree like that, and not use it..."

And then I couldn't hear anymore. The white noise drowned him out. Each breath I pulled in felt faint and inadequate, and my face burned with shame. Scorching. Unbearable. And worse than that, I could hear my mother laughing at me, the week after I graduated. There was nothing harder to listen to than what she had said. *You went all the way to college to get a job washing dishes? At The Caroline? And you think I ought to worry about Richard? You think he can't go wash dishes somewhere if he drops out of school? You're an idiot, Mary Jane. A complete idiot.*

I shifted away from Carver, as close to the passenger side door as I could get. I leaned my brow on the window, hoping to cool my skin off.

I tried to take a deeper breath—a normal breath—and kept failing. Failing, failing, failing... just like my whole life.

My mind drifted and lingered, and came to rest in a place where my misery dwelt. My searing pain. My regret. I knew that this was what happened when I lost my grip on denial. And I knew I couldn't stay in this place where I was nothing but broken. I knew I had to pull myself out. I had done it before.

But it took me a long time, sitting there, to return to myself. To remember that I was not money, or a job, or a college degree. I was none of those things, however much my mind tried to trick me into believing it. However much society wanted me to believe it. To take things that weren't me and link my identity to them—that was how I ended up in the place that was broken.

Dignity did not come with money. Or a job. Or a college degree. Dignity came from within. Straight from God, and the universe, and the magic of life.

So when I managed to sit up straight again, and pick up my chin, and take a deep breath, what came out of my mouth wasn't going to be pleasant.

Because when I picked myself up from the well of my pain—

I returned with things from my visit.

Revelations. Insights. Secrets.

Dark things.

Carver had stopped speaking, having realized sometime ago that nothing he said was going to make me respond. And maybe he'd realized I'd stopped listening to him, and regretted admitting he had seen my diploma. Maybe he wished he'd never asked me why I was living on tips.

I regarded him now, this unlucky ballplayer who'd lost his wife and his brother and stopped hitting homeruns. This man who had a contract with the St. Louis Cardinals, but it was a contract I knew—with *absolute certainty*—was going to be dropped at the end of next season. Dropped and not picked up again. Carver wasn't just limping along. He was doomed.

Once upon a time, Carver Greyson had been magnificent. He'd broken records, like hitting three homeruns in a game four times in one season. At twenty-five, he'd stolen more bases, hit in more runs, had a higher batting average than anyone his age ever had before. He'd been destined for Hall of Fame greatness. He'd been someone breathtaking. Amazing. Inspired.

And his brother had been the person who had taken him there.

Ben Greyson was the ghost Carver lived with. His childhood companion, his best friend, his ally, his agent of hope and dreams… how could Carver have ever repaid Ben for all he had done? His savvy kid brother who'd loved politicking so much. And baseball.

Only Ben had loved something more than baseball and politics. The person sitting beside me had meant more to Ben than anything else.

I knew now why Carver couldn't get out of his slump.

And I knew why he'd be out of a contract by the end of next season.

"You were saving all your money for him," I said quietly. "Filling up a campaign chest… for a seat in the House… or the Senate… or whatever it was that he wanted…" I could feel the air in the cab grow tense, like the crackle of a charge before lightning strikes. My words were having a huge impact on Carver. And I knew I should stop.

But he hadn't stopped.

So neither did I.

"And now that he's gone, you're giving up. Like this was all in the plan. You can't find a way to be happy without him, so when your contract runs out, you'll tell yourself that it's over. And you think you'll be happy again. You even want to tell yourself he'd be proud. That he would look down on you now, and find this acceptable."

I glanced at Carver, and saw he was clenching his jaw and staring ahead, not looking at me. The sight of him like that made me strengthen my voice. To make sure he heard me. To make sure he would not block me out. "But what he loved in you, Carver—it had nothing to do with the money. He did that for you."

I fixed my gaze on the dashboard, and summoned the words I knew I had to speak, like a great weight on my shoulders I had to shrug off.

"So don't tell me… Don't tell me how easy you think this should be. When you lose the one person who ever believed in you. There's nothing here that is easy. Not even what you want to believe."

We had finally arrived at my building, and as Carver parked outside my apartment, I didn't waste time pushing open the door and jumping out of the vehicle. He called, "Mary Jane," at the same time I cried, "*Thanks for taking me dancing!*" like everything was just fine, and shut the door. Done. We were done. I started across the parking lot to the stairs, holding onto my blanket and walking with purpose.

I heard Carver's door open and close, and he called my name again, but I didn't look back.

Go on, Carver, I said in my head. *Go on and find someone else. I wasn't going to sleep with you anyway.* At the base of the stairs, I turned back a little, but not enough to look at him, and said, "I'll see you around. Maybe I'll be your driver again when you fly home next week." I kept the ice from my voice, though I felt icy. I needed to get ready for work, and put this whole misguided date far behind me. I should never have taken him to my Hole-in-the-Wall. I should never have let him into my house.

I hurried up the stairs, taking them two at a time—when Carver ran after me. I turned in surprise, I was so startled to hear him leaping the stairs to catch up—and then he grabbed me and yanked me right off my feet. I was too shocked to scream, though a strange, panicked noise slipped out of my throat, and I dropped the blanket because I thought I might fall.

But Carver clutched me against him, held me bound up so tightly I couldn't breathe for a second, and I knew I wasn't in danger of falling.

"I wasn't trying to hurt you," he said. "Please, Mary Jane. Please don't run away." His voice sounded raw with anguish, like a man who'd been crying, though Carver didn't have any tears on his face. He was plenty upset though. He lowered my feet to the platform, but kept his arms wrapped around me. I wanted to yell at him, but I wasn't sure what to feel. Angry? Forgiving? Hopeful? Relieved? Wasn't this display of brute male force just a misogynist ploy to manipulate me? Should I slap him and threaten to call the cops?

Oh my God, this was weird. Everything about Carver was weird. He'd canceled his trip to St. Louis, he'd taken a bellhop out on a date, he'd chased me up the stairs and then *grabbed* me—what was wrong with this man?

He hadn't put on his coat before he'd come after me, and I felt heat rise off his body like I was pressed to a woodstove. I could smell his cologne again, too, which was—oddly— extremely comforting, and I closed my eyes for a moment, trying to figure out what to do.

I was reminded of the children I watched at the daycare, especially all of the fights that erupted. When they tried to share toys, tried to play together, tried to have a conversation. Things were often so inscrutably hard for young children—which was what made watching them so comical. A few weeks ago, one five-year-old boy had asked his favorite toddler companion what her religion was, and when she'd responded, *Purple*, he'd been quick to tell her, *Purple is not a religion.* So she'd flung her Tonka truck aside and said, *It is! It is! It is!* When the five-year-old refused to believe her, she stormed away. And he was left with nothing to do but chase after her, and then he grabbed her and hugged her and refused to let go... until she returned to the sandbox to play.

Which seemed to be the same thing Carver was doing. He wanted to grab me and hug me until we were okay.

The idea that Carver might be so overwhelmed —maybe more overwhelmed than I was—made me laugh, a soft, private laugh against Carver's shirt. We'd gone dancing together, we'd tried to make conversation… and ended up at the same destination as those two children in the sandbox. Sometimes people asked questions that couldn't be answered. And sometimes people died, and dreams failed, and love disappeared. And sometimes purple had to be a religion.

Carver continued to hold me, and I didn't like to admit it— but it felt *nice* to be held. No, more than nice. The warmth of his body, the sweet smell of his cologne, the way his big massive arms kept me close—he was a gentle giant right now. And I couldn't remember feeling this good in a long time.

"Oh, Mary Jane," Carver sighed. "Please don't run away. Please, darling. Please don't."

I felt a sunburst through my heart, I was so awed by the prospect that I still wanted to spend time with him, and that Carver still wanted to spend time with me—and I suddenly wished I could just stand here forever—against his warm body, with his arms braced around me, sheltered in the soft sound of his voice.

"You're the most beautiful woman I've ever met in my life," Carver said. "The most beautiful, amazing, intelligent young woman I could've ever imagined would be on this earth. If you refuse to ever see me again, I will regret this moment for the rest of my life."

"All right," I said softly. "I won't run away from you." He took a deep breath of relief, and I asked, "You still want to play baseball today?"

He laughed. Laughed and hugged me until my feet left the ground again. "Of course I still want to play baseball."

I leaned back to look up at him, and sent him a smile. "Want me to call when I get off?"

"I'll just meet you here," he said. "Twelve o'clock."

I pulled away so I could get ready for work, and then I gazed up at his face and said, "Bye, Carver."

He planted a kiss on my cheek, and the press of his lips on my skin made me shiver. I touched the place where he'd kissed me, covering my cheek with my hand, like I'd suffered a burn and wanted to hide it.

Carver started down the stairs, and when he reached the concrete at the bottom, he turned back to smile at me with that grin like the devil. He called, "Bye, Mary Jane," so I dropped my hand, swept up my blanket, and finished running upstairs.

22

BASEBALL

I drove in to work with Steve that morning, and I drifted along, tired and tense, and thinking about my night with Carver the whole time. Especially that weird episode I'd had. Shutting down on him like that. I regretted that now.

I didn't like that I couldn't remain calm when people asked me personal questions. *Where is your father? Why aren't you using your degree? Why are you taking care of your siblings, when that is your mother's job?*

I often found a way to dismiss such queries—usually with a little white lie:

"My dad? Oh, he's in Phoenix, working construction. And Mom just needs a hand, that's all. We're working things out. She'll be back on her feet soon. No big deal."

I didn't like to admit why I chose lies over truth, but I knew why I lied.

Because the truth was uncomfortable. And when I shared the truth, people looked at me like I was making a shameless attempt to be pitiful. And I didn't like that look whatsoever. I wasn't asking for pity. But people always looked at me like I was demanding it. And I hated that.

So why hadn't I fed Carver one of my little white lies? Why had I reacted with silence—and then brought up his failing career and his dead brother like that?

I'd never used the word *pain*. I'd never said, *Carver, those questions are too painful to answer*. That would have been the logical thing to do.

Instead, I'd tapped into the sorest place in his heart, and made it clear that I wasn't the only one who possessed something valuable that was not being used.

Part of me was glad I had done that—part of me was *viciously happy* I had. But part of me worried I'd been petty. And cruel. Carver had been asking me a question. He honestly couldn't understand what I was doing in Riverdale, living with my mother, and working a low-wage job.

But I hadn't asked Carver *a question* about why he'd stopped hitting. I'd just slammed him with the truth.

Or what I believed was the truth.

Ask a hard question, and you found a hard answer. And now I wanted some answers about Carver.

So while Steve and I were at work, and I was running the shuttle and hauling luggage, I asked Steve to search the internet for me, and find out how the sports world explained Carver's slump.

A few hours later, when I saw Steve again, he said, "The guy's wife and brother were both killed in a car accident. Some semi-truck driver fell asleep at the wheel, and plowed into them after one of his games. Everything online says that's why the Grizz stopped hitting."

"Does anyone talk about his brother at all?" I asked.

"Sure," Steve said, "He was Carver's agent, helped him get his first contract, and he managed Carver's career—interviews, appearances, all that stuff. What else were you wanting to know?"

"Did Carver and Ben have plans together?" I asked. "Plans outside of baseball?"

"Not that I could tell," Steve said. "Ben wanted his brother in the Hall of Fame one day, and they were making donations to charities, visiting schools together, helping with fundraisers and such. But a lot of celebrities do that. Ben's only agenda was running Carver's PR campaign, and Carver's hitting streak made his job easier. After the accident, Carver didn't even play ball again for a month—and this was in July, in the middle of the season. There's stuff online that says he cost the Yankees their bid for the postseason that year. Kind of unfair, don't you think, to blame something like that on one guy? He's just one person, not the whole team."

I nodded, but felt too distracted to speak for a moment. So there was no mention of Ben's political ambitions, but I was sure that someone as smart as Ben Greyson would have been thinking about his own political career while he was helping his brother. Or had I been wrong? No, I still felt certain I was right about this. I just had the feeling… that I didn't have the whole picture yet. Maybe I never would. I'd taken something private and used it as a weapon against Carver, so why would he want to share anything further with me? I sure wouldn't.

I said, "Thanks, Steve. For reading all that."

"Something else, too," Steve said. We were standing together at the front desk, in one of those rare spaces of time in which the main entrance was empty. I stood with my hands on the desk, still thinking about Ben and Carver Greyson, while Steve typed on the computer keys, playing a game of solitaire as he spoke. "That house Carver bought here—it's always been in his sister's married name: Clarissa Thornton. Which means we're probably the only people who work here who know her brother's a ballplayer."

"Us, and The Summit's executives," I said.

"Well, yeah," Steve laughed. "Just saying. I mean, the NFL players here would never pull something like that." He meant the three football players who'd bought houses on the other side of the golf course. Those men liked to swagger around and be worshipped. Flying under the radar was not in their DNA.

"There's a baseball player here, too," I said. "That guy who plays for the Mets is pretty full of himself." All those men drove black Escalades with tinted windows, and they never stayed on the premises long. Other vacation homes to visit, other parties to crash. What a life.

Steve snorted. "Every time I see one of those Escalades, I just want to gag." Steve disliked football—and probably all team sports—with a passion. He'd been picked on by jocks pretty ruthlessly growing up. "Carver doesn't drive an Escalade, does he?"

"No," I said. "You're safe from rap and chrome hubcaps," and Steve grinned. He was excited about this trip to play baseball today, which surprised me. Steve seemed like the kind of person who had hated P.E. But then, playing baseball at the community center with my family was hardly P.E.

And Steve craved camaraderie. All his, "leave me alone, I just want to play chess by myself," talk was a bunch of baloney. He wanted friends. Not just a girlfriend, but a group to belong to. But he got so sullen sometimes, that even the other geeks at his high school had shunned him. Poor guy. One good thing about Steve smoking pot with my mother: it was definitely helping him loosen up and stop taking life too seriously.

A woman stepped out of the elevator and called for a bell cart, so I left the desk and went to fetch one.

Steve tried to clock out at noon, so we could leave and play baseball as planned, but the earliest anyone could come in to relieve him was twelve-thirty. I didn't have Carver's number to warn him, so when Steve and I left work, I was worried.

I hated being late. What if Carver had waited a half hour outside my apartment, and then bailed? What if I never saw him again? What if he'd changed his mind about playing baseball, and found some other woman to spend his time with?

I sighed, and Steve said, "I bet he's there. He seemed like a good guy. He probably knows why we're late."

"I hope so," I said. But I doubted that very much.

So when we pulled up to my building, and I saw Carver's Lincoln Navigator already parked in the lot—

My heart *soared* in relief.

Carver wasn't in his vehicle, so I bounded up the stairs, opened my door, and found everyone inside—the kids, Mom, Gandhi, and Carver—hanging out in the living room, talking and laughing. Carver stood beside Ethan, showing him something about holding a baseball, and when I stepped inside, they both turned to smile at me.

"Hey, Mary Jane," Ethan said. "Carver's showing me Beau Rieson's curveball—here, look at this." Ethan brought the baseball to me and held his fingers around it in a bizarre way. "That's how he grips it right there," Ethan said. "I bet I could learn how to throw one."

I nodded and said, "I bet you could, too."

Mia frowned at me and asked, "Why are you late?"

Steve rushed to say, "Sorry, that was my fault," and as he explained why we'd been held up, I glanced over at Carver again.

He wore blue jeans and a faded red t-shirt—a Cardinals shirt—and I was hit again by the fact that this was a *major league ballplayer* standing in my apartment. A huge man with a body full of muscle and power, who could sprint around bases fast as a hurricane—and there he was on the other side of the room, smiling at me with his bright silver eyes.

"How are you?" Carver asked.

"I'm yeah," I blundered, and then corrected myself. "I mean fine. I'm fine, Carver. How are you?"

"Hungry," he said, and I realized I smelled food, like someone had already fixed lunch—a really *nice* lunch. I turned to my dining table and found it covered in large plastic trays.

"Carver brought all this stuff!" Mia said, hopping over. She pried a lid off one tray, exposing several enchiladas. "We waited for you though—aren't you proud of us?" To the boys, Mia yelled, "Okay, time to eat!" and she went about pulling the rest of the lids off.

While the kids, Mom and Steve grabbed plates and started dishing up food, shouting stuff like, "*Thanks again for the grub, man! This is awesome!*" to Carver, I took a deep breath, crossed my arms, and cocked an eyebrow at him. I would never have asked him to bring us all lunch. But he only sent me another smile and shrugged his shoulders a little.

Mia asked, "Aren't you gonna eat something, Mary Jane? We're not sitting around here forever!"

Which made me remember I was still dressed like Sasquatch. I hurried to unzip my vest, blushing at the idea of Carver seeing me in this getup again. I needed to change. I also needed to ask the kids where their manners were, since they were digging into the food without any regard for the man who had brought it. But then Ethan took Carver a plate and asked, "You want Pepsi or tea? I'll pour you a glass." I didn't have Pepsi or tea in my house, which meant Carver must have also brought drinks. I cast him another look.

He just smiled at me, and when Mia said, "Carver, come sit by me!" he said, "Sure," and made his way to the table.

I still wasn't sure about all of this—Carver coming into my apartment without me and bringing in all this food—but the only thing I said was, "I'll be right back," and walked down the hall. Once I was in my bedroom, I shut the door and leaned against the panel. My stomach felt fluttery, and my knees jittered.

Why had Carver brought all this food? Did he think I needed his charity, or had he wanted to make some kind of peace offering? And should I be worried that Mom and the kids had let a strange man into the house? Or had their time talking to him last night made this visit okay? He'd come to take them out to play baseball, after all, just like he'd promised. Was it really so shocking that the kids had let him in? I'd gone dancing with Carver, I'd taken him to my vapor cave, I'd told him about Hanna. My time with this man last night had been anything but a casual date.

I remembered telling Carver he was *pretty* last night, and felt my face burn. Why couldn't I have come up with something clever to say? Why couldn't I have been like the women in the movies for once, the ones with sharp eyes and perfect lipstick, who let men light their cigarettes and then murmured things like, *Thanks for the drink, tiger.* Those women never leaned over the bar and said, *Great job tanking your baseball career.* A sophisticated bar maven would *never* do something like that.

I sighed and ran my hands through my hair, and then took a seat on the bed. I hadn't been that mean to Carver, had I? I hoped not. I hadn't been motivated by cruelty. I just wanted him to know that I was already aware I wasn't using my college degree.

Just like Carver was already aware that he was no longer hitting homeruns.

But how could he have known not to ask me those questions? Grit and denial were my homeboys, but they didn't strut around, out where anyone could see them.

Well, I had a second chance now, didn't I? Carver was here. That crazy man had come back for more. So I needed to get a move on.

I stripped off my uniform, put on a pair of khakis and a clean shirt, and rejoined the mob around the dining room table. They'd moved the trays to the kitchen, so there was enough room at the table for everyone, and the kids were just starting to eat. Carver rose and gestured for me to take the empty chair next to him.

"Did we settle on Richard's plan?" I asked, and Richard said, "It's all settled!"

Carver winked at me before I sat down, and while he kept up a rousing conversation with the kids over lunch, I kept glancing at him, unable to stop.

I studied the width of his forearms, and the layers of tan in his skin, and the line of his throat when he laughed. I studied the scars on his knuckles, and the size of his wrists, and how he always leaned forward before he answered a question. He smelled like soap and clean laundry, and I wished I could lean in close and inhale the scent of his skin. I wanted to reach out and place my hand on his knee, just to know he was real, just to feel him—even though he was sitting right next to me, and I knew he had to be real. Every time that he spoke, his voice slipped along my skin like a gentle caress. But whenever he smiled at me, I looked away. I felt more nervous than I had before we'd started dancing last night. I didn't like it.

When everyone finished eating, I asked Ethan and Mia to clean up, and Gus wiped down the table. Poor Gandhi had to stay behind when we left, because we couldn't take a dog inside the community center.

The kids insisted that we all ride together, so instead of taking Steve's car, I sat in the back seat of the Navigator this time, and let Mom ride shotgun. Mia shared a seat with me, and sat on my lap, but everyone else had their own seat.

The community center was on the south side of town, a great big facility with a huge climbing wall and an Olympic-sized pool. It turned out Carver had already been there today and paid for our passes. When we walked inside, the man at the front desk just waved us on through. Carver carried a bag with the bats, and he let the kids carry in the rest of the gear, which they were thrilled about. They kept calling it "real live baseball equipment" which was kind of embarrassing and kind of funny together.

Carver was like the coach that afternoon, and once we were inside the big room with the track, he had everyone pair up for batting practice. All the pitching was underhand for Steve and Mom, though Mia and the boys started throwing each other fastballs. Ethan, Gus, and Richard made a loose group of three, and Steve, Mom, and Mia made the other. Mia and Ethan traded places a few times. Everyone took turns batting, pitching, and catching. Carver and I fielded balls. It felt so good to have a glove on my hand, to run around and chase after baseballs, that I found myself smiling and laughing all afternoon. And whenever Carver stood next to the kids, leaning over to show them something about gripping a bat, or setting up for a swing, my heart pounded so hard I felt breathless.

Some women found men in dark suits, swirling glasses of whiskey, to be the ideal of sexy. Or men with flashy convertibles, or sleek motorcycles. Or men with tattoos and come-hither stares, or long hair and jewelry and suede jackets… or surf boards, waxed chests, hemp bracelets. Black Escalades. Chrome hubcaps. Rap on the stereo.

But I looked at Carver in his faded red shirt, helping the kids figure out how to hit—the the way he knelt when he spoke to them, so gentle and patient—and the memory of dancing with him, how his body felt against mine, and the tenderness in his voice—the effect of all this was more devastating to me than any sweet-nothings he could've whispered in my ear. And the more I tried to distract myself, by chasing after baseballs, or showing the kids how to throw when they weren't talking to Carver—the more I found myself wanting him. I tried to tell myself that I had to be stronger than this. That the last thing I needed in my life was to sleep with a man who I'd known for two days. A man who was leaving next weekend. A man who did not even live here.

But the desire I felt was a hot, melting thing: a plaintive, pleading, inescapable heat. Longing rolled through my body and pushed on my bones.

I could have said no to a dark suit or a whiskey glass. I could have said no to long hair and jewelry, or tattoos, or a flashy convertible.

But this man who smiled at the kids? And said things like, "There you go, Mia! There's your power swing! Keep doing that!" and laughed with a sound that tickled my skin—

This man was turning into someone I couldn't say no to.

Part of me hated that.

But another part of me loved it.

23

THAT OTHER HIM

The kids, Mom and Steve had so much fun with batting practice that two hours went by before Richard pointed out that we should play a game. By this, he meant he wanted to throw the ball to Carver, so he could see Carver hit. So Ethan rummaged through a duffel bag and found the rubber bases, and we assembled the diamond and started a game. I was the permanent catcher, while Carver made one team, and everyone else made the other. Carver could hit all the crazy pitches that came anywhere close to his bat, and he hit them as grounders or pop-ups to the kids. Then he ran the bases so slowly, that even when one of them missed the ball or dropped it, they could still throw him out at second base, or maybe third. He always kept going until somebody caught him. It was an extremely comical sight.

Whenever Carver returned to home plate, he'd ask, "Want to bat?" and I'd laugh and shake my head no. I just liked being close to him, watching him swing at the kids' pitches. Richard yelled once, "I bet you could break out a window!" and pointed to the highest windows in the building.

Carver only laughed and told Richard, "You'd better throw harder, if you want destruction." So Richard threw harder fastballs, hard enough that he finally wore his arm out, and I knew that no matter what, Carver wasn't going to break any windows. His level of mastery with a bat was just too profound, and his goal was to hit balls to the kids to catch, not to knock holes in the wall.

When the kids, Mom and Steve left the outfield, and came up to bat, Carver pitched and I remained catcher. Carver could play the whole field on his own, and it shocked me sometimes, seeing how fast he could move. Not just his speed, but his grace. Carver had beautiful form when he stood on a diamond... even now, when he was fooling around. His body had ease and precision, and his mind had a laser-sharp focus on where his pitch would end up as soon as the ball neared the plate. Before the bat even made contact, Carver's feet would be moving, taking him to the place he'd already determined the ball would end up.

And that was Carver's true talent. It was the way his mind worked: calculating the speed and spin and trajectory of a baseball. Then deciding how the ball would be affected by a particular swing. All of which happened in fractions of seconds.

Those split-second judgments gave him foresight, which gave him speed, which gave him power. And grace.

His fielding skills weren't products of muscle mass. They were a gift of his mind, and his passion for anything involving a baseball in motion.

I imagined him again in his uniform—not this relaxed, laughing Carver—but the one who wore pinstripes under stadium lights, and stole bases, and made double plays, and wiped sweat from his brow. The one who stared down his pitchers, and knocked in runs every inning, and finished games with grand slams. The one who played to win.

That Carver was as equally real to me now as the one in jeans and a t-shirt, pretending to drop Ethan's pop-up, pretending to let Mia outrun him, pretending he couldn't stop Richard from making it home. And I suddenly wished I could see him—that other him—playing one of those games. With his jersey and cap and his desire to win.

We played until seven that evening, which was when the community center closed. Even Mom was sad when it was time to pack up. We loaded into the Navigator again, and were on our way home, when Carver took a wrong turn.

I said, "Carver, you—" but he smiled and caught my gaze in the mirror.

"I thought we could go have some pizza."

The kids cheered and bounced in their seats (Mia bounced on my lap), but I only felt terror at the thought of dining out. I didn't have enough money for this, and even though Carver had given me that extra cash yesterday, I needed to spend that on my Buick. Not pizzas.

When we parked at the restaurant and the kids raced inside, followed by Mom and Steve, I stood by the driver's side door for a moment, alone with Carver. I frowned.

"Carver… I can't—I mean—pizzas, and everything… You already paid for lunch, and bought everyone passes—it's too much. I can't afford dinner here, and I can't expect you to just pick up the tab. You have your own kids to take care of."

Carver shrugged. "Paying for a couple of meals and some passes is not going to land me in the poorhouse, Mary Jane. If that's what you're getting at."

I scowled. "It adds up," I said. "You gave me all that money yesterday, you took me to Goldking last night, and now you're driving us all around and—"

"And I'm having a good time," Carver said. He put his hands on my arms and stepped closer to me. I remembered the way he'd held me that morning, and my heart pattered hard in my chest in hopes he might do that again. "Yesterday, I asked you out for a drink," he said softly, "and now I'm asking you to come have some pizza."

"But my whole family's here," I said. "It's not a date if you feed an army."

He chuckled and slid his hands down my arms, cupped my hands in his, then lifted my hands to his mouth and kissed my fingertips. "When I'm around you, Mary Jane, I feel like… I feel like I'm awake. Like I can just be… me, for a change. I'm more alive right now than I have felt in… forever, it seems."

I smiled. "You just say that cause you like playing baseball."

Carver laughed. "Mary Jane, I haven't liked playing baseball in years. Why else do you think I'd let my contract run out?"

I stopped smiling. "That's like chocolate chip cookie dough saying he doesn't like chocolate chips."

Carver nodded. "You see my dilemma."

Mia opened the door of the restaurant and yelled, "Are you guys coming, or what?" before starting toward us. "Mary Jane, Richard said he's gonna order a soda, and I told him he couldn't—but he said he's still going to order one! So you better get in there and tell him he has to get with the program—"

Before I could tell her I'd deal with it, Carver told Mia, "It's all right. You guys order whatever you want. We're celebrating your last day of Christmas vacation."

Mia's eyes widened, and then she did a little victory dance for a touchdown before shouting, "Okay!" and running inside.

Carver faced me again, and the way that he smiled at me made me shiver. "It's still a date, Mary Jane. Small army or not. Come on," and he tugged my hand so I'd walk toward the building. "I'm starving."

***

Supper played out the same way lunch had—though I didn't sit next to Carver this time. The kids were just too keyed up and boisterous, so when they squeezed into the booth around him, I didn't protest. And maybe… maybe I was also a bit scared of him. About the effect he was having on me. After watching his body all day, my mind had fallen into the gutter. I kept thinking about Carver's hands, and how they'd feel on my skin, once he'd pulled off my clothes… and this was damn inappropriate for hanging out in a pizza place with my family. I kept trying to clean up my act, but then I would wonder if Carver had thoughts like that when he looked at *me*. He might. Then again, we'd only known each other two days, and I mostly dressed like a Yeti. So that was doubtful.

But maybe Carver was secretly into Yetis… and that's why he'd asked me out. Or maybe my brief time in a sundress had bowled him over. I hoped he had noticed my breasts in that dress—or maybe in this shirt I had on? And then I felt angry for even having this thought.

I should've never gone on that date. I wouldn't be having this problem, if I hadn't agreed to go dancing.

As we were leaving the restaurant, Carver placed his hand on my cheek and sent me a smile, and part of me wanted him to keep touching me, while the other part said, *this man is just going to hurt you.* So I returned his smile, but I didn't touch him back.

"Thanks for supper, Carver."

He ran his hand through my hair in a loose, playful gesture. "You're welcome, Mary Jane. I wish you'd sat next to me though."

I crossed my arms and nodded, and then skittered away from him as fast as I could.

When we were on our way home, the kids asked Carver if he'd come upstairs and play video games before bed, but I told the kids it was too late to play video games, and Carver said he had some errands to do.

"We could play ball again though," he said, with a swift glance at me. "If that's okay. Maybe later this week?"

I said, "That sounds great," and the kids whooped and hollered. The noise made me laugh, since it was nice to hear the kids so… happy. Downright bubbly. All afternoon, all through dinner, and even now… It made something hard and painful inside me feel a little bit softer.

When Carver parked at my building, he left his vehicle running, but hopped out to give the kids high-fives and man-hugs before they went upstairs. Once everyone else had departed, I said, "Thanks again for supper. And lunch. And playing baseball today."

"My pleasure, Mary Jane."

I made sure I wasn't close enough that he could reach out and touch me, since all I could think about was how much I *wanted* him to touch me. I also kept glancing at his lips, and wishing he would kiss me. A real kiss. Holy cow, did I want to kiss him.

I also knew I didn't just want a kiss. I wanted to tear off his clothes and throw him down on a bed, and tell myself that nothing else mattered, not even waking up to cold sheets.

So I kept my distance.

"I'll be home around six-thirty tomorrow," I said. "Do you want to come over for supper?"

"Maybe," he said. I could tell by the light in his eyes that he was trying to tease me.

"Maybe, what? You'll fly home early?"

Carver laughed. "No. It's not that."

I took another step back.

"I just want to be friends, Carver. We're just friends."

The way he smiled made me strongly suspect that he wasn't fooled. "Are you still upset with me, Mary Jane?"

"No," I said.

"You're still running away."

I turned my gaze to the building, too embarrassed to speak for a moment. "Am not."

Carver found this amusing. "You've got more of a lead-off right now than I take on first."

I stomped my foot. "Carver, I'm not running away."

He laughed. "Maybe we should go have a nightcap."

"No," I snapped. A brief silence followed, so in a softer voice, I added, "The kids have school in the morning."

"I know, Mary Jane. I'm just teasing you." He put his hand on the door of the Lincoln, preparing to climb back inside. "All right, friend. I'll come over for supper tomorrow."

I stood for a moment, wishing I could be someone else. Someone who could jump in the passenger seat and go have a drink. Someone who could tell a man, *Why don't you come on upstairs, and we'll see where the night takes us. I don't want to be Cinderella. I just want to have a good time.*

Only I wasn't that someone. I had four kids who'd play video games all night if I didn't tell them to go brush their teeth and lie down.

And I didn't just want a good time. I wanted a man who loved me.

So I turned and hurried upstairs, so I wouldn't have to watch Carver drive away.

24

EXPECTATIONS

The next morning, I struggled to stop daydreaming about Carver and get down to business again. Mondays required all of my focus, especially a Monday after vacation. And I needed to pick up my car before I went to work, which required even more juggling than usual.

I woke the kids for school, made sure they ate breakfast before they went out to the bus, and then I had Steve give me a ride into town. At the repair shop, I looked over my Buick, which now had a new radiator as well as a few other parts. The total came to $456.85.

I flipped through the bills Carver had given me, and then I stood at the counter another moment. My hands shook.

What was I *doing?*

Was I really going to spend this money?

I glanced at those hundreds again, and struggled to pull in a breath. Why had I ever taken this cash to begin with? I felt lightheaded, and placed my arm on the counter to steady myself.

Was I really going to stand here and lie to myself?

How much had Carver spent on my family yesterday? All that food, and those passes… quite a lot. Maybe not six hundred dollars… but a few bills, to be sure.

And now I was going to take this money he'd given me?

Was I out of my mind?

"Payin' cash, ma'am?" the man behind the counter asked.

I shook my head no, and stuffed the money into my coat pocket again. "Credit," I said, and handed over my MasterCard. My hands were still shaking as I signed the receipt, but this time, I knew what I felt was relief.

I didn't take money from men and then go to the bar. How had I come so close to forgetting that?

I tucked the receipt in my wallet, drove to a gas station to fill up the tank, and then headed to work at Happy Garden.

Stella was back from her trip to Nigeria, but she seemed depressed and didn't want to talk about it. She drank coffee non-stop. After the children all arrived and we served morning snack, I noticed that Grace hadn't shown up.

"Where's Grace?" I asked Linda, since Linda and Grace ran the toddler room.

"Grace no longer works here," Linda said. "Stella's friend Reagan is going to fill in this week until she can find someone."

"Oh," I said, and then I felt a stab in my heart when I remembered the episode with Stella and Grace right before Christmas. I had a bad feeling about this. "Do you have her number?" I asked Linda. "She, um… borrowed some CDs of mine." That was a lie, but I hoped Linda couldn't tell.

"You'll have to ask Stella," she said. "She'll have it." So I waited until that afternoon, and when the children were all playing happily, and there weren't any parents arriving for pick-up, I asked Stella if I could have Grace's number.

"I just need to get my CDs back," I added.

Stella said, "Oh, sure. When I get a minute, I'll take care of it." But the rest of the day went by, and almost all of the children were picked up by five-thirty, and Stella still hadn't brought me that number. When I asked her about it again, she sighed and said, "It's just been a long day. Remind me tomorrow." Then she smiled at me and blinked her eyes a few times, before she walked into her house. Stella could leave the daycare whenever she wanted to rest, and she usually stopped work around four-thirty most days. But we'd been shorthanded today, on account Grace was gone, so Stella had been forced to step in. She left me alone at a quarter-till six, when I finished mopping the floor and signed the last two children out.

After work, I drove to the grocery store and bought everything I needed for tacos. Not with Carver's money, of course. With my own.

By the time I got home, it was past six-thirty, and Carver was already there, sitting at the dining table with the kids. They were bent over papers and worksheets, with pencils and calculators scattered around them. The kids were *doing their homework*. I was so stunned by this that I nearly fell over and dropped all the groceries.

"Hi, everyone," I said, recovering from shock. Mom came over and peeked into one of my sacks, while Carver rose, took the bags from my arms, and carried them into the kitchen for me.

"Did you buy any pie?" Mom asked.

"I bought ice cream," I said.

Mom clapped her hands and shouted, "Hot *dog!*"

I left my coat on, gestured for Carver to step outside with me, so he slipped on his jacket and obliged.

I closed the door behind us, and he asked, "How was work?"

"Fine," and I studied his face, wondering why he'd made the kids start their homework. "Carver, you don't need to—I didn't ask you over for supper to make you—"

"Work on algebra problems?" he mused. "Proofread essays?"

I covered my eyes for a moment, unsure how to handle this. "Carver—I don't know what to say. When you asked me out for a drink, I thought—I thought you'd be off at the bar by now." I dropped my hands and looked up at him again. "You know, flirting with… Enjoying the Riverdale night life. Not hanging out in my apartment with my family. You know?"

He leaned against the wall and sent me a smile. "I want whatever night life you want." He tilted his head toward my door. "But my vote's on the algebra problems in there, and whatever you were fixing for dinner."

I reached for his hand, and he straightened, looking curious. But when I pushed those six hundred dollar bills into his palm, his expression turned to one of concern.

"That's yours," I said.

"Mary Jane, what are you—"

"I told you, Carver. I don't take money from men and then go to the bar. I don't need your charity. I don't need anyone's charity."

"It wasn't charity," he said. "It was a gift. I just wanted to do something nice for you."

"And if we'd met at the bar, and I'd worn a nice dress and gold earrings—would you have still left me six hundred dollars to fix my car? God, Carver." My face felt hot, and my throat felt tight. "I almost took that from you. *I almost took that from you.*"

Carver stuffed the money away, and grabbed my hands. "I'm sorry, Mary Jane. I'm sorry. I wasn't judging you." His voice sounded heated with worry. "I've never once looked at you and thought about charity."

I almost laughed. "Then why did you bring over all of that food yesterday? And buy all those passes? And then—"

"Because I wanted to," Carver said. "And we could have met in a bar, and I still would have brought over lunch. And paid for those passes. And paid for dinner." I tried to pull my hands free, but Carver held on. "I didn't think twice about leaving that money for you—because I *have* done that before. I've left tips like that plenty of times. But no one—no one—ever put the money back in my hand."

"Because they slept with you," I said.

"Mary Jane." He sounded angry. "That's not fair. I've tipped men more than that—for multiple reasons. Do you really think I'd want to give a woman money so she'd climb into bed with me? Do you think that's the kind of person I am?"

"I don't know what to think of you," I said. "I just know you're a ballplayer. And ballplayers go to strip clubs. And have sex with women whenever they feel like it. Even their teammates' girlfriends and wives. Women throw themselves at athletes, Carver. I'm not stupid."

"I have never had sex with a teammate's girlfriend or wife," Carver said. "And I'd never give a woman money and expect her to sleep with me. And as to all the women who want to have sex with an athlete—I'm not the kind of man who plays with fire like that. I married Audrey when we were eighteen, and I never cheated on her. I never would have cheated on her. And in the years since she died, I just… I just… I can't bring myself to…" Carver paused for a moment, and stared at the ground before he could continue. "I've had two girlfriends since then. And neither one of those relationships lasted more than a month. I'm not out there chasing women, Mary Jane. I tried to… I tried to tell you that. I told you about my sister, and how she… I never took… any of it… casually to begin with, and ever since Audrey… and I have my three boys… I just haven't wanted to be with anyone. Not like that."

Now it was my turn to be stunned. I blinked up at Carver, too astonished by this information to speak, and he wrapped his arms around me. I leaned my cheek on his chest, struggling to find something to say.

"I was supposed to be with Matt Daughtry this week," Carver said. "To work on my hitting. Do you know how many weeks I've spent in my off seasons, since Audrey and Ben died, trying to work on my hitting? Trying to get out of my slump? Can you understand how trapped I am, Mary Jane? Only when I'm with you, I forget I want to escape. Because I'm not Grizz Greyson, the great disappointment, the famous failure of baseball. I'm just me, Mary Jane. Just a man. Why would I ever want to risk that? Why would I ever want to hurt the one person who makes me remember I don't live in a cage?"

Somehow, I found my voice, though my words sounded meek with surprise. "Matt plays for the Cardinals?"

"He does," Carver said. "Third base."

"Where does he bat in the lineup?"

"Last year, fifth," Carver said. "His two children and mine play together a lot."

In a steadier voice, I said, "Thank you for telling me all of that." I wasn't talking about Matt Daughtry, but I knew Carver would understand.

He squeezed my shoulder, and I felt him take a deep breath to say something else, but Mia yanked open the front door and said, "Mary Jane, do you want me to start dinner or what?"

I hurried to step away from Carver, and told Mia, "I want you to finish your homework." Mia left the doorway, and I glanced at Carver, trying to determine if he wanted to say anything else, but he only smiled and pushed the door open a bit wider, waiting for me to enter first.

I stepped inside, hung my coat on the rack and walked into the kitchen, and Carver returned to the dining table. While I worked on supper, the kids finished their homework and put up their book bags, and then they sat at the table again and begged Carver for stories. He shared tales of different games he had played and things about his friends on the team, and they asked him about what it was like to play baseball for a living.

"Spring training starts in February," he said, "and that's a great time. Unless you're really out of shape, and then it's not so fun. But I love spring training."

"The Cardinals train in Florida, right?" Richard asked.

"That's right," Carver said. "We have practice all day for a while, and then we start playing games."

"You have to travel a lot?" Ethan asked.

"Almost nonstop," Carver said. "I feel lucky when I'm home and I can spend time with my boys. I try to take them with me in the summers, when they're not missing school."

"I bet they love having a dad who plays baseball," Richard said.

"I hope so," Carver said. "Because I'm not going to quit."

I felt a pang in my heart when he said that, realizing the extent that Carver had learned to lie to himself: because he didn't sound at all like a man who had lost all his passion. He sounded like a man who loved what he did.

I recalled that he'd taken a month off after his wife and brother died. Now I knew Carver hadn't just taken a break. He'd wanted to quit. He'd wanted to walk away from his career right then, but something had made him return.

No wonder he had said he felt trapped.

"Are your kids in St. Louis?" Ethan asked.

"They're in San Diego right now, with my sister," Carver said. "She has four children, and the oldest two are big enough to ride the kiddie coasters at Disneyland. So tomorrow, they're all driving to Anaheim, and they'll probably ride the teacups and spin themselves sick."

"Don't they miss you?" Mia asked.

"Sure," Carver said, and by the sound of his voice, it was obvious that he missed them, too. "But I was going to be in St. Louis this week, anyway, and they have their cousins and Grandma and Grandpa all with them. I'll see them on Sunday."

"Do you get used to being away a lot?" Richard asked.

"Depends," Carver said. "Sometimes it's nice to be out, playing games. Sometimes it just about breaks my heart."

"Did you always want to be a ballplayer?" Mia asked.

"Always," Carver said. "It was the only thing I was ever good at, so of course it was the only thing I ever wanted to do."

Mia asked him if he had a brother, and Carver said, "I had a wonderful brother. He was my manager, my agent, and my very best friend. I'd probably be working on an oil rig right now, if it wasn't for him."

"Where is he?" Mia asked.

"He died in a car accident," Carver said.

"Man, that is terrible," Richard said. "That is really... really... God..."

Carver leaned his elbow on the table and smiled at Richard. "Yeah," he said. "That about sums it up."

I finished my preparations for supper, stepped out of the kitchen and said, "Dinner's ready. Go wash," and the kids trooped off to the bathroom. I sent Carver a smile, and he smiled back. He wore a blue collared shirt this evening, and a dark pair of slacks. His grey leopard eyes seemed brighter than ever. "Are you hungry?" I asked, and he laughed.

"I'm always hungry," he said.

I shivered and laughed, unsure whether he'd meant for that comment to have a double meaning or not. Then I looked over at Mom on the couch and asked, "Mom, you want to make the first plate?" So Mom came into the kitchen and started dishing up tacos.

I'd shredded cheese, diced tomatoes, chopped lettuce, made guacamole, cooked five pounds of burger and seasoned it, found a tub of fresh deli salsa in Green Grocer—in short, I had everything ready for a big taco feast. I even had Spanish rice and a pot of beans, although the kids were so sick of rice and beans that I knew they would pass.

We feasted, and when we were finished, I had Richard help me dish up bowls of ice cream. I'd even bought chocolate sauce, which Mom offered everyone. She said, "Now *this* is a party! Now we're having some *fun*."

I was so relieved that Carver never gave me puzzling looks over Mom. Because I wasn't anywhere near ready to try to explain her. I felt tremendously thankful each time Carver took it in stride when she repeated herself, or when she made strange announcements that came out of nowhere. For instance, if Mom suddenly shouted, "I told those Vultures to go to hell!" while everyone else was talking about Gus trying to get his driver's permit, Carver would say, "Good for you, Miss Preston," and Mom would smile.

After dinner, Steve volunteered to wash dishes, Gus wanted to show Carver his baseball cards, and Mia wanted everyone to watch *Gladiator*. So we hung out in the living room, and Carver and I sat on the couch—with Mia between us—because she'd seen him with his arms around me outside and she was feeling jealous. So she wriggled against me and hugged me in a way that meant, *You're mine, you know that, right?* while she looked over Carver's shoulder, watching as he went through Gus's cards. Gus sat beside Carver, pointing out his favorites while they discussed different players.

At one point during the movie, Mia cupped a hand to my ear and whispered, "Carver's like Maximus!" and I tipped my head back and laughed. She meant his body, I guessed. His great big biceps and shoulders and everything else. As soon as I laughed, Mia glanced over at Carver in dismay, and I knew she was worried he'd figure out what she'd said. Mia was weird about her infatuation with *Gladiator*. So I pressed a finger to my lips to assure her I wouldn't repeat it.

Carver's phone rang, and he went outside for a time while he talked, and when he returned inside, he said he had to leave.

"It's bedtime, anyway," I told the kids, and I stood and flipped off the TV. "Go on, do your thing," and the kids slumped out of the room. It was only nine o'clock, but the first day of school after vacation always wore them out.

"Everything okay?" I asked Carver as he pulled on his coat.

"Branch got some stitches tonight," he said. "Playing Superman on the stairs at the house."

"Are you going to San Diego then?"

Carver grinned and shook his head no. "I'm just going to call him in a few minutes, once they get home. He's worried about missing Disneyland tomorrow, that's all. He'll be fine."

I nodded, and then I went to stand by the door so I could tell him goodnight.

"I'm glad you came over for supper."

Carver smiled again. "Me, too."

I clasped my hands together, ready to make an announcement. "I'm going to work four tens this week, so I'll have Friday off."

"That sounds nice," Carver said. He kept his voice light, like he was teasing me.

"I would say let's go skiing, but I know—"

Carver said, "I'll go skiing, if you want me to."

"I thought you…" I began, remembering he'd told me he didn't like skiing.

"I can manage the easy runs fine," Carver said. "I'm just not gung-ho for the sport. So as long as you don't leave me behind for a double-black diamond—"

I laughed. "I don't even ski those runs, Carver. We'll do blues and greens all day, I promise."

"Then it's a date," he said, and I knew he might've kissed me right then, but the kids were watching us. Not directly. There was just an awful lot of mingling going on in the hallway.

"Goodnight," I said softly, and he gave me a wink before he slipped out the door.

***

I turned in early that night, but around four in the morning, I couldn't sleep anymore. I left the bedroom, wandered into the living room, and took a seat on the couch where Carver had been.

I thought about his conversation with the kids before dinner, how he'd told them he wasn't going to quit baseball. I hoped that was true. I knew from his rookie card that his birthday was in December, which meant he wouldn't turn thirty until the end of this year. So if the Cardinals were planning to drop him at the end of this season, Carver was in that perfect storm of risk, since baseball statistics showed athletic performance declined after age thirty.

There were exceptions, of course. Some men were better ballplayers at 35 or 36 than all the players on their team in their twenties. So youth didn't always dictate performance.

But it sure was a factor—a huge one—in deciding who would be cut from a roster. At 29, Carver was up against—not just all of those younger guys—but who he had been at their age. All the potential he'd lost. That's what he really faced, at the end of this season. Money was one bottom line. But failing to live up to expectations was another.

I leaned my head back and gazed up at the ceiling, and thought of our night in the vapor cave, and how Carver had rested his cheek on my leg… and how he had told me tonight that, around me, he was only a man.

But that wasn't true.

I might not see him under the mantle of what he had been— as the Grizz—but Carver was definitely a baseball player to me.

And maybe that was what Carver really needed. To remember that his heart had always been in the game, long before he had a title, or fame, or expectations to meet.

The Carver who'd played baseball in the streets after school, with his sister on third so she could heckle the batters… that was the Carver who'd gotten lost in the contracts, the publicity, and the deaths of the people he loved.

Not everyone found what they most wanted to be when they were a child.

But Carver had.

I was sure that hadn't made it any easier on him, when he had wanted to quit.

And then I realized—I *did* know why Carver was still playing baseball.

Not everyone Carver loved dearly had died in that accident. The tough little girl who'd played street games with her brothers... she had grown up into someone Carver trusted and needed. She even had his three boys with her now. *My sister says desperate is my middle name.*

She was the reason Carver had gone back to baseball. And she was probably the reason he had tried to start those relationships. But the thing Carver needed to find wasn't there, so he gave up.

Dignity came from within... and so did joy. And passion. And the desire to win.

And maybe Carver was closer now... closer than he had been in a long time... to remembering that.

25

DARK, SECRET PLACES

At five-thirty that morning, I showered and dressed and woke the kids up for school.

While they ate breakfast, I wrote some checks to pay bills, and Mia asked, "Is Carver leaving on Friday?"

"Sunday," I said.

The kids eyed each other with significant glances.

I set down my pen, waiting for someone to speak up.

Richard cleared his throat. "Well, if you guys are going skiing on Friday... Then we uh, we were thinking..."

"You want to play baseball again," I supplied.

Four heads nodded up and down.

"I'll bet Carver's up for that," I said, and the kids practically jumped for joy at the news—which was bizarre behavior for them at this hour. So I added, "But if you give me a hard time this week, forget it. We'll stay home." I even put my hands on my hips so they knew I meant business. They finished eating breakfast without another peep.

After they'd all left for school, Steve came into the kitchen for some cereal.

"I heard you get up early," Steve said.

"I had some thinking to do."

"About Carver?" he asked.

I smiled. "About a lot of things."

***

As I was leaving for work that morning, I bumped into the Iranian man who lived two doors down. He was whistling and carrying a basket of clothes downstairs to the laundry room.

"Good morning, Miss Logan!" he called. "How are you feeling today?"

"I feel great," I said, and that was no lie. "How are you?"

"Very good," he said. "How are your children?"

I smiled at this. "The kids are all good," I said. "You remember they're not actually my children though, right?"

"Of course," the man said, and he waved me goodbye. "Many pleasant returns on your day, Miss Logan."

I waved and said, "Same to you."

I took my time driving to Happy Garden that morning. As I passed through the valley, I gazed around at the mountains, and spotted a cluster of deer on the road. I slowed down and then stopped. They were crossing the road about twenty feet in front of me, and as I was waiting, a few more in the ditch leapt onto the asphalt to follow the others.

A man in a Toyota Tundra arrived, barreling down the road in the opposite direction, and I flashed my lights at him twice. He didn't slow down. He wasn't paying attention, and if he did notice the deer on the road, he didn't give a damn. Two seconds later, he'd come up on the deer, and I screamed. A doe jumped out of the ditch and darted right in front of him, and he hit her so hard that her body flew up and landed on the hood of my car. She smashed into the metal with a sound like a bomb going off.

The Tundra slowed down beside me, its whole front end crushed in, but since the engine hadn't stopped, the man gunned it again. I jumped out of my car as he took off, so fast I couldn't even read his license plate number. I cried out again, and then I turned to the deer on the hood of my car.

I'd never hit a deer before, or anything else. The doe twitched as she died, and her hooves scratched at my hood. I watched the light fade from her eyes as her body went still and blood oozed from her mouth. I noticed a fawn stood nearby, cowering in the ditch, and I knew he must belong to this doe. I continued to stand there in shock, staring at the deer on my car, until another man arrived in a pickup. He stepped out of his vehicle and came to stand beside me.

"You all right, miss?" he asked. "You need some help?" He walked toward the front of my car before I could answer. "Here, let's get her down," he said, and he gripped the deer's legs in his hands. He was a big man, older than my father would have been, and built like a bull. He reached under the deer's belly and lifted her up like a sack of sand. Then he carried her away from the road and into the field, laid her down in the snow and returned to my side.

"Is your car all right?" he asked. "How hard did you hit?"

"I didn't hit her," I said. "A man in a Tundra did," and I pointed down the road where he'd disappeared. Then I inspected the damage on my car. The Buick had never been pretty, but now the hood was crumpled and there were tufts of hair clinging to the metal.

I turned to the man and said, "Thank you for helping me."

"You sure you're all right?" he asked. "You want me to call someone?"

I shook my head no, and said, "I'm Mary Jane Logan. It's nice to meet you."

"Doug Johnston," he said, and tipped his hat. "I'm sorry this had to happen to you. I don't know anyone around here who drives a Tundra."

I gestured toward the fawn standing lost in the ditch. "I think he was hers."

"Yes'm," Doug said. "It's a pity."

A few vehicles passed by, and I talked to Doug for a couple more minutes, and then we shook hands goodbye. I sat down in my car as he pulled away, but I didn't turn on the engine. I waited until Doug was gone, and then I left my vehicle again, and walked along the ditch. The fawn jumped away from me, and darted toward his dead mother.

The wind sliced at my skin, and my boots sank in the snow as I moved.

I knew I should leave for work. Stella would be furious with me for being late. She'd give me her most evil expression and make it clear to me that *tardy workers* became *unemployed*. I'd never been a "tardy worker" before, but Stella wouldn't care about that.

I ought to be racing to Happy Garden, and begging Stella's forgiveness for missing the first five minutes of my shift.

But I wasn't ready to leave. I wasn't finished here. With this deer and her death. With the chilling significance of watching her die. Today was a Tuesday. Hanna had died on a Tuesday.

Hanna with her lovely brown eyes, like that deer's.

Hanna would have cried as she watched that doe die.

I kept walking. The sky was overcast, pale white with grey shadows, like sad little bruises. I listened to the sounds my boots made as I passed through the snow.

The fawn watched me a while, and then he tucked his legs and lay down by his mother. I turned to observe the other deer, at least a mile away now. I counted fifteen, though a few had already passed out of sight. I wondered if they'd come back for him. I wondered if he'd get up and follow. As I stood there and pondered all of the things that could happen, I reached into my coat pocket and took out Hanna's badge.

I traced her name in the pieces. The scar I kept picking at.

Hanna. My Hanna.

My wonderful Hanna, who had loved life so much. Who had been such an incredible basketball player. Who had traveled, and read poetry, and swum in the ocean. Who had always been full of ideas. *We'll make a documentary together, right after we graduate—*

Some people came equipped to dream big, no matter the circumstance. Hanna had been one of those.

I knew why she'd taken her sheriff's badge and snapped it apart. I knew what she'd been trying to say. Dreams died like stars, burning out from the core. Taking the light as they vanished. Leaving the silence of space.

Hanna had only been telling me that I had to start dreaming. I had to find a new way. Because her life, and her dreams, had winked out with her cancer. The path we had chosen together was gone. Which meant I had to look past her death, into something greater than the two of us.

She'd be so mad, if she knew I'd kept her broken badge and given up. I could see her frowning at me, and I found that funny—Hanna frowning—and I almost laughed.

I held the pieces against my heart and gazed up at the sky. I tried to think.

I wasn't sure how I was going to figure out a way to film a documentary in Africa, when I was already broke with four kids to take care of. But I knew that those things were only excuses. The will made the way, and I was willing myself now to come up with something.

The answer, I knew, wouldn't arrive in an instant. But somewhere, out in that dark, empty space where stars came to life… somewhere out there, I'd find it.

I glanced at Hanna's badge one more time. All those sharp, broken pieces. How many times had I studied this badge and thought about crying? How many times had I wished for the one thing I would never have again?

I knelt in the snow beside the field, and arranged the pieces in front of me. I wrote the word *Love* in the untouched powder. Again and again, until those broken pieces were surrounded. Then I leaned back on my heels, with my hands on my knees. The snow soaked through my jeans.

I didn't want to leave Hanna's badge.

But I had other things I wanted now. A great many things. More than making sure the kids finished school. More than keeping our house. More than getting my bills paid.

I was ready to dream bigger than that.

***

A few minutes later, I arrived at work. Stella already knew why I was late. A Happy Garden parent had seen my car and the dead deer, and told Stella. I still had to inform her myself, and make sure to act overly apologetic and fix her extra coffee, and let her know how much I valued my job, and promise her that I would never—*ever*—be late in the future.

Which was tiring. But I felt stronger today than I had in a long time, so kowtowing to Stella didn't wear on me as much.

I was also extremely relieved to spend the next ten hours around young children, even if they were screeching and yowling and wetting their pants at naptime. Because children were undeniably, spontaneously *alive*, and I found myself more grateful to have this job than I could have ever thought possible.

And there were a *lot* of children in the daycare today. We were actually over our staffing capacity. In the rush of activities and the grind of the day, I almost forgot to ask Stella for Grace's phone number again. I didn't remember until almost closing. "I really need those CDs back," I pressed. "Especially after my drive in this morning."

Stella said, "Oh, yeah! I forgot all *about* that. I'll go find it now," and she disappeared into her house. When she reappeared later, she kept to the toddler room and ignored me.

I walked in, smiled and asked, "Do you have that number now?"

Stella frowned. "I had a call from the bank, and I'm going to have to search through my *papers*. It's been such a *stressful day*. I'll have to finish looking for it tomorrow."

"Sure," I said, and ducked out of the room. I realized that Stella was never going to give me that phone number. And if I continued to ask her for it, I was going to get myself canned, as I was certain now that Grace had been canned. I couldn't afford to lose this job.

But I knew Grace's last name was Wolcott, and I knew she'd been on a Verizon plan with her phone, because she'd complained to me once about how high her bill was. So I reasoned there was probably another way that I could track down her phone number.

I left work at six o'clock, and I searched for the fawn near the accident site, but he was not with his dead mother. I hoped the other deer had come for him and he was off with the herd. I was so distracted thinking about this, that I was almost home before I realized I'd forgotten to ask Carver if he wanted to come over again tonight. I'd only asked him if he wanted to go skiing on Friday. I hadn't mentioned having dinner this evening. I slapped my forehead and felt so dumb for forgetting. Maybe I wouldn't see him again until Friday. Damn.

When I arrived at the apartment and found the place empty, my heart sank. I walked to the table and picked up the note I'd been left.

I recognized Ethan's handwriting.

> *Dear Mary Jane,*
> *We went to play baseball.*
> *Don't cook dinner.*

I knelt to pet Gandhi a minute, hoping this meant they'd gone to the community center with Carver, and then Mia burst through the door.

"Hey, ready for dinner?" she asked. "We're going out." She kind of bounced as she said it. "Everyone else is down in the car." She had to mean Carver's Lincoln.

"Did you guys walk Gandhi?" I asked.

"Sure, after school," Mia said. "Then Carver came over and took us out to *play baseball again.*" She half-roared, half-giggled those final words. "And now we're getting supper. With *you.*" Mia grabbed my hand and pulled me out the door.

Carver stood waiting at the bottom of the steps. He wore his dark woolen trench coat and black scarf. The wind tugged at his tawny brown hair, and he was so lovely when he smiled at me, I had to catch my breath.

"How was your day?" he asked.

I laughed and said, "Oh, it was a day," in a tone that implied it had been far from usual. *I realized I'm going to make that documentary. Not six years from now. But now. I'm going to start working on it again.* But I didn't say that out loud.

He searched my face for a moment, and I smiled to let him know we could talk about it later. "Olive Garden okay?" he asked.

"Olive Garden sounds great," I said, and as I stepped toward the Navigator, he placed his hands on my shoulders and gave me a kiss on the cheek. I made a giddy little sound when he touched me, wishing everyone wasn't already in the vehicle, waiting on us. He opened the back passenger door for me, and I clambered inside. Mia hopped on my lap. Everyone was pretty much shouting about what an awesome baseball game they had played at the community center, and I found myself smiling again.

Inside the restaurant, I sat across from Carver—and this time, I reached across the table and clasped his hand. He laced his fingers through mine. "You look… different," he said.

I touched the tip of my nose and said, "I hope that's not code for *bad.*"

"No," he laughed. "Lighter, somehow. You look lighter."

"I feel it," I said. "I feel lighter." I ran my thumb along Carver's knuckles and asked, "How's Branch?"

"Riding the teacups," Carver said. "Out-spinning his cousins, I'm sure. Those stitches aren't holding him back one bit."

"I wanna go to Disneyland," Mia said. "You should take us there, Mary Jane."

"I should," I said, and sent Mia a smile. Coming up with the money for a trip to Disneyland was no more ludicrous than paying for a documentary in Africa. Strange that I didn't think of such a thing as insurmountable now. If I really wanted to take the kids to Disneyland, I could. I was sure I could find a way.

Carver squeezed my hand. "So what happened today?" and I told him about the man hitting the deer, and how Doug Johnston had shown up to help me.

The kids were stunned, and gave me horrified looks, and Carver placed his hands flat on the table, like he wanted to stand up and go hit something. Or someone.

Richard asked me, "Were you scared?"

"I was in shock for a while," I said. "I was glad Doug stopped to help. I might've been there a long time, if he hadn't been there."

Ethan put his arm around my shoulders. "Sometimes, I think: for every bad person out there, there's always a good one."

"I think you're right," I said, and gave him a hug. Ethan was such a sweet boy.

But Carver still looked… angry and troubled. "You should file a report with the police, and maybe they can find him. His insurance should have to pay for the damage."

I laughed. "My car isn't worth it. Crushing the hood in simply gave it more character. Isn't that right, Mia?"

Mia rolled her eyes. "Drug dealers put bags of meth in that car. That's why she calls it her Candy Man Cadillac."

"Mia!" I pulled her toward me and lowered my voice. "*You shouldn't tell people that stuff.*"

But Mia was looking at Carver and laughing, and he was chuckling, too.

I was just getting over my embarrassment, when Mom chose to pipe in. "Their father sold meth," she said to Carver, gesturing around at the kids. "That's why he's in prison."

As soon as Mom said the word *father*, the whole ambiance of the table changed. Mia stopped laughing, Richard's face turned dark red, and Ethan lowered his gaze, and then dropped his head, like he'd rather melt into the floor than remain in his chair. Gus reached out to pat Ethan's shoulder, but then let his hand drop without touching him. Carver glanced around at the kids with a worried expression, but Mom pressed on with her story with lightning speed, with no concern for the effect she was having on anyone.

"The first time I met that man, he told me we were gonna be rich. *Hey, honey, let's get married, and you can come live with me.* Did he buy me a ring? No. He opened a can of corned beef hash and fried some eggs. I didn't even have flowers. Or a cake. And I wasn't there two weeks before that man burned a hole in my dress—just dropped his cigarette one night, and didn't even say he was sorry. After he was convicted, I divorced him. I said, No more *hey honey* for me. Burning up sheds. Stealing money. Wrecking my car. He can rot in that jail cell, for all I care. He never once took me to the movies. Or bought me flowers. Not once. Dole Preston was an absolute loser. Of all the men I've known in my life, he was the dumbest."

Then Mom gave Carver a playful look, as if to ask, *How do you like that?* She stirred her drink and asked me, "Can I order another?" To Carver, she lowered her voice and added, "Mary Jane never takes us out like this. She's so selfish."

I said, "Mom, you don't need another drink."

"Fine," Mom snapped. "Fine. Just ruin all the fun, why don't you." Anger flashed in her eyes. "What's next, huh? What's next? You think you can make me stay home with your mangy old dog? Is that the plan now?"

I was still holding onto Mia, but I released her and stood. I walked over to Mom, placed my hands on her shoulders, and then leaned over to give her a hug. I spoke close to her ear, low enough that I hoped Carver couldn't hear. But given the silence that had descended upon the whole table, I guessed he probably could.

"I really like how you fixed your hair tonight, Mom. You look really pretty. And there's a guy at the table behind us who keeps looking at you. The four-top with the suits. I saw him elbow his friend and point at you earlier."

Mom smiled and glanced around, pleased when she spotted the group of four men. She fluffed her hair and ignored me, and I returned to my seat.

I patted Ethan and Richard on the back before I sat down, and I squeezed Mia's hand. Then I looked up at Carver, who was gazing at me with a solemn expression. I smiled and kept my voice easy, since we needed to move on and change the subject, or risk Mom flaring up again. "Did the kids ask you about playing baseball on Saturday?"

"They did," Carver said, and at the mention of baseball, he gave a smile and a nod.

The kids started grinning as if nothing had happened. Little gremlins. Good thing gremlins bounce. These kids had quite a school of hard knocks to live through.

Richard blurted, "And he said we could, Mary Jane! He even said we could have pizza again!" He drummed his fingers on the table, excited.

"As long as you're good," I said. "Like I told you at breakfast."

"We'll be good," Richard promised.

"We'll be good," Gus echoed, and I sent Gus an extra smile, because it was brave of him to speak up in a public area like this, with so many strangers around. Carver even gave Gus a thumbs-up, which made Gus blush and hide his face for a moment. Not out of fear, but with happiness.

Our food arrived, and for the rest of our meal, Mom kept sending the four suits furtive glances, the kids talked about baseball and the St. Louis Cardinals, and I enjoyed being able to sit so close to Carver. When he flew home this weekend, and returned to his life, I wondered what would become of him at the end of the season. If his contract was dropped, would he start coaching, like he planned? Or would he decide he still had a few more years of baseball inside him, and try to negotiate a place with another team?

I hoped he kept playing baseball, of course. The real Carver, that is. Not the one who was trapped. But the Carver who lived with his passion. The one who only felt joy when he picked up a bat.

And every time he caught my gaze across the table, I shivered with pleasure. Carver wore a black collared shirt tonight, and black was the most dangerous color I had seen on him yet. It set off his tan and his jaw line and the silver shade of his eyes, and made me want to put my hands on his skin and kiss him in dark, secret places. He made me feel desperate to love him, and heat coursed through my body with the force of a storm. If he asked me out for a nightcap again later, after the kids went to bed—this time, I wasn't going to say no.

26

GRACE

When we arrived home after dinner, the kids took out their papers and books and did their homework, and Carver helped Richard with algebra again. Mom went into the bedroom and smoked pot, which meant she had the back window open. I would have yelled at her about that, but leaving her alone now was a small price to pay for peace and quiet in the living room.

Steve came in after his shift, and Richard asked him to play chess, so they did. Mia turned on *Gladiator*, but chose to play chess with Ethan in front of the TV. Gus finished showing Carver his baseball cards.

I kept looking at Carver and sending him smiles… and he kept meeting my gaze, and smiling right back.

The kids went to bed before ten, and while this was happening, Carver called his boys, and talked outside on the phone. Mom announced she was going down to the bar, and left the house, and Steve decided he'd tag along and see what was happening. Since Mom had inducted him into her pot-smoking ways, he was far more curious about Riverdale night life. Which meant he was on the prowl for a girlfriend, of course. And this more relaxed, humble Steve made much better boyfriend material.

After the kids were in bed, and Carver stepped back inside, I worried he was only going to leave again, so I wrapped my arms around him. He hugged me against him, and I nestled my cheek on his shoulder.

"I was thinking about you today," Carver said.

I made a sound that was part sigh, part giggle. "And?"

"And you're twenty-two."

"Mm-hmm." I wasn't sure where he was going with this. He just smelled so delightful, and felt so good in my arms. I was suffering a bout of euphoria.

Carver didn't sound happy though. He sounded worried. "So when I was signing my first contract to play for the Braves—you were only eleven years old."

"I know." My euphoria started slipping away.

He scooped me up and I yelped, and then Carver walked to the couch and sat down with me on his lap.

"It's very strange," he said. "To think of you like that."

I rested my cheek on his shoulder again. "Not so strange."

"Where were you, when you were eleven?"

I thought for a moment. "Richard was almost two. Ethan was brand new. We lived with Dole then. In Alabama."

"You moved a lot," Carver said.

"I did."

"I don't know how you grew up the way you did."

I buried my face in his chest. "Please let's not talk about this."

He rubbed his hands on my back, which felt lovely, but I knew he was not ready to let this go. "At least tell me what's wrong with your mother," Carver said. He ran a hand through my hair, and I met his gaze.

"I don't know, Carver. No one does. Name a disorder, and she's been diagnosed with it. Locking her up makes her worse, not better. She's happiest when someone supports her, and she can drift around, smoking pot. That's about it."

"She doesn't work?" Carver asked.

"She's tried," I said. "And failed. She can't keep a job for more than a few days at a time. Employers just get too fed up with her."

Carver remained pensive, and glanced up at the ceiling. "That man—Dole Preston—is he really in prison?"

"He's serving another ten years in Cañon City," I said. "And the kids have never once asked to see him. Though I offer, sometimes, to drive them over there."

"He was arrested in Colorado?"

"That's right. He lived in the Springs for a while. That's where he was sentenced."

Carver clasped my hand in his, and then kissed my fingers. "How did you... how did you end up at Swarthmore, Mary Jane? When this is... your family is... This is not an Ivy League environment. To say the least."

I laughed. "I told you. I helped win a state softball tournament, and aced the SAT. With my grades and athletics, I got a full ride. I was in."

Carver hugged me against him. "It's not that easy."

I laughed again. "You play major league baseball. Your idea of easy might be a bit skewed."

"What I do and what you do are not even on the same planet," Carver said.

I put Carver's hand on my thigh, hoping to steer him in the direction I wanted to go. But he was too distracted right now, thinking of all the differences between us, and unnerved by the idea that I was a child when he was a man. I knew what he was probably doing: calculating my age against his life milestones, and determining where I might have been at the time. There was the fact that he was married with a child before I was even in high school. The fact that I'd been in eighth grade when he'd started playing in the majors. And the fact that when his wife and brother had died, I had just graduated high school. I wasn't even in college yet. I hadn't even met Hanna.

Such a depressing thought, to remember my life before Hanna.

I didn't like all this thinking. It was totally killing the mood.

I swung my feet to the floor, left the couch, and paced to the dining table. I crossed my arms and glanced at Carver again. "You were right about me," I said. "I did give up on it."

He rose and walked toward me, stopping about three feet away. "Your documentary?"

I nodded. "I think I forget how close... my own death... always is," I said softly. "Watching that deer die today reminded me though. I'm here in Riverdale to take care of my family, sure—but that's not all I'm here for. So it's time I stopped messing around."

Carver smiled and shook his head. "You're the last person in the world I'd ever accuse of messing around."

I quirked an eyebrow at him. I almost managed to say something clever—something a sophisticated bar maven would say—but then Carver took a seat, looking serious, and I knew it wasn't the time for bar maven banter. He leaned an elbow on the table and turned his gaze to the floor, and it was obvious he was grappling with something he wanted to share.

I sat down and propped my chin in my hand, waiting for him to speak up. When a minute passed by, and he still looked tense, I said, "Tell me."

He met my gaze for a moment and sent me a smile. "I spent a lot of time praying today," he said softly. "Praying and talking to God." I heard a mixture of things in his voice: sadness and hope, old memories… peace. This had not been a normal day for Carver. Not at all.

I waited for him to continue, and then I nudged him along. "And?"

"I felt better," Carver said, and he sent me another smile. He turned his gaze to the ceiling, and his next words were measured, more solemn. "I was… I was thinking how… Things had started falling apart in my life… before the accident. When Audrey and Ben died, it felt like… It never felt like an accident. It felt like God's judgment. It felt like I had been judged."

He was quiet a long time, and I wasn't sure if I should prompt him to continue or not, so I kept my voice gentle. "And when you prayed today?"

Carver's face changed, took on a quality that was almost imperceptible for me to notice, even though I was only a few feet away. His eyes became softer and his muscles relaxed just a fraction, and I would have missed it entirely if I hadn't been watching so closely. Carver had become so adept at hiding his feelings, that even something this profound was almost completely concealed.

Pain hurt. And the body had to manage it, no matter what caused it. Release from pain—whether with medicine, with music or prayer, or a new idea about love—usually brought a physical change. And I knew that's what Carver was feeling right now: release.

He gazed at the wall, deep in thought. Trying to put this in words. His voice was heavy and light, full of wonder and sadness. "It was like… I've carried all of these—things—inside me, for so long… and today, it was like… something else came in… and filled me up."

He still wasn't looking at me, and I kept my voice tender. "What filled you up, Carver?"

"Grace," he said softly. The tone of his voice found a new harmony. No sadness. No regret. This was a sound without pain. "Absolute grace. Like there was nothing else. Like there'd never been anything else."

I let the silence wrap around us, and it was a beautiful, comforting quiet. I drifted around in my own memories a long time, thinking of people I'd known, and things I had done.

I remembered singing psalms in church as a child. The old woman who smelled like wild onions and read me the Bible. The Southern Baptists who came to our house one Christmas and brought over a big pot of soup and cornbread and a sack full of candy canes. I had so many memories like this, experiences I had collected in my mind, and I knew each of them shared an essential ingredient: these were all of the ways I had been taught to have faith in God's love. In any love. These were memories about love.

I asked Carver, "You remembered that you were forgiven?"

He nodded and turned away from me, wiping his eyes with his hand. "I remembered," he said. "I don't know why I would ever forget."

I reached out and took his hand. "We all do, Carver. It's what makes us human."

He laughed and gazed up at the ceiling again. His eyes were still wet, despite how much he was fighting those tears. "I don't know why it's so easy to talk to you, Mary Jane. But I'm glad that I can."

"Me, too," I said. I stood and stepped close to him, gave him a kiss on his brow, and then I left the table and walked into the kitchen. I ran the sink for a minute—just to give Carver some time to himself—and decided to wash the glasses that had been left on the counter.

When I finished, Carver was standing with his hands in his pockets, and I knew that our evening together had come to an end. Men rarely displayed what they viewed as weakness and then felt jacked up on testosterone. I knew Carver's emotions tonight had not left him feeling like Superman.

I still felt like Wonder Woman though. But that was okay.

"Want to come over for supper tomorrow?" I asked. "I'll make spaghetti."

He laughed. "You had pasta tonight."

"Pesto," I amended, recalling my meal at Olive Garden. "I'll make red sauce tomorrow. Truth be told, I'd rather serve pork chops. But I've already thawed the meat for spaghetti."

Carver chuckled again and nodded. "I'll be here."

He turned to leave and placed his hand on the doorknob, but I walked over and took his wrist. I pulled him down toward me, and then I stood on tiptoe to kiss him. I pressed my lips against his, hoping I could share enough heat that even this brief little kiss would have an impact on him.

"Goodnight," I said, stepping back. "Don't be late for supper tomorrow."

He sent me a smile, and something passed through his eyes. Something I hoped meant he'd stop thinking about me like some eleven-year-old kid, and remember that I was a woman who wanted to love him.

"I'll be here," Carver said.

After he'd gone, I flipped out the lights and started getting ready for bed. I kept Carver's voice in my mind, and the things he had told me tonight, of his prayers and God's grace… and then I remembered Grace from work, and how I still needed her phone number.

I couldn't have explained why I felt such a need to contact her. But I did. Grace had loved working at Happy Garden, in a deep, resounding way that had always shown on her face. Children were her calling, and if Stella had fired her right before Christmas, I was worried that Grace was not in a good place. The thought of losing a job I loved right before Christmas made me shudder.

So I reminded myself to track down Grace's phone number tomorrow, and then I went to sleep.

I had a dream about Carver. He wasn't wearing his black collared shirt though, or playing baseball, or dancing with me.

He was stretched out on a bed with black satin sheets. Wearing nothing but a smile.

It was a very good dream.

27

TWENTY-FIVE CENTS

On Wednesday morning, I packed the kids off to school, and then I left early for work. I drove into town, still thinking about my dream with Carver, and I stopped at the library to use a computer. I found Grace's phone number online.

I walked down the street to the Riverdale Diner, which had an old-fashioned pay phone in back. I dialed the number I had, and Grace answered after two rings.

"Grace, it's Mary Jane," I said.

"Hi, MJ," she said.

"What happened?" I asked.

"At Happy Garden?" she sighed. "Stella told me not to come back after the holidays. She also told me not to use Happy Garden as a work reference, because she'd have nothing kind to say about me to another employer. So I found a job at Burger King."

"Burger King?" I squeaked. I was trying not to gasp, this came as such a shock. I knew it was hard to find employment in Riverdale, but *criminey*.

"I couldn't get hired on without a reference anywhere else in town," Grace said. "Sunny Days Kindergarten needed a teacher's aide, but I didn't qualify without someone to vouch for me. It's been really stressful." She sounded like she was ready to cry. I felt horrible for her.

"You're a great employee, Grace—and you did great work at Happy Garden. I'll be your reference. Stella can't stop you from putting the truth on your resume."

Grace sniffled. "That's not—you can't be my reference."

"Sure I can," I said. "You let me know which job you want to apply to, and I'll set up a meeting with the person in charge of hiring. Then I'll go in and tell them what a great coworker you were, and how sad I was to see you go, and that the circumstances of your dismissal had nothing to do with your work ethic."

"I still have to list my supervisor," Grace muttered.

"That's fine," I said. "Everyone here knows Stella McLaughlin runs Happy Garden. But some of them are also going to know that the woman's got issues. And people who hire employees appreciate personal visits—no one wants to hire a bad worker. Stella is costing herself time and money by firing good employees over her own garbage. It's why she'll probably be out of business within a few years."

"Happy Garden makes tons of money," Grace said.

"You would think," I said mildly. "But here's the funny thing about people who get businesses handed to them: those people often drive them into the ground. And that's exactly what Stella is doing with Happy Garden. You know why she refuses to pay the closer past six? She's taking her company money and spending it on herself—on her car, her vacations, her night life in Riverdale—and she can't figure out where her bottom line is."

"How do you know that?" Grace asked.

"Because Stella is a mess," I said. "And messy people keep messy books. So will you go ahead and apply for another job, and put me down as your reference? I promise I'll go in and speak to whoever I need to. Not every childcare facility in Riverdale is going to let Stella McLaughlin dictate their business decisions."

Grace was still hesitant. "You'll just be wasting your time."

"I won't be wasting my time," I said. "But if you keep working a job you don't want to work, you'll be wasting yours."

There was a long moment of silence, so long that I thought the call might have been dropped. But then Grace said, "Okay, Mary Jane. I'll put you down as a reference."

"And you'll start applying again?" I asked.

"I might not find anything," Grace said. "But I'll try."

***

Working at Happy Garden that day, it was hard for me to look at Stella and not feel a raging hatred toward her. I wanted to shake her and yell, "Why did you fire *Grace?* Right before *Christmas? What is wrong with you??*" but I managed to keep myself under control. Knowing that I planned to disrupt Stella's nefarious plot to hurt Grace made me feel better, since it was the mental equivalent of drop-kicking my boss.

Stella had a few ideas of her own that day, and she made several announcements at lunchtime.

After her trip to Nigeria, Stella had been blessed with several epiphanies. As a result of this newfound enlightenment, she'd come to the following conclusions:

1. Happy Garden should open its doors to poor children who lived on public assistance. Because poverty should be stopped, and there was poverty here in Riverdale.

2. Happy Garden staff were now mandated to attend weekly staff meetings, which would take place on Thursday nights. The first such meeting would be held tomorrow. Failure to attend the meeting would result in instant dismissal.

Stella looked right at me as she shared point number two, and I knew this was because I'd asked for Grace's phone number. She obviously didn't want anyone to know that she'd fired Grace, and since I'd been unintentionally stirring the pot, I was officially on warning.

I decided Stella was a world-class nitwit. I knew that these late-night staff meetings would go on my list of things that were an absurd waste of time. And if I didn't arrive home until eight or eight-thirty at night, I would barely have any energy left to fight the homework battle, much less fix dinner.

After her two announcements at lunchtime, Stella beamed around the room at us, especially me and Izzy, and said, "I want to assure you *all* that you'll be *paid* for your time at these meetings, from *six-thirty* to *seven-thirty* each Thursday night."

I felt my hands start to shake, so I pretended like I had to sneeze and left the room. I walked outside for a while, until I'd calmed down.

Later that afternoon, Stella called me into the house for a "quick meeting," which was such odd behavior that I worried she was going to fire me. I followed her through the laundry room and into her office, which held a desk so heaped with papers that she couldn't sit down and see over the top of it. I remembered telling Grace that Stella's books were a mess, and at the sight of this office, I almost laughed.

She moved her chair to the side of her desk and smiled at me sweetly. She'd put on a few extra pounds during her trip to

Nigeria, as her tank top seemed even tighter than usual. I didn't know why Stella wore skin-tight clothes all the time, but it was obvious her favorite store was PacSun.

"Mary Jane, you've been such a *huge* asset to Happy Garden," Stella said. She paused to smile. "Usually, after *three months* of successful employment, I offer my staff a *raise*. But as I was busy last month preparing to leave for *Nigeria*, I didn't have time to *meet with you*. Now that I've returned, and since you've been a *solid* employee for *four months*, I'd like you to know that you've *qualified* for a *raise*. Your *hourly wage* will now be *$8.25*."

"Thank you so much," I said, and forced myself to look happy. I couldn't quite manage the level of gusto this situation required, but I sure did my best. I tried not to think about what this raise meant for my paycheck, but of course I already knew: an extra ten dollars a week. And that was before taxes.

"That's really great news," I continued, because Stella was staring me down, waiting for me to show her some more genuine appreciation for this windfall of cash. "I'm so... *glad* that I've found a home here. Happy Garden is such a... *delightful* place to work. It's such a *great* opportunity for me, and a *wonderful* learning experience."

Stella gave me a self-satisfied grin. She knew she was making me grovel, and found pleasure in that. "Your next paycheck won't *reflect* this raise, but starting next *Thursday*, you'll start to see your income go up."

I wanted to yell, "*Starting* next *Thursday??* For an extra *ten dollars* a *week?* You called me in here for *this??*" but again, I held my tongue.

I rose, shook Stella's hand and said, "Thank you so much, Stella. I really appreciate it." Then I bolted from the office and returned to helping Izzy.

I thought of the couple I'd picked up on their own private plane, and how the man had tipped me a dollar. I wished he'd simply said thank you, and kept that damned bill. I felt the same way about Stella.

Only I couldn't afford to light my paycheck on fire.

So messing up Stella's vindictive plans for Grace was my consolation prize.

***

When I arrived home that night, I found Carver at the table with the kids, doing their homework together and eating popcorn. Carver was taking their math and reading problems and turning them into baseball stories, which held the kids enthralled. To him, all numbers, statistics, even literary concepts, existed for the sole purpose of informing the game and discussing its history. And for whatever reason, the kids never grew bored with this logic. Steve even said, "Carver and I are a lot alike. Only my obsession is chess."

I made spaghetti for dinner, with hamburger and Italian sausage in the sauce, served with steamed broccoli and fresh bread smeared with butter. I sliced apples for dessert.

I told the kids what had happened to Grace, and why she'd been fired, because I wanted them to be aware that they could also lose their jobs for saying the wrong thing at work. Carver shared a similar story of a ballplayer who was dropped from his team for telling the owner he was thinking about converting to Islam.

"So that guy was supposed to hide his religion?" Mia asked.

"He wouldn't have known to do that," Carver said. "You just can't take getting fired too personally sometimes. Some people in charge are idiots."

"Because they hate Muslims?" Richard asked.

"Because they hate about anything," Carver said.

I was so happy to hear Carver say this that I reached over and squeezed his hand. I also sent him a big smile, though I was trying not to look at him too much, because every time I did, I remembered my steamy dream about him on those black satin sheets, which caused me to blush and feel overwhelmed. So I worked hard at distracting myself, but I couldn't stop thinking about him without any clothes on. I so wished my mind would get out of the gutter.

After dinner, I started to clean up the kitchen while the kids finished their homework, and Mom told us a story involving an astronaut and a trip to Mercury with a bushel of grapefruit. I thought she might've really been talking about Richard Nixon.

When Mom's tale was finished, Carver stepped into the kitchen and started scrubbing the dishes, and I tried to push him away. "I don't want you to do this," I said, but he just hugged me.

Heat slipped through my body, and I felt such an ache for him, for so much more than a hug. I couldn't think for a minute.

Mia cried, "I'm done with my problem set!" So I walked to the dining table to check over her work, and then returned to the kitchen to dry dishes. Carver was scrubbing the last pot.

"Guess what I did today," he said.

I caught his gaze and asked, "What?" with a smile.

He had the last pot in his hand, which he raised and lowered like it was really a dumbbell.

"You started training again?" I asked. "Weight lifting?" I hoped he wanted those twenty-six pounds back, for the extra power that muscle would give him.

Carver nodded. "I always stay in shape. But I thought it might be time to get serious again."

I patted his shoulder and gave him a kiss on the arm. "I'm glad to hear that," I said. "Because I prefer a man with a little more muscle. You're actually on the puny side, for my taste." Carver's shoulders shook with his laughter.

Mom called, "Mary Jane! Stop being a cuss!"

***

With homework done, the kitchen clean, and the kids playing chess, I decided that Carver and I should go for a walk. I clipped Gandhi's leash on his collar, and we headed out.

The night air was bracing, but I felt too happy being with Carver to mind the cold. We walked Gandhi a few blocks to the river, and then followed the bike trail. The path was lit with infrequent lamplights, which cast a brighter glow in the winter, on account of the snow. I took Gandhi off his leash and let him romp around.

"How was your day?" I asked Carver.

"Great day," Carver said. "I knew I'd see you tonight."

I grinned. "I felt the same." We ambled along in companionable silence another minute, and then I said, "I had a dream about you."

Carver sent me a smile. "Good one, I hope?"

"Mmm…" I said, noncommittal.

"You're not going to tell me?"

I shook my head no. "Mm-mm."

"How is that fair?"

I laughed. "Fair?" I was really teasing him now.

"I had a dream about you, too," he said.

"Did not."

"I wouldn't lie about that."

"Oh, Carver," I sighed. "You are no match for me. Don't even try."

Now it was Carver's turn to laugh. He reached for my hand, and though I tried to evade him, he was faster. He gripped my fingers a moment. "Why don't you want to tell me your dream?"

I gazed up at his face, and all I could think about was how soft his lips were, and how his five o'clock shadow would feel against my skin. He smiled at me again, and I made a high little sound in the back of my throat. Then I tugged my hand free. "Come on, we need to catch up to Gandhi."

Carver grabbed my waist though, and pulled me toward him. I found this funny at first, and we both laughed, and then I put my arms around his neck and we stopped laughing.

The way our lips touched was too raw and hungry for a sweet little word like *kiss*. My desire for him had started burning me up, and I wasn't the only one who felt so much heat.

Being alone with Carver hit my system like the strongest jolt of adrenaline. I couldn't catch my breath. I couldn't stop wanting more. We might have struggled to learn how to dance together, but there was nothing awkward about us when we kissed.

When my hands started to roam over his body, and his kisses trailed down my neck, I stopped thinking. My body knew what I was doing. And my body was reckless with how much I wanted him.

I kissed him with every part of me that was desperate to love him, and whenever he pressed his mouth to my neck and whispered my name, his voice rolled against my skin like we were naked together.

"Come with me," he said. "Mary Jane... Come home with me tonight."

"I... Carver, I..." I forgot what I was saying, and kissed him again. It felt like ages until I remembered I had something to do. "It's a school night, Carver. I need to make sure the kids go to bed."

"After that," he said. "Come with me."

I thought of my day tomorrow, of my ten-hour shift, that new staff meeting to follow, and then supper and homework with the kids. It felt like a lot.

"Not tonight, Carver. I have too much to do." I made his hands stop roaming, and then I leaned against his chest and closed my eyes. His heartbeat against my cheek was like the pulse of a steam locomotive, powerful enough to send tremors through my body. Did my heart feel like that? Could he tell? "I'll go home with you Friday," I promised. "Friday and Saturday. And I won't work this weekend. I'll take this weekend off."

"Mary Jane," he sighed, and I felt his body tremble. He ran his hands through my hair and kissed me again. "I'm going to have to run five extra miles tonight, just to sleep."

I giggled. "Go home and have a dream," I said. "I recommend that."

***

Later, after I told Carver goodnight, put the kids to bed, and went to sleep, I did have another dream about him.

He stood on a baseball diamond this time, in his uniform, with his cap and his glove.

It took me a long time to orient myself to this dream. I didn't realize for quite a while that I stood on the pitcher's mound, and I wore my white sundress. Carver wasn't far away. He was in place to play shortstop, which was not a position he played in the majors. I suddenly worried I was supposed to be pitching—but I didn't have a glove. Or a ball. And there was no one else on the field. The stands were empty. The dugouts were vacant. All of the lights were on for a night game, but there was no one else in the stadium. Just Carver and I, on a field that almost stretched into forever.

I'd never stood on a professional ballpark before, and it was… beautiful and frightening. The size of it. And the energy around me… Hushed. Expectant. Like we were waiting for something. The stars were out overhead. I felt the stadium lights on my skin.

I glanced at Carver again. "What are we doing here?"

He laughed and tapped his glove on his thigh, gazing around at the wide open space of the ballpark. He looked impressively happy, and his voice was expansive. "I don't know, Mary Jane." He removed his cap and smiled up at the lights, at the sky. "But it sure is a nice view."

28

AW, CHUCKWAGON!

When I opened my eyes Thursday morning, that strange baseball dream was still with me. I didn't know what to make of it—but I knew I liked the dream with Carver and the black satin sheets a lot better. That one had been far more... *exciting*.

I hurried to get the kids off to school and drive to work, and when I arrived at Happy Garden, I discovered that Stella was in full-on psycho mode.

As part of her plan to "help the poor" of Riverdale, the first two poverty-stricken children were inside the building. One of them was a little boy named Tuffy, and Tuffy had decided to break out a window and pee on the wall. Stella's response was to tackle the boy, pin him to the floor with her legs, and yell, "Don't you ever—*ever*—*do that again! Do you hear me??*"

I waited for her to stop crushing Tuffy to the floor, and then I asked the boy to put on his coat and follow me outside. As I expected, he was smirking at Stella the whole time and totally enjoying himself. He gnashed his teeth at the other children as he put on his coat.

I took Tuffy to the maypole with me, and I asked him how old he was, where he lived, and a few other questions until I felt like I understood him a little. Mom always called me a mean little pill or a cuss, but I wasn't really that bad. Tuffy was though. Tuffy was hell on wheels, and he knew it. He enjoyed damaging property and hurting people. He mentioned that he'd already been told he wasn't welcome in public school.

I asked Tuffy what he liked to do more than anything, and he said, "Play soccer."

"Well, I don't know a whole lot about soccer, but I know some-one who does." One of the parents of a Happy Garden child had played soccer in college. "He can come and show you some moves, but I can't ask him about it if you keep breaking Stella's windows."

"Stella's a cunt," he said.

Hearing a five-year-old say that word shocked me so much, I said, "I need to sit down." I walked over to one of the fallen trees by the river, brushed off the snow, and took a seat. Then I asked, "Will you do me a favor?"

Tuffy stared me down. "What?"

"Will you please not use that word around me? It makes me feel sick inside, and then I can't think about soccer. And if I can't think about soccer, I won't remember to ask that man to come and show you his moves."

"Who is this bozo?" Tuffy asked.

"Olivia's father," I said. "She's four. I think she's here today."

Tuffy scowled. "I already play good."

I shrugged. "Anyone who wants to play has to practice. I don't make the rules. If you don't want to practice, you'll never be good. No one can get around that."

"Ah, fuck you," Tuffy said, and he walked down the river a ways. I kept an eye on him, but I let him go. I wondered if Stella would come out to check on us, but when she continued to remain in the daycare, and none of the other children came outside to play, I knew that Stella was scared of Tuffy and wanted nothing to do with him now. So much for helping the poor.

I decided I'd find a soccer ball and play some soccer with Tuffy. I started back to the daycare and called, "Tuffy? You coming?" and he followed me sullenly. I found a soccer ball in the playground box, and we played one-on-one for a while. Normally, I'd have let a child beat me and score points. But, with Tuffy, I had to school him again and again.

"You know, Tuff," I said. "I think you need some practice. You kind of suck at this."

"Ah, fuck you," he said again, and he stalked off to the swing set.

I walked toward the fence and called the horses over. I said, "Hey, Tuff, come check out these horses." Tuffy scampered to my side and glowered at the animals. They frightened him.

"You want to ride one?" I asked.

"No!" he yelled.

"Why not?"

"Because they're stupid!" he shouted.

"That's what you think," I said.

I climbed over the fence and walked through the field. The two horses followed me around, and even the little burro came trotting over to see what was up. Tuffy watched this, still scowling.

"Why do you think they're following me?" I asked.

"I don't care!" he shouted.

"Could be they think I have apples," I said. "Could be they're just lonely and want to be petted." The burro was closest to me at the moment, so I stroked his face. The donkey gave a little nicker.

I asked Tuffy, "You know what it means to be lonely? When you're by yourself, and no one's there to love you?"

Tuffy stared at the ground.

I patted the horses and donkey goodbye and climbed back over the fence. I asked Tuffy if he wanted me to push him on the swing, and he said, "Sure." So I pushed him on the swing for a while, and timed him when he went down the slide, to make it a game, and then I invented some soccer drills, and had him practice his footwork. My entire concept of childcare followed one simple motto: when in doubt, wear 'em out. I was so successful at this that Tuffy announced he was tired sometime after lunch, so we went inside and I put out a cot for his nap. Even with all of the noise in the room, Tuffy went to sleep.

Stella watched this activity from the hallway, with an anxious expression I'd never seen on her face before, and I decided I could get away with drinking a cup of her coffee today. So I went into the kitchen and made some.

Stella joined me, and I noticed her eyes were red. It looked like she'd been crying.

"I shouldn't have done that," she said. "Tackled him, and... and all that... I think I was wrong about this... about the public assistance children. I don't want him to come here tomorrow unless you work with him again. You're the only one who can handle him."

I said, "Stella, he's still a good kid. You don't need me to be here." If there'd been the possibility of overtime pay, I might've considered this offer. But Stella didn't pay overtime, and Carver was taking me skiing tomorrow. And if she really wanted to help these children, then it was up to her to dig deep. I'd grown up with kids like Tuffy my whole life. Meanness and poverty were not news to me.

"Well, I've been thinking this through," Stella said, "and I think I was just too hasty to invite these children in... I mean, I want to *help* them and everything, but this is just... I'm not making any *money* on these kids, and...Well, I'll have to pay for the *window* now... And I didn't even get to have *drumming* class today, because the *other* one had a screaming fit and tried to attack Izzy." Stella ran her hands through her hair, probably as stressed relating this news as she'd been when it happened. Then she smiled at me with a pleading expression, as if she needed my reassurance that she was right, and that Happy Garden was no place for kids on public assistance.

As she'd already decided to stop her campaign to fight poverty, I knew there was only one response I could give her. "You have a wonderful program here, Stella. You've worked very hard to make Happy Garden the loving, creative place that it is. I'll respect your choices, whatever you decide."

Stella smiled again and nodded at me. She looked immensely relieved. I poured myself a cup of coffee and checked in with Izzy on which of us needed to fix afternoon snack, and then I helped her lay out the other cots for naptime. The rest of the day followed our usual routine.

When Tuffy woke up later, he seemed dazed, and he followed me around groggily and kept a hold of my belt loop. I asked, "Hey, Tuff, you hungry?" and he nodded. I fixed him a late lunch, and once Tuffy was adequately rested and fed, he transformed into the docile, loving child I knew he still was. The child he always could be, if someone ever bothered to take care of him. He volunteered to help me in the kitchen a while, and when it came time to mop the floor, I found a mini-mop for him to use, and he mopped beside me. I did not keep a grudge against Tuffy, or snap at him or cut him down, and he responded by showering me with love and respect. I returned the goodwill by listening to him chatter about soccer.

When we were done with the floor, I had him give me a high-five, and then I taught him a cool handshake, which I called a man-shake, and I told him everything I knew about David Beckham. I didn't know much, but I said that David Beckham practiced soccer every day, and that he never used bad words unless he dropped a hammer on his toe, in which case, he yelled, "Aw, chuckwagon!" I made Tuffy practice saying it with me.

When his mother arrived to pick him up, it was ten minutes past six. She was a short woman, about fifty pounds overweight, with the prematurely aged skin that meant heavy drinking and hard living. Tuffy was so mellowed out by his day that he walked over to his mother and asked her to hold him, so she scooped him up and propped him on her right hip. He leaned his head on her shoulder while Stella came out to talk to his mom. Stella informed her that Tuffy had broken a window, peed on the floor, and would not be welcome back tomorrow at Happy Garden.

"I'm really sorry," Stella said with a smile. "We wish you all the *best* in your search for a new daycare provider."

I was almost done with the last of the closing duties, but I decided to stop checking over the cubbies, and fetched the soccer ball from the backyard. As Stella returned to her house, I brought the ball to the woman, and told her it was for Tuffy. "We had a really nice day together," I said. "Tuffy was a big help. He worked in the kitchen, he helped me pick up all the blocks and put them away, and then he helped me mop the floor."

The woman nodded at this without listening, so I looked at Tuffy and asked, "What does David Beckham say when he's angry?"

"Aw, chuckwagon!" Tuffy cried happily, and he took the soccer ball from me and kissed it.

I watched him leave with his mother. It was dark outside, but I could see them in the parking lot, visible in the light from Stella's windows. As soon as the woman thought she was out of sight, she plunked Tuffy down on the gravel and slapped him across the face. The blow sent him sprawling, and he dropped to his knees.

"How *dare* you *embarrass* me!" she yelled, and she leaned over and slapped him again, several times. Then she threw open the sliding door of the minivan and shouted, "Get the hell in the car!"

Tuffy didn't cry as he climbed into the vehicle. His mother knocked the soccer ball out of his hands, and it careened into the shadows and disappeared in the parking lot. So I picked up a sweater from one of the cubbies, opened the main door, and walked out.

"*Hi there!*" I called cheerfully, waving one hand, and the woman froze as I approached with the sweater. "Tuffy forgot this inside. Sorry about that!" and I walked up to hand him the sweater. It wasn't Tuffy's, of course, but that didn't matter. Then I said, "Hey, Tuff! Your ball rolled away!" and I searched around in the dark until I found it. I scooped it out of the ditch, said, "Here you go," and passed it to him. He wasn't smiling anymore, but he took the ball and held it in his lap.

His mother had taken a seat in the van, hoping to make a quick getaway, but I caught the driver's side door with my hand before she could close it.

She hid her face from my gaze, sitting there with her shoulders hunched over. She looked broken and vulnerable and pathetic, but I still crossed my arms as I studied her. She knew I had seen her. She knew I could file a report. But I had something better than cops on my side: I had shamed her. Normally,

I didn't agree with making people feel low, but in this situation, I thought it was necessary. I could stand there and stare her down for an hour, but she finally said, "It's been a long day," in a timid little voice. She wanted me to smile and forgive her. Because nice people did that.

Problem was, sometimes I wasn't so nice.

I knew this woman and I could have grown up as sisters. She'd been abused growing up. One look at her sorrowful, ugly face told me that. But I also knew that getting whaled on as a kid didn't give someone a pass to beat her own children.

I said, "Hey, Tuff, will you go inside for a minute? I need to talk to your mom."

So Tuffy went inside, where it was warm. He peered through the glass in the door and watched us. I turned back to his mother.

"You need to sign this boy up for soccer," I said, and she gave a meek nod. "Whatever school he goes to, he needs to play soccer. You owe that to him as his mother." I had her full attention now, throwing out the word *mother* like that. Hit a nerve. She had more going upstairs than my own mother did. Tuffy had that in his favor, at least.

I kept my voice low and steady. "He wants to be a good kid. And he *is* a good kid. He's a great kid. But you brought him here hungry and tired—and starving for someone to care about him. So he broke a window and peed on the floor. And what happened? He got someone's attention. We fed him a meal. We let him sleep. And if he'd known he could have our attention without breaking a window, he wouldn't have done those things. You're teaching him to act like this. You are. And when you hit him, you're teaching him something else. You're telling him that you're out of control. That you have no respect for yourself. So why should he?"

The woman's face and neck had turned dark red while I spoke. I waved for Tuffy to join us, and while he was crossing the gravel, I added, "You can be a better mom. If you want to be."

I picked Tuffy up, hugged him goodbye, and placed him on his seat in the minivan. Then I pulled the sliding door shut and returned to the daycare.

Their van pulled away and I finished locking up. I walked out to my Buick before I remembered that tonight was Thursday night, which meant I had that new mandatory meeting. The clock on my dashboard said it was 6:23 p.m., so I sat outside in the cold and waited.

I thought of the way I'd spoken to Tuffy's mother... and then I remembered throwing those three men out at The Caroline last summer. Carver had described that behavior as *powerful* and *free*, but I still had trouble accepting that those descriptions were accurate. It was easy to stand up for someone who was being abused. Like Tuffy with his mom, or Justice Garcia with those idiot customers, or Grace being fired by Stella. It always felt easy to help other people.

Much harder to stand up for yourself.

Stella had wanted me to grovel for a raise, and I had. I played her games to keep this job, and I hated it.

Groveling to Stella made me weak, but calling Tuffy's mother out on her shit made me strong—so the fact was, I would never truly be powerful and free while I was tied to Happy Garden. Because the price I paid for keeping this job was too steep.

So I sent another request to the universe: to find a way to escape Happy Garden. To be able to earn a paycheck and still be home at night with the kids.

At 6:28, two other vehicles arrived. Izzy and Linda both stepped out of their cars, and I followed them into Stella's house to attend our first staff meeting.

The next hour of my life felt every bit as pointless as I had guessed it would be.

***

By the time I made it home after eight, I discovered the kids had already eaten. They'd cooked mac 'n cheese and hot dogs with Carver, and they'd eaten at seven and then finished their homework.

I smelled all the food in the house—food I didn't have to worry about cooking or washing up after—and collapsed on the couch, so bottomed-out by my day that I needed to sit for a while, and just be. Well, sit and ogle Carver, of course. He wore a black polo shirt and dark slacks, and he was picking Gus up and down, so that his head touched the ceiling. Gus was having a ball. Gandhi sat at Carver's feet and gazed up at them, wagging his tale and wriggling his body.

"I think Gandhi wants a turn," I told Carver. So when Carver put Gus down, he knelt beside Gandhi and rubbed his belly a while.

Mom was doing something that might have been Tai Chi in the corner. She had an intense expression on her face and kept swinging her hands around in strange poses, doing odd little kicks. Richard and Ethan were debating baseball statistics, and asking Carver to chime in now and then. I kept my place on the couch and felt too tired to move.

Mia gave me a curious look. "You're getting lazy, Mary Jane," and she poked my arm. "You know what I want to do now…?" She drew out the question in a singsong voice.

"Watch *Gladiator*?" I guessed.

"Play Monopoly!" Mia shouted. She ran to get the game board. Sometimes it surprised me how much energy kids had, even after a whole day of school.

Mia set up the game board, and I made some coffee for myself because I wanted to brighten my mood. Seeing Tuffy's mother had made me remember my own childhood, and sometimes that put me on edge.

We played a rousing game of Monopoly until ten o'clock, when I made Mia pack up the game board and call it a night. The kids went to bed, Mom retreated to the bathroom to smoke pot, and I sat on the couch with Carver and told him about my day with Tuffy.

"That's terrible, about his mother," Carver said. "It's too bad people can't adopt parents in this country. That woman needs to be straightened out more than her son at this point. It's no wonder so many people are trapped at the bottom, when they treat their own children like that."

I winced at his words. I knew he wasn't trying to hurt me. He didn't know, couldn't know… what he was really saying to me. How personal all of this was.

But I winced just the same.

"It can happen to anyone," I said. My voice remained quiet, and I thought for a moment. "Poverty might run in cycles, but giving up on yourself is an equal-opportunity Suck Fest."

Carver smiled. "That it is."

I didn't want to talk about work anymore, so I asked Carver if he'd like to stretch out on the couch, and just lay with me for a while. Steve wasn't home yet, so we had the living room to ourselves.

Carver moved his body without answering, and I quickly discovered that the couch was too small for us both. Carver said, "Just lay on top of me," so I did. I nestled my head on his shoulder and said, "Tell me about your three boys."

I couldn't see his face at the moment, but I felt him smile with his whole body, and I heard his voice change. "They're all smarter than me," he said. "And more trouble than a pack of monkeys." He reached into his left pocket and pulled out his wallet. Then he opened his billfold to show me their pictures. "Jackie… Christopher… and my youngest, little Branch." He pointed to each one in turn, and I thought they were beautiful boys, with blond hair and blue eyes. They looked strong and assertive, like their father.

"I think Christy will grow up to be the tallest of the three," Carver said. "He was the biggest at two. They play baseball, they love to fish… My father takes them fishing a lot. They're obsessed with Legos. And computer games. They read more books than I ever did."

I propped myself up on his chest so I could see his face while he spoke. "Tell me some stories about them," I said, and he did. Playing baseball, going fishing, learning how to ski… Carver had no shortage of humorous tales involving his sons. I listened for hours, and laughed quite a lot.

"You're a great father," I said.

"I just copied my own dad," he said, and he took my right hand and linked our fingers together. "I never would've made it without my parents. I'd never make it right now, without them."

I could tell by the tone of his voice that he was trying to point out how different we were. Especially how different my parents were from his own. And maybe he still wanted to know where my father was. But I was more comfortable discussing Carver's folks than my own.

"What about Audrey's parents?" I asked. It was the first time I'd ever said his wife's name aloud, and I felt my skin tingle with apprehension. I wasn't sure if I was delving into forbidden territory or not. But when Carver spoke again, his voice remained light.

"Audrey's older sister had four children right out of high school and no husband to help her, so she's always lived with her parents. They're still in Port Arthur. My parents take the boys down to visit them every chance they get."

"Cousins," I sighed, picturing all the time I'd spent with my own family growing up. When I'd been little, I never had so much fun as when I was out with my cousins. Swimming holes, trampolines, bike riding. I curled up against Carver again before I said, "Heaven on earth, right?"

Carver laughed. "Heaven exactly."

The front door opened, and Steve walked in. It was after two a.m., and I sat up in shock. "Were you at the bar?"

"No," and Steve laughed. "I mean, I was. Then I… um," and he blushed. He ran a hand through his hair and asked, "So, what are you guys doing? Just hanging out?"

I struggled to hold back my huge smile. "We're going skiing tomorrow."

"Yeah, the kids mentioned that," Steve said. "Sounds like you guys picked a good day. I hear the powder's great."

He must have been hanging out with snowboarders or something, since Steve never said things like this. I left the couch and Carver followed me, probably as amused by Steve's behavior as I was. But he was hiding it better.

"Are you hungry?" I asked Steve. "There's food left."

"Nah, I'm fine," Steve said.

I knew it was time to call it a night, so I gave Carver a big hug and asked, "Pick me up at nine?"

"I'll be here," he said.

"Sweet dreams," I giggled as he put on his coat and opened the door, and Carver sent me a look like he'd bite my neck if he could. I laughed and blew him a kiss.

29

LOVE

Friday morning, I cooked the kids scrambled eggs and bacon for breakfast.

"No fair you get to go skiing," Mia whined. "I don't want to go to school."

"Stop it," Ethan told her. "We're doing fun stuff tomorrow."

"And we'll go see a movie tonight," I said, since I felt guilty about having a day off and spending it without them. "We'll even buy popcorn." The kids gaped at me in shock.

Richard said, "Who are you, and what have you done with our sister?"

I ignored this. "You have to get your homework done right after school though." I glanced at Ethan and said, "After practice," because he had basketball practice right after school. "Or we won't go."

"We'll do our homework," Gus said. "Don't worry."

After the kids left to meet the bus, I showered and dressed. Steve went to work, and Mom skulked around the living room, looking pouty.

The sight of her so sad and forlorn made me increasingly miserable, until I finally just caved and asked her, "Mom, you want to come skiing with us?"

Her answer was to jump up and yell, "Whoo—*hoo!*" and she was ready to run out the door in two seconds flat.

"You don't need to fix your hair?" I asked. "Or your nails or your makeup?"

Mom shook her head no. She seemed scared I might change my mind. I glanced out the window and saw Carver's Lincoln pull up.

"Time to go," I said, and we walked down to the car. Well, *I* walked to the car, and Mom bounced like Tigger.

Carver raised his eyebrows when he saw Mom, and I knew he was shocked, but he still said, "Morning, Miss Preston."

"Good morning!" Mom beamed. "Mary Jane invited me," and she pointed at me, in case Carver might've forgotten who I was.

"Mom's a good skier," I said nervously. "She really loves it." I studied Carver's face for a moment, almost sick to my stomach that he might be upset with me, but he didn't seem angry I'd brought Mom. He was giving me a curious look with those bright silver eyes, one corner of his mouth curled into a smile, so if anything, he found this amusing. I opened the door so Mom could climb in.

"Buckle up," I told her. Mom grumbled at me, but a second later, I heard the lock click in place. I hopped in front, and we were on our way.

***

Twenty minutes later, we arrived at Riverdale Mountain Ski Resort, which was every bit as ritzy and glamorous as a ski resort should be. It was also a bright, sunny day, perfect weather for skiing. Carver found a parking space close to the base, and we rode the shuttle bus to a rental store. Soon we had skis, boots, poles, and everything else we needed for a day on the mountain. Mom had brought her own goggles, which were the same ones she used on her cleaning sprees. They smelled like ammonia, of course.

We chose several green runs to start off the morning, which were the easiest slopes to ski down. Carver had led me to believe he wasn't much of a skier, but that turned out to be false. He was a very fine skier, and I had to admit, he was as beautiful to watch skiing as he was anywhere.

After we skied down each run and queued at the lift, Carver would pull me against him and kiss me. If Mom was behind us, we always waited for her, and she'd ski over talking about national politics and the lessons of the sixties and why it ought to be easier for people to buy valium. Other times, Mom skied so fast that she beat us both down, and then she'd call us slow-pokes and announce we needed to drink some beer.

We ate a big lunch at a restaurant halfway up the mountain, and spent the rest of the day on blue runs until the mountain shut down and it was time to go home. Then we returned our equipment to the rental store, rode the shuttle to where the Lincoln was parked, and headed into Riverdale. It was one of the most perfect days I'd ever had in my life.

"Thank you for taking us skiing," I said.

"Yes, *thank you!*" Mom shouted.

She didn't need to shout, but Carver just smiled and said, "You're welcome, Miss Preston. The pleasure's all mine."

At the apartment, I cooked pork chops for dinner, the kids did their homework, and after we ate, we all piled into the

Lincoln and went to the movies. The kids picked something from Disney with a lot of action and ribald one-liners, and Mom chose a romantic comedy, but Carver and I decided to wait outside. We sat in the backseat of the Lincoln with our arms around each other, and listened to the radio.

Even though I was happy to have time just to sit with him, I wasn't feeling contentment. Sunday was starting to seem like it was only seconds away, and I didn't like the way Carver's pending departure was pressing against me, making me anxious.

"Tell me about your documentary," Carver said.

So I did. I told him all about *Brighter Than Stars*, everything Hanna and I had planned in advance. That helped calm my nerves, and made me feel a lot better.

In the quiet that followed, Carver asked, "Why didn't you want to marry the Cowboy?"

I sighed and pulled away from him. I wished he'd forgotten all about what I had said in the vapor cave. "Can we just make out now?" I asked, and Carver laughed.

Then he turned serious again, and put his hands around my face. "Did he do something to you?"

"No," I said. "The Cowboy is wonderful. He was the perfect guy for me."

Carver considered this for a moment. "Then why break it off?"

I shifted away from him, out of reach. I had no desire to admit the truth. None whatsoever. But it was probably better this time to just come out with it. "The Cowboy wants children. And I don't."

If Carver was surprised by this news, he masked it. "You don't think you'll change your mind?"

I shook my head. "I will never—*never*—change my mind."

"Because you have to take care of your siblings?" Carver asked.

In a quieter voice, I said, "It's more than that."

"What?" he asked.

I shook my head again. I couldn't have voiced this answer, even if I'd wanted to. The place where the real answer lived was a very dark place indeed.

"Do you not want to get married?" Carver asked.

I leaned against the seat, remembering the times Mom had been married or we had lived with a man. How she used to rant and rave at those men until they started to hit her. How desperate she was for someone to support her.

Marriage seemed like so much… dependency. And pain. In the fairy tales, the *Just Married* sign flashed at the end of the movie, while everyone was still smiling—but what happened after that? Did Prince Charming sit down with a bottle of whiskey, yelling at Cinderella to get out of his house because he was sick of footing the bills for her and her brats?

Who knew. The prince rescued her, sure. But he could always dump her again. I had witnessed firsthand how often this happened.

I glanced at Carver and tried to muster a smile. "I don't know, Carver. My mom married four times, and… well…" I shrugged. "Duck was an alcoholic, Dole was a meth dealer… the Prince Charmings Mom found were not very… inspiring."

Carver raised his eyebrows in shock, and rubbed his brow with his wrist. "It's so hard for me to… wrap my head around the things you tell me sometimes. You are nothing like the picture of… the picture of your background… that I have in my mind. It still amazes me that you've gone on to do the things that you have. How in the world did you do it?"

I stared at my hands for a moment, thinking about all of the ways I might have turned out. "I never started smoking," I said. "Smoking, drinking, hard drugs, ditching school... cigarettes were always the gateway activity for the life I didn't want."

"You were a kid, and you knew that?" Carver asked.

I caught his gaze with a smile. "Of course. It's why I really lay into Richard sometimes about smoking. He's the prime age to start. Even the industry is gunning for him to light up, on top of all of his friends. Except for Gus, thank God. Gus hates cigarettes. But peer pressure and money—that's a tough combo to beat."

"That woman who slapped her child," Carver said. "Do you think she ever saw smoking that way?"

I shrugged. Yes. No. "Maybe," I said. "Hanna told me something once about life: You have to be very brave to be happy. I think, when you grow up as a kid, and all the adults in your life are drinking and doing drugs, spending everything they have on a fix, whatever—if all the adults in your life are miserable, you learn that misery is the price you pay to belong. To fit in. And then if all of your friends are drinking, doing drugs, and they're miserable—then you're really in a bind. Then you have to decide if you want to be happy, or if you want to have friends. Because you have to drink and do drugs and be miserable if you want to keep those friends. Or you have to be lonely and outcast and go meet some new people if you want to be happy. It's a tough choice to face."

"That's how I felt about steroids," Carver said. "When I was a freshman in high school, all of the juniors and seniors on my team were taking them. But the first time someone ever gave me a needle, I took it home and showed it to Ben. Ben looked at that needle and just said, *No*, and he took it from me and I never saw it again."

"He was a year younger than you, and he already had that figured out?" I asked.

Carver laughed. "Oh, Ben was a miracle boy. He was almost as smart as you are," and Carver leaned over and planted a kiss behind my ear. His lips tickled, and I laughed.

"I wish I could have met Ben," I said. "He had so much character."

Carver tensed and drew back. A shadow passed over his face—and then he smiled just as quickly, trying to hide what he felt. "The two of you would have hit it right off. Ben would have taken to you like… a wizard to magic."

I smiled and said, "He does sound a bit like a wizard to me."

Carver took my hand and laced our fingers together. "Then say you're the magic. Because that's how I feel around you."

I leaned over to kiss Carver's lips, and then I ran my other hand through his hair. "You're magic yourself, Carver. Two-hundred-fifteen pounds of it, sitting here next to me."

Carver laughed. "I wish it worked like that," he said softly. "I wish being bigger meant I had more." There was a sadness to him now, a sadness that seemed part of that shadow that had passed over his face. Something was wrong, but I couldn't guess what.

"How did your sister react?" I asked. "Losing Ben."

The shadow left Carver's face, as well as that tension. I felt relieved, since Carver's uneasiness worried me, and I was grateful he seemed relaxed again now.

"Clarissa is a rock," Carver said. "I've always been so grateful to have her… I often think what a terrible thing it must be, to be born without a sister. Even annoyingly over-competent sisters like mine."

I laughed. "I'm sure she loves hearing that."

Carver grinned. "All the time." He thought for a moment, and added, "That woman you saw who slapped her child… She would never be able to do such a thing if she'd grown up with Clarissa."

I smiled and nestled against Carver again, resting my cheek on his shoulder. "The world is quite the garden, isn't it? Everything growing wild all together. Mercy and cruelty, kindness and misery. You never know what you will find. Out there in the jungle of people."

"I found you," Carver said, and he rubbed my back with his hand. "I'm starting to wonder… what I'll do now… when I leave."

I put my hand on Carver's chest, above his heart. "You'll play baseball," I said. "You'll play baseball again."

He kissed the top of my head. "That's not what I meant."

He was about to say something else, but the kids arrived then, running up to the vehicle and laughing about the movie. Mia opened the door and shouted, "You were just sitting in the car the whole time? That is so weird."

"Yeah," I agreed. "Where's Mom?"

"Talking to some guy," Mia said. "Want me to get her?"

"Sure," I said, and Mia ran back inside the theater. A few minutes later, she returned with Mom. After we had everyone in the Lincoln again, Carver drove us back to my apartment. I decided to change and put on my sundress, so while the kids and everyone else played chess and watched television, I checked over my safety pins, and then put on some mascara and lip gloss.

When I stepped out of the bedroom, I told everyone good night and slipped into my coat. Carver opened the door for me, and as soon as we were outside, he said, "I like your dress."

I laughed. "You've known me a whole week, and that's all you can say?" It was also the same thing he'd told me before we went dancing, and I knew he remembered, because Carver laughed.

Then he gave me that grin like the devil, and stopped me to nuzzle my neck. He lowered his voice. "I don't care what you have on. I just want your legs wrapped around me."

I gripped his jaw and pushed him away. "Better."

When we arrived at his house, Carver parked the Lincoln in the garage, and I followed him inside. He helped me out of my coat, and then he shrugged out of his own jacket and hung both our coats in the hall.

We walked into the kitchen, and it felt—so *different*—to be in this house again. It was such a spacious, exquisite place, with tall windows and track lights and artwork on the walls. But none of these things could ever be as lovely as Carver.

He asked, "What would you like to drink?" as he stepped around the island toward the fridge.

I wondered how I could have ever looked at this man and not wanted to love him. To make love to him. To fall in love with him.

I had been so scared of those things.

But all of my earlier fears about him seemed so ridiculous. And not even the fact that Carver was leaving—that he would soon be back in the travel rotation of baseball, playing games every day, flying from city to city for months on end—even this seemed inconsequential, compared to how much I wanted him.

I should walk to a bedroom right now. All that heat in my skin. How much I ached for his body, so much that I felt light-headed. I should grab Carver's hand and lead the way.

But I was nervous. I didn't know which room was his. And I didn't want to ask.

He caught my gaze and smiled, and I remembered he'd asked me if I'd like something to drink.

"Water," I said.

He filled a glass at the sink and brought it to me, but I didn't remain at the island. I walked toward the living room, which was not a separate room in this house, but a shared space with the kitchen. I was almost to the couch when I turned around. Carver put down the glass, and started toward me.

As he closed the distance between us, he seemed uncertain at first. Maybe he thought I wanted to explore the house. Or turn on the TV. Maybe he thought I wanted to talk about something.

I studied him as he made his way toward me. All the lines of his body that made him so perfect. Those bright silver eyes. The dark fringe of lashes that framed that pure color. The wide plane of his shoulders. The layers of muscle that defined his tan skin. The scars on his knuckles. The way his brown and blond hair looked rough and unkempt. The sharp line of his jaw. His five o'clock shadow. The shape of his mouth. His soft lips.

I took a deep breath as I waited.

He stopped in front of me with a puzzled expression. Did I want to see the house? Did I want to talk about something? His gaze asked the questions. He smiled shyly, like a boy. Like a man who wasn't sure what I wanted, but was up for anything.

When I put my arms around his neck and pushed up against him, a change swept over Carver's whole body. He embraced me and kissed me, and it was almost frightening, the amount of strength he had. How fast he could move. How hot his skin felt. That shy boy disappeared. And this was a man who knew what he wanted.

When I released my hold on his neck and knelt on the carpet, Carver sank to his knees. I helped him peel off his shirt, and he unzipped my dress and slipped it over my head. He placed his hands on my hips and pulled me against him, and the longing I felt burned my skin with white heat.

We kissed like we would never hit ground, like something would always be there to catch us, and I wasn't sure which of us needed this more, needed to love and be loved so much that it hurt. Carver's mouth traced the curve of my neck, and when we dropped to the floor, my name in his throat was the deep growl of a panther.

30

BATTLE

We went to sleep in Carver's room, on a king-size bed with a puffy blue comforter and plenty of pillows. Heaven.

I opened my eyes again around four in the morning. A light had been left on in the hall, but it cast only a faint glow in this room. Enough that I could see Carver clearly, but little else. Framed pictures, two dressers, a baseball glove on the desk—these were outlines of shadows, absent of detail.

I kissed Carver's shoulder, and he stirred awake. He gave me such a sweet, tender smile, and cupped my cheek in his hand. He turned on his side to kiss me, and then he pulled me beneath him, and we made love again in the darkness.

Later, I lay with my head on his chest, listening to his heartbeat. Feeling the warmth of his body. The even rise and fall of his breath. I said, "Tell me what you love about baseball."

Carver's voice sounded thick with happiness, a sound that made something deep in my body purr like a wildcat.

"Being outside," he said. "Feeling the weather. Even bad weather. Rain, wind, sleet… springtime, sunshine… days so hot my skin melts."

I smiled. "What else."

He ran his hand through my hair. "Slides," he said. "Perfect throws. Lead-offs. Triple plays. Tagging a man out at home. Fastballs. Changeups. Getting dirty."

"Your coach?" I asked.

Carver chuckled. "Sometimes."

"Your teammates?"

"Yes," he said. "Definitely."

I sat up on my heels, so I could gaze down on his face. Carver slid a hand along my arm, past my shoulder, across my collarbone. He rubbed his palm over the skin of my heart. "I love the speed," he said. "The speed of the ball. The speed of the game. The long minutes of waiting. The split second when lightning strikes."

"Like falling in love," I said. "Like living a life. Long minutes of waiting. And then lightning strikes."

Carver touched my face with his fingertips. "That's what I love about baseball."

His bed had dark blue sheets. They looked black in the night.

"I had a dream about you," I said.

He grinned. "So you say." He slid his hand to my belly, and circled my hip with his fingers.

"Did you ever play shortstop?"

"In high school," Carver said. "First base for the Braves. Third for the Yankees. Left field, center, and second for the others."

"Do you miss playing shortstop?" I asked.

Carver laughed. "No. There isn't a place on the diamond where I wouldn't be happy."

He curled forward and sat up, and I felt the light press of his teeth as he nibbled my shoulder. "Do you love the battle, Carver? Do you love playing to win?"

He gripped my upper arms and laid me down on the sheets. His gaze traveled over my body, and he pulled my hips closer. "The play is the win, Mary Jane. The scoreboard just tells me how much I wanted it. How much I wanted to play." He kissed the tops of my knees, and then he pushed my legs apart and placed his mouth on the softest place on my thigh.

Later, as the sky lit with dawn, we made love again.

***

Carver cooked quite a spread for breakfast—steak and eggs and waffles—and we drank orange juice from champagne glasses. We ate at the dining room table, on heavy white plates, and Carver kept leaning forward to tug on my ear, or loop his feet around mine.

Then I drew us a bath in the claw foot tub, and once we were in the water, I let Carver hold me. I thought of asking him about his life before the accident. I wanted to know why things had been falling apart. But Caver touched the back of my neck and asked, "How did you get this scar?"

The question made me start—*my scar?*—and then I blushed and covered the back of my neck with my hand.

I often forgot about that scar. I hardly ever noticed it, since I had to turn around in the mirror to see it—and I didn't spend a lot of time in front of my mirror.

I also willed myself to forget that scar as much as possible. It ran across my neck and one shoulder. Long and jagged. White with age.

My face burned, and I avoided meeting Carver's eyes. He took a deep breath, but he didn't ask again. I finally lowered my hand and leaned against his chest again.

I should have guessed he wasn't about to give up though. He slid a hand down my back, and I felt him touch the other scars that I had, around my tailbone, and along the backs of my thighs.

His fingers traced the question, but he didn't ask me again.

The answer was in me… but it was buried so deeply… in a hollow, empty place. Too empty for a word. Too hollow for my voice.

I took hold of Carver's hand and drew it away from my leg. I rested his palm on my belly and placed a kiss on his throat. We didn't speak for a while, not until I asked Carver, "How about this one? On your knee?" and ran a fingertip down the long scar on his knee.

"Surgery," he said. "Three years ago."

Carver had never taken steroids or human growth hormone, so his skin wasn't marred by needle marks or any of the other side effects drugs like that would have caused. He did have a faded scar on his elbow though, which I touched and asked, "And this?"

"Bike crash," he said. "I think I was ten or eleven. Something like that."

I took his hands in mine, and kissed his knuckles. Then I sent him a grin, and a questioning look.

Carver laughed and glanced at his hand, like he wasn't quite sure what I meant. Then he chuckled again. "Roughhousing, that's all." He caressed my shoulder, and then he lifted me up from the water and gazed at my body. He nestled his face between my breasts, and I hugged him. "Mary Jane," he sighed. "I'm so happy you're with me."

"Me, too, Carver." I ran my fingers through his hair and kissed the top of his brow. "Me, too."

When we stepped out of the water, Carver dried me off with a big white towel, and I followed him to his room. I perched on the bed and watched him dress. The way he slipped on a shirt, the way he pulled on his pants and threaded his belt. There was something erotic about seeing Carver's routine—the way he moved as a man through the world, completely separate from me. I thought of all the mornings beyond this one, mornings when he would wake up without me, and get dressed in this way. Carver the man, who would stroll into a locker room, change into his uniform, and become Carver the ballplayer.

All of that was waiting for him. His uniform. The batter's box. The title he felt trapped inside. The last year on his contract. His teammates. His fans. All of those high expectations. The numbers on the scoreboard. The stadium lights.

And right now, he looked so incredibly powerful. He looked like a man who belonged on a diamond.

Carver had hung up my dress last night, and I finally willed myself to walk to the closet and slip it on. I fiddled with the zipper, and Carver stepped over like he wanted to help. But he just gripped the hem of my dress and pulled it back off. He swept me into his arms and placed his mouth on my breasts... and soon I was back on the bed, twisted up in those dark blue sheets.

31

WILDFIRE

It was almost noon before we managed to keep our clothes on and leave the house.

Carver drove us to my apartment, and once I was home again, I changed into a t-shirt and jeans. Then we took the kids, Mom and Steve to play baseball.

Richard decided I had to bat in this game, and I hit several pop-ups to the kids, which they had no trouble catching.

"Mary Jane, you aren't even trying," Richard said in frustration.

I said, "Of course I'm trying. You're just one hell of a pitcher." He knew I wasn't swinging as hard as I could, and he knew I was trying to hit balls to the kids. But I also didn't have the muscle power I'd had in high school and college. I'd just lost too much weight.

So Richard kept throwing to me, trying to strike me out. He never did, but I found it endearing that he worked so hard. Carver and Gus kept consulting with him, whispering differ-ent pitches Richard could try to trick me up. Whenever Carver left the mound after one of these visits, and sent me a grin, I thought of all the ways he had kissed me this morning… and felt myself blush.

We played until four o'clock, when Mia announced she was starving, and that if we didn't get some food soon, she'd start eating her glove. "Seriously, I will bite into this freaking leather. We need to get out of here."

So we packed up and went out for burgers at a kid-friendly place called Seth's Pubby Pub. I sat beside Carver, and he kept his thigh pressed against mine under the table. Sometimes he leaned over and planted a kiss behind my ear, and sometimes he took my hand and rubbed his thumb in my palm, and I knew he would have kissed my fingertips or nuzzled my neck, if we hadn't been in full view of my family.

While we were eating, the kids begged me to take them to the hot springs. "Let's go swimming tonight, Mary Jane. Please?"

"Please?"

"Please?"

"*Please??*"

I opened my mouth, unsure how to answer, but Carver smiled and said, "That sounds great—let's go."

I felt a rush of relief. I loved the idea of soaking with Carver again, and I was thrilled that he'd agreed to do this. It made me so giddy that I almost told him, *I love you*, right then. The words filled my chest, like a sudden pressure that needed released, and I knew that soon—before he left—I would voice these words to Carver. I would tell him I loved him, and I wouldn't be frightened.

Because Carver had always been loved. By his family, his friends… and by all of those people he played for. The ones who came to see him under stadium lights, or out in the sunshine… The ones who loved him because he was part of their team. Carver had earned love for hitting grand slams… and now he'd earned mine for being the person he was. For teaching the kids about baseball. For being so sweet to my family. For reminding me that I was powerful and free.

"What are you thinking about?" he asked.

"You," I said, and he leaned over and kissed my cheek. Such a chaste little kiss. But so full of heat.

After supper at the Pubby Pub, we went home for our swimsuits, and then we headed up the mountain to visit the hot springs.

The Riverdale Hot Springs was a beautiful facility, with thirty different pools of water of varying temperatures. The pools were built into the mountainside, each with its own unique shape and size, and decorated with the natural rock. There were potted plants everywhere. They thrived in the hot steam from the water, so that strolling the grounds at night felt like being inside a rain forest. The cabana was closed in the winter, but all of the pools were open, and at night the lights were kept so dim that the stars seemed brighter than the lights in the water.

The kids and Gus spent their time jumping in and out of the pools, from hot to lukewarm to an icy-cold pool that was made of snowmelt. I thought the half-frozen pool was probably their favorite.

Mom and Steve smoked pot in the parking lot before they came in, so Mom was pretty mellow while she soaked in the water. She and Steve found a group of hippies to talk philosophy with. Carver and I sat in a pool with a waterfall, and whenever we were alone, we kissed and ran our hands over each other. I wore a blue bikini and Carver wore a pair of black swim trunks, and sometimes I worried he was going to pull my top off.

"What time is your flight tomorrow?" I asked.

"Four o'clock," he said, and I felt some relief. An afternoon flight was much better than saying goodbye in the morning. He leaned over and nuzzled my neck, and the water lapped around us and splashed my hair.

"You taste better than winning," he said, and I laughed.

"Nothing tastes better than winning." I could see his grey eyes in this shadowy light, and he was smiling at me with that grin like the devil. I placed my hands on his jaw for a moment, and then I ran my fingers through his hair while I kissed him. If anything tasted better than winning, I'd have said it was Carver.

He rubbed his thumbs along my hipbones, slow circles that hit several pressure points, enough that I leaned my head on his shoulder and sighed with pleasure. "God, Carver. You're about going to kill me."

I felt his body tremble as he laughed. "There's not a man alive who could knock you out, Mary Jane."

Except maybe this man.

Those words in my chest were fighting to escape. I wanted to tell him. I needed to tell him.

But I said, "I should check on the kids," and he gave me a kiss before I left the pool. I stepped into my flip flops and set off to find them.

The kids were all fine, still hopping in and out of that icy-cold water and a tub called the Craw Pot, which was one-hundred-eleven and too hot for me. Richard had come across some classmates from school, so he and Gus were showing off for the girls. There were quite a few people at the hot springs tonight, and by the time I could see Carver again, still seated in the pool with the waterfall, several people had joined him. Four young women and two men, all of them about my age, which meant they were probably students at Colorado Plateau.

I decided to spy on them. I wanted to see Carver when I wasn't with him, have a picture of him in my mind in which I played no part. He was sitting on the lip of the pool, gazing into the valley. Steam curled off his skin and mixed with the vapor rising up from the water, and the two guys beside him were talking to him about football. The girls were clustered together, giggling and casting furtive glances at Carver. Another woman joined the pool—a woman in a red fringe bikini with a sparkling necklace and earrings—and she drifted closer to Carver and tried to flirt with him. But he kept talking to the boys without paying attention to her.

I shivered as I thought of all the women who probably hit on Carver. The woman in the red bikini was beautiful, with that cool, haughty air of money about her, and even if Carver hadn't been ripped, he was stunning. Gorgeous enough that this woman with expensive jewelry wasn't wasting any time. It might not even matter to her if he was married or not. Sex didn't care about rules. Good people did. Biology, not so much.

And when Carver returned to his baseball career, I wouldn't be with him. But biology would. And women. Lots of women. A man in a uniform was a strong aphrodisiac. Especially a lonely, single man with a five o'clock shadow, eyes like a leopard, and a dark voice like a secret, a sound that licked against skin like a kiss.

I knew that Carver wasn't lonely right now. He was expecting me to return. He was going home with me tonight.

But two months from now… three, four… eight… He would be lonely again. Lonely and forgiven. Full of grace. Ready to let someone back into his life. Someone who might wear red lipstick and earrings, and sit with him after a game in the bar, having a drink. And she might say something clever like, *Thanks for the drink, tiger*, while she sent him a smile and crossed her legs like an expert. I could not be that woman. But I knew she would be there for him. Women like that had always been there for him.

Carver must have grown tired of discussing football with the boys, because he left the pool and stood at the top of the steps, searching over the grounds to find me. So I stopped hiding and came out. He smiled with relief when he saw me.

"Where'd you go?"

"I was spying on you," I admitted, feeling proud of myself.

Carver laughed. "I missed you," he said, a comment that made my heart pound with happiness. He glanced at the pool with the waterfall, and said, "Let's find another one." So we relocated to a place where we could be alone again. Carver took a seat in the water, and I curled up in his lap, and we put our arms around each other and our lips touched with fire… but then that same group of college students came and joined us. They were pool-hopping, being loud and boisterous, so I stopped kissing Carver and leaned my cheek on his shoulder. The college students piled into the water around us.

They'd smuggled in alcohol, probably whiskey or rum, and the boys offered us drinks from their water bottles. Carver said thank you, but declined. The boys wanted to talk about football again, and they called their buddies over to join them. Two more boys came and sat down beside us, and Carver obliged them by discussing more football. It was clear the girls felt put-out by this whole conversation. I could see them pouting and shooting angry looks at the boys. Here they were in bikinis, trying to flirt, and these guys were more interested in football.

After about twenty minutes, one of the boys asked Carver, "So, do you play?"

He smiled and said, "Not football." He glanced around at the guys and asked, "You all play for the Mavericks?"

Colorado Plateau's teams were called the Mavericks, and I was well aware that their football team was no Crimson Tide. This was not Alabama, and people here did not flock to their games. But the boys had a lot of pride in their team, no matter how many times they lost.

"Oh yeah, we all play," the boy said, and he named their positions. Then he told us about their last season and how it had ended. I could tell they were all sad to be graduating this April. They wished they could go back in time and keep playing football.

I knew that Carver was trying to find a polite way to excuse himself so we could be alone again, but these boys had locked onto him. They were hooked into sports, and somehow they knew he belonged to that world. I thought maybe boys were like bloodhounds that way, and they'd sniffed Carver out. He did know quite a lot about football. But that only made sense, as he'd grown up in Texas.

The boys wanted to analyze NFL teams, and they asked Carver several questions and listened closely when he voiced his opinions, until one of them asked, "Do you, uh, play hockey or something? You seem kind of familiar."

Carver wiped his face with his hand, smiled and said, "I like hockey a lot. But I think a giraffe would skate better than I do."

This brought some laughter. "I feel like I've seen you before," the first boy continued, and he shook his finger at Carver. "Didn't you play for the Cowboys one year? I could've sworn…"

Carver laughed. He tipped his head back against the rock wall behind us, and gazed up at the stars. "I never played football," he said. "Not even in high school."

"Yeah, but seriously, man," the boy pressed. "I know I've seen you on TV before—"

I stood then and tugged Carver's hand. I smiled around at the boys. "Excuse us, fellas, but I'm too hot to stay in this pool—I need to find a cooler one," which made them all chuckle, but when they watched Carver leaving, the smiles left their faces. They turned glum. The girls drifted over, suddenly excited again to be in the pool with them.

I walked Carver to the far end of the hot springs, out of sight of the college students but within view of Gus and the kids. They were leaping out of the Craw Pot, making gasping sounds.

"Why didn't you want to tell them?" I asked, stepping into the pool. We were alone again here.

"I don't know," he sighed. "I just wanted to be here with you." He wrapped his arms around me in the water, and I rested my head on his shoulder.

"I'll miss you," I said.

"I'll miss you, too," and he ran a hand through my hair. Then he tugged on the ends until he had my hair sticking up in all the wrong places. I probably looked like a goof. I wriggled away from him and smoothed it back down.

I felt those words pressing against me again, urging me to speak. So I evaded his arms for a while, under the pretense that I thought he wanted to mess up my hair. He trailed after me for a time, his arms making huge waves in the water whenever he moved, and then he finally lunged for me so fast that I couldn't escape him. He kissed the back of my neck and my shoulders. I felt his teeth on my skin.

"I love you, Carver. I love you."

He turned me around in his arms and kissed me, the sort of kiss that left my whole body trembling. The sort of kiss that made me forget where I was.

"I love you, Mary Jane." His voice sounded low and rich as the deepest part of a melody, the stormiest part of a song, and I knew we had arrived at the place we'd been least likely to meet. Not just on the edge, but falling. We'd gone over together. And I knew I couldn't keep Carver with me, but I suddenly wanted to keep him so badly, I felt lost.

Love might move mountains, and bring happiness, and help dreams come true—but sometimes, love just made a mess. Sometimes love burned like a wildfire just so something else had room to grow.

Maybe I had helped burn Carver down, so he could have something else. Maybe he would find it when he started playing again.

So I said, "Hold me tight," and he did. He bound me against him with those two massive arms, and that felt as perfect as making love to him did.

32

THE HUMAN CONDITION

The hot springs closed at eleven p.m., but around ten o'clock, the kids decided to join us. So Carver and I talked about school with them, until Mom and Steve drifted over and joined us as well. They all knew Carver was leaving tomorrow, and wanted to let him know they'd be rooting for him. Richard and Gus especially wanted to wish him good luck with his season. Carver smiled and told everyone, "Thank you for that."

When it was time to leave, we dressed again in the bathhouse, and then rode back to my apartment. Everyone told Carver goodbye. Ethan even gave him a card he had made, with a homemade picture of Carver playing baseball. The words *Good Luck with Your Season, Carver* filled the inside of the card.

"Not the same as a Cabbage Patch doll," Ethan said. "But maybe not as weird."

Carver laughed and pulled Ethan into a hug. "This is perfect. I'll keep it taped in my locker. Thank you, Ethan."

It was hard to watch the kids tell Carver goodbye one more time… bittersweet to think of all of the fun they'd had this week, and to know that they might never see him again. I was glad that Carver didn't rush them in any way. He was as gracious and patient with them as he had been all week, until the kids said everything they needed to before they trooped off to bed.

Steve and Carver shook hands goodbye, and Mom said, "So long, buddy. It was nice to meet you."

"It was very nice meeting you, Miss Preston," Carver said, and he gave her a little bow, since Mom was standing in the kitchen, dishing up a bowl of ice cream.

"You gonna be here tomorrow?" Mom asked me.

"At suppertime," I said. "Carver's flight leaves at four."

"See you later then," Mom said.

I left my apartment with Carver, and we drove to his place. I felt very solemn, thinking about our own farewell tomorrow. Thinking about how much I would miss him.

In the dark, quiet space of the Lincoln, Carver said, "You could come with me, Mary Jane."

It took me a minute to register what he had said—and then I had to repeat those words a few times in my head.

Go with him?

It took me time to process. Not just to understand what he meant, but to get over my shock. I hadn't expected Carver to ever propose such a thing.

Some ballplayers traveled with their girlfriends or wives, or their families, the way Carver sometimes did. If I went with him, I would travel to his games and watch him play. Fly from city to city. Stay in pretty hotels, eat in nice restaurants. Curl up in bed with Carver each night. Be there to love him.

I turned this idea in my mind. And then I discarded it. That was not what I wanted.

I'd made a vow that Richard and Ethan and Mia weren't going to drop out of school. And I also had Gus, and Gandhi, and my mom to take care of. And I had my documentary project to start planning. I was not now, nor would I ever, contemplate walking away from my whole life. Especially not when I finally felt like I wasn't some powerless victim, but a person setting out to get what she really wanted in life.

I *did* want Carver. That was true.

But I wanted the kids to graduate a lot more.

"I'm sorry, Carver," I said. "I can't go with you."

"I'll come and visit then," Carver said.

Another shock.

I hadn't considered this, either. For good reason.

Professional ball teams traveled almost nonstop. They typically played three games per stadium visit, and they might visit three different stadiums in a travel rotation. Then they'd fly home, and play about a week's worth of games in their own stadium, before boarding an airplane again to repeat the whole process.

Carver had about four days a month when he wouldn't be in front of a crowd—four days off that were travel days, anyway—and he had to perform at that level for six straight months. Seven, if his team made the playoffs.

He was not a man who would have time for trips to a remote place like Riverdale. Athletes only missed games if they were on the Disabled List, and there was no way I wanted that to happen. Only severe injuries landed players on the DL, and I wanted Carver to have a great season. Not sit in the dugout or the stands, healing from surgery, even if that meant he would have time for a visit.

"I want you to play baseball," I said.

"I will play baseball," Carver said.

I sighed and closed my eyes for a moment. "You know what I mean. I want you to be there. One hundred percent. Every day. It takes six to ten hours to fly into Riverdale, depending on layovers. This isn't a place for a day trip."

Carver knew this, of course. But when I admitted these things aloud, I felt him grow tense. By the time we reached his garage, his grey eyes looked stormy. I kept my thoughts to myself as we walked into the house, and then I stood near the kitchen counter, wondering what would happen. This conversation was a drastic mood-killer, almost as bad as the one we had suffered the other night. Maybe worse.

Carver took a seat on a tall kitchen chair, leaned over the island, and buried his face in his arms. "I'll come back before spring training then." He knew as much as I did that this wasn't practical, either—which had to be why his voice sounded so rough with anxiety.

"Your training starts now," I said. "As soon as you're home. That's why you started lifting again. You're ready to get back to your hitting size. And Matt is waiting on you, so you can practice your swing before you guys get to Florida."

"I still have one more month," Carver said.

I shook my head no. "You have a lot to do in one month. Transforming your body, putting in practice time… and you have your boys, your family… And I'm going to apply for the grant money I need to film *Brighter Than Stars*. It'll take a long time to put a proposal together. It's a massive amount of work. With the kids and my jobs… it'll be a lot to pull off."

He glanced up, looking hopeful. "Then please visit me, Mary Jane. I'll pay for your tickets—I'll pay for your family to come with you—and you can work on your proposal at my place—"

I stepped over to him and ran a hand through his hair. He felt overheated, like he hadn't cooled down after his time in the hot springs.

"I don't have any vacation time," I said. "I work seven days a week. I should have been working this weekend, but I called in sick. If I do that again, I'll lose my job at The Summit, and I can't afford to get fired. I missed a day of work at Happy Garden already, to have my teeth pulled. Stella will fire me if I miss again. I need two jobs to make ends meet, and I can't work at night."

"Then I'll give you the money you need," Carver said. "I'll make it so you don't have to work."

I dropped my hand and stepped away from him, uneasy that he would even say such a thing. "No. I told you. I can take care of myself."

"You're not taking care of yourself," Carver said. "You're taking care of—a lot more than yourself."

"I think that's the human condition," I joked, trying for levity. The conversation was starting to feel too intense, too unwelcome, for my last night with Carver. I thought of Tom Morbun in Goldking, offering to give me those thousands I needed for the property tax. Tom with his pearly white dentures and his big house on the hill. His bouquets of pink flowers. His quick, easy deal.

And now Carver was doing the same. I felt so dirty and gross, trading sex for money like that. I didn't want to be Tom Morbun's mistress, and I certainly didn't want to be Carver's. A kept woman was the opposite of someone who was powerful and free. The life of a mistress was tied to a man's, and it reminded me of a damsel in distress tied to the railroad tracks of an oncoming train. If the man found another woman, or grew bored of his lover—what happened to the damsel?

The train ran her over, that's what.

I had been in charge of my life before Carver skipped his flight last weekend and told me he loved me. And I would be in charge of my life after he flew home tomorrow. Love made life messy, but it didn't have to destroy me. I wasn't getting hit by a train.

So I hugged myself for a moment, and then said, "I'll wait for you. I'll be here when your season is finished… in October. November, if you make the postseason." That was as much as I was willing to risk. I could stand by the train tracks to see what would happen. But I wouldn't lie down on the ties.

Carver looked so torn up and sad. He wanted to make this work out. But the truth was, it might not. This week together in Riverdale might have been all that was meant for us, and that was a hard thing to face.

Sometimes the truth was a warrior goddess, clad in white robes with a sword, ready to let justice be done. And sometimes the truth was something much smaller. Sometimes she was shabby and tired, and so diminished that people preferred to push her away. Keep her far out of sight.

There were plenty of times in my life when I had done such a thing. Hiding the truth took almost no effort. It was easy and quick. Like Tom and his deal.

But I didn't want to do that anymore. Truth might be shabby and tired and sorry to look at sometimes, but pushing her away was never a good thing to do.

So I met Carver's gaze and said, "I know you might find someone else. Once you're playing again. That might be why… falling in love with you this week… maybe this means you're ready now, to have someone else… and this week was… This week was incredible. And perfect. Nothing can change that. So that's why I think… it will all be okay."

"Nothing about this is okay," Carver said.

"All right," I sighed. "Then it won't be okay."

I didn't want to talk anymore. I wanted to make love, or put some distance between us so Carver would feel better. And since Carver was far from feeling romantic, I said, "I'm going to watch a game."

I walked into the living room and scanned the DVD shelves. I didn't see any cases for baseball games, so I went into Carver's bedroom and searched his bookshelves. I found a cupboard of DVDs. I skimmed the titles until I found one with a game Carver had played for the Tigers. Not a game from his glory years, but that was fine.

If he was going to sit in the kitchen and mope, then I might as well watch him run bases and catch balls and slide into home. And then maybe he would remember that I wanted him to slide into me. I didn't want our last night together to be a disaster. But things were not looking up.

33

WAVES IN A STORM

In the living room, I fiddled with the television and the DVD player, and once I had the screen showing the right feed, I dropped on the couch.

The game began, and I spotted Carver on left field, just by the way he moved. At the first sight of him in his uniform, I sat up straight and bit my lip—because, *wow*—he was even more gorgeous in uniform than I had imagined. I often thought baseball uniforms had been designed for the sole purpose of turning men into sex objects. But seeing Carver in one? This was a whole different level of hot.

"Wow, Carver," I said. "You look so…" My voice trailed off because Carver had reappeared on the screen, and I forgot all about what I was saying. When he caught a fly ball in the first inning, I rewound the video so I could watch it again. The way his body moved on a diamond made me wonder if I could jump his bones yet. I glanced over at him, but he wasn't looking at me. He was messing around in the kitchen, fixing something to eat. I turned back to the TV.

When Carver played baseball, he had such a laziness to him, the way a lion can sprawl out and sleep on a rock before a hunt begins. Some people have so much confidence in what they do, they don't seem to care about anything, and that was how Carver played, like everything was a foregone conclusion. He'd wait until the last second to turn up his glove to catch a fly ball, and he'd barely pay attention to what he was doing. He'd be smiling at someone, or listening to someone talking in the stands, or whatever it was that kept him so cool and careless out on the field. You would think he had nothing on the line when he played.

When Carver threw a ball, it shot across the field with the speed of a missile, graceful and smooth and perfectly aimed. He usually threw from his left, but in the fourth inning, he switched his glove hand, and I saw him bare-hand a ball and throw from his right, with the sort of natural talent that explained his switch-hitting.

But this game took place after the accident, and when Carver came up to bat, I watched him strike out twice before he knocked in two runs. As a young rookie moving up in the world, Carver had been an explosive hitter, but the only evidence of that earlier power was his assurance in the batter's box, which was something like a requirement, anyway, when you played for the Majors. I watched him hit a fly ball into left, which was caught, and I saw him hit a grounder that made it to first for the out. Even out at first, walking back to the dugout, he was a man who melted my bones.

He was twenty-six years old in this game, and he already had those streaks of grey in his hair. They were even more visible when he took off his cap. Losing Audrey and Ben, I realized, had put the grey in his hair. Funny that I hadn't figured that out before now.

Carver brought me a sandwich and sat down beside me.

"Thank you," I said, and set my plate on the coffee table.

I hadn't been paying attention to the announcers, but as Carver joined me, a sportscaster was saying, "*And what is going on with the Grizz?* Another lackluster performance today. His fielding is there, but that isn't helping the Tigers. Hard to believe the kid with all those homeruns is barely able to find the ball anymore. What happened to the power hitter who thrived under pressure? It's like he just ran out of talent."

I leapt up, grabbed the remote and switched off the TV.

Carver laughed. He seemed much more relaxed, and sent me a smile. "Nothing I haven't heard before, Mary Jane."

"Maybe so," I said. "But you don't need to hear it right now." I glanced at my sandwich and asked, "Did you eat?"

He shook his head no. "I just needed something to do with my hands. To help myself think."

I nodded, and then quirked an eyebrow at him. "Want to help me do some thinking?" I asked. He caught my gaze, curious, so I leaned over and kissed him. "I've really got a lot on my mind," I said, and kissed him again.

Carver smiled and ran his hands down the sides of my body. His voice remained mild. Hopeful. "When your grant proposal is finished, will you come for a visit?"

I turned away in frustration. Could we not just have sex? Man oh man.

I left the couch and paced around in front of the TV. I couldn't believe he still wanted to talk about seeing each other, when we could be making love. To hell with the talking. I wanted to rip his clothes off.

And as to visiting him: I might not be a professional athlete, but my goals in life were no less important than his. In fact, they were *more* important to me. Because my goals were *mine*.

"It's not just a proposal," I said. "I have to earn funding. Anyone can write a proposal. Not everyone can write one good enough to do anything with."

"I need a window," Carver said. "I need something more than waiting."

I continued to pace with my hands on my hips. "I can't promise a window. I love you, Carver. I love you very much. But I told myself years ago that I was going to escape the Place with No Hope. And it still almost trapped me again. I can't put everything at risk—the kids' schooling, my work, my dreams—when you might find someone else, someone whose life is more compatible with—"

"I won't find someone else," Carver said. Heat flashed through his voice.

I stopped pacing and faced him. I took a deep breath and lowered my hands. "Anything can happen. You know that. You're out in a bar, you meet someone, you hit it off. Of course no one plans those things—"

Carver stood. "I'm not going to stroll into a bar and forget that I love you."

I crossed my arms and stared at the floor. He might. The truth was, he might. But arguing about it wouldn't solve anything.

Carver walked over to me and sank to his knees. He gripped the back of my legs and pressed his cheek to my hip, like he needed something solid to feel. "Tell me we can work this out," he said. "Tell me I'll see you again before the end of the season."

I ran my hands through his hair and took another deep breath, and something hard and brittle in my chest finally decided to soften. I wasn't sure why I was being so rigid. But finding an opening in this situation did help me feel better. "All right, Carver. All right. If I can miss a weekend of work and not lose my job, and if my grant proposal is finished… I'll come for a visit. You might have to buy tickets for everyone—"

"Of course I can do that," and he smiled up at me. He was so happy and relieved that I shivered a little. Maybe our last night together wasn't doomed to be awful.

I cupped his jaw in my hands and rubbed my palms on his stubble, and then I knelt and kissed him. Touching him, tasting him… I felt flames in my skin. Carver tried to slip off my shirt, but I wouldn't let him. I pulled off his though. I removed all of his clothes. I felt such a rush at the sight of him. All that skin.

I placed my hands on his shoulders and pushed him back, pushed him until he realized I wanted him to lie down. So he leaned on his elbows and studied my face for a moment. His chest rose and fell in bursts, since his breathing had quickened. His gaze traveled over my body. Those silver eyes asking me why I hadn't taken my clothes off.

I placed a kiss on his shoulder and said, "Lie down, Carver." I could tell he was fighting this. He wanted to grab me. His muscles flexed, and I braced myself for a pounce.

"Carver," I said, before he leapt up. "This isn't going to kill you." I pushed on his shoulders again. Maybe the full impact of this being our last night together had finally hit him. Maybe he had decided he wanted a throw down, and being docile just didn't fit with his plans.

But I didn't care what he wanted. He'd been moping around tonight and making me wait, and watching him play baseball had not helped at all.

So when he finally lay down, I ran my hands along his body a while. I did whatever I felt like. He kept trying to unzip my jeans, but I wouldn't let him. I took my time undressing. I took my time with everything.

Tomorrow he would board his flight out of Riverdale. And he would be with his boys again, and he would play baseball, and when he fell asleep at night, he would be alone in his bed. And maybe he would find someone to be a cure for his lonesome. To be a mother for his boys. To help him remember he was always full of God's grace. And maybe this other woman would love Carver as much as I did right now.

But tonight, he was mine. All mine.

He pulled me down for a kiss. A hot kiss. Sweet and melting. But I slipped out of his hold. I called the shots. I wanted what I wanted. All that heat in my body. The release I was craving. When I finally perched on his hips, he gripped my thighs with his hands and tipped his head back. He said, "Mary Jane, Mary Jane…" in such a dark, aching voice, and his fingers dug into my thighs deep enough to leave bruises. But I didn't feel any pain, and I didn't stop. His breathing turned ragged, he started to writhe underneath me, and the sounds in his throat were like a caress. I took pleasure in every one of his moans, every twist of his body. He was at the mercy of my love, and my love was not merciful.

I only stopped when he thrashed and bucked his hips, and he clasped my shoulders and pulled me against him. His heart was thumping so hard that it drummed through my body. He ran his hands through my hair and kept saying my name, and his chest rose and fell with each breath like waves in a storm. Several minutes passed before he lay still, before his heart settled down and no longer thumped on my ribcage. I could smell the iron in his skin from the hot mountain water, and I closed my eyes for a moment, feeling heavy and perfect.

Then Carver rolled forward and scooped me up in his arms, and he carried me to his bedroom. He laid me down in the blankets and buried his face in my belly, so that all I could see were the messy tufts of his hair.

"Carver," I said, and I ran my hand along the plane of his shoulders. "What's the matter?" I remembered our night in the vapor cave, when his body had tensed like he had something to tell me, and that was the way he felt now. He was stressed about something. Something other than leaving tomorrow.

He lifted his head and studied my face for a moment, and when he lay down beside me, he wrapped me in both of his arms, kissed the top of my head and the tip of my nose. I knew he was holding back something. Something he had been hiding a long time. Maybe something that explained why his life had been falling apart. Or maybe this was the reason a shadow had crossed his face at the mention of Ben.

Once he shared this with me, I would have to carry it always. And it might not be something I wanted to carry. It might be something I was better avoiding.

I could fall asleep now. I could pretend I didn't notice how anxious he was.

But I kissed him and said, "Tell me."

34

THE WRONG QUESTION

I waited several minutes before I felt Carver start to relax. The tension drained out of him like fizz from a bottle. His voice sounded deeper, but his words were precise. He was committed to sharing this with me. There was no going back.

"My sophomore year in high school, our team hit a winning streak and Ben was on fire. He was a freshman that year, on top of the world, and he talked half the people in Texas into attending our games. He had the mayor, county commissioners, store owners, all my father's coworkers, the women who bought makeup from my mother—anyone Ben could find, he convinced them to come to a game. Our district Representative even made it to one. Ben bragged to everyone that I was on my way to the Majors, and that they could all tell their grandkids one day they'd seen me play back in high school."

Carver linked our fingers together, and it was clear by the tone of his voice that he was as amazed by Ben's prescience about his baseball career now as he had been back then. "Ben's dreams were so powerful that he could make strangers see them.

It was like getting high sometimes, just being around him and listening. By my junior year, we had such a home crowd you'd have thought we were a Minor League team. And of all of the people Ben talked into attending a game, one of them was a girl from my class I'd always been sweet on. Audrey Lynn."

Carver fell quiet a moment. "We dated for two years, and I married her right out of high school. I planned on working part-time that summer, and we shared an apartment with Ben. But I drafted out in June to play for the Braves, so we rented a house in Atlanta, and Ben found his own place. A year after that, Jackson was born. The following summer, we had Christy, and I moved us to New York and played for the Yankees. I had everything I wanted right then: my family, a contract, money to help Ben get into politics." Carver paused, and kind of chuckled at something, perhaps a fleeting memory of how happy he'd been. "I was gone so much that it took me a while to figure out… to figure out that… We had three children together before I was sure… before I even asked her about it… but I think I always knew when it started… when she and Ben… it was the year I signed my first contract… that was when it began."

Carver struggled so much to admit this to me, I thought he'd probably willed himself not to see that affair for as long as he could. He must have been desperately lonely, to finally admit what had happened. I didn't know who to feel sorrier for in this situation—for Carver, for Ben, or for poor Audrey Lynn—because I couldn't imagine loving any other man if I'd been married to Carver. How heartsick did a person have to be, to leave a husband like Carver for the arms of his brother? But then I thought, maybe Audrey had fallen in love with Ben first, before she even knew that Carver was sweet on her and that he was going to ask her to marry him one day. Maybe Audrey started loving Ben on that day when he'd talked her into going to that first ballgame... but when Carver had shown his feelings for her, she'd been too dazzled to say no. In which case, I felt even sorrier for her.

Carver said, "I waited until a night when we were alone... and I asked her where I'd gone wrong... and did she want a divorce... By the time the sun rose, I was convinced she had always loved Ben. And I think she only married me because..."

Carver's voice trailed off into silence, the kind of silence that tells you the sentence will never be finished, so I decided to finish it for him. "...because Ben loved you so much."

I let those words fade away, and then I propped myself up on one elbow to peer down at his face. Carver ran his hand through my hair, pushing my bangs away so he could see my eyes. "Branch Rickey is Ben's little boy," he said softly. "Audrey made me promise never to tell him. She didn't want our boys to think she'd betrayed them, or that she wasn't a good mother. She was so scared I would divorce her, but I never would've quit Audrey. I'd have had to die first, I loved her so much. If I'd been killed in that accident, and could have traded them places, then Audrey would've married Ben. But she wouldn't divorce me for him. And I wouldn't quit my brother, even for stealing my wife."

I tried to put myself in Carver's place, and imagine how I would feel if I learned that my husband had slept with my sister, had conceived a child with her, but didn't want me to divorce him.

I could not imagine keeping a husband like that.

But Carver had gone on with his life... knowing about his brother and Audrey... knowing the truth about Branch. Why had he done that? I searched around for a reason, and then I wondered if Carver had blamed the affair on himself. Maybe he decided he'd been a terrible husband. Or maybe he thought that because Ben had given him so much, how could he ever begrudge his kid brother for taking something from him?

But maybe Carver had also been filled with rage. Before he forgave Audrey and Ben, maybe he cursed them. Maybe he had wished them both dead. And that's why their accident never felt like an accident.

But Carver had not killed his brother and wife. A man who fell asleep at the wheel of a semi had done that. No amount of anger, no sense of betrayal, could have ever caused that to happen. But it was no wonder why Carver had lived with that guilt for so long.

Hanna had been right about life: you had to be brave to be happy. You also had to be brave to feel God's grace.

I leaned down so I could kiss Carver's brow, and then I rolled onto my side so he would turn over and hold me, which he did. "I won't ever tell," I said, referring to the news about Branch. Who his real father was. That had been Ben and Audrey's truth to tell. And they had already chosen.

"I know, Mary Jane." I felt Carver's body grow heavy, like he was falling asleep, and when he spoke again, his voice had dropped even lower. "In those years when I played… as the Grizz… all the attention I had, all those fans… it was so much bigger than me… and when I knew Audrey didn't love me, when I knew she wanted to be at home… home with a man who would be there to love her… I started to hate my whole life."

I kissed Carver's hands and said, "You're wrong about Audrey. She loved you, Carver. She would never have stayed married to you, if she didn't."

He released me and sat up enough to rest his body on his elbow. His voice sounded rougher, more alive now with anguish. "I swore to myself I would never do it again. I swore I'd never find myself… asking my wife… why I wasn't enough."

I rolled onto my back and gazed up at Carver. "Of course you were enough," I said. "You were more than enough. She couldn't help loving Ben. I bet no one could."

Carver closed his eyes. His cheeks were wet with tears, but he didn't wipe them away. I ran my hand along his shoulder, and touched the back of his neck.

"They still left you behind though, didn't they," I said. "I bet you really hate them for that. Leaving you here to go on without them."

The words had the effect I wanted them to: Carver's pain broke, and he laughed. I felt relieved to see him smile, and he opened his eyes again, directing his gaze toward the ceiling.

I asked, "What did you say to him, when you found out?"

"I said he could go to hell. And I wanted to hit him."

"And what did Ben say?"

"Nothing… for a while. And then he finally said he was sorry. And that I should go ahead and hit him."

"Did you?"

"No," Carver laughed. "I never hit my brother. Not since we were kids, fighting over toys."

I rubbed Carver's cheeks with my fingertips, drying his face. "You asked Audrey the wrong question," I said. "You should have asked your wife why she always loved you so much. You should have asked her why she would never have quit you, not even for your brother."

Carver swept me up then and hugged me. Not a gentle hug. It was closer to a bear mauling, with a fierce clumsiness to his grip that was all that remained of his tenderness.

"Mary Jane," he said roughly. "Mary Jane." He eased the strength of his hold, and I breathed a bit easier. "I might never have found you. What if I'd taken that flight? What if I'd spent this week in St. Louis?"

I wriggled loose enough to put my arms around him, so I could hug him back. I rested my cheek on his shoulder, and he squeezed me again.

"I will always love you, Mary Jane."

I planted a kiss on his cheek. Then another and another. I wanted to tell him I loved him. That I would love him forever. That I was so grateful he had gone on with living. That he had listened to his sister and kept playing ball. That he had skipped his flight last weekend and taken me dancing. But those words never came. When I opened my mouth to speak, it wasn't to tell him I loved him.

"I want you to be the Grizz again, Carver. I want you to be who you are."

"I'm not the Grizz anymore," he said thickly. "Ben made the Grizz. And the Grizz died with him."

Which was so untrue. What a lie. What a great, killing curse.

"Ben's body died," I said. "But Ben didn't die. All the best parts of him—everything he created—everything he made—survived. You will always be the Grizz, Carver. You thought you lost your reason to win—but you didn't. You couldn't. You always wanted to win. And you know where Ben lives now—" I tapped my fingers above Carver's heart. "And Audrey. And they're still here in your boys. They will always live on in your children. You never lost your reasons to win. You just keep gaining more."

Carver hugged me against him, his emotions past the point where I could decipher them. Grief and longing and memories... and all of that love. Had he listened to what I said? Or had someone tried to tell him before, and my words fell on deaf ears? Should I have simply told him I loved him, and held him close?

I would never have spoken to him like that if I hadn't done such a poor job myself. At least Carver had kept playing ball. I had quit my dreams altogether. And I hadn't wanted to believe that Hanna was not really gone. That I would always carry her with me. I wouldn't have clung to her broken badge for so long, if I'd been willing to accept such a thing.

So now I was giving Carver the advice that I had needed to hear for myself. Only it had taken an act of violence and the death of an innocent animal to help me understand. For Carver… maybe love was enough. Love and violence were such similar creatures. Powerful. Wordless. Intrinsic to life.

I rested my cheek on Carver's shoulder again, and while I couldn't know what he was thinking, he did not seem upset. He felt far away though, far away from me and this bed. Someplace with his brother, maybe. Someplace where the two of them walked a diamond together, sharing a dream.

And maybe their children were there. Maybe Audrey was, too.

Carver had to return to a place where he still had the power to dream. Only he could ever say where that was.

But I knew where that place was for me: inside of a mountain called my Hole-in-the-Wall, where the heat of the earth filled the air. With Hanna beside me. And years before that… as a child… it was me and the sunshine, and all of those people who brought me their love… and that bright thing called hope.

I closed my eyes, and in the easy quiet that followed, I drifted to sleep. I stirred when Carver moved again, cradling me against him, and he seemed such a gigantic, warm presence beside me that I heard myself murmur, "I called you the bear-man. The first time I saw you."

I felt Carver laugh, a tremor that passed through his body, and I went back to sleep. But then his voice skimmed along the darkness again, finding me in that place between dreaming and waking.

"Will you watch my games, Mary Jane?"

I nestled my cheek against his chest, and felt the steady thump of his heart. "You better want to play pretty bad, if you expect me to watch." I wasn't sure if I said that or not, or if I imagined those words. The lines between joking and seriousness felt all blurred, just like my consciousness. I kept dipping into sleep, and then waking again. But after Carver asked me if I would watch his games, I did fall asleep. A deep sleep.

I dreamed of him though.

That weird stadium dream.

Standing on the diamond. Waiting for a game to begin. The lights on around us. The stars overhead.

Carver in his uniform. Me in my sundress.

Only Carver and I stood near home plate this time. He did not wear his cap or carry a glove. Were we supposed to bat? I glanced around, but there wasn't any equipment. No bats, no helmets, no batting gloves. The dugouts were empty.

I gazed over the diamond, so massive and beautiful. The grass vibrant and green in the stadium lights. The bases gleaming white, waiting for a game to begin.

And then I realized that the stands were full of people this time. So many people—and they were screaming and cheering—but the field was empty. No coaches. No ballplayers. Just Carver. We stood near home, without even holding bats in our hands.

I felt panicky. All those people. The empty diamond. The sense that I was supposed to be doing something. But what was I here to do? Why were they cheering? The noise was a pressure, something almost hurting me. I wanted to run away.

Then I thought, No—Carver was supposed to be doing something. Carver was supposed to be playing.

I turned to him, but he wasn't looking at me. He was staring off above center field, up into the stands. Had he already hit a homerun? Had I missed it?

The scoreboard wasn't lit. The people kept cheering.

Carver smiled and placed his hands on his hips. He seemed three times bigger than me. Larger than life. Where was the pitcher? Where was his bat? Why were these people all cheering?

If Carver had hit a homerun, why wasn't he running the bases? Why wasn't he on his way home?

"Do you have to run?" I asked. My voice sounded so strange in this dream. Warped by the sound of the crowd.

Carver glanced at me then, still smiling. "Not yet."

35

SPLIT OPEN

My strange dream woke me up. When I opened my eyes, I discovered I was alone. The sun had come up, but it was still early. I slipped out of bed to find Carver.

I remembered I was naked. So I took a shirt from his closet, which hung on me like a dress.

I found Carver in the living room. The TV was on, with the sound turned low. He didn't seem to be watching the screen. He heard me get up though, and sent me a smile.

I smiled in return and walked toward the couch.

He'd put another game on. I glanced at the TV and saw he was playing for the Yankees this time, against the Angels. I lay down beside Carver, using his lap as a pillow, and he ran a hand through my hair.

The roar of the crowd on TV was like the sound in my dream, and I wondered if I'd dreamed all those people in the stadium because Carver had been in here watching this game.

After a minute, an announcer said, *"And here is the Grizz stepping up to the plate.* Batting an incredible .421 through the first half of this season. Twenty-three years old, and this man is a cyclone. Some of the pitches he hits, I'd swear he has a crystal ball in the dugout. The highest-paid player with the Yankees this year, Greyson leads the division with RBIs and homeruns. It's simply astounding how much power this guy has. With the Yankees down by two runs, and Ricardo on second, we'll see if the Grizz can close the gap in this game."

Carver combed his fingers through my bangs and said, "Your hair used to be long."

I wasn't sure how he knew this. Maybe one of the kids had shown him a picture. I said, "I cut it. After Hanna died."

"Will you let it grow out again?" he asked.

"Maybe," I said. On the TV, I watched Carver foul his first ball, and then miss the second pitch.

The sportscaster said, "And that's strike two for the Grizz. We'll see if Dianda will get a strike three or not. That last fastball he threw was ninety-six miles per hour…"

The announcer's voice trailed off as Dianda prepared for his pitch. He threw Carver another fastball. Ninety eight miles per hour.

Carver swung. And hit. The fastball sailed out of the park. Tie game.

The sportscaster hollered, the crowd roared, and I found myself smiling. Not just because Carver had hit a homerun. Which was definitely great. Definitely enough to make me smile. But I was also incredibly happy that it had been captured on film. I loved that moments like this were preserved, remembered, and witnessed again. It was the reason why I wanted to film documentaries so badly. To remember a piece of history. To tell a story. To commemorate an event. To create something beautiful.

I felt Carver trace a fingertip along that old scar on my neck. I wondered if he would ask about it again. But he rubbed my back with his thumb, and it felt so good, I closed my eyes.

I wanted to stay awake. I tried. But I was too happy and sleepy to keep myself present.

***

When I opened my eyes, sometime after eleven, I found myself in bed with Carver. He was awake, and he smiled when I tried to sit up. I blinked a few times, and then snuggled against him and put my head on his chest. Sunlight brightened the slits through the blinds, so I knew there was no chance that his flight would be canceled.

"Did you pack yet?" I asked.

"I did," he said.

"Want to take a bath with me?"

He laughed. "I thought you'd want to go skiing again."

"You have to wear your clothes to do that," I huffed, and I left the bed and walked to the bathroom.

Twenty minutes later, I had the bath ready, and Carver came in and felt the water with his hand. "Pretty hot," he said.

"You sure are," I agreed, and he laughed. I wriggled out of his shirt and stepped into the tub. I gave Carver an appreciative smile when he stripped and slid in behind me. He nibbled one side of my neck for a minute, and I nestled against him.

I thought of my dream again, and wondered if Carver believed he would ever hit another homerun. I was about to ask him why he'd put on that game against the Angels, when he asked me, in a tender voice, "When did Hanna die?"

I blinked for a moment. I wasn't surprised by the question. I was surprised by my reaction to it. I didn't flinch. I didn't hurt. It was like a small miracle.

I said, "A year ago. Christmas morning."

"She had cancer?" Carver asked.

"Brain cancer," I said. "It spread to her lungs… her kidneys, her liver, her bladder. All of her lymph nodes. Her bones."

"Sounds… painful," Carver said.

"Yes," I said. "Even with all of that morphine. I know that she hurt."

"Were you with her?" he asked.

"Her aunt didn't want her to die in the house," I said. "So Hanna died in a hospice. I slept on a cot in her room."

"You were still in school?" Carver asked.

"Still in school," I said. "I almost didn't graduate. I was with Hanna in Cincinnati almost my entire fall semester, so I couldn't attend class. But two of my professors let me sign up for independent studies, to keep me on track with my credits. There were so many hours when Hanna was unconscious, those days of just waiting for her body to shut down, and I would read to her. Watching her die wasn't even the hard part though. The hard part came after."

"After she was gone," Carver said.

"I lost my will to go on for a while," I said. "School seemed very… unimportant. Everything seemed unimportant. I destroyed my GPA. I blew off the exam for grad school. I slept on the floor of my room and just barely managed to drag myself to class. I was late all the time. I struggled to write papers. I struggled with everything. I felt like a zombie."

"I'm amazed by you, Mary Jane."

I tipped my head to look at him. "Why's that?"

Carver laughed, like he was shocked I would ask. "By every-thing," he said. "That you grew up the way you did… and went to Swarthmore… and then to lose your best friend like that during your last year of college… My God, Mary Jane. It's amazing that you earned your degree. And then you came home to take care of your family. And you still want to make your film."

I placed a hand on Carver's chest, and left an outline of water on his skin. "I told you I always wanted to escape the Place with No Hope."

"Death kills hope," Carver said.

"People kill hope," I said. "I killed my own dreams. And then I started dreaming again."

We were quiet a long time. I traced the muscles in Carver's arm for a while, remembering how big he had seemed in my dream. How big he seemed now. I felt very primal around him. More animal than person. I wondered if he felt that way when he looked at me.

Carver asked, "Where do you see yourself in ten years?"

"At a black tie awards banquet," I said. "Giving a speech about my latest film project."

Carver grinned and kissed my cheek. "No doubt," he said. "I have no doubt you'll be there."

I smiled for a minute, and then asked, "What about you?"

"I'll be coaching a team," Carver said. "Winning a World Series." He slid his hand from my knee down the length of my thigh. "Would you still love me, if I didn't play ball anymore?"

I laughed. "You will always be a ballplayer, Carver. It's part of your DNA. Coded into your marrow. Stamped into your blood cells." I shifted onto my knees and turned to kiss him. "You could never put on a uniform again, and you would still be a ballplayer. You will always be the Grizz."

He placed his hands near my throat, and then slid his palms along my breasts, down my stomach, and stopped on my hips. He studied my body with a thoughtful expression, and I wondered if he was thinking about being primal with me. I hoped so. But then he said, "You're so thin, Mary Jane. I wish you didn't have to push yourself so hard. Just to get by."

I felt sad he had said this. I was *thin?* I was *just getting by?* Was he trying to insult me?

I slipped out of his hold and left the tub. He watched me leave the bathroom, but he didn't say anything. I walked to his bedroom and hid in his sheets. I buried myself in all of those blankets and pillows and felt a bit better. Carver's skin smelled like white sand and pure heat, and so did his sheets.

I heard water splash. I heard him step out of the tub. Then I heard his voice in the room.

"Want some breakfast?" he asked.

I felt too sullen to answer. I wasn't hungry. Not for food.

The mattress tilted when he sat on the bed. He slid a hand under the blankets and gripped my ankle. "I'll pull you out of there," he said.

I laughed. I tried to yank my ankle free. But Carver held on.

He drew me toward him, and I scrambled to stay hidden. He uncovered my legs though, and I felt his teeth on my thigh, like he was trying to bite me. It tickled.

"Carver!" I yelled. My heart raced and I tried again to break free. But he grabbed my waist and yanked me out of the blankets, and then he dropped to the mattress and pulled me on top of him. He lay with his back on the pillows, gazing up at me.

He ran a thumb along my jaw line, and I thought of the night he had seen me after my teeth had been pulled. When my face had been swollen and red, and I was dressed like a Yeti.

How embarrassing. I hoped that wasn't what crossed his mind now.

I wanted Carver to know I wasn't just getting by. Not anymore. And he didn't need to tell me I looked thin. I could see myself in the mirror.

So when he rubbed my chin with his thumb, I nipped at him, the way a turtle might snap at something. "I'm smaller than you," I said. "But I'm not weak."

Carver smiled. "You're the strongest person I know, Mary Jane. I would never say you were weak."

I felt some relief, hearing this.

"I just meant… I can see your bones," Carver said. "That's all I was trying to say. You're so thin you look brittle. Like a starved ballerina. Nothing but sinew and bone."

I glowered at this. "Ballerinas are beautiful, Carver."

He laughed. "If you say so."

I was shocked. "Who could possibly be prettier than a dancer?"

"You," he said. "You're more beautiful than a dancer."

"But you just said I look starved."

"You do look starved," Carver said.

I felt annoyed. "I'm not starving myself."

He laughed again. "I know."

"Then what are you trying to say?"

"That I wish you had some meat on your bones," Carver said. He squeezed my thighs. "More muscle. Enough to fill you out a bit more."

"Are you trying to give me a complex?"

Carver laughed. "I'm trying to give myself more to hold onto in bed."

"Well, take it or leave it, Carver. This is all you get."

He sat up and hugged me and pulled me on top of him. "I'll take it," he said.

I lay on his chest for a while, and he spread his hands across my back and ran his palms down my skin… and eventually, his fingertips found that old scar on my neck.

I knew he would ask. I braced myself. But he formed a new question this time.

"Did your father give you this scar?"

"No," I said. I found the question repulsive. But I knew that if I had told Carver the truth to begin with, he would never have asked me this. So I kept my voice neutral. "My father never laid a hand on me."

"Where is he?" Carver asked. "Does he live in Colorado?"

"He died in Colorado," I said. "In Denver. He stole a shipment of jewelry and lied about how much it was worth. Some men killed him over it. They stabbed him."

"Your father was a thief?"

"A very good one," I said. "But a miserable liar."

"Did you ever help him on jobs?" Carver asked.

I almost laughed at the idea. "My father had no honor. But he loved me. He loved me too much for that."

Carver kissed the top of my head. "I don't think I will ever understand you, Mary Jane. You're so far out of my league, I worry I won't ever catch up."

I laughed. "You play for the majors, and I'm out of your league."

Carver chuckled and ran his hands down my back. "That's right."

I caught sight of the clock on the table, and realized it was almost one.

Carver would board his flight in three hours.

In three hours, he'd be gone.

I suddenly wanted to panic. The idea of saying goodbye made me lightheaded. And frightened. I didn't want him to go.

I sat up enough to give Carver a kiss. An urgent kiss. My mind raced.

I wanted to make love one more time. But I knew I really wanted to keep him forever. I wanted to wake up every morning and find him beside me. I wanted his body, his love. All of his tenderness.

I plucked his hands from my shoulders and moved them over my breasts.

I felt a jolt in his body, and then he rolled me beneath him and pushed me down in the sheets.

My panic subsided. I stopped feeling so frightened.

I did have his love. I did have his tenderness. There was no forever. There was only right now.

He leaned down to kiss me again. Kiss me and touch me like he would never let go. I sighed with pleasure and relief when I linked my arms around his shoulders. I wrapped my legs around his hips.

He was mine again now. Aching, split open, and feverish. Mine.

36

FLYING

By the time Carver and I were dressed and ready to leave the house, I was starving. It was two o'clock, and as we opened the doors to the Lincoln, I said, "Wait—don't you want to call a cab?"

He said, "No, we'll just drive."

"But the Lincoln—"

Carver smiled and said, "Come on and hop in. I'm hungry."

So I guessed that he wanted me to drive the Navigator back here and park it, which was fine. I didn't want to wait around on a cab, anyway.

Carver drove us to a place called Annabelle's, which I had never patronized before because the prices were outrageous. I was glad I was wearing my khakis and my favorite sweater, as most of the people in Annabelle's wore business casual. Carver had dressed in slacks and a collared shirt for his flight, and we were on our way to our table when a man in a sports jacket came over and cried, "Carver Greyson! How are you, old man?" and pumped Carver's hand like they might want to arm wrestle later.

"Fine, Dale," Carver said. "How are you?"

"Spring training next month," Dale beamed. "Won't be long now." He was taller than me, but he still had to look up at Carver. He had a big mustache and dirty blond hair. "Clarissa came by to see me last week," Dale added.

"I'm flying out to meet her today," Carver said. "She took the kids to Disneyland."

"And you didn't go with them?" Dale laughed. Then he turned to me and asked, "Who's this pretty young lady?"

Carver grinned and said, "This is Mary Jane Logan," so Dale and I shook hands. "Mary Jane, this is Dale—"

"Lehman," Dale added.

"He owns the Ford dealership in town," Carver finished.

"It's a pleasure to meet you," Dale said. Then he told Carver, "I'm going to tell Suzanne that I saw you. Good luck with your season." He waved once in farewell and returned to another area in the restaurant.

When we arrived at our table, Carver pulled out my chair and waited to push me in like a gentleman.

"I think that man's probably one of the biggest busybodies in the entire free world," he said. "But he does a good job with his dealership. If you have any trouble with the Lincoln, just take it to him."

I cocked my head slightly and said, "Carver, I drive a Buick."

He took his keys from his pocket and tossed them to me. "Now you have a Lincoln."

I felt my heart slow down and then stop. I glanced at the keys in my hand and felt too stunned to speak. I gave Carver my best what-in-the-hell-is-*wrong*-with-you?? look.

He laughed and picked up my hands, keys and all. "Take it, Mary Jane. You need a better vehicle to drive your family in.

Something big enough to fit everyone. Something with enough seatbelts. At least let me do this for you. I wanted to surprise you at the airport, but… Please don't look at me like that." He kissed the tops of my hands.

I sucked in my breath, dropped the keys on the table, and pulled my hands out of reach.

Carver looked worried. "It would just sit in the garage, Mary Jane. Waiting for Clarissa's friends to visit the house—and they can rent their own cars this year. If you take the Lincoln to drive your family in, Gus can have your Buick when he gets his driver's license. And if Gus has his own car, you'll have someone who can help you get groceries and take care of things. Someone to help free up your time so you can work on your grant proposal."

I stared at the keys again, so torn up inside I didn't know what to do.

"Please take the Lincoln," Carver said. "I will worry about you so much less… if I know you're at least… in a vehicle that… Oh, Mary Jane. I can't stand when you look at me like that."

"I don't need you to worry about me," I said.

"I know," he sighed. "I know I don't need to worry."

I poked the keys on the table.

What had I worried he would leave me?

A diamond necklace.

A diamond necklace, I could have turned down in a heartbeat.

But a vehicle? Something I could drive all the kids and Gandhi in? And Mom? Something with enough seatbelts for everyone, something that I never had to worry about breaking down?

He had picked the right tactic with me, bringing up my family like that.

Where the kids were concerned, I lost all my pride.

Damn it to hell.

I didn't see much difference between taking a man's money or taking a vehicle. They were equally property. Property gained for something I had given him freely. But maybe there was a way around this dilemma.

"I could borrow it," I said. "And when you come back to Riverdale, I can return it to you."

Carver studied my face a long moment. "All right," he said gently. "I'll come back for it then."

I knew Carver would never take this Lincoln from me. I also knew that I could leave it parked at his house, and force him to deal with it later. He could buy twenty more Lincoln Navigators right now, if he wanted to. This did not make me feel any better.

Our server arrived at that moment, looking harried. "I'm so sorry to keep you waiting!" she chirped. "Can I take your order?" So Carver and I ordered, and then he leveled his gaze at me.

"I want to see you again before spring training starts."

I thought about repeating what I told him last night. About needing time for my grant proposal. Needing time to follow my dreams. But he'd heard those arguments. And we were back here again.

So I went with levity.

"I already told you I need a man with more muscle."

This made him chuckle. "I bet if I showed up on your doorstep next month, you'd take me in."

"I own a gun," I said flatly. "So you had better not try it."

Carver started laughing again. Then he tried to plead with me. "I'll make sure you won't miss any work—"

I cut him a look, though I kept my voice light. "I don't think so."

He ran his hands through his hair, and he seemed pretty stressed. I muttered, "Buck up, or I'm taking those keys and ditching you here," and he laughed again.

"Mary Jane," he said, though it was more like a sigh. "I don't want to wait that long."

"You're not going to be *waiting*," I reasoned. "You're going to be pumping iron. And taking batting practice. You don't need me around to do that."

Carver leaned an arm on the table and searched over my face. "A week was never enough."

"We get what we get," I said softly.

"I know," Carver said.

Our lunch arrived and I ate mine with gusto, but Carver seemed a lot less hungry than he had earlier. When the bill arrived, he left cash on the table, while I scooped up the keys and said, "I'll drive," with a grin. I still wasn't sure that "borrowing" Carver's vehicle was the right thing to do, but having a way to tease him at the moment was nice.

He held the door for me as we left, and when we arrived at the Navigator, he grabbed me and kissed me.

I had my arms around his neck in an instant, I was so into that kiss, but then I pushed him away and said, "Stop it, Carver. I'm not changing my mind," and stalked around to the driver's side door. I started the Lincoln and listened to the engine purr for a moment, while Carver sat smiling beside me, looking more amused than upset.

"You really won't have me back?" he asked.

"When your season is over," I said. "I'm all yours."

***

When I parked in front of the airport, I stepped out of the Lincoln to tell Carver goodbye.

We stood in the same place where we'd been a week ago. But I was not the same person. And neither was he.

Carver left his carry-on bag on the seat, so his arms were free when he hugged me. We kissed one last time.

"I love you, Carver."

He embraced me like he had that first time, standing on the stairs outside my apartment. He swept me up off my feet.

"I love you, Mary Jane."

He wore his dark woolen coat with the long black scarf. His body so familiar to me that it hurt to let go. When he finally released me, he picked up his bag, kissed my cheek, and walked through the sliding doors into the airport.

I tucked my hands in my pockets, and turned my gaze to the Rocky Mountains. The peaks were brilliant with snow, the winter sky cloudless and purpling as the sun approached the horizon.

I thought of my goodbye to Hanna on Christmas. *I love you, I love you, I love you.* And now I had used those words to say farewell to Carver.

I walked around to the driver's side door and climbed in the Lincoln. It was the first time I'd been in the vehicle without Carver. I glanced at the backseat where we'd sat talking on Friday. I wished he could walk out of the airport again. Ask me for a ride to The Summit. Promise me he wasn't a serial killer. Tell me that we should go dancing.

I felt very alone right now. Very small.

But this was not a Square One.

I had a future again. I had a vision for myself that pulled me forward, pulled me with such force that I wondered how I had ever felt stuck. How I had ever believed I was so weak and defeated that all I could do was crawl.

And maybe, I realized, I had gotten good at goodbyes. I would love Hanna forever. And I would love Carver forever. And love could mean a farewell, but it was never the end. Love was momentum. It was the force that kept pulling me forward. Into my vision. Into my future. Not so I could crawl. But so I could fly.

I turned the key in the ignition and listened to the engine a minute. I gazed over the display on the dash, and something struck me—so I jumped out of the Lincoln. I ran to the back door and threw it open—and there were the bags of Carver's baseball equipment. I knew he hadn't simply forgotten those bags. He had left his gear for the kids.

I leaned my face on the door for a moment. Even though Carver was gone, I felt so incredibly happy. No matter what happened between us—if I never saw Carver again, and we weren't meant to last—he had shared with my family the best part of himself.

I shut the door, and my knees wobbled a little from the rush of emotions, but I managed to return to the driver's seat and head home without incident. I thought of Carver on his flight. I wondered if he talked to the people around him. I wondered if they asked him what he did for a living, and how he would answer. I wondered if he missed me as much as I missed him.

By the time I reached my apartment, it was almost five o'clock. I opened the front door and stepped inside, and found Landon and Janine in my home.

Janine smirked when she saw me, and then laughed. A dirty little laugh that was filled with contempt. I crossed my arms and turned to my brother.

"What are you doing here, Landon?"

37

SPLITS-VILLE

"What am *I* doing here?" Landon scoffed. "Man, you've got some nerve."

The kids sat on the floor. Landon and Janine had the couch. Mom was wandering around with a deflated balloon in her hand, and Steve was at the dining table, worrying one of his chess pieces in his hands. Gandhi padded over to lick my fingers. I petted his head a few times.

Landon was giving me his most pissed-off expression as he said, "Some fucking *linebacker* shows up at Tom's house on Thursday—*pays off the taxes*, even stops by the *courthouse* and lays down *this year's* fucking bill, so I come here to see what's going on, and Richard tells me he's some *Major League* fucking *ballplayer??* What the hell, Mary Jane? A *ballplayer?* You figure the guy can't get enough at a *strip club*, you might as well throw yourself at him? Join the crowd and be some fucking groupie?"

While Landon was yelling, I covered my face. I wasn't ready for this. I wasn't ready to have all this dropped on me at once.

Carver had paid the property taxes?

How had he found out about the past due property tax?

Had he gone through my paperwork? Had he asked the kids questions?

My heart pounded so fast I felt faint. I leaned my back against the door and focused on not blacking out.

I had to get Landon out of my house. Regardless of whatever Carver had done—if he really had gone behind my back and paid this bill—I knew Landon was only furious because he'd wanted Tom Morbun to buy him a truck. Creepy Tom Morbun. I'd never mentioned Landon's deal with Tom to Carver. Why the hell would I?

The whole situation made me sick. I suddenly wanted to throw up.

But the kids were all watching me. And Steve. And that wretched Janine. I wasn't going to stand here and fall apart in front of Janine.

I lowered my hands, and struggled to keep my voice level. Determined. "He fell in love with me, Landon. So if he paid off the taxes, I'm glad. It's one less thing to have to worry about."

Did I mean that? Wasn't paying a woman's property tax just another way of handing her cash? Or a diamond necklace? Or a car? Was I a hooker now? God, I felt horrible. What was this teaching the kids? That Mom had been right all along—that it was up to a man to step in and pay all the bills—was this what I was showing them? Did they think I'd spent the week with Carver so he would give us this money, and save our house?

The idea that the kids would think this made me want to black out again.

I wished I could run away, run away from all of this.

Landon was so pissed to lose out on that truck, he'd driven all the way to Riverdale to lay into me. "Are you for *real?* Because you never had to pay off that money, I already had it worked out—"

I raised my voice. "You didn't have shit worked out, Landon. Get out of my house."

Landon stood and held up his fist, and it was times like these I was glad I owned a gun.

"You think you're so fucking *smart*," Landon shouted. "You think you've got some fucking diploma, you can tell us all what to do. You even drag these kids down here, like some pack of dogs—"

I said, "The high school *closed*. You can take that up with Bunker Wilson."

Landon kept trying to steamroller me though. "And now you're *fucking around* with these men down here, telling them to pay our fucking property tax and then sucking them off—"

I threw open the front door and shouted, "*Get out!*"

As soon as I yelled, Mom and Gandhi went to hide in the kitchen. Steve stood up, but he seemed ready to pee his pants. The kids were cowering on the floor. They knew what Landon could do when he decided to hit you. I was lucky I still had all my teeth. William had lost two of his in a fight with Landon one time, and Jeff had had his nose broken.

I pointed out the door and shouted, "I'm not *sleeping around!* So don't trouble yourself protecting my *honor*. Just get out!" I could see Janine standing and smirking at me, like Landon's evil shadow.

"You're just some fucking *dog*," Landon bellowed. "Just some fucking dog after any *prick* with some money—"

I wanted to grab Landon bodily and hurl him out of my house, but the second I laid a hand on him, we'd be in a fight. And Landon had Janine here to help him, so I knew I would lose. I couldn't touch him. I had to go to work at Happy Garden tomorrow, and I wasn't showing up with a couple of black eyes or a busted nose. That job was hell enough on me, even when I wasn't in physical pain.

So I stepped away from the door and waited for Landon to leave.

"*Get out*," I yelled, and when Landon finally left, Janine stood in the doorway a moment.

"I bet you were just *begging* him for it," she laughed, and I grabbed the door and swung it against her. The force of it knocked her outside, and I slammed the door shut and latched the deadbolt before Landon could hurt me.

He beat the door with his fist though, and screamed, "You *are* a fucking *whore, Mary Jane!* You *fucking cunt!*"

I waited for Landon to stop pounding the door, and listened for the sound of his feet on the stairs. A minute later, I heard an explosion of shattering glass, and figured that Landon had broken one of the windows on my Buick. I sat down in the armchair and dropped my head in my hands.

After ten minutes of silence, in which nobody moved, Mia came to the armchair and curled up in my lap. She wrapped her arms around my neck and rested her cheek on my shoulder.

"You okay, Mary Jane?" she asked softly.

"Sure, I'm all right," I said.

She sat with me for a while, and then she asked, "Did Carver leave?"

I leaned back in the chair and put my arm around her. "Of course he left, baby," I sighed. "He had to go see his boys."

"Is he ever coming back?" Mia asked.

I felt my voice waver. "I don't know." My body seemed so weak at this moment, I almost trembled. When I realized how sad Mia was though, I kissed her brow and told her, "He might come back."

She released her breath like she'd been holding it in for a while. Mia wanted to believe Carver would come back so badly, I could see it in her face like a bruise.

I glanced around at all of the kids and asked, in a cool, even tone, "How did Carver find out about our property tax?"

Four heads dropped and stared at the floor.

Mom poked her head out of the kitchen and looked at me, still holding that deflated balloon. "Tom Morbun was here one night. With flowers."

I was almost too shocked to ask, "*What?*"

Mia hurried to explain. "We forgot to tell you, Mary Jane. We're sorry. Tom wasn't here very long. And I threw those flowers in the dumpster."

"It was the day Carver took us out after school to play baseball," Ethan said. "We were putting our shoes on to leave, and Tom knocked on the door. Carver didn't talk to him at all. Richard and Mom did."

I felt horrified. Too numb to speak.

Mom said, "I told Carver you and Tom had a deal. *And that's all.* I never said what. I never told him one word about that property tax. So you can't blame this on me."

My stomach lurched like someone had punched me. I put Mia down and stood. I needed to be on my feet or I would be ill.

Ethan was frowning at Mom as he said, "We told Carver that you and Tom did not have a deal. But Richard said you were making sure Tom didn't take our house. That must be how Carver found out. We never said anything about the property tax."

"Tom can't take our house," Mom snapped. "That's a bunch of shit. Tom doesn't even *need* the money. So he can't take the house."

Richard lost his temper and yelled at Mom. "It's not about needing the money! Goddamn it! You don't even know what you're talking about!"

Richard knew he shouldn't be yelling at his mother like that. But Richard yelled at everyone when he was mad at himself. And he knew he'd told Carver something I hadn't wanted him to. I could tell Richard felt bad about that.

"Why didn't you tell me?" I asked him.

Ethan answered. "We forgot. We all went to play baseball, and just forgot."

But Carver hadn't forgotten. He could have said something to me. He could have asked me about Tom. He hadn't breathed one word about it though. Not one word.

And Landon had said Carver had gone to Tom's house. And to the courthouse in Goldking. Carver had done all of that, had paid all that money, and failed to mention it to me.

What would I say to him now? How was I supposed to react? I had told him I did not want his money. And still he had done this.

"You want me to start dinner?" Mia asked.

"Sure," I said, and she slid to her feet and walked to the kitchen. She had to squeeze past Mom, who was standing in the doorway, smacking her hands on that balloon. I guessed she liked the sound it was making. I sat down in the armchair again.

Richard brought something to me, and held out his hand. I glanced up at his face before I reached out to take it.

"I found this in the cupboard," he said. "About an hour ago."

I thought he was handing me a video game, but I looked down and saw a brand new iPhone, shiny and white. The screen held one text message: *I miss you, sonny.* My poor heart tried to beat faster, despite how worn down I felt, despite how stunned I was to see this phone.

"It was underneath your diploma," Richard said. "You think Carver put it in there?"

"I'm sure he did," I said.

"Who's sonny?" he asked.

I sort of laughed and said, "Why don't you go and help Mia?" So Richard went off to the kitchen, and then I asked Ethan to tell me about their day. I wanted to make sure they'd walked Gandhi and eaten lunch, and he told me they had.

Ethan still looked shaken though, so I said, "Landon's pretty scary, huh?" and Ethan hid his face in his hands. He seemed ready to cry.

He mumbled, "I shouldn't have let him in."

I patted his shoulder and said, "Don't worry about it. I might've let him in, too."

***

I'd never been able to afford a cell phone before. As I stared at the screen that evening, I wondered what I should say to Carver.

I wanted to call him. I wanted to hear his voice. I wanted him to explain why he'd paid that property tax.

But I didn't call him. I tucked the phone in my pocket before dinner was ready. Then I went to check on the Buick.

Landon had smashed in a back passenger window. I'd have to vacuum the interior tomorrow, but at least I could sweep up all the broken glass on the asphalt right away. I taped a garbage bag over the hole. That was the best I could do until I had the money to fix it.

After supper, I sent Richard and Gus downstairs to wash laundry, Mia cleaned the bedroom, Gus vacuumed, and Ethan scrubbed out the tub. It was a typical Sunday night.

Except for the phone in my pocket.

I took Gandhi for a walk. I still didn't call Carver.

After the kids went to bed, I finally sent him a text.

Landon was here when I came home today. He told me you paid the property tax. Why did you do that?

It was an hour earlier in San Diego. Only ten o'clock, not eleven. I wondered what Clarissa's beach house looked like. I wondered if Carver could see the ocean. I wondered if his boys were in bed yet.

He sent me a response within seconds.

I paid that tax because I could.

I frowned and typed, *I told you I didn't want your money.*

I didn't give you any money, Carver texted. *That bill was in Gilly Preston's name. I paid the tax for your mother.*

Well, he was right about the name on the bill. The house in Goldking was in Mom's name.

I typed: *I never made a deal with Tom.*

I know, Mary Jane.

Then my phone rang, and I answered.

"Hi, Carver." The words caught in my throat.

"Hi," he said. "Are you angry with me?"

Just the sound of his voice made tears well up in my eyes. I wiped them away. "I don't know. Yes."

"What happened with your brother?"

"He was upset."

"Why?" Carver asked. "Doesn't he live in that house?"

How did he know this? "Did the kids tell you that?"

"Your mother did," Carver said. "She wanted me to know all about… your three older brothers." His tone implied he didn't know what to make of these siblings.

"She's very proud of them," I said.

"I gathered that," Carver said. "So why was your brother upset?"

"Because Tom was going to buy him a truck."

"If Landon paid off the taxes?" Carver asked.

I said, "Tom never expected that bill to be paid. Landon told him… I mean, Landon thought he could convince me to…" I almost couldn't get the words out. I struggled to finish. "I was supposed to make it worth Tom's while to forgive the debt."

Carver didn't say anything for a long time. I didn't know what to make of his silence. Just that he knew what kind of family I had now. I would have rather told him the truth about my father again than share anything about Landon. My brother's behavior seemed far more barbaric.

"Did your brother do something to you?" Carver asked. "Should I come back?"

"I'm fine," I said. "I'll be fine."

"You don't sound fine."

"Well, I am."

"Your mother gave me the paperwork," Carver said. "One night when we were waiting for you. I never would have gone through your things."

I didn't say anything, though I felt relieved to hear this.

He said, "Now I wish I had told you."

I felt tears in my eyes again, and brushed them away. "Why didn't you?"

He sighed. "Because I wanted to help you. Help your family. Not because you needed my charity. But because it makes me sad that you're doing this all by yourself."

I heard a young boy call, "*Dad! Dad! Come look at this!*" on the other end of the line. Then I heard the boy squeal and laugh, like Carver had scooped him up.

"I should go," I said quickly. "I have things to take care of."

"Will you call again later?" he asked.

"Not tonight," I said.

The boy had fallen quiet. So had Carver.

"I'm glad you're back with your boys."

"I love you," Carver said. "I miss you."

The boy asked, "*Who are you talking to? Aunt Deedee?*"

Carver told him, "My friend Mary Jane."

I tried to picture them. Carver and his son. In a pretty house by the sea. With hardwood floors and white curtains and book-shelves in the walls.

They seemed so far away. So far away from a place where brothers smashed out car windows in rages. Where old men brokered deals with young women because they wanted to know what it would feel like to sleep with their daughters.

"I love you, Carver," I said, and ended the call.

***

When my alarm went off the next morning, I still wasn't sure what to do about the property tax.

I knew that Carver, like Tom Morbun, would not suffer any consequences over this money. Spending money when you had plenty in the bank was easy.

Taking money from someone when you were broke was not.

And mixing sex with money felt so abhorrent to me, that it didn't even matter that my mother's name had been on the paperwork for the property tax. I had still paid this bill through-out college. It was the biggest reason I had student loans—and I was paying those off as well. I'd been sending Tom two hundred dollars each month, the same amount I paid on my loans. I knew he'd been hoping I would get so worn down, I'd take him up on his offer.

But I was Mary Jane Logan. I did not have sex with men for money.

My mother did.

But I was not my mother.

It was hard enough that I had allowed myself to borrow Carver's vehicle. And use the phone he had left.

For him to go around me and pay the property tax was too much.

So in the ledger where I kept track of my student loan debt and the outstanding property tax, I cleared the old entries for Tom Morbun and the Goldking County Treasurer. I wrote a new total beneath Carver Greyson's name: $6,142.75.

Then I slammed the notebook shut and pushed it away.

I left the table and woke the kids up for school. I went to work.

Later, on my way home from Happy Garden, I drove to the library. I checked out every book I could find on how to apply for grant money.

I might not have six thousand dollars to clear that debt to Carver, but I could certainly get moving on writing my grant proposal.

At home, I made dinner and the kids did their homework.

My phone chirped. I didn't look at the screen. I switched the phone off.

I wasn't sure who I was punishing more. Carver… or myself.

While the kids played chess with Steve after supper, I sat at the table and started reading my books.

I stopped when it was time to put the kids to bed. Then I returned to the table and read until midnight.

Once upon a time, I'd been a girl who lived with grit and denial. And I had wanted a man who would love me.

But love brought new problems. Love complicated everything.

And as to denial, I wasn't getting along with that old buddy of mine. He and I were in splits-ville, for sure.

Which left me my grit. And I had more of that now. A lot more.

38

SILENCE AND MAGIC

For the rest of January, I worked at Happy Garden and The Summit, the kids went to school, and every night, Carver texted me. And the first text always read: *Please forgive me. I didn't mean to upset you.*

Then he would send: *I missed you today.*

I typically responded by typing out: *You'd better be pumping some iron.*

He sent me other messages.

I'm sorry.

I wish I knew how to fix this.

Please call, Mary Jane. I miss the sound of your voice.

But I couldn't lift my spirits enough to call. Or tell him anything beyond my hopes that he was putting on weight and getting back to his hitting size.

I wished Carver had just listened to me when I returned his six hundred dollars. Because now I owed him six thousand, and owing money like that made me feel weak.

I had to remind myself I would take care of all this. These bills, my film project, making sure the kids finished school. I would strive for the things I wanted in life—and I would find success on my terms. In a way that made me feel strong.

I didn't hate Carver. I didn't even blame him, really, for what he had done. Most people borrowed money for college to pay for *college*… not to pay their mother's property tax and utility bills.

But there were plenty of people who lived the way I did. Maybe Carver didn't understand that because he had grown up in a world where parents took care of themselves. Which was why I couldn't be angry with him, but also why I was dragging my feet calling him back.

So here was the tired, shabby truth again, inviting herself into a life where she was unwanted. But I had a new deal with the truth. I didn't kick her out of my house anymore.

But it still took me a long time to figure out how to explain this to Carver.

Weeks, actually. It took me three weeks.

But I forced myself to try one night. I put the kids to bed and sat on the living room couch. I started a text:

My mother never paid her property tax. Her great-uncle left her that house five years ago. Before that, my mom needed a boyfriend or husband to keep a roof over her head.

I stared at the screen, gathering strength for what I needed to say. *When I was young, we lived in a car for a year. A 1981 Chevy Impala. Me, Mom, Landon, William, and Jeff. And then Mom met Dole, and we moved into his house. But that year in the car was the scariest time of my life.*

I sent Carver this message, and then I composed a second one.

You wouldn't have known I always paid the property tax. And you couldn't have known how much I fear being homeless. But I do. I never want the kids to be homeless. And I never want to be like my mother.

I read over this second text and realized I had never shared this with anyone before. Not even Hanna. With Hanna, there had been an understanding. A way of knowing between us that didn't need words. She and I… we knew the same pain. Pain we didn't discuss. We communicated history in body language, in silences, in the things that made us laugh. Some horror is only funny within a certain context of hell. And Hanna and I always got the joke. We had known the same hell.

I had always hidden myself. From everyone. Even Hanna. Only with Hanna, it didn't matter. She had been able to read me. And I could read her.

But I wasn't hiding now. I was about to tell Carver what I feared most in the world. And until a few seconds ago, I hadn't even known what it was. Not consciously. Not with words.

I had spent my whole life running from it. But I'd never actually turned and faced it.

And now I was looking right at it. There on this screen. I held it in my hands. And it was just a few words. A few words that held all of my fear. My horror. My despair.

And it was not being homeless. If I was ever homeless again, I knew I could survive it, because I already had.

I wasn't terrified of being homeless.

I was terrified I would turn into my mother. I was terrified. Because turning into my mother meant I would die. Not my body, but my soul. My faith in myself. My love for myself. My hope. Those were the things I would lose.

I had told Tuffy's mother the truth. A parent who had no respect for herself… taught her children not to have respect for her, either.

I still loved my mother. But that was love. Love and compassion did not occupy the same place respect did.

Respect had a code. And I could not love myself if I didn't live by that code. Because those were the rules. That was the deal I had made to survive. And not just survive, but to *thrive*.

I read over my message for Carver again.

I still wasn't sure if I should send this or not.

A tremor passed through my body. My hands shook.

I was about to tell Carver my deepest fear. And fear was a weapon. A weapon much more powerful than a gun.

I had loaded Ravi and fired bullets plenty of times. But I'd never loaded a gun like this. Why would I ever want someone to know something so dangerous? Something they could use against me. Something to hurt me. Life was so full of pain. Overflowing with pain. So why would I give anyone the ability to hurt me even more?

I put the phone down, and started to cry. I pressed my hands to my face, and I fought to hold back those tears a long time. But I had cracked something open inside me, and the tears kept falling.

Between fear and love, I always knew which one was stronger. But sometimes I didn't think clearly.

I could delete this message. Or I could send it to Carver.

My phone rang. I glanced at the screen and saw Carver's number.

I didn't answer. I couldn't have spoken to him, anyway, when I was crying like this.

But I read my text one last time. I took a deep breath. And I sent it.

Maybe I wasn't as strong as I wanted to be. Maybe sharing my fears made me weak. Maybe I ought to still be protecting myself. Because Carver could hurt me now. Really hurt me. And I already hurt. I was sitting here, crying over nothing, which was the worst kind of hurt I could be. Carver had already bruised me when he'd been trying to help me. And now I had loaded a gun and put it into his hand, and he could pull the trigger anytime. Anytime.

I hated that I loved him so much. I hated risking all of this pain for something that might not even work.

The phone rang. I saw Carver's number again.

I switched the phone off.

Here was the truth: I was gutless. And tired. I wiped my face dry and stopped crying.

I had to find the place inside me that overcame fear. The place where I asked myself, *So what, Mary Jane? What's the worst that can happen? You turn into your mother? You lose all respect for yourself? Is that the worst that can happen?*

The answer was *yes*. That *was* the worst that could happen. And I could not let it go.

I was going to keep my self-respect. And the second Carver told me, *Oh, Mary Jane, you're overreacting. It's only money. You're blowing this out of proportion*—I would smash this phone he had given me, and be done. Done trying. Done with him. I wouldn't even care what he did with himself. If he quit baseball, if he found someone else, if he started hitting again.

I could never be with a man who took my gun and pulled the trigger. A man like that was not worth my love.

Maybe Carver was calling to tell me that now: that I was overreacting. Blowing things out of proportion. And when I answered the phone and heard him trivialize my fear—heard him trivialize *me*—then I would know we were done.

Or maybe he was just calling to tell me he loved me. That he hadn't understood that he'd been paying my bill. Even if it was in my mother's name.

Whatever Carver wanted to tell me, I was too scared to find out.

I left the phone off.

✳✳✳

On the last day of January, I had a long talk with Steve. I knew he was happy living in my crowded little apartment, and did not want to leave.

I didn't mind that he was still living with me. He was actually a huge help to me now, assisting the kids with their homework, and driving Ethan to basketball practice and games. Steve paid for a lot of groceries, too. He bought fresh fruit and vegetables, so many that the fridge and countertops were always loaded, and expensive things like unsalted almonds and cashews and Tillamook cheddar cheese—expensive items I could never afford on my own. Crock-Pots of rice and beans became a food of the past. I was addicted to salads, and I made them all the time.

The kids complained the first night, and I told them, "This is what Carver eats." Which was true. He always ate healthy, and now that he was trying to put weight on again, his diet was all superfood smoothies and protein shakes—and this information, thank goodness, made the kids stop their grumbling.

I was so grateful to have all this fresh food in my house, and not just live on beans and bananas and apples and eggs anymore. I knew Steve bought all these groceries for me in exchange for putting him up, and in hopes I'd let him stay. He liked being with my family, and I guessed he felt he belonged. He was a help to the kids, and to me, and my mother. He had friends to play chess

384

with. And he joined the kids for baseball on the weekends, when he wasn't at work.

So after we had our talk, I told Steve, "As long as you keep helping around the house, you're welcome to stay." I thought this was a pretty square deal, and so did Steve. He stayed.

Steve wasn't the only one who had a sunnier outlook on life. The kids were different now, too. Our homework battles had stopped. They sat down and did their assignments with minimal prodding, sometimes without any reminders at all, and they talked about baseball while they worked. They told each other *Remember when?* stories about Carver, and repeated things he had said, or recalled all of his antics at the community center. Sometimes Richard would get to laughing so hard, he'd fall out of his chair, and then Mia would fall out of her chair, too. The *Remember when?* game could last hours, all through dinner and homework and putting the dishes away. The kids often went to sleep at night still playing this game.

They were trying to conjure him back, of course. Tell enough stories, and he might reappear. I knew magic when I saw it.

But even if Carver and I didn't work out as a couple, practicing magic was never a bad thing. The kids had discovered a purpose in schoolwork outside of the work in itself—which was the whole point of education. I hadn't been able to teach them this. But I was grateful someone had. Someone I still loved very much.

39

AN ACT OF PRECISION

On Valentine's Day, I came home from work to find three *huge* vases of roses on the dining room table. Two of the vases held pink roses, and one held red. Mia jumped around like a spaz, and hugged me as soon as I walked through the door.

She pointed to a vase of pink roses. "Carver sent me those!" she yelled, and she held up a card. "See, Mary Jane? *To Mia*," she read. "*Beautiful flowers for a beautiful girl. I hope you're still playing baseball!*" She burst into that half-roar, half-giggle she used when she was really excited. "I want to take them to my room—can I?"

I said, "Sure," so Mia grabbed her vase off the table and high-tailed it to the bedroom. Those flowers were bigger than she was.

I put down my bag and pulled off my coat. Mom stepped out of the bathroom, and I guessed she'd been smoking a joint, since she looked spacier than usual and her makeup was perfect. She held a card in one hand—a card like the one Mia had shown me.

"How much money do you think these are worth?" Mom asked, and she touched the other vase of pink roses. I assumed those must be hers, and Mom wanted to know how much money Carver had spent on her. How much *did* a man spend on a vase of four dozen pink roses on Valentine's day?

"A lot," I said.

"More than the balloons I gave you?" she asked.

"Definitely," I said.

Mom smiled and giggled and bent her head to smell her flowers. I didn't see another card on the table, but there was a cardboard box on the floor. And it was already open.

The boys were sitting around this box, peering inside of it, and they were excited to show me what it contained.

A video game for each of them. A box of dog treats for Gandhi. A chess set for Steve. And one more valentine card. Not like the cards for Mia and Mom. This card had a red envelope. And Carver had drawn a bunch of hearts on the outside. They were slanted and angled, like man-scribbles. The sight of those hearts made me smile.

"Can we open these games?" Richard asked.

I said, "I don't see why not," and the boys erupted in cheers. Gus gave a dog treat to Gandhi.

Then I took a seat at the table—next to my roses—to examine my valentine.

The card was heavy cream cardstock, with a sparkly red heart in the center and a dark crimson border. He'd folded a letter inside.

> *Dear Mary Jane,*
>
> *I'm so very sorry I have hurt you so much. I understand why you don't want to talk. But I hate that we're not talking right now.*

I told you before I left that you were out of my league. I meant that. That's why I don't know what I can do to make things right between us.

You said I couldn't come for a visit. But every day I want to get on a plane and come see you.

Whatever I need to do to fix this, please tell me. I can't find the answer.

I hope you're working on your grant proposal. I hope you haven't changed your mind about visiting when your proposal is finished.

I'll be in Florida by the end of this week. I wish you could be there with me.

I've gained five pounds since I saw you. It's harder to put on weight than it used to be. It's taking me longer. There are some days when 241 seems so far out of reach. But the scale keeps ticking up.

You are one of my reasons to win, Mary Jane.

I love you so much. I think about you all the time. Please call me. Please talk to me again.

> *Love,*
> *Carver*

I folded the letter, told the kids to start dinner, and then I took Gandhi for a walk. We started down a side street, toward the river.

I called Carver.

When he answered, he said, "Mary Jane," and he sounded anxious as well as relieved. "Don't hang up, all right?"

"I won't hang up."

"You promise?"

"I promise."

I wondered where he was. St. Louis was an hour ahead. Where would Carver be at seven-thirty on a Wednesday night? At home? Out to dinner? I wanted to ask, but then I just blurted, "I've been working on my proposal."

"I'm glad to hear that," Carver said.

I smiled. I glanced at my valentine letter again, and smiled some more. "I'm happy you're putting on weight. Your flowers arrived. They're lovely, Carver. Thank you."

He didn't say anything, and I could feel all the tension between us. The pressure of those weeks of not speaking. Carver had done a lot of thinking since the last time we'd talked. Which had been—I was astonished to realize now—*five weeks ago*. We hadn't spoken to each other in more than a month. Text messages, sure. But not a real conversation. I was the world's biggest coward sometimes. And I could tell by Carver's silence that he had a lot of words trapped inside him. Words he was still holding back.

"Did you get my card?" I asked. I had mailed him a valentine five days ago. Just a card though. No roses.

He made a sound that was part laugh, part sigh. A soft, easy sound. "I got it."

I blushed. I had written some really steamy things in that card… things I was always thinking about, even if I didn't have the guts to call him. I'd even told him about my dream with the black satin sheets. I couldn't believe I had shared that with him. I kept blushing and wondering what he had thought when he read it.

"I have dreams about you, too," he said, and the tone of his voice made me think of his hands on my skin. The way I felt when he kissed me. I shivered and hugged myself and tried to stay focused.

"I'm sorry I didn't want to talk for so long," I said. "I just needed time to myself. To figure things out."

"Did you make a decision?" he asked.

"I'm going to pay back the money," I said. "Sooner or later, I'll pay it all back."

Carver was silent a long while. I waited him out.

"I wasn't trying to make it harder on you, Mary Jane. But that's what I did."

Gandhi and I arrived at the river, so I stood and gazed out on the current. The sun had set, and the water looked black. "Are you at home?" I asked.

"With the boys," Carver said. "Building some sort of… Star Wars Lego thing. Jackie's idea. Christy's really into it. Branch just wants to play with the dolls."

"We ought to trade kids," I joked. "Because your house is silent."

Carver laughed. "I'm in the den. I came in here when I saw you were calling." He was quiet a moment. "Where are you?"

"At the river," I said. "With Gandhi." I knelt to pet him a minute. "I miss you."

"So you said." He meant my valentine, of course. I never put stuff like that in my texts.

I heard Carver take a deep breath, and I knew he was ready to be serious now. Even so, his question surprised me. "Why did you fall in love with me, Mary Jane?"

I flushed a little. "You tortured me into it."

"Torture?" He sounded amused.

"That's right, Carver. You're just so sweet that it's torture. I couldn't say no."

391

"I didn't think women fell in love with sweet men."

"Not just sweet," I amended. "You're tender and patient. You spent time with the kids doing homework. You took us all out to play baseball. And you promised me you weren't a serial killer. How could I say no to all that?"

Carver waited a moment before he spoke again, and his voice sounded sad. "But I hurt you sometimes. And I don't even know that I do it."

I'd been worried that Carver would diminish me by casting aside my concerns. But he had taken me seriously. And I was relieved.

"I think I hurt you, too," I said. "Avoiding you all this time. Carver, I… I don't know if love ever means you don't get hurt now and then. If we didn't want to be close, we'd never have so many misunderstandings. Real intimacy is…" I thought for a moment. How did I describe how much I had to understand myself before I could understand a relationship? How some pain in a relationship seemed inevitable? The world was not perfect, and neither were we. I said, "Real intimacy is an act of precision."

"Sounds like work," he said.

"Right now—yes," I laughed. "In bed with you—no. I think our bodies have the precision-thing pretty well mastered."

I could tell he was grinning. I could hear it in his voice like a hug. "Loving your body is definitely easier… when the words don't get in the way."

"Exactly," I said. "Probably why the long-distance thing hardly ever works out. Too many misfires. Too few chances to fix them."

"I wish I could pull you into bed with me now," Carver said, and I smiled.

"Who needs the bed?" I asked, and Carver laughed.

"Mary Jane," and something about the way he said my name made me pause.

I waited for him to go on. "Mm?"

"Would you…" he trailed off. "When you decided not to get married—was it really just because you didn't want to have children?"

I thought for a minute. The ghost of my denial drifted into my mind. And then I remembered I was spending time with the truth again. Even if she was broken and ugly.

"I always thought that was why," I said. "But the Cowboy told me once I wouldn't have to have children. And I still told him no."

"You thought he might change his mind?" Carver asked.

"Maybe," I said. "But I have a different theory now."

We didn't speak for a time, and I thought of those two texts I had sent him. I thought of my deepest fear. I knew the real reason why I'd turned down the Cowboy. It was true that the Cowboy would be happiest once he had his own children, and it was also true that I recognized that I could not give him that. I wasn't meant to have babies and live my whole life in Goldking. My path and the Cowboy's were totally different.

But there was something else, too.

I thought of my mother's four husbands, and how none of those men—including my father—had given her what she wanted: security and unconditional love. Quite the opposite. Mom kept having babies, trying to convince one of those men to stay and take care of her if she gave him a family, and none of them would. And now that she had her own house, a home that no one could kick her out of (outside of not paying her taxes), was Mom looking to marry again? She dated and had boyfriends, and she still wanted someone to love her, but marriage was no longer required.

So what was the point of a marriage license, if a woman had her own house, didn't want to have children, and took care of herself? Mom had only chased after a husband because she needed a sense of security, and her prime tool for marrying a man was to tie her self-worth to her looks… and I'd always been against doing that to begin with. Being the prettiest girl at the ball had brought my mother nothing but hardship and abuse, and the men in her life never hesitated to dump her whenever they wanted to.

I knew that my mother had always wanted to be Cinderella. And once upon a time, I thought I had, too. Thinking about it now made me sad. Why had I ever believed I was waiting for Prince Charming to come along with a white horse and carriage? Hadn't I had enough proof growing up that this was not a good plan?

The truth was: I had a documentary I needed to film. And it wasn't set in a castle.

I wondered if Carver had guessed that he had been right… that evening we sat talking outside the movie theater. I had the sneaking suspicion that he had actually known before I did that I simply didn't want to get married. Maybe Carver was savvier about this than me because he had already played the part of Prince Charming—in his story with Audrey—and that fairy tale hadn't turned out so well.

Carver had sworn he would never find himself with a wife who was in love with somebody else—and his almost total avoidance of women made it clear he probably had no desire to ever marry again. We had fallen in love in a week, and now that we were back to our lives, we were like an affair that hadn't quite fizzled out. Far from a committed relationship. Farther still from the idea of marriage—or even living together, for that matter. We were a couple in limbo—two people in love, but without any logistics on our side, which meant the odds were against us that we would be together that long.

Carver waited me out, wanting to hear my new theory, so I finally said, "The Cowboy proposed when we were sixteen… and I was already struggling so much taking care of the kids, and trying to keep up with high school, and wondering if I might go to college—and I didn't want to repeat any of my mother's mistakes. Getting married meant… putting myself into danger… and living at the whim of somebody else. I don't think marriage is the right path for me. I can take care of myself, and I'd rather stay single."

Carver's next question surprised me even more than the first one. "What happened to you, Mary Jane, when you lived in that car?"

I held my breath for a moment, and tried to recover from shock. From marriage to homelessness—okay, maybe we *were* still on the same subject. In my warped view of the world, one thing obviously led to the other. Marriage=chaos=divorce= homelessness. So what *had* happened to me the year I lived in a car?

"Nothing good," I said. "My father ran off and left us. And my mother couldn't pay rent. So we lived in the Impala for a year. My brothers and I kept to the backseat. Unless Mom showed up with a man. Then we would have to clear out for a while. I usually just hid under the car for an hour, and I'd climb back in once Mom was asleep. We had to stay on the move, park in a different place every night so the cops wouldn't catch us. It was always a struggle to find the money for gas."

There were other nightmares involved. Other pieces of hell. But sharing that was enough. It was all I was ready to share.

"I hate this story," Carver said.

I laughed. "Good thing it's mine then, and not yours."

"I don't want to believe you," Carver said.

"Then don't. There's a reason I never talk about this."

"People don't want to believe you?" he asked.

I smiled, and then sighed. "It's their pity. I don't need any pity."

"But I hate that this happened to you."

"That's fine," I said. "I just... I don't want to be pitied. Especially not for things outside my control."

"I know you don't want to seem weak," Carver said. "But you will never be weak, Mary Jane. Anyone who would think that—well, who cares about them?"

I almost laughed. That was the crux of the problem, wasn't it? I *did* care. I cared when I shouldn't. I had to learn to stop doing that. "I'm getting there, Carver. I am. I'm just... I still have some growing up to do."

"You and me both," Carver said, and I laughed. So did Carver.

After a minute, I said, "It's hard to open up. And it's hard to remember that some people have opinions that don't matter." I wished I could be in the same room with Carver. I wished I could hug him. I really wanted a hug. But I just lowered my voice and said, "Your opinion matters though. A great deal."

"Mary Jane, I..." He sounded so tense again, and I had the sense he was pacing, like he was all worked up and didn't know what to do. His voice held uncertainty, and a whisper of fear. "I think about you. Even when I'm out on the field. I've never thought about anyone like that before. It's... distracting. It's not how I play. It's not how I've ever played."

This made me giggle. "You are the laziest-looking player I've ever watched, Carver."

He laughed, and the fear slipped away from his voice. The uncertainty remained. "It takes a lot of focus to look lazy. Believe me. My head is in the game. Even on a bad day, I'm always right there. Only now, it's… It's the strangest thing, Mary Jane. The strangest thing."

"What?" I asked.

"My focus is different. Sometimes I think about you on the field, and it doesn't matter. I mean, it doesn't matter to my concentration. I'm not used to that."

"Sounds like you're obsessed," I said.

Carver laughed. "Yeah, I… I guess I am." That tension returned to his voice. "It worries me though. What if I'm losing my focus? I can't be a good player unless I can concentrate."

"Are you hitting again, Carver?"

He knew I was asking if he was hitting homeruns. And his answer surprised me, but not the answer itself. It was the tone of his voice.

"Yes," he said quietly, and I had never heard him sound so… small. He didn't sound like a major league player who'd rediscovered his power swing. He seemed… almost frightened. Like he didn't know what to do. And this was *fantastic news*. I wanted to ask who had been there when he hit it out of the park—had Matt seen it? Or another teammate? Had they cheered? Had Carver cheered?

But there was no triumph in Carver's voice. His focus felt different, so he was different. Identities were such worrisome things when they changed. And Carver was definitely worried.

"If you're hitting again, you're not losing your focus," I said. "But you might be expanding it. You still feel like you can concentrate?"

"It's better," Carver said. "It's stronger than ever. That's what I don't understand."

"And how do you feel when you're out there?" I asked.

The worry left his voice. And all of the fear. I heard the rough sound of surprise, and happiness. Amazement. "I feel like a kid again. Like I just… like I just can't wait to get out there and slam the ball. I feel like I'm having the time of my life."

I smiled and closed my eyes for a moment, aware I'd been wishing and *wishing* for this, and was almost overwhelmed with hope that *my wish would come true*. I wanted to jump up and down. I wanted to scream and cheer and act like a lunatic.

But I kept my voice calm, and asked, "When you were a kid, did you think about other things when you played? I don't know—maybe comic books, or getting your driver's license, or girls—and you could still pick up a bat and hit the ball?" I waited for Carver to respond, but he seemed intent on listening. So I said, "Maybe you stopped doing that when you made the big leagues. And maybe a little distraction right now… maybe it means you're just growing again, like when you were a kid."

Carver was quiet a long time. Not a bad sort of quiet. When he spoke again, he sounded so peaceful. There was an ease in his voice that hadn't been there before. "How did you figure that out?"

I giggled. "Mind-reader," I said. "I was born with superpowers."

Carver laughed. "I believe it."

I heard the patter of feet on the other end of the line— the sound of a small child running—and then one of Carver's boys cried, "*Come on, Dad! We need you to be the Ewoks! We're ready to play!*" Then he harrumphed and whined, "*Aw, Dad!*" and stomped away, put-out to discover his father was still on the phone.

I had to smile at the idea of Carver playing with tiny Lego Ewoks. I loved that he was the type of dad who got down on the floor with his kids. He needed to get back to it though, and I needed to do the same.

"I'll call you tomorrow," I said. "The kids are making dinner, and I should get back. Happy Valentine's Day, Carver."

Carver's voice was soft. So much deeper and rougher with longing. Still as tender as a kiss. "Happy Valentine's Day."

40

HEROES AND RISK

The kids brought home sign-up sheets for baseball the next night. Mia had even decided to try out for softball. So I read through the forms and arranged for them to have sports physicals. Steve volunteered to drive the kids to the clinic for me, since I couldn't get that much time off of work. I knew there was no way Stella would let me run around taking the kids to all of these physicals, and I was so grateful I had Steve there to help me, I said, "I don't know what I'd do without you. I really don't."

Steve said, "Hey, what are friends for?" and that made me smile.

Carver left for spring training, and he sent me a text one afternoon to say: *I'm in Florida.* The Cardinals held spring training in Jupiter, Florida, and the team shared a stadium with the Florida Marlins. I wished I could go watch them play, because one of the Delaware cops at The Summit told me that spring training games were as much fun to watch as the games in the season. But a visit wasn't possible right now. I still had work to do on my proposal.

Carver took his family to Florida with him, a decision he did not come to lightly. The boys had pressed him to go, and while he didn't like to make them switch schools for a month and a half, in the end, he was glad that they'd pushed him so hard. He was happiest with his gremlins. I could empathize.

By the end of February, I decided to splurge and purchase a laptop. I'd owned a laptop in college, but it had been stolen one night, on a train ride back to Pennsylvania after Hanna had died. I'd accidentally fallen asleep with my computer beside me, and when I woke up, someone had taken it. So I used the iPhone and ordered another one, and once I had a laptop again, I started formatting business letters at night, trying to perfect my proposal to make *Brighter Than Stars*. I was usually so tired from working at the daycare all week that sometimes I couldn't even type out a sentence. But I managed to push my way through it most nights.

I mailed Carver a card on March first, to his address in Florida. Inside, I drew a picture of us skiing with Mom, only Mom was saying, "Let's buy some beer!" as she went down the mountain. It was a goofy picture, and I knew he would laugh.

Since the iPhone could be used as a portable wireless router, I could access the internet on my computer. One night in mid-March, I took a break from my work, and searched for articles about the St. Louis Cardinals. I found a website that posted spring training scores—and there was a picture of Carver taking a swing. I studied that image a long time. This was not an old picture, but a photo someone had taken in the last two weeks. Carver was definitely hitting again—and people were noticing. He also looked more handsome than ever. He seemed radiant. Part of this glow was his superfood diet, part of it was his increased muscle mass—but most of it was his renewed belief in himself. Nothing made a person so lovely as self-confidence. And Carver had plenty right now.

I finally clicked away from that picture, and read an article about him on another sports webpage:

> One veteran player of note this spring is Carver Greyson, whose batting average dropped in the last five years from an astounding .397 when he played for the Yankees, to a lackluster .239 last year.
>
> But the Grizz seems to have returned to his power swing, and Saint Louis might reap the benefits of having another year on his contract.
>
> Greyson is one of the few players in history to have homered four times in a single game, and the only player in history to have hit three homeruns in a game four times in one season. Redbird fans will be eager to see if the Grizz has still got what it takes to knock it out of the park.

I scrolled though a few more websites, and then I found an interview Carver had given two days ago. A man in a blue suit and tie had brought a microphone into the dugout. Carver wore his uniform, and held his glove propped on his leg. His hair looked as unkempt as always.

The first part of the interview was garbled a little, enough I couldn't quite hear what was said. Some sort of technical error that took the cameraman a minute to fix. When the sound came back, I was astonished to hear what they were talking about.

"Ever since that tragic accident five years ago," the interviewer said, "you've struggled to perform successful at bats—why the sudden change this year?"

I would hate answering a question like that in front of a microphone. God. Carver had done this before though, and he was a pro.

He kept his voice quiet and low. "I don't think anyone's prepared to lose their loved ones so soon. I know I wasn't."

"So do you think you've had time to heal?" the man asked.

Wow. If someone asked me that about Hanna, I'd probably want to punch him. Or at least tell him to shut the hell up. But Carver wasn't about to punch anyone.

He looked very tired though. Like he'd rather talk about anything than his grief. And then it passed, and he looked like himself again. "I don't know if anyone really heals," he said. "I think you feel the presence of God's grace in your life again. You reach a point where God helps you remember you're whole. And you stop feeling lost. I can't take credit for that."

"So you attribute your success to God?" the man asked.

Carver shrugged with a smile. "My success and my failures are all God's. I try to give my best every day, and I'm thankful when I can perform in a way that makes people excited to watch a game, makes them appreciate what I do for my team. But I'm not the one in control, and there are times when I forget that and have trouble."

"You're saying, God's in control?" the man asked.

Carver smiled and rested his hands on the bench. "Absolutely," he said. "I live within the grace of God, and that frees me. I think, as an athlete, when I forget that, then I stop meeting potential. I can see something in my mind, but I can't make it happen, and I struggle against something I don't understand."

Then the man asked, tongue-in-cheek, "Would you say that God's sending the Cardinals to the World Series this year?"

Carver laughed. "I'm playing ball with a great group of guys, so I'd love to see us make the postseason together. But as to the will of God, I leave that up to God."

I loved that Carver was hitting homeruns again—and that he was still so humble. As to why he was hitting again, Carver could have told that man, *Well, I'm working my tail off here. I'm practicing every day. I have to eat the right foods. I have to spend hours in the gym. I have to dedicate my life to this sport.*

But he never said anything like that. About his personal sacrifice, or his work ethic, or all of his time in the gym. He simply said he needed God's grace to play ball. And I thought that was a beautiful answer.

I visited other websites, and saw numerous interviews like this one—older videos, filmed in the years before Audrey and Ben died. And Carver always said the same things, about God, God's grace in his life, and his love for his family. He'd been twenty-five years old when his wife and brother had died, when those streaks of grey in his hair had appeared, and sometimes his teammates referred to him as *the old man* because of them. The term made Carver laugh, and sometimes the interviewers asked him about it, especially if he was growing a beard, because he had streaks of grey in his beard as well as his hair.

"Yeah, it's growing in like my father's," he'd say, and his eyes would be bright, genuinely amused. "I keep holding out for the respect that's supposed to come with age though. So far, nothing." Then one of his teammates would hurl a glove at his shoulder, or fling a ball toward his chest, which he'd catch with one hand. Off-camera, I'd hear people laughing.

I liked those moments a lot. But that sort of humor was rare. In most of those earlier interviews since Audrey and Ben died, Carver was often asked why he'd stopped slugging the ball, and what steps he was taking to get over his slump. He struggled with those questions a great deal. He'd stare at the ground, as beaten down as I'd ever seen a man. Those interview questions seemed to break him apart.

"I pray," he'd say thickly. "I spend time with my family. That's about all I can do." Then he'd glance up at the person who was asking the questions, and smile in a way that meant, *Can we please change the subject?* But that never happened. Failure was as compelling as victory sometimes, and in the last four seasons of baseball, Carver had been a poster-boy for dashed hopes. For a man who'd seemed destined for Hall of Fame greatness, it had come as a shock that after the death of his wife and his brother, he'd only just barely managed to keep playing ball. After one interview last fall, a sportscaster said, "Well, it's a shame. I don't think the Grizz will ever recover from this. His career could have held so much more. But it's doubtful at this point he can even stay in the majors. This is more than a slump. It's like he just ran out of talent."

I remembered hearing this line during that game with the Tigers, the one I had watched after our night at the hot springs. Carver had *run out of talent*. I started to notice this phrase was used quite a lot in reference to Carver and his hitting career. And it made me sad that he had listened to people say this about him for almost five years.

Carver had never run out of talent. He had only forgotten his reasons to win. He lost his faith in himself. Talent and faith were not the same thing. Talent gave you ability. Faith gave you the power to do something with it.

I was feeling disheartened by all of this *run out of talent* talk, and then I discovered someone had posted a video compilation of Carver hitting homeruns, and set it to music. Watching this

YouTube clip made me so happy, I watched that video three times before I finally went to bed.

As I lay on my cot and waited to fall asleep, I kept thinking about the person who had created that video. Someone named Grizz4ever. I wondered if this person had ever met Carver, or if they had just watched him play in a stadium. And then I thought of all of Carver's fans. All of the people taking notice that he was hitting again. The people who had kept watching him play these past seasons, hoping for the Grizz to return.

Those people thought of Carver as a hero. And the more I considered this fact, the more I thought about heroes in general. Heroes and leaders. The people who inspired us. And where inspiration truly came from.

Ken Burns was a hero to me, and I had never met him. But I loved him. I loved him so much that I wanted to make documentaries one day—because his films inspired me. They made me remember that all of life was significant. And when I watched a film by Ken Burns, or I watched Fred Hampton's *Eyes on the Prize*, I knew I was significant. To witness their creation made me feel important. I loved that.

And I loved that people wanted to find heroes in life. We seemed so hardwired to seek them. Athletes. Singers. Musicians. Political leaders. Scientists. Doctors. Artists. Actors. Teachers. Coaches. And some heroes touched our lives in other ways. Parents. Neighbors. Friends. Children. Even pets. We needed them on every scale, like our laws and our government: local, state, and national. And a few heroes became international. A few belonged to the world.

The real job of a public hero was not very heroic though. The public hero lived in risk, constant *public* risk. They lived the same life we all did, but they lived their lives with everyone watching.

And when they stumbled and fell, we all witnessed their failure. We could not look away. We clucked our tongues and said, *What a shame*. Or we said, *I guess he just ran out of talent*. And what we really meant when we watched a hero fail was, *Thank God that didn't happen to me*. Failure scorched a person with shame. But *public* failure—oh, that was worse. Much worse. Public failure was self-immolation. And the greater the fall of a hero, the greater the fire. A roaring bonfire was a spectacle.

And the truth was: we wanted our heroes to fail. Not because we were evil. It was more like we just wanted proof that these people were no more invincible than anyone else. And failure was a gift, really. Failure was just a beginning. Because we really wanted something else from our heroes. Their success wasn't even the point. When life knocked down a hero, and made him bleed, we wanted something a lot more compelling than blood on the ground. The magic was not in his pain. The magic was in what he did next.

We wanted to see him get up. Because if our hero got up, if he put out the flames and moved on, then he was really showing us that we could all get back up. Over and over again.

Carver had lived as a hero. His rise to success had been breathtaking: his youth, the broken records, the wins. And his beauty. Carver had always been handsome and gracious, a combination that was an immense part of his charm.

And then his success had disappeared overnight. When one drowsy truck driver nodded off at the wheel. Tragedy and pain avoided no one in life. Especially not heroes. And who could be a real hero, anyway, unless life dealt its blows? We were all knocked down at some point. We all left our blood on the ground. That was living.

And life would always keep breaking our heroes. And us. We were all facing pain. We were all trying to figure this out. This thing called life. We needed inspiration. We needed joy. And when we looked to our heroes, the more broken they were, the more we would love them. It was how much we loved them that made us significant. We were greater people inside, when we loved. When we loved so much that it hurt.

And now it was Carver's turn to pick himself up. He would play his first game of the season in two weeks. Would he continue to hit, once the real pressure was on? I hoped so. But there were 180 days in a baseball season. Anything could happen.

And then I thought of my grant proposal, and how close I was to sending my letter off in the mail. The future was as undetermined for me as it was for anyone else. Anything could happen.

41

SKIN DEEP

High school ball games started in March, and Steve had his work cut out for him, helping me shuttle the kids around to play baseball. I put Mom in charge of watching their home games, since I was usually at work when they started. Steve thought she did a good job of cheering them on. Richard told me she almost got busted smoking pot under the bleachers one afternoon, but for the most part, she behaved herself. Steve even bought her some blue and white pom-poms at Walmart, which Mom waved around whenever anyone scored, no matter which team made the run. She also invented cheers to perform in the house, which were pretty annoying but sometimes made me laugh.

On the last day of March, the St. Louis Cardinals played the San Diego Padres at home to kick off their season. I sat on the couch with the kids, and we watched the game on my computer.

Carver played left field that night, batted fourth in the lineup—and when he *hit a homerun* at the top of the seventh, the kids jumped off the couch and *screamed*. Then they ran around the apartment like maniacs. Gandhi barked and barked and hid under the table, he was so freaked out by the noise and the kids' whacked-out behavior. I called him onto my lap and petted him until he calmed down.

Mom came and hugged me and said, "How about that? Your boyfriend hit a homerun!"

I was almost too happy to speak. "He sure did." I was so proud of Carver, I couldn't stop smiling and laughing.

The Cardinals won, and Mia begged me to let her text Carver. I said, "Of course you can text him." So she sent him this message:

Congratulations, Carver!!
That was amazing!!! From your friend, Mia
        (plus Richard and Ethan and Gus)
        (and Mom and Steve and Mary Jane, even Gandhi)
        Except I wrote this message, don't forget—Mia

Carver sent a reply about an hour after the game: *Thank you, Mia. Thank you, everyone*, and he added a smiley face.

Mia was ecstatic. She wanted to take the phone with her to school and show everyone in her class. The boys wanted to do this as well, but Mia growled, "*No!* He wrote *my* name on the message!" She even tried to punch Richard when he attempted to take the cell from her.

"Give me the phone," I said before she could hurt someone, and she handed it over. "I'll print copies of the message tomorrow, and you can all have one to take to school. Okay?"

This earned me a round of dirty looks and several snarls from the kids, but I just made them all go to bed.

When the living room was quiet again, I sent Carver another text.

Great game, with a row of red hearts.

Within a minute, he called me. I answered, "Hi, Carver!" and right after he said, "*Mary Jane!*" I realized there was a racket on his end, with lots of people talking and shouting.

"Are you still in the locker room?"

"No," he laughed. "I went out with the team. They wanted to go have a drink."

"Are you drinking?" I was genuinely curious about this. Carver lived on such a strict diet.

"I've got my double-shot of wheatgrass right here," he said.

I laughed. "Are you really drinking wheatgrass in a bar?"

"It was this or a kale smoothie," he said. "I might switch to lemon water."

"How can you order wheatgrass in a bar?"

"I don't know," Carver said, "I think a couple from California own this place," and I laughed again. Carver laughed with me. And then we kept on laughing like we were both nuts.

"Do you feel awesome right now?" I asked.

"I'd feel really awesome if you were here with me," Carver said. "Having a shot of wheatgrass with me."

I burst into laughter again, picturing him in some ritzy bar, the place packed with people, and Carver just standing there with his shot of wheatgrass, laughing on the phone. I heard people calling for him, wanting to have his attention. But he kept laughing with me, like we were sharing the best joke ever.

And when we were ready to talk again, I said, "I'm really proud of you, Carver."

"Proud enough to come for a visit?" he asked.

"Definitely."

"Really?"

"Maybe in a month?" I said. "When I'm done sending my letters out."

Carver was so happy, I thought he might pop. "Okay, Mary Jane. Okay. This is great news. This is really great news." He sounded a little delirious.

"Enjoy the party," I said. "Kale smoothies and all. I'll call you tomorrow."

"Mary Jane, I couldn't have done this without you."

"You could have," I said. "Although… maybe I ought to threaten not to see you again unless you keep hitting homeruns."

Carver laughed and laughed, and he told me he loved me again and again, and when we ended the call, I remained at the table a while, staring down at the phone.

I wondered what it would feel like to have just hit a homerun in a major league game. To be out in a bar with a bunch of teammates, drinking and yelling and talking. How amazing would that feel? How exciting?

What if I had been there today—in the stadium? After the game, would Carver have hugged me and kissed me? Would I have gone to the bar with him? Would he have taken me home? Would we have made love? I wondered what his bedroom was like, and what it would feel like to be with him now.

I thought about visiting him in a month, and wondered if Carver would feel different about me, when he finally saw me again. Maybe when he was on top of his career, when he was truly back as the Grizz, he wouldn't need me anymore. And maybe seeing me again might help him realize that—that he could find another woman who would be there with him— watching his games, going out with his team, going home with him at night. He didn't need to wait around on a girl who had… so many things in her life that she couldn't even come for a visit. Maybe Carver's impatience would finally kick in.

But if he did let me go, I knew I would still love him. Carver had appeared in my life like the sun, bright and warm as pure hope. He'd told me I was powerful and free, and then he had fallen in love with me… and during the time we spent together, I remembered to have faith in myself. Faith was a gift that love made, like sunshine and water creating a rainbow.

Love was such a… physical *force* in our lives. Love could burn like a wildfire, and it could spread like one, too: with sparks on the wind, or with a great sweep of fire. As sudden as lightning, or as steady and slow as a cook stove. And once you were burned, that was it. You never forgot. Some part of that fire would always stay with you… and that was how I felt about Carver.

✳✳✳

By the end of April, my life outside of work was filled with baseball. My apartment was littered with mitts, cleats, and dirty baseball bats, and constantly smelled like grass. I often left work and tried to catch a game one of the kids might be in, and when I wasn't sitting in the bleachers, I was listening to a Cardinals game on my phone, usually while I fixed dinner and the kids did their homework. Sometimes I listened to one of Carver's games while I sat in the bleachers and cheered for the kids. Carver was back to slamming the ball again and scoring runs right and left, and the kids were full of their own heartaches and joys of the game.

I had so much baseball in my life, I almost felt a bit crazy. And I would never have juggled getting the kids to all of these games and practices if I didn't have Steve. The two of us were a team, making sure the kids were all where they needed to be every day.

On the last day of April, Gus received his driver's license, and I let him start driving the Buick. I had repaired the window in March, and Gus loved the hell out of that car. He helped me run errands, and he started taking Richard, Ethan, and Mia home after practice—the biggest single stress relief I could have asked for.

If I had still been making payments to Tom Morbun and the Goldking County Treasurer, and if Steve hadn't been able to help out with groceries, I would never have been able to afford to have four kids playing sports. There was not only the cost of their cleats and sports physicals, but also the five-dollar allowance for food money on game days. Sometimes I had to give them each ten dollars, if they were gone for lunch and dinner both. I averaged about $500.00 a month in extra expenses related to baseball games, and that was after spending around $600.00 on physicals and equipment. So by the time May arrived, I still had a sizeable MasterCard bill, which was a bummer. But at least I was making my student loan payments. I never missed a due date, and that was a comfort.

I sent a check for fifty dollars each month to Carver, which was all I could afford at the moment. I worried he would send my checks back, or not deposit them. But he never did either. I knew he hated taking that money from me. I knew it must hurt him. But pain was a relative thing—and in this situation, mine felt greater. So Carver took the checks, and each time they cleared, I was relieved.

***

On the morning of May fourth, which was my twenty-third birthday, I was working at Happy Garden, helping a little boy learn how to tie his shoes.

Stella appeared in the hallway. It was such a brilliant sunny day that she had to shade her eyes when she looked at me.

"*Guess* who I ran into *yesterday!*" Stella said with an exaggerated grin.

I felt a flicker of apprehension before I asked, "Who?"

"Grace!" Stella chortled. "She was in the supermarket with her *boyfriend!*"

I was happy to hear that Grace had a boyfriend. "That's great!" I told Stella.

"Guess where she's *working!*" Stella laughed.

I gazed at Stella expectantly, though I already knew the answer. I had helped Grace find a job at Sunny Days Kindergarten. As a teacher.

I opened the back door so the little boy could run out and play.

"She's over at Sunny Days *Kindergarten!*" Stella beamed. I wasn't fooled by her smile. I recognized malice when I saw it. "She's actually teaching *kindergarten!* Can you *believe* it? I was just so *happy* for her. Isn't that *fantastic* news??"

"Definitely!" I said. I tried hard to sound perky.

"You know that Grace mentioned she put you down as a *reference?*" Stella asked. "To help her get that *teaching* position? Isn't that *great??*"

I felt the blood draining out of my face. "Really?" I gulped. Then, more brightly, I said, "I had no idea!"

"Yeah!" Stella gushed. "She said that she saw you back in *January*, after she stopped working *here!* And she told me you'd been dating a *baseball* player! She even said she'd seen him on *television!* She told me his name was *Grizz Greyson!* Isn't that *funny?*"

"Yeah, that's pretty funny," I said. I had forgotten that Grace had come over for dinner one night, the day she had gotten that job, and the kids had been eager to tell her about Carver. When she'd asked me later if it was all true, I'd told her it was, but that we probably wouldn't see each other again.

"I mean, you don't even *talk* about sports!" Stella laughed. "And how could *you* meet a Major League player like that? You'd have to live near a stadium, wouldn't you?"

"Sure," I said.

"And you would have to—*you* know—move in those *circles*," Stella said.

"Of course," I agreed.

"Grace is so funny!" Stella gushed. "I mean, you've never mentioned a *boyfriend* in all the time you've worked here! You've always been *single!*"

"That's right," I said.

"I *thought* so!" Stella crooned. "You just live with some *kids*, right? In middle school or something?"

"Two in junior high, two in high school," I said.

"And the younger ones are like—*yours*, right?" Stella asked.

"No," I said quietly. "Two brothers, one sister. And one family friend."

"Oh, *right!*" Stella laughed. "I knew it was something like that." She cast me one of her fake-pity expressions, the sort of look that let me know how pathetic I was, and then she sauntered off to the kitchen. I breathed a sigh of relief and hoped that was the end of it.

I couldn't understand why Grace had told Stella I had helped her find a new job, and then mentioned Carver. Why did Grace not understand these things? She had asked Stella a question about missing Christmas with her family to fly to Nigeria, and then been fired. And I had *told* Grace that Stella was a mess. This was not a woman to share personal information with. This was a woman you watched yourself around. Had Stella pressed Grace for something to use against me?

I sighed. Probably. Women like Stella knew an easy mark when they saw one. And Grace was an easy mark. I could imagine Stella talking to Grace in the supermarket: *You know, I was almost wondering if Mary Jane was gay, you know, cause she never has a man in her life.* And unsuspecting Grace: *Oh, Mary Jane's not gay, she had a boyfriend in January.* Yeah, I could just imagine Stella pulling something like that. Say something untrue about someone, and then wait for her friend to jump in and clarify.

So I wasn't really surprised when Stella called me into her office for another "quick meeting." It was late afternoon now, and the air in the house felt stuffy.

I hadn't been inside Stella's office since the day I'd been given a raise. Her desk was still heaped in papers, and Stella had to move her chair to look at me. She seemed uncomfortable, and she wore a forced smile. I walked in and took a seat.

"Mary Jane," she began. "I wanted to tell you what a pleasure it's been to work with you here at Happy Garden. The children really love you and you've been a *huge* help to the staff. But… due to the *recession*, I've had to take a hard look at my finances, and I simply can't afford to keep you on." Stella smiled in a way that meant I should nod my head in understanding, but I was too numb by this point to follow her cues. My stomach felt cold, like I'd swallowed a handful of ice cubes.

"I would like you to finish out this week," she continued, "but starting next Monday, your services will no longer be needed." She smiled brightly again. "And *do* let me know if you need a letter of reference to find new employment. I would be *happy* to do that for you."

I wanted to say I'd rather eat nuclear waste than ask Stella for a letter of reference, but I was too upset to speak. I stood to leave. I didn't smile at Stella, and I didn't pretend to be happy. As I made my way to the door, Stella blurted, "I had the *funniest* conversation with *Dale Lehman* this morning! I had to drop off my *Lexus* for some routine repairs, and wouldn't you know it, but Dale has actually *met* that *baseball player* Grace mentioned! Remember how she thought she saw you with that one guy? Grizz Greyson? Well his *sister* keeps a vacation home here, and Dale told me he knows her! Isn't that *interesting?*"

I stopped with my hand on the door, and turned back to Stella. Stella with her Lexus. Her house. Her own business. Her friends she went out with every night. And all of that lovely free time to have fun. Stella smiling at me. Because she had control over my job, and I didn't.

And here was the truth about Stella: she had all of those things. All of those things that I didn't. And she still wanted to be Cinderella. Stella was lonely, and sad, and desperate for companionship. She was desperate for love. And maybe she thought a man could help her get her finances in order, help her make her business profitable, help her to be a real leader, and not a petty wretch of a boss.

But Stella did not look like Cinderella. And that was the whole point of the story, wasn't it? All of that physical beauty. Stella didn't have a smile that sparkled, or a trim, slender figure, or long glossy hair that fell down her back. But it was more than that. Even in the fairy tale, beauty was never beauty when it was only skin deep. The truth was, Stella could have been beautiful with no teeth in her smile, no figure to speak of, and no hair on her head. But Stella scowled, and complained, and fired people without cause.

And she hated me. Not because I had helped Grace. Or because I had had an affair with a man who was handsome and wonderful and everything Stella wanted in life. Her hatred ran much deeper than that.

Stella knew that she was alone. And she was lonesome in a way that made her sick inside.

And I was alone, but I wasn't sick. And that was why Stella hated me.

Maybe that sounded absurd. Maybe I was just being foolish. Maybe I should simply chalk up this firing to my overdue comeuppance for going behind Stella's back and helping Grace. Because people running businesses didn't fire workers over dark emotional turmoil and petty jealousies. No one could ever run a business and function like that—right?

Well, that was the thing about life: nothing easy here. Not even what you want to believe.

So I faced my boss one last time, this woman I had groveled to so many times, and said, "Stella, you're a terrible boss. You're bad with money. You're selfish. And you only have a Lexus and a house and a business because your parents paid for it all. So keep telling yourself that you're better than me. Maybe one day you might really believe it."

Stella's fury was immediate: her red face, her eyes flashing fire, her lips drawn back in a snarl. She started yelling at me, calling me a filthy whore—a filthy whore!—and I laughed, because Stella was ridiculous. I opened the door and added, "You can mail my last check."

I passed through the laundry room, walked into the daycare, and called out to my coworkers, "Hey, everyone!" Once I had their attention, I cheerfully announced, "Stella just fired me! So I'm leaving. I've enjoyed working with you all! Good luck with everything!"

I picked up my bag that held my lunch and my wallet, and walked outside. The other women didn't follow me, because such an action would probably get them fired as well. But the children didn't understand what had happened, and I ended up with a sea of little heads traipsing behind me. I had to walk them all back inside, a few of them crying as they grabbed my legs, and I had to promise them all I would see them again. Then I had to give them hugs, kisses, and several high-fives, before I could leave and start my search for a new job.

As upset as I was to be out of work, I didn't have any desire to cry. I had asked the universe to get me out of this job—and it had. Never mind that this was a *horrible time in my life* to get fired. Never mind that I would have rather been fired in June or July, when the kids were out of school for the summer. Never mind that getting fired was *not what I'd meant* when I'd asked to be free of this suck job.

At least I didn't have to attend those damn staff meetings anymore. That was one happy thought. But I couldn't make rent without constant full-time employment. I couldn't pay the electric bill, I couldn't keep the water on. I had two days, tops, to find another job. As I drove away from Happy Garden for the last time, the clock was definitely ticking.

42

THE THING ABOUT BABIES

I spent the rest of my afternoon walking through downtown Riverdale, going in and out of businesses, trying to find a job that didn't require me to work weeknights. The kids had one month of school left, and with so many practice times and ball games to coordinate, on top of putting on dinner, checking over homework, and making sure bedtime was followed—there was no way I could take on a night shift.

But I couldn't find anything. Waitressing, dishwashing, cashiering—every service job in town required evening hours. The railroad wasn't hiring. Neither were the insurance companies, the colleges, Office Depot, or the carwashes. After a coffee shop turned me down, a man drinking espresso offered to pay me $150.00 for some nude photographs, which I thought was a low blow. I didn't need any more reminders that I could sell my body for cash, and yet, life kept throwing this disgusting thing at me. When the Riverdale Diner turned me down, another guy said I could be his muse and he'd give me free drugs. I said, "Do I *look* like I do *drugs?*" and he returned to his burger.

I visited thirty-five businesses before I had to head home. When I checked the mail, I found my first two responses to my grant proposal: rejection letters. I read over them quickly, and—just as quickly—tucked them away in my bag.

As I walked up the stairs to my apartment, I found Landon sitting outside my door. He didn't even look at me as I came up the steps.

I crossed my arms and said, "What are you doing here?"

Landon stared down at his hands, unresponsive. His blue jeans were dirtier than usual. His t-shirt had two more holes than it used to.

"Where's Janine?" I asked.

Landon shrugged, which probably meant they were having issues. They might have split up.

"What do you want, Landon?"

He only shrugged again. I said, "You're not welcome here," and went inside. I locked the door behind me. I guessed he wanted some money. But he'd picked the wrong sibling to come beg for cash.

The kids were inside with Mom. Steve was at work. A large vase of blue and white flowers sat on the dining table.

"Carver sent you flowers!" Mia said, and I found myself smiling. I had already forgotten that today was my birthday.

"Why would he send more flowers?" Mom asked.

"Cause it's her birthday," Mia said.

"Oh, God," Mom muttered. "Another birthday."

"Who told Carver my birthday?" I asked the kids.

Mia raised her hand with a grin, which made me laugh and hug her.

A small package lay on the table as well, and I opened it. I found a pretty card with a love letter, plane tickets that could be redeemed anytime, and a gift card to an expensive restaurant in town—enough that I could take the whole family to dinner.

Mia caught sight of the gift card. "You wanna use that?" she asked. She had already started making a huge salad for dinner—her present to me. I knew she'd be sad if I turned her meal down.

I tucked the card away. "We'll save it," I said, "and celebrate the last day of school this year." I chucked Mia's chin, and she smiled with relief. I asked Ethan and Richard to clean up their baseball gear and vacuum the grass off the floor, and then I retreated to the bedroom to read my love letter. Gandhi came with me, and once I stretched out on my cot, he rested his head on my shoulder.

I read Carver's letter and forgot about being fired. I forgot about my rejection letters, my bills, and Landon sitting outside my door. Carver had written a letter full of passion and heat, and his words rolled through my body like the sound of his voice: *Sometimes I can't sleep, I can't stop thinking about you. Sometimes I dream you're in bed with me. I pulled off all the blankets and pillows once, trying to find you, those dreams are so real…*

I could have remained on my cot for the rest of the night, just reading this letter and daydreaming about Carver. Lost in one of my fantasies about visiting him. But someone knocked on the door, and Richard said, "Mary Jane, food's ready." So I reluctantly tucked Carver's letter away and joined my family for supper.

The stressful parts of my day all hit me again. Getting fired. Rejection letters. And Landon sitting outside.

Ethan pointed to the salad Mia had made, which was loaded with chickpeas and sunflower seeds and at least ten different vegetables. "I peeled the oranges," Ethan said. "And look—almonds." Ethan knew I loved almonds.

"Awesome," I said, and perked up.

"Richard made the dressing," Mia added.

I could tell he'd made one of my favorites: ground cashews and orange juice and rice vinegar. I gave Richard a hug, and then Ethan and Gus. I saved Mia for last.

"I hate eating salad," Mom said, and she gave me a dirty look. "Let's use that gift card and buy steak."

"No way," I said. "This is the best meal in town," and Mia laughed as she sat down beside me.

We lingered a long time over dinner, and then the kids did their homework. Around nine o'clock, Mia peeked out the front door and said, "Landon's still here."

I called, "What do you want, Landon?" I was trying to get the dishes done.

When Landon didn't answer, I told Mia to lock the door again.

The kids went to sleep at ten, and I sat at the table with my bills box, calculating how much my last check from Happy Garden would be. At eleven, Steve came home and asked, "What the hell is *he* doing here??"

"Money," I said.

A few minutes later, Landon started sobbing. A blubbering so loud that I could hear it with the door shut.

Mom paced through the living room, glaring at me. "Your brother is out there crying. *Crying*. And you won't let him come in?"

I shrugged. I sat at my computer, searching over job postings, and trying to keep up my spirits. Those two rejection letters were really weighing me down.

"What's the matter with you, Mary Jane?" Mom snapped. "You don't give a shit about your brother now, is that it? You don't give a shit about your *family?*"

I ignored Mom, finished my futile search for job postings, and opened a sports website. I watched highlights of Carver's game tonight with the Yankees, which the Cardinals had won, 2-1. Carver batted in the winning run, but not with a homer. He hit a line drive that let the runner on second score. I checked another website, and saw that Carver's batting average had shot up to .388. There was also another new fan site proclaiming *The Grizz is BACK!* It was fun to read. I forwarded it to Carver, to make sure he'd seen it. I also thanked him for my flowers, my letter, my gift card, my tickets.

Landon continued to blubber outside.

Mom shouted, "He made a *mistake*, Mary Jane. He didn't mean to knock out your window. Jesus Christ. Can't you just forgive him this one time?"

"You love him so much," I said, "you give him some money."

"I can't believe you!" Mom yelled. "Your brother is *sorry!* He's here to ask you for help! But what are *you* doing? Sitting in here with your stupid computer, in your stupid house, while your *brother* is out there *sobbing!* I can't believe I raised such a… selfish *bitch* for a daughter!"

She was pissing me off. "Landon isn't *sorry*," I said. "And I don't have any money to give him."

My phone chirped. Carver had sent a text to say happy birthday, and thanks for sharing the website. Then he sent another to ask: *Can you visit now?*

I smiled and typed, *Sorry. I lost my job today.*

Mom kept shouting at me. "Your brother needs *help!* He needs *help*, Mary Jane! Goddamn it!"

Carver sent: *What happened?*

I replied, *Stella fired me. I was a bad egg.*

Carver asked, *Did you mention Jesus or something?*

I burst into laughter. Then I typed, *In a way.*

Mom yelled, "You think you're so smart? You think you're hot shit?" She picked up my computer, and held it over her head like she wanted to throw it. She was gritting her teeth, on the brink of a rage.

I put down the phone and grabbed my laptop. "Knock it off," I snapped. "You want to help Landon, go help him yourself."

"What am *I* supposed to do?" Mom shouted. "I'm not the one with a *phone.* Or a *laptop.* Or some hotshot boyfriend who plays games on TV. *Oh, look at me.* I'm Mary Jane. *My boyfriend is on TV.* Isn't that wonderful. Aren't I so *special.*"

I carried my laptop into the bedroom, and placed it under my cot for safekeeping. Mom followed me, and her tantrum woke Mia up.

"Did anyone give *Landon* money to go to college?" Mom yelled. "Did he get a free ride? Did anyone take care of *him?* No. But my stupid daughter. My stupid daughter, she can listen to her brother crying out there, and not lift a *finger* to help him."

I hurried out of the bedroom, and Mom followed, shouting all the way. I closed the door behind her and hoped Mia would fall back asleep. Mom wouldn't go in there again until she was ready to sleep, which was the only reason I'd had to stash my computer under my cot.

"No one takes care of me," I told Mom.

"Yeah, right," Mom snarled. "How about Mr. Moneybags, huh? How about the guy on TV? Here, honey. Here's some money. Here, I'll pay your bills. Here's some flowers. Here's some video games. Here's your property tax. You think *Landon* would like someone who could pay all *his* bills?"

I was sure Landon *did* want someone who could pay all his bills. Except Janine worked as much as he did: hardly ever.

In the living room, Steve was putting his coat on again. He couldn't stand listening to Mom throw a fit. He left any time she flared up.

"Wanna come with?" Steve asked.

I shook my head no. I couldn't leave Mom here alone while the kids were asleep. Without her basement grotto to hide in, she was unstable here. No telling what she would do.

Landon was still crying outside. He didn't even look up when Steve left. The blubbering was so loud, I felt bad for my neighbors.

"You could give him some gas money!" Mom cried. "You could feed him some dinner!"

"I'd rather die," I said. I stepped outside and told Landon, "Feeling sorry for yourself is not an apology. Unless you're here to take Mom back to Goldking, I have nothing to say to you."

I shut the door and picked up the phone again. I sent Carver another text. *Landon is here. I'll call you tomorrow.*

Then I pocketed the phone and went to grab Mom, who was in the kitchen now, pulling my pots and pans from the cupboards. She was making a mess, throwing things and slamming doors shut.

"Your brother has *nothing,*" Mom screeched. "And what do *you* have? You and all your *money.* All your money, Mary Jane— your dirty, filthy money. And you can't spare a penny on your brother. Your brother who *said he is sorry* and is asking for *help.*"

I pushed Mom out of the kitchen, and put away the pots and pans. I said, "He didn't say he was sorry. Those tears are for himself. And he can keep crying. He can sit out there and cry all he wants. I *work* for my money. And so can he."

Mom grabbed my diploma while I was putting the last of the pans away. "What the hell did they teach you in college? To turn your back on your family? To treat your family like *shit?*"

I scrambled out of the kitchen and tried to save my diploma, but Mom opened the front door and hurled it outside before I could stop her. I heard the case crash and split apart on the concrete below, but I didn't run to retrieve it. The second I left the apartment, Mom would lock me outside, and probably barricade the door—and then I'd really have problems.

I was tempted to shove her outside, but she had that look in her eye like she was ready to slug me. She wanted a brawl, she was so worked up over Landon, and I was in no mood for a fight with my mother. So I glanced down at Landon and said, "I hope you're happy out here. I hope all that bawling makes you feel like a man."

Then I shut the door again and sat on the couch. I tipped my head back, wondering how long Mom's fit would last. I also hoped someone didn't steal my diploma. I hated that it was sitting out there in the dark, like trash.

That diploma had separated me from my family. From my mother and my three older brothers. And there was no going back. Mom knew what she was doing when she tried to destroy it. We were really fighting a war here, with the kids in the middle. I wanted them on my side, and Mom hated that.

She kept shouting and shouting about what a bleepity-bleeping bleep I was, and Landon kept crying outside on the steps, egging her on.

Mom pulled her hair, stomped her feet, and fell into The Abyss. Also known as the most dead-end of all subjects: The Past. "And you know what your *father* told me? You know what he said, Mary Jane? I should get an abortion. Because he didn't want any damn kids. He didn't want *you*. But no. No. I had you. Didn't I? I kept you. *I* kept you, Mary Jane, not your worthless father. And this is my thanks. This—*thing*—sitting here. This self-righteous… piece of… *shit*… child. That came out of my body. This is my thanks for bringing you into this world."

I hated when Mom had her tantrums. And I hated when she brought up my father like this. But Mom despised all her Prince Charmings, and ran them down equally. My father or Landon's, the kids' dad or Jeff and William's old man—all of them were targets of scorn.

Maybe my father *had* told Mom to get an abortion. But what did that matter now? He'd tried living with Mom, he'd taken care of us all for a while, and then he left—but he had come back for me later. Me, Richard, Ethan, and Mia. He took us all to Goldking. He tried to give us a better life. He had been a thief and a liar and far from an honorable person, but in the end, my father had loved me, and I hated listening to Mom bring up garbage that didn't matter anymore.

I felt very drained, waiting her out. Waiting Landon out. So when I heard Landon's old diesel start up in the parking lot, I was relieved.

"He's leaving," I told Mom, and she began to calm down. She stopped ranting and raving and hid in the bathroom. I knew she went in there to cry. She hid in there to sob and be miserable, and wade through the immense confusion that was her own mind.

I could not cure her misery. I often wished that I could. Misery leaked out of my mother like battery acid, and it was toxic as hell. She would cry herself to sleep tonight, and wake up tomorrow feeling lost. She wouldn't remember what she had said. She might not even remember that Landon had been here.

I went outside and found my diploma. I worried Landon had kicked it, but I didn't see any boot prints. The case was ruined, but the plastic sheeting had kept the paper safe. I brushed off the dirt and folded the case around the paper again. Then I brought my diploma upstairs, and returned it to its place in the cupboard by the dining room table. It wasn't the same as hanging my diploma in a frame on the wall, but right now, putting it on display in the cupboard was the best I could do.

I listened to Mom cry in the bathroom. Even as I child, I had pitied her. My pity for Landon was limited though. Nonexistent at times, like right now.

I used to think Mom had ruined Landon. That all of the times she had screamed at him, and called him terrible names, and beaten him black and blue as a child—I used to think she had broken something inside of him. Something Landon would never heal.

But Mom had beaten me, too. And I wasn't like Landon. Or William. Or Jeff.

I could see my reflection in the glass of the cupboard, and I was suddenly compelled to reach up and put a hand inside my shirt collar. I touched the back of my shoulder, and felt that jagged white scar that crossed over my skin.

I could hear Carver asking me, *How did you get this scar?* And I knew why I hadn't been able to answer. I couldn't bear to hear what he might say. How he might think I was… damaged. Like a broken chair in a store no one wanted to buy. Sometimes the truth could kill romance. Maybe Carver wouldn't have sent me a love letter today, if I had told him the truth when he'd asked. Such was the power of fear.

But if he ever asked me again, I would tell him. I would never bring it up on my own, but I wouldn't hide from it, either. I had told him the truth about my father, and Landon. The truth about the scars on my body was no worse than that.

I had always hated the scar on my shoulder. Even more than the others. Mom had made this one with the claw end of a hammer. I had never felt a rage black enough to ever pick up a hammer and strike a small child, but my mother sure had. She had hit me with the face several times, and those bruises had all disappeared. The claw end left this scar though. I couldn't say how old I was when this happened, maybe four or five. I only knew that I had all of my scars before we lived in the car. By the time Mom made that Impala our home, I was big enough—fast enough—to escape her. I could read her moods by then, and I could run.

I was still running. Maybe I would always be running. Childhood had held so many dark days of terror. Days of hunger. Days of pain. And as I touched this ugly scar, I knew that here was the imprint my childhood had left upon me: I had promised myself I would never do this to anyone. I would never make anyone suffer the way I had. I would never bring a child into this world, when the world was so full of nightmares and pain.

As an adult, I knew that a life full of pain was not the way every child grew up. I understood that I could have a baby and not beat my child black and blue. My oath not to have children was just part of my character now. I had fused it into my soul. Maybe that was the price I had paid to survive.

I was still scared of Carver's opinion of me. If he really thought to himself, *There's something wrong with a woman who doesn't want to have children.* God, how I hated how often people said that to me. Whenever I admitted I didn't want to have children, I always heard that remark. People were so quick to judge. So quick to decide what made a *real* woman… and what made a damaged one.

Some women were born infertile. Some women could never conceive. And some women were biologically ill-equipped for childbearing. Pregnancy sometimes killed the baby, or the mother, or both. Nature made them this way. It had nothing to do with choice.

So I didn't think God had created all women to have babies. I didn't want to have a child, and I felt fine with that choice. I felt only peace. Contentment. I felt like it was the right decision for me. When I thought of my life and my future, I felt happy. I felt excited. How could anything be wrong with me, if I felt this good about my decisions?

At least Carver had his three boys to care for, and I had already told him I didn't want to have babies. Whatever his private thoughts were, maybe he would never judge me so harshly. Never tell me he thought something was wrong with me. That I had to change to be loved.

But I was scared he would. I was scared he might have the power to make me unhappy. I didn't want to lose Carver's love. But my decision to avoid having children was not a choice I would change.

I knew why my mother had children. And it had nothing to do with nurturing life. Nothing with hope for our futures, or hope that we would be happy. We were simply her insurance policy. The policy that never worked. Men didn't stick around for babies. I wished my mother had figured that out.

But that was old history. Mom couldn't have any more children. And the ones she had were almost all grown. Mia was in junior high now. She'd be in eighth grade next year. I would be twenty-seven when she graduated from high school.

And Mia *would* graduate. I could see her graduation day in my mind. I could see all the kids graduating. I wanted my will to be strong enough to guarantee that this happened. I might not have the ambition to bring new life into the world—but I certainly had the ambition to protect the life that was already here.

I straightened my shirt, turned off the lights and went to bed. Mom remained in the bathroom, crying and muttering. "He told me he *wanted a baby*... he told me, he told me... And where am I now? Who's here to love Gilly? Who's here to love *me?*"

I closed the bedroom door, and the sound of her voice faded to a soft, incomprehensible sound.

As I lay on my cot, I prayed and prayed that Landon wouldn't come back. For money. For anything. I hoped he stayed gone. I also prayed and prayed I'd find a job tomorrow. As far as I was concerned, looking for work was more stressful than clocking in at Happy Garden. But I had end-of-year field trips to pay for, and rent, and the water bill was due. I had to get a job. I just had to.

43

RESISTANCE POETRY

The next morning, I woke the kids up for school, watched them leave for the bus, and then I sat outside on the stairs. I listened to the birds chattering in the oak trees nearby. It was warm enough in Riverdale now that I could wear shorts and a t-shirt without feeling cold. I stared down at my bare feet and wriggled my toes for a while, because sometimes it brought me good luck to wriggle my toes.

When the Persian man stepped out of his apartment to go to work, he spotted me and called, "Good morning, Miss Logan!" and I smiled, even though I felt beaten down. Between Mom breaking my diploma case last night, my rejection letters, and the sudden loss of my job, I was not feeling very perky.

But I cheered at the sight of my neighbor and said, "Hi, Mahmood."

I'd finally committed Mahmood's name to memory that winter, when he and his friends threw a party and shared some of their food with us. They'd brought over a pot of stew called *khoresht* and a bowl of fresh fruit, which had been awesome.

His full name was Mahmood Abbasi and he rented one of the larger apartments across from mine. He lived with his lover, a man named Javad, and two other Persian men who I guessed were also gay. They all worked at that big home for the elderly in Riverdale.

Mahmood walked over to me and said, "You are looking sad this morning, Miss Logan."

"Yeah," I sighed. "I'm kind of bummed."

"You are not working today?" he asked.

"No," I said. "I got fired."

Mahmood sat down beside me and rested his elbows on top of his knees. He wore his blue scrubs and white tennis shoes for his shift at Tucky Hilson's.

"You will find new employment?" he asked.

"Sure," I smiled. "I'll figure something out."

Javad stepped out of their apartment, looking a bit more harried, and when he noticed Mahmood on the steps, he said something in Persian.

Mahmood told him, "Miss Logan has lost her job," and Javad cast me a look of concern.

"You will find new employment?" he asked.

"Definitely," I said. "There are lots of jobs here in Riverdale."

Mahmood stood and returned to his apartment, and then he carried out a porcelain bowl that held several apples, two bananas, and an orange. "Miss Logan," he said, "you will need to keep up your strength."

I took the fruit bowl he handed me and said, "Thank you, Mahmood. I'll bring this back," and he patted my shoulder. Then he and Javad walked out to their Honda and left for work.

I continued to sit outside and listen to the birds sing. I ate one of the apples. I thought I was really lucky to have these

Iranian neighbors. They were so generous and kind, and with several hours of job-hunting ahead of me, I had definitely needed a dose of kindness right now.

***

My first full day of searching for work was dismal. I gave up visiting businesses around four o'clock, and went to the middle school to watch Mia play softball. She rode home with me after her game, and when we arrived at the apartment, Mahmood's apartment door was open. When he heard the sound of Mia's voice, he came out to see if I'd found a job yet.

"Maybe on Monday," I said, since tomorrow was Saturday and I had my weekend shift at The Summit.

Mahmood nodded, and then he said, "Miss Logan, we are all hoping you and your family will join us for dinner tonight. We have made a very large feast."

I stammered, "That's… that's… You made everyone *dinner?*"

"Yes, Miss Logan!" Mahmood beamed. "Won't you please join us tonight?" He smiled and nodded encouragingly at Mia, so she would help talk me into it.

"I'm all for it," Mia said. "Those guys can freaking *cook*. Let's do it!"

So a few minutes later, I gathered up the kids and Gus and Mom, made them all wash up and put on some nice clothes, and we walked over to Mahmood's apartment for dinner. I wished Steve could've joined us, but he was working a shift at The Summit tonight. Mom ranted for a while about how she thought Mahmood and his buddies were all involved with the Taliban and plotting the end of America, but eventually she calmed down enough to come with us.

As we walked toward Mahmood's door, Mom said, "If they start building a roadside bomb on the table, I'm *outta* there!" and she jerked her thumb backwards for emphasis.

"Sounds like a plan," I said.

***

Mahmood's apartment was in the building on the other side of the stairs, and his apartment was much larger than mine, spacious and beautiful. He had a huge dining room table surrounded by paintings, and a cupboard full of ivory sculptures and a leather-bound copy of the Qur'an. He also had an entire bookshelf full of poetry, most of it printed in Arabic or Persian.

The other two men who lived with Mahmood and Javad were named Habib and Bijan, and all four of these men were well-groomed and polite. They also had swarthy dark skin and shiny black hair, and I guessed Mom found them handsome, because she eventually decided they might not be Taliban. I thought she found Bijan the most attractive, because at one point she whispered to me, "Are you *sure* these men are *gay?*" and she was looking at Bijan as she said it.

I told her, "I'm pretty sure," and Mom turned a bit surly. But for the most part, she was a good houseguest.

Mahmood and Javad were the ringleaders of this party, and together they served up roasted chicken, rice, stew, vegetables, fish, pastries, and so many other delicious things that even Mom tucked in and had seconds, and then thirds.

The kids and Gus did most of the talking, so the conversation centered around: (1.) baseball and (2.) Carver's homeruns. Since Mahmood and his friends didn't follow baseball, they found the kids' fanaticism amusing as well as educational. They sure learned a lot about the St. Louis Cardinals.

Around nine o'clock, the kids went home with Mom, and I stayed to talk to Mahmood and Javad at the table. They'd made an entire jug of mint tea, and we drank several cupfuls while they told me about the current problems in Iran, such as the government suppression of human rights. As I was well aware that Iran's fundamentalist-run theocracy and pseudo-democratic constitution were the causes of profound misery in that country, I mostly smiled a lot and nodded my head in agreement.

"I tell you, Miss Logan!" Mahmood cried at one point, "Iran needs *democracy!* Our country needs *freedom!*" I thought he was a little hyped-up on account of all the caffeine he'd been drinking, though I sure loved his enthusiasm. Javad even had a little American flag that he waved around whenever the word *democracy* came up.

While we'd been talking, Habib and Bijan had been putting the food away and washing the dishes, and when they were finished, they took out several books of poetry from the shelf on the wall.

"We will read you some poetry!" Habib said, and he and Bijan thumbed through the books to find the poems that they wanted.

They proceeded to read aloud what they called Resistance Poetry for the next half hour. First, they would recite the poem in its original Arabic or Persian, and then Mahmood would translate the poem into English for me as best he could. They read these poems so passionately and with such conviction, that the men turned misty-eyed within the first five minutes, and Javad waved around his American flag quite a lot. Their Resistance Poetry used coded language for government oppression and

Iran's seemingly hopeless and brutal struggle for freedom, so I frequently turned emotional right along with them. They were really beautiful poems. Mahmood was certain that this poetry would bring Iran's callous leaders to their knees, and transform the entire country into "a brilliant hope, shining brightly," as he put it.

"Long live *freedom!*" Bijan cried. "Long live *democracy!*" and Javad waved his flag again.

Sometime after midnight, I was drying my eyes for around the fortieth time, Mahmood said, "You know, Miss Logan, something Iran could really use? A *Daily Show.*"

I said, "Daily Show?"

"*The Daily Show* with Jon Stewart?" Mahmood clarified. "Political comedy show? Iran should have one of those."

"I love that show," I said, and everyone nodded their heads.

"We have been planning to make one," Bijan said.

"In Persian," Habib clarified. "And Arabic."

"Mahmood would be our Jon Stewart," Javad said. "We will call it *The Daily Show with Mahmood Abbasi.*"

Bijan nodded. "And put it up on the internet."

I considered this for a moment. Would Jon Stewart mind these guys using his show like that? He knew Iran was full of young people and intellectuals yearning to be free to speak their minds… people who were often imprisoned, tortured and killed by those fundamentalist leaders. I bet he'd be happy about this project.

"When will you start this—er—Persian Daily Show?" I asked.

Mahmood laughed and held up his hands. "We have purchased a camera. That is all."

"Where's your camera?" I asked.

Javad went to a cupboard and removed a Sony Professional Widescreen Camcorder. He brought it over to show me, and as I took the camera from him, I felt stunned. This camera cost four or five *thousand* dollars. These guys were serious about filming this show.

"Have you started writing yet?" I asked.

The men turned solemn. "We cannot figure out the camera," Javad said. "And how would we put the pieces together? We don't know how we would make a complete show."

I turned the camera in my hands, and set it down on the table. "I can teach you how to use that."

Mahmood sucked in his breath and looked shocked. "You know how to use this camera?"

"I've never used that particular camera before, but sure, I can teach you," I said. "And if you buy a Mac and the editing software, I can teach you how to edit your film."

The men glanced around at each other. They looked nervous, stunned, and amazed.

"You would do this for us, Mary Jane?" Mahmood asked.

I laughed. "Of course. I want to make movies myself one day. I want to film documentaries. Why wouldn't I help out?"

There was a flurry of Persian and Arabic in the room, and then the men started to cry out in happiness, and Javad waved his American flag in exuberance. Mahmood sang a song, and after a minute, the others joined in. I wasn't sure if the song praised God, or country, or both, but it sure was pretty.

Mahmood knelt in front of me, and took my hands. "You are a very great woman, Mary Jane. Very great." He kept smiling up at me, and the others were smiling, too.

"Filming and editing is the easy part," I said. "You'll have to do all the writing and make up all the skits. And you might want to build a fake newsroom set."

Mahmood nodded with passion. "We will do this."

They were so committed to this project, and so oddly adorable—that the consequences of what they were planning to do finally hit me. If these men publicly trashed Iran's fundamentalist leaders, they would never be welcome in Iran again.

"Are you all U.S. citizens?" I asked. They nodded. "You know you'll be permanently banned from your country, if you do this?"

Mahmood nodded again. "Of course."

I sighed. "Okay then. I'm in."

So by the time I left their apartment that night, Mahmood and his friends had resolved to buy the editing equipment they needed, and set up their living room to resemble Jon Stewart's sound stage.

Later, when I was home again and looking over my mail, I found another rejection letter for my grant proposal. I folded the paper with a sigh.

As I turned out the lights and went to bed, my heart sank as I remembered that I still needed a job. I *really* needed a job. There was no way I could help Mahmood and his friends, or send in any more grant proposals, if I didn't have the money for rent.

But as long as I found new employment, things were looking up. I was excited to work on this show with Mahmood. For the first time since I graduated, I was about to take part in the trade I loved most: filming and editing, and that felt like such a huge win. A win I had almost given up on after college. After Hanna. And I knew she'd be happy, if she could see me right now.

If things would just fall into place, I could visit Carver this summer. Sometimes I felt like I wanted to visit him even more than I wanted my grant proposal accepted. I missed being held, and I missed making love, and I longed to be near him again. Watching him play baseball at night, or reading his love letters, or hearing his voice on the phone, I knew that this ache in my body kept growing worse.

So I prayed again that I would find a job soon. I prayed and prayed that I would see Carver this summer.

44

A NEW DREAM

After working my shifts at The Summit that weekend, I returned to job-hunting on Monday. I revisited every place of business that was currently hiring, and tried to talk my way into a position that didn't require me to work nights. I eventually found myself in the Riverdale Diner that afternoon. The diner was owned by a man named Bob Mudd, and his establishment served the greasiest food for two hundred miles. When I'd visited the diner on Thursday asking for work, Bob had been flirty with me, so I reasoned I might be able to win him over on a morning shift. Bob Mudd didn't need any help, either with waitressing or in the kitchen, but if he had something open up, he told me he'd call.

So I went home to my apartment that night feeling glum. I answered a knock on the door around seven, and found Mahmood waiting outside.

"Good evening, Miss Logan!" he said.

I smiled. "Hey, Mahmood."

"We found these for you!" he said, and he held up a pair of black tennis shoes. The sides were decorated with sparkly silver lettering that spelled out *USA*. I thought of Javad waving his American flag and laughed.

"Wow!" I cried, taking the shoes. "Mahmood, these are great!" I checked the size, and when I saw they were in my size 9, I put them on.

"We have ordered all of the editing equipment," Mahmood said. "So we should be able to start filming next week."

"That's fantastic!" I said.

Mahmood asked me to follow him, so I went to see the work on his living room. Habib and Bijan were constructing a news desk shaped like Jon Stewart's, and they'd already painted the walls and moved the furniture.

"You'll need to make sure to add a copyright disclaimer," I said, "and send Jon Stewart a DVD of the show. Subtitled, of course."

"Our dream is coming true!" Mahmood laughed. "Miss Logan, this is wonderful!"

"It sure is," I said.

I still hadn't found a new full-time job, but I was excited enough for this film project to calm my anxiety. For the moment, at least.

***

At five o'clock the next morning, my phone rang. I worried immediately that something had happened to Carver—and I answered in a panic—"*Carver?*"

"This Mary Jane?" a man asked.

"Yes," I said. I recognized the voice of Bob Mudd, from the Riverdale Diner.

"Turns out my head cook came down with TB. So if you still want this job, I'll see you in twenty minutes," and he hung up.

I jumped off my cot and hurried to dress. I had to leave Steve in charge of getting the kids off to school, and then I grabbed the keys to the Lincoln and headed out the door.

***

The Riverdale Diner was about the grimiest hole I had ever worked in. The time clock alone held so many layers of filth, the green metal had turned sepia. Once I clocked in, I spent the morning cooking platters of eggs, hash browns, corned beef and green chili, and switched to burgers and fries at eleven. My shift ended at one, and I smelled like grease so badly by then that I almost felt nauseous. I now had a layer of fry oil stuck to my skin, so I stopped by Walgreens and bought a sugar scrub that smelled like cinnamon and vanilla. Once I was home, I hopped in the shower and scrubbed off the stink. Then I poured a tall glass of water and called Carver. He was getting ready for a game in Chicago against the Cubs.

I was so relieved that Bob was paying me $10.75 an hour, a full $2.50 more than I'd made working for Stella—that the first thing I told Carver was that I had a job cooking.

"How about your proposal?" he asked.

"Rejection letters so far," I said. "I'm not working in the film industry, so that's not unusual—though I *am* starting a project," and I told him about The Persian Daily Show with Mahmood and his friends. "They're really great guys."

"Are they trying to steal you away from me?" Carver asked.

I laughed. "They bat for the other team."

Carver sighed with relief.

That evening, the kids and I watched his ballgame in Chicago. Carver hit a homerun in the third inning, and stole base after base throughout the game. I loved seeing his lead-off, and the speed of his sprint. The way he slid for a base. And when he stood up with dirt on his jersey and that grin like the devil, my heart would slam in my chest.

Maybe now that I was working again, and the kids were almost finished with school, I could pick a weekend this summer to visit. I remembered the sound of his voice when he told me what he loved about baseball. *Fastballs. Changeups. Getting dirty.*

Well, he was certainly getting dirty tonight. And I wished I could be with him after the game, to help clean him up.

***

For the rest of May, Steve had to make sure the kids were up for the bus every morning, and I cooked at the diner and came home smelly and sticky with grease. The odor continued to put my stomach on edge, so I had to scour my skin each day after work. The smell of that fry oil was as hard on my nerves as the sound of screaming toddlers at Happy Garden had been. But at least Bob Mudd was decent and rational, and the hourly wage was so much better, that cooking at the diner was easily a million times better than working for Stella.

Mom was the only one of us who could tolerate the food from the diner, so I usually brought her home a green chili burger after my shift.

On May thirtieth, the kids played their last baseball games of the school year, and the Rockies played St. Louis in Denver. Even though Carver hit two homeruns in this game, the

Cardinals lost. But the score seemed irrelevant, since all I could think about was how Carver was only *eight hours* away… how I could drive for eight hours to see him.

I knew I couldn't miss work, and I had no money for gas.

But the entire time the Cardinals played at Coors Field, I was obsessed with the idea that I *could* visit. And when I spoke to Carver on the phone at night, I struggled not to fixate on the issue. I didn't want him to say, *Well, I could just give you the money for gas, and after you lose your job, I could support you until you find another one*—because I felt razors slice my heart at the very idea.

I still battled against the urge to drop everything and run to him. For one night in his bed, throwing my whole life away seemed worth it sometimes. My skin felt flushed, my body felt jittery. I was light on my feet, calculating how many seconds it would take me to reach him.

I hated that desire could make me so crazy, make me want to wreck my entire life for *one night* in a hotel room with Carver. But I just kept fantasizing about showing up at the ballpark and surprising him at the end of the game, and how he would hold me and kiss me, and the things we would do once we were alone… and sometimes I just wanted to beg him to skip a game to fly down and see me. I felt like I lost my mind for three days.

I was relieved when the Cardinals finished their rotation at Coors Field, and went on to play somewhere else. My ability to think about something other than driving to Denver returned.

After the first week of June, the kids attended their last day of school, and we used the gift card from Carver for a celebratory dinner that night. The next morning, the kids packed up their things and I drove them to Goldking with Mom. Gus followed in the Buick. Once the kids were in town, they dropped their bags at the house and set off in search of summer employment.

Landon had moved out. He was back with his father, in Duck's trailer across town, and I hoped he stayed there. Forever.

The kids would make enough money this summer to pay for their food, electric, and water. It was the first time they had ever done this before—paid all their own bills—but I had coached them enough that they felt sure they could do it. So as long as Landon stayed away, I knew they'd be fine.

I realized I was still calling the kids *kids*, even though Richard and Gus were both bigger than me, and Ethan would be a freshman in high school this fall. They were teenagers now. And even Mia was old enough to get a good summer job. Then I thought, *whatever, they're still kids*. Even if they could pay their own bills for a summer.

Mom was thrilled to return to her basement grotto. Her herb garden had withered, so I let her have ten dollars in credit at the hardware store to buy seeds. Then she strolled downtown to the S.O.S. Bar, on the prowl for a man. There were always a few single men in Goldking at any one moment, all of them guys Mom had slept with before. But lonely was lonely, and Mom's standards weren't high.

I returned to Riverdale that evening, where it was just me and Steve and Gandhi in the apartment.

Throughout the month of June, I continued to work on grant applications and help Mahmood and his friends film the Persian Daily Show. I wasn't sure we were actually being funny at all, as most of the skits Javad and the others came up with made no sense to me. In one show, Habib dressed up like a general and we filmed him giving orders to Javad, who was dressed like a soldier. The subtitles read like this:

GENERAL: I *order* you to buy a lawnmower and ride it over the desert!

SOLDIER: Yes, sir!

GENERAL: I do not care if your lawnmower breaks down! You will cross the desert!

SOLDIER: Yes, sir!

GENERAL: Take this can of petrol, and get out!!

The gas can was decorated with a picture of some Iranian official who ran a petrochemical company in Tehran. Overall, I thought these skits were beyond weird, and either something was lost in translation, or I just didn't get Persian humor. Not even Mahmood could explain how that lawnmower skit was funny.

But I managed to edit the segments together and turn them into a show, and Mahmood and his friends put the clips on YouTube, and emailed the links to everyone they knew. While I worked with the sound equipment and spliced the shows together on the computers they'd purchased, I taught Mahmood and his friends how to edit. I knew the episodes would turn out better if I wasn't part of the process, though it took more than three weeks before they started to get the hang of it.

Despite all my doubts, Mahmood assured me that their Persian Daily Show was a hit. And I could see for myself that thousands of people were watching the videos on YouTube. The show was also amassing a huge following on Facebook. "We are helping to spread revolution," Mahmood said, and I thought that was awesome. Iran deserved a democracy, and helping Mahmood and his friends made me feel good.

✳✳✳

On the Fourth of July, Carver played a game in Cincinnati. I was home alone with Gandhi that afternoon, and though I listened to the broadcast on my phone, I really thought about Hanna. I thought about her gravesite. I wondered if I should've asked Carver to fly me out to that game, so I could visit the place where my Hanna was buried. I felt so sad about it that I drove out to a canyon and shot several Coke cans, until I ran out of ammo. Then I sat on a tree stump and threw sticks for Gandhi to fetch.

My grant proposal had been rejected forty-two times… and there were no other sources of funding for me to apply to.

It meant I had to shelve *Brighter Than Stars*, and come up with something else.

I would have to create an entirely new project to film. Something that might have a chance of being accepted.

As I sat throwing sticks to Gandhi, I thought about taking a break from work to clear my head. Not to visit Carver, but to think of a new project. The more I thought about it, the more I decided it was the right thing to do.

I needed some time in the mountains. I wanted to ride King and sleep out under the stars. With the kids home in Goldking, I could afford to miss work and still make my rent and my student loan payment. Carver would be sad if I didn't visit him. But I wouldn't be much of a companion, if I went to see him when I felt down on myself.

So I made up my mind to spend a weekend in the mountains. To get away and just think.

When I walked into my apartment that night, I received a text from Carver that said he had finally reached his goal hitting weight of 241 pounds. I called him to say congratulations, and we talked for a while.

"Ready to visit?" he asked.

"I sure want to. But I have to take King into the mountains next week. So I can come up with a new project to film. I need a place where I can just... think. And clear my head."

"Are you all right, Mary Jane?"

"I will be."

45

ABIGAIL'S RING

Missing work without vacation time was my biggest obstacle. But at this point in my life, I was desperate. I was ready to beg.

After five days of pleading with people, I finally found someone to cover my weekend shift at The Summit, and Bob Mudd decided to cave and give me a Friday off at the diner. It was such a massive amount of effort to receive three days off—but if I came up with a new film project, I wouldn't regret it.

I drove up to Goldking on the second Thursday in July, after my shift at the diner and a sugar-scrub shower. I wore a flannel shirt, jeans, and my black cowboy boots. On the seat behind me, my pack held a change of clothes, a bar of soap, toothbrush and paste, ten cans of soup, two sacks of apples, a big bag of nuts and seeds, dried strawberries, seven oranges, a cantaloupe, and green tea. I also took my coat, my gloves, and my straw cowgirl hat with the fake turquoise on the band.

Once I was in Goldking, I went to the Cowboy's house first. He was finished with work, drinking Mountain Dew in the backyard, and tinkering with a dismantled PlayStation. I guessed he was repairing it for one of his friends.

He smiled and stood up from the picnic table as I came over to join him.

"Hey, MJ," he said.

"Hey, Cowboy," and we hugged. "I'm going camping."

He studied my face for a moment, and then asked, "You want to borrow my stove?" and I nodded. The Cowboy had helped me on my journeys before. He collected hunting equipment the way some women bought shoes, and he wasn't stingy with his supplies. "Well, come on," he said, and I followed him into the house.

The Cowboy kept all of his camping gear in the workroom, a space that always smelled like oil and venison, on account of the machinery that hung on the walls and the butchering that was done on the table. He reached up on a shelf and pulled down a two-burner camp stove.

"You asked Abigail to marry you yet?" I asked, since I knew they were still dating. The Cowboy blushed. I took that for a no. "Are you going to?"

He shrugged, placed the stove on the table and took down a couple of butane canisters, and then a mess kit. "How's the ballplayer?" I'd told the Cowboy about Carver a while ago, when he had stopped by my apartment to check in on me. He'd found out that Landon had broken my window, and wanted to know why.

"Carver is good," I said. "Busy with games." I gazed at the floor for a moment, and added, "I'll show you something," before leaving the workroom to walk back to the Lincoln. I retrieved ten of the rejection letters I'd accumulated, carried them inside and held them out to the Cowboy.

"There's my documentary project," I said. "D.O.A."

The Cowboy glanced through the papers and frowned. "No marketability…" he read aloud, scanning various paragraphs. "No perceivable audience… The design of this project displays an obvious lack of foresight and structure…" He folded the papers together until they were wadded into a mass that resembled a softball. "What are you going to do with this garbage?"

I removed a box of matches from one of his shelves. The Cowboy stuffed the papers into a cooking pot, and we lit them on fire.

"Good riddance," he said, watching them burn. "Now what?"

"I have to think up a new project," I said. "Something with marketability, foresight, and structure."

The Cowboy rapped his knuckles against the wood table. "Want me to go with you?" he asked, gesturing through the open door with his chin.

"Not this time," I said. "I feel too barbaric right now. Even for you," and I smiled at him, so he'd smile in return.

"You already talk to Don?" he asked, since I usually took King and a pack horse named Nikki. But I followed the motto that it was easier to ask forgiveness later than permission up front, especially when it came to Don Doonan.

"Nah," I said. "I'll just check their shoes aren't loose, and leave a note."

I borrowed the following supplies from the Cowboy: stove, fuel canisters, matches, mess kit, knife, sleeping bag with a pad, tent, first aid kit, headlamp, three water bottles, and one transistor radio about the size of my fist. He wanted me to take one of his rifles, but I told him no. I would have Ravi, and he was enough.

"How about pepper spray?" I asked.

"You got it," said the Cowboy, and he handed me a canister of it and stopped trying to make me take another gun.

When I had all of this gear in the Lincoln, I said, "Show me the ring you bought Abigail." I knew he hadn't bought her a ring, and I knew this subject made him uncomfortable. But I also knew something was bothering him, which meant I was better off being pushy.

The Cowboy returned to the workroom and opened an empty box of ammo. Inside was the same diamond ring he'd tried to give me six years ago.

"Cowboy," I sighed, even though I knew the Cowboy had never intended to give Abigail this ring. He was telling me something else by showing it to me—that he was terrified of being turned down again. He was so scared Abigail might tell him no that he wasn't even going to ask. He looked so sad now. So young. Afraid to admit he didn't know what to do. So I picked up a pen and paper and leaned over the work table. I drew a picture of a ring with a ruby in the center—for Abigail's birthstone—with clusters of three diamonds on each side. I labeled the band to be made of white gold.

"Here, Cowboy," I said, handing him the paper. "There's what to buy." I took the old diamond ring from his hand. "This one is mine. Go find me a chain, and I'll wear it."

The Cowboy walked into the main part of the house, went upstairs, and returned with a slender gold chain, probably from his mother's bedroom. His mother never wore jewelry, though she'd amassed quite a collection over the years. The Cowboy handed me the necklace, and I threaded the ring and fastened it around my neck.

I wouldn't wear it forever. The Cowboy understood that. Some objects in life just seemed to anchor us to our fears. And that's what this ring was doing to him. So I was taking it from him, and letting him know I would always honor what we had once had together. When he smiled, he smiled with relief. He looked like The Cowboy again.

"Now give me a hug and invite me to your engagement party," I said. The Cowboy hugged me without speaking.

"Be safe up there," he finally said.

As I was leaving the work room, I called, "Drag my carcass out of the canyon, if I fall off a cliff." The Cowboy laughed.

46

NINE WEEKS IN NAIROBI

After I had all of my camping supplies, I drove to the house. The kids were home, hanging out between lunch and dinner shifts. I told Mia she could keep the phone for the weekend, and I asked Gus to drop me off at King's pasture, in the Lincoln, since my supplies were in back. I asked Gus to park the vehicle at the house and to hide the keys for me, and he said that he would.

Once I was down at the pasture, King ran over to greet me, and when he spotted my pack and the camping supplies, he started prancing around. King loved pack trips, so he kept tossing his head and snorting. He hated riding equipment more than ever though, so when I tried to saddle him, he sucked in so much air, his stomach swelled to five times its size before I could cinch him up properly. I thought that his attitude was completely uncalled for.

"You better knock it off, King," and I shook my fist at him. "I'll eat your apples if you don't cool it." Mollified now, his ears drooped and he frowned. He knew I wasn't messing around when I threatened to eat all his apples. So he stopped bloating his gut and let me tighten the girth.

My favorite pack horse was a black mare named Nikki, and Nikki was sweet as could be while I loaded her up with all our supplies. I gave Nikki an apple, and told her, "You are such a great horse," which made King turn sorrowful. He really wanted an apple, but that was too bad.

Nikki had my camping gear, two sacks of grain, and the apples, while King would carry me and a few things in his saddlebags.

Both horses had been recently shod, and their hooves were in perfect condition, so it was lucky for me that Don took such good care of these horses. He also kept a nice tack room. King's saddle and bridle were in the best condition, but that was because Don never rode him. I finished adjusting my stirrups and hoisted myself into the saddle, and Nikki followed us on her lead line to the gate. As we headed east of town and rode into the canyon, I felt happier than I had in a long time. My whole body changed, because I knew I was free. I wasn't going to smell like grease tomorrow, or hustle for tips, or look at my bills, or any of the other chores that had come to define my life. And when I knew I was free, I was all steel. I felt the iron in my blood, and that made me happy.

Mountains made me remember that nothing could ever damage my soul, not petty bosses, not fatigue, not even rejection letters. I gazed around at the peaks, and I was in heaven.

King wanted to run, but I kept him reined in and we followed the river. We didn't start climbing until the turn after Primrose, which took us into a gulch known as Broken Rock. I had a particular meadow I wanted to camp in tonight, a stretch of grass with a smattering of Columbine flowers and a waterfall nearby.

Nikki and King made good time, and we arrived a little after eight o'clock that evening. I walked both horses for a while and checked they'd cooled down, and then I made camp in the twilight. Nikki and King drank water from the stream while I ate one of my oranges and heated a can of soup on the stove. Then I fed both horses some grain on a smooth stretch of granite, and King proceeded to sort the seeds with his lips into organized piles. King refused to eat oats and corn mixed together, like a child who screamed if his potatoes touched the peas on his plate. He had the equine equivalent of Asperger's syndrome.

While King was sorting his food, I decided to spread the sleeping bag outside of the tent, so I could gaze up at the stars. I could hear creatures scurrying around in the trees, and the sound of King's munching when he finally started eating his seed piles. I picketed both horses, and then turned on the radio and found KTUR Rock. I listened to Cat Stevens and Fleetwood Mac and the weather report. Then I switched off the radio and enjoyed the quiet again.

I thought of the times I had brought Hanna camping up here, when I'd built fires and we'd poured rum and Cokes. But on this trip, I hadn't brought any liquor, and I didn't build a fire until my very last night, when the temperature dropped low enough that I needed one just to sleep.

After three days in the mountains, I had thought of a new project to film. My new idea was to spend nine weeks in Nairobi next summer with a group of five high school seniors. I'd film them learning about Kenya, living in a dorm together, and volunteering in orphanages, health clinics, and schools. These high school students could be of any ethnicity or family background, but they all had to have one goal for their college experience: they all wanted to get into Stanford. The film project would be called *I Want to Get into Stanford: Nine Weeks in Nairobi*. The audience for this show would be all of those upper-middle and middle-class families who worked so hard to help their kids earn admission into top universities.

I figured that designing a show for these parents would give the project market appeal, as these people spent loads of money on admissions advisors, SAT practice sessions, and tons of other extras for their kids. They also had the money for cable, Wi-Fi, and everything else that drove consumer culture.

When I'd been in high school, I'd had no idea some kids were given so much help to score a place into college. Not until Hanna mentioned it while we'd been in India. She told me how a wealthy girl named Chloe had gotten into our school—her parents had moved the whole family so that Chloe would shift up in class rank, from her place of 27th in her large, urban school district, to become the valedictorian in a smaller public school. With parents going to such lengths for their children, there had to be a market for a film highlighting the current challenges of college admissions.

I'd chosen Nairobi for its infrastructure and relative safety, and I'd chosen Stanford because California was sunny and warm, and I reasoned that the kids who wanted to go there might be more outdoorsy and talkative than, say, students whose top pick was Harvard. The biggest draw of the show would be to find out if any of the five students actually made it into Stanford, and whether they thought their nine weeks in Africa had tipped the scales in their favor. If America was perpetually going to be split into the haves and have-nots, then a documentary like this would surely hit a nerve.

And if this show was successful, then I might earn the money I needed for *Brighter Than Stars*. So I would put everything

I had into *Nine Weeks in Nairobi*, to make that documentary the best it could be.

I turned in my sleeping bag and gazed into the fire. As happy as I was to have a new project to work on, I was not really content. I kept wishing Carver was here. I wouldn't have needed the fire if he'd been beside me. And he was such good company. We would have had a long conversation, about all sorts of things. He was the first person I wanted to tell about *Nine Weeks in Nairobi*. I knew he'd be excited about it, just because I was excited.

I remembered those dreams I'd had about him—the dreams of him in a stadium. I had hoped he would rediscover his joy of the game… and he was the Grizz again now. A powerhouse, a force of a man. And sometimes he felt so incredibly far away. And then other moments, like right now, he felt so close. Like he might appear any moment at the edge of the firelight, and slip into my sleeping bag with me.

The idea made me glow. Sooner or later, I would see him again. Not on TV, but in person. The real him. Not the uniform, not the ballplayer. Carver the man. The one who wrote me love letters, with man-scribble hearts in the margins, and had dreams about lying in bed with me, running his hands down my body. That was the Carver I wanted to visit.

***

On the afternoon of July thirteenth, I rode out of the mountains, and returned Nikki and King to their pasture. As soon as I'd unsaddled the horses, they went straight to their hay. I borrowed another horse, a brown mare named Daisy, to ride to the Cowboy's house. He agreed to drive out in his truck to pick up my gear, and chose to idle along beside me as I rode Daisy back to the pasture. We talked to each other through the open window.

"Did you find a ring?" I asked.

The Cowboy smiled. "I found one," he said. There was a light in his eyes that hadn't been there a week ago. So I knew he'd proposed, which made me so happy I laughed. So did he.

"Engagement party?" I asked.

"Sure," he said with a grin. "Let's drink some beer tonight."

So that's what we did. After I returned the Cowboy's supplies to his workroom, and went home to shower and put on some clean clothes, I met up with everyone at the S.O.S. Bar.

The S.O.S. was a dive, with peanut shells on the floor and flickering neon signs, but they served great margaritas and they hosted live bands. By the time I arrived, the Cowboy and Abigail were already there, as well as all of the people in town who called themselves friends. Abigail told everyone she and the Cowboy would get married on the first Saturday of October, when the fall colors peaked. She was pleasant to me, and I was grateful for that. I refused to dance with the Cowboy, even when they played his favorite Tim McGraw song. I told him, "That's her song now," and nodded toward Abigail.

"Never," he said, and he waited out the song at the bar, ordering another round. He returned to Abigail after it ended, and danced with her for the rest of the night. As I watched them together, I thought they made a great couple, and I knew the Cowboy loved her, even if it had taken him so long to propose. The music made me keep thinking of Carver, and how we had danced together that night in Muldoon's. I had been so nervous that evening, and I realized now that Carver had, too. Why else would we have struggled so much to do something so simple?

It was funny to think of him being anxious like that. Nervous about taking me out on a date. My wonderful Carver, who was probably hitting another homerun tonight.

The band in the S.O.S. played Garth Brooks and Alan Jackson, and I danced with men who might or might not have been alcoholics, and who might or might not have had all their teeth. For a night out in Goldking, I had a good time.

***

Before I drove home that evening, I read through my phone messages and checked my voicemail. Carver had left one or two each day, usually after a game, mostly to say he hoped I was all right. He sounded worried, so I replied to a message to let him know I was fine.

He called me immediately, so we talked for a few minutes on my way home.

"Was the trip a success?"

I laughed. "Definitely. It was perfect."

"You'll tell me all about it?" he asked.

"Tomorrow," I promised, since I knew I would lose my cell signal soon. A hazard of life in the mountains. "I love you, Carver. I miss you."

He laughed. "Not half as much as I missed you, Mary Jane."

Once I was home, I spent a few minutes online, and discovered the Cardinals had won three of their last four games. Carver had hit three homeruns in one game, a grand slam in another, and double homeruns in the others. His name was all over various sports websites—and ticket sales had gone up.

I saw a picture of a group of his fans, people who called themselves grizzlies and sometimes painted their faces white with black lines on their cheeks, to look like claw marks. During games, they held up banners with a stylized picture of a bear's head. The image was sort of like Japanese writing, composed of a few graceful black lines on a white background. The bear was showing his teeth and taking a swipe with one paw. I thought it would make a great t-shirt, and sure enough, I found a photo of two people who'd gotten creative with a screen printing machine.

With every game Carver played, his fan base grew larger, and I thought it might be approaching what it once must have been, back when he was younger and slugging balls left and right. He usually went out to say hi to the grizzlies, and they often passed him baseballs to sign or held up their children to shake his hand. Several people uploaded photographs of the Grizz with their children, either onto the fan site or the Facebook page someone else had set up, and I loved to study those pictures. I could stare at Carver for hours on end.

The next morning, I went to work at the diner, and that evening, I watched the Cardinals play in Pittsburgh. My heart always skipped whenever Carver was on screen. He made two dramatic catches in the second and third innings, one of which propelled him into a somersault, and one that sent him sliding across the grass at least fifteen feet. The broadcasters replayed both those catches a few times. He hit two homeruns in this game, and I thought if there was any man having a better season than Carver, I was hard-pressed to name him.

The Cardinals beat the Pirates that night 6-4, and I texted Carver to congratulate him on another great game. He called me sometime after ten.

"You were spectacular," I said. "Your fans are going nuts tonight. Are your boys with you?"

"They're here," Carver said. "Asleep." It was almost one in the morning in Pittsburgh, and I wondered if Carver felt tired. "Tell me about camping," he said.

I felt myself blush. How did camping compare with the Major League game I'd just watched? It didn't even feel like the same universe.

"It was great," I said. "And I'm really excited about my new project."

Carver said, "Tell me about it," so I did. I explained the concept for *I Want to Get into Stanford*, and Carver listened with interest.

"How much will it cost?" he asked.

"A lot," I said. "I have to show the grant committee I'm willing to front part of the bill, or at least fifteen thousand dollars, in order to stand a chance to win anything. So as long as I don't run into any problems, I should be able to charge the airline tickets myself, which would satisfy that requirement."

"I'll underwrite what you need on the form," Carver said. "As long as you promise it's nothing political."

I laughed, astonished and touched by his offer. "It's not political. Just five kids trying to get into Stanford. There might be some politics of entitlement going on, but that's about it. It would be a PBS show."

"Then I'll underwrite the cost of the tickets," Carver said. "At least let me do that, Mary Jane. I want to help with this project."

I blushed and tried to think. "I don't know."

"Just consider me... an extra source of funding," he said. "Without the red tape."

I bit my lip. "Let me think about it."

I could tell he was smiling. "All right. Then tell me more about camping."

I didn't know what to say. "It was um, you know… I ate soup. King stepped in a bee hive. That sort of thing."

"Mary Jane," Carver sighed.

So I told him about the trip in some detail, and I added that the Cowboy had finally proposed to Abigail Turner, and that I'd attended their engagement party at the S.O.S. Bar.

"I wish you could have been there," I said.

"I could miss a few games, and come see you," he said.

I sat up straight. "I don't want you to miss any games." The All-Star Game was coming up in four days, and since Carver would be playing for the National League, this was no time for him to be ditching games.

"I almost blew off those three games in Denver," he said. "I wanted to see you so bad."

I giggled with pleasure, remembering my own hell and how crazy I'd felt when he'd played at Coors Field.

"Are we beating the odds?" he asked.

"What odds?"

"That a week was all we would get."

"I don't know," I said softly. "Are you seeing anyone?"

"*You*," he laughed. "I'm waiting for you to visit."

He knew why I'd asked though. Carver wasn't just appearing on sports pages online. His name was frequently being added to "Hottest Bachelor" lists on the internet. The fact that he was hitting again had given people permission to ask about his dating status—and Carver offered up nothing other than, "I'm seeing someone," in response. But since no one had been able to find this mysterious someone, many people believed Carver was still single. Especially women.

Even sportscasters wondered if Carver was really attached. An interviewer had asked his teammate, Matt Daughtry, what he thought. Matt replied, *Greyson just gets up in the morning and drinks his go juice. As long as he keeps hitting the ball, I'm not too concerned about his personal life.*

As Carver's "go juice" was made of wheatgrass and kale smoothies and protein shakes, Matt escaped further questioning, and people kept speculating that Carver was single. He never went anywhere with a girlfriend, so it was a logical conclusion to make.

I knew he was protecting me from the noise and clamor surrounding his life. He knew what fame meant, and I was sure he remembered that he had hated it, once upon a time, when his wife was alive. Fame had given Audrey the wish for something much simpler in life: for a man who came home every night, a man who didn't live in the spotlight. Dreams coming true often brought unwanted consequences—and Carver's fame had definitely been one.

"After the season, I want to go to Tahiti," Carver said. "Just you and me for a week. I want to lie in the sand with you on top of me. Wearing as little clothing as possible. And I want to fall asleep under the stars, listening to the sound of the ocean."

I couldn't spend a week in Tahiti. How would I ever get so much vacation time? It had been such a struggle to escape for a weekend. And how could I miss a week of work during the school year, when I had the kids with me again? But this was Carver's fantasy, and he was welcome to it.

"Then I want to go on a cruise," he said. "A big family cruise. I want to see the Galapagos Islands, and travel around Italy, and then see the Greek Isles. We could take all the kids, Mary Jane. They'd have a blast."

I smiled, since the kids *would* have a blast on that trip.

"And I want to make love every night," Carver said.

I laughed. "Sounds good to me."

But I knew I couldn't go. While Carver might be able to dream about vacation time, I only kept thinking about the bills I was struggling to pay off.

As I went to sleep that night, I decided it was time to pick up a night shift in town. I needed to pay down my MasterCard and be ready for the kids to return to the apartment next month. The monthly interest on the balance was brutal. And Steve had met someone this summer, a pretty girl named Emma Quinn, and he was with her tonight, on a date. If Steve moved out, and was no longer helping with groceries, I was going to be pretty strapped this winter. So it was time I picked up a third job.

47

BAD LUCK

Carver helped the National League win the All-Star Game, which was held in Cleveland this year, and one week later, on July 22nd, he was home in St. Louis for a game against the Astros. I sent him a text early that morning: *Thinking of you today, xoxo* because this was the anniversary for the event that had changed his life completely, the way losing Hanna on Christmas Day the year before had changed mine. He replied: *Thank you, Mary Jane* with a heart.

The Cardinals lost that game due to a series of errors on the field, though Carver played well and knocked in several runs. He had the most Runs Batted In of any player this year.

Steve and Emma ended up falling head over heels for each other, and they decided to move in together. On the last day of July, they signed a lease for an apartment on the south side of town. Emma came over to help Steve move out, though he didn't have much, outside of a few chess sets and his clothes.

I was so incredibly sad to see Steve moving out, though I did my best to be happy for him. He had wanted a girlfriend so badly, and I knew he was brimming with joy to have found one. I thought Emma was a lot like Steve, geeky and shy and sweet. After they'd loaded Steve's car, I sat outside with them on the sidewalk, and we talked about Emma's plan to become a hairdresser. Then I had to leave for my new waitressing job at Serena's on Main.

Serena's was one of the best restaurants in Riverdale. The dining room held mahogany tables covered with ivory linen, fine china, and small vases of peach-colored roses. I served a lot of wine and champagne, along with $30.00 glasses of cognac and $75.00 plates of prime rib. I had picked up the job on a lark, after one of the waiters left for Costa Rica, and the manager asked me if I was single. "My boyfriend's out of town," I replied, since I really wanted the job, so the manager said, "Well, that's good enough," and hired me. He asked me out on a date at the end of each shift. I always told him no. I knew at some point he'd get angry that I kept turning him down and probably fire me, but the money at Serena's was too good to worry about that.

The manager's unwanted advances were tiresome, but nowhere near as bad as putting up with the tirades of the chef, who was a complete rageaholic and total asshole, prone to flinging dishes at people and hurling food on the floor. He pretty much suffered nonstop tantrums, maybe from all of the coke he was snorting. He offered me a line in the bathroom one night, which he obviously intended as a prelude to sex. The chef was beyond gross.

Waiting tables at night, I wore a white collared shirt with a red silk scarf, dark slacks, and a long black apron that tied at my waist and fell past my knees. I usually left work at Serena's around eleven or midnight, which made waking up for my five a.m. shifts at the diner a struggle, though I managed to get by. After cooking all morning, I'd nap in the afternoon, and that always helped. Waiting tables at night was a fairly easy job. No harder than grilling burgers at the diner or a shift at The Summit. And I never left Serena's smelling like grease, which was nice.

I didn't have time to watch Carver's games anymore, though I skimmed through the write-ups late at night and kept abreast of the scores. And I worked on my grant proposal for *Nine Weeks in Nairobi* every free second I had. Having gone through the process already with *Brighter Than Stars* made this second proposal much easier, and within three weeks of my trip to the mountains, I was mailing off letters. I felt much more confident as well, much more certain I had discovered a subject with market appeal. I felt like I was closer to yes.

Sometimes on the weekends, if I didn't work a shift at Serena's, Mahmood would invite me over for dinner, and I would watch clips from the Persian Daily Show and listen to Javad and the others exclaim that over three million people had seen every episode. They were so proud of their comedy show that they practically jumped around when they talked. I thought their newest videos were much better than the ones we'd filmed in June, but I still didn't understand the humor at all. The Facebook page for the show had more than two million followers. We'd only subtitled a few of the shows into English— like the episode we mailed to Jon Stewart—so when I watched the videos, Mahmood had to translate them for me.

***

One hot afternoon in late August, a few days before the kids would arrive to start school, I was preparing to leave for a shift at Serena's, when someone knocked on the door. I assumed it was Mahmood, come to ask if I wanted to join them for dinner tomorrow. But when I opened the door, I found two police officers standing outside, along with two men in black jackets marked FBI.

Somewhere in the distance, I heard Mahmood calling, "*I am so sorry, Miss Logan!* I am so very sorry! But I am *not a terrorist!* I do not support *terrorism!*" He screamed the last part.

One of the officers in the doorway said, "Mary Jane Logan?"

I took a step back. "Yes?"

Fear gripped my body, squeezed all of the air from my chest, and I stared at the police like I'd opened the door to find two hungry tigers. It sounded like Mahmood was being arrested, sounded like he was being accused of being a *terrorist*, and if he was being taken into custody, then—

The officer in front of me said, "You are under arrest for supporting terrorist activities against the United States government." He held up a paper. "This is a warrant to search the premises. Please turn around and place your hands behind your back."

My breath came short and fast, my hands clammed up, and I suddenly wanted to run—but my legs gave out underneath me. I fell over and hit the side of the armchair, and my head smacked the wall. I collapsed on the floor.

"Wha—" I gasped. "What did you say?"

"You are under arrest for supporting terrorism," the officer repeated. The FBI men walked past him, entered my apartment, and began searching around. No one seemed at all concerned that I had fallen over. "Please stand up and put your hands behind your back," the officer said. The other one stepped toward me with a pair of handcuffs. The sunshine through the window made the cuffs sparkle like jewels.

Then my vision darkened, like I was about to black out. I covered my face with my hands. "I'm not a… not a *terrorist*…" I said. "There's been a… this is all a *mistake*…"

"Miss Logan, please stand and put your hands behind your back. Don't make this any harder than it needs to be."

I heard the scorn in his voice—like he actually thought I was guilty of this terrorism charge—and then I did black out. I came-to on the floor, on my side, and the officer with the handcuffs pulled me up to my feet. I managed to stay upright while he cuffed me, but I nearly passed out again. I wavered and dropped to my knees. I felt like I couldn't breathe.

Gandhi cowered under the kitchen table, but when I fell over again, he ran out to lick my face.

"I can't... I can't go to *jail!*" I said, but the officer wasn't paying attention. He hauled me onto my feet and pushed me toward the door. I stumbled along, and realized he was taking me to a squad car.

"My dog!" I said, twisting around. "I can't leave my—"

"Your dog will be at the pound," the man said. "You can call someone at processing to go pick him up."

I almost fell over again. I tripped walking downstairs and skinned my knees on the concrete.

"I'm *not a terrorist!*" I yelled.

"Ma'am, you'll have to save that for your lawyer," and he shoved me into the back of a squad car.

I thought, *Oh God, oh God, oh God. I am going to jail. I am going to jail.*

How could I possibly be going to jail?

***

I almost blacked out again while I rode in the squad car. I couldn't handle the idea that these men thought I was a terrorist. I also couldn't handle the idea of going to jail. I searched around for my steel, but came up with nothing. My body was a loose mass of goo, all quivering horror.

I wondered for a second if maybe I'd been duped this whole time, and perhaps Mahmood and his friends really *were* terrorists pretending to love democracy and hate Iran's fundamentalist leaders—but that was ridiculous. I knew those four men were not terrorists. Someone in the FBI must have spotted the Persian Daily Show videos and mistranslated them. This all had to be a mistake, and as soon as the English subtitles were added, I'd be let out of jail.

But how long would that take? How long would I have to sit in a cell, not working my jobs, not earning my rent? I was going to be fired. I'd probably lose my job at Serena's just for missing work tonight.

I had nothing in savings. I had $2,436.00 on my MasterCard bill. My rent was due in two weeks. If I lost my three jobs, I was…

I was screwed.

***

When the squad car parked in front of the jail, I was taken inside to a dismal room with a long concrete bench. My handcuffs were fastened to a metal ring behind me, and then I was asked a series of general questions. The officer running the interrogation typed my answers on a laptop.

He asked for my full name and address, how long I'd lived in Riverdale, and if I was currently employed. Did I have any serious medical conditions? (No.) Did I take any medication? (Birth control.) Did I have any STDs? (No.) Did I take any illegal substances? (No.) Had I ever had suicidal thoughts?

I pondered this question a moment. I would have answered no, except I knew the FBI was searching through my apartment. And that meant they would find my journal, where I'd written several things after Hanna had died. Things like, *I can't go on without her. I wish I'd died with her.* Stuff I'd had on my mind at the time of the funeral. I didn't think I'd been suicidal, but I'd certainly thought a lot about death, and I'd written things in that journal which probably seemed suicidal.

I worried that if I made a statement that later seemed like I'd been lying, then I'd rot in jail longer.

So I finally said, "When my best friend died, I thought a lot about dying. I thought I wanted to die. But I never actually tried to kill myself."

The officer typed on his keyboard, and continued through his long list of questions. Almost two hours later, I was allowed to use the telephone.

I called the manager at Serena's first, to tell him I'd been arrested and would not be showing up for work. This did not go over well.

"You were arrested for *what?*" he snapped.

"For supporting terrorism," I said.

My manager snarled, "You expect me to *believe that??* That you're in *jail* for *terrorism?* What in the fuck do you *take* me for?"

"It's the truth," I said.

"You are *fired*, Mary Jane! Turn in your scarf and your apron *tomorrow.*"

"I'll be in jail tomorrow," I pointed out.

"*You're fired!*" he shouted again, and hung up. I had known that was coming. That was exactly what happened when you turned down dates from your boss. Men took that stuff way too personal. I thought the manager at Serena's and the chef should probably hook up, as they were both about the biggest babies I'd ever met.

The police allowed me to keep using the phone, so I called Bob Mudd at the diner, and then my boss at the Summit, to let them know where I was. They both managed not to fire me on the spot. After that, I called Steve.

"Hello?"

"Steve, it's Mary Jane."

"Hey. What's up?"

"I was arrested today, and—"

"Arrested?? Are you all right?" He sounded panicked.

"The FBI made a mistake, and they think I'm a terrorist," I said. "The police took Gandhi to the pound. Will you go pick him up for me? I'm worried they might put him to sleep. If you can't keep him, I'll give you the number for the house in Goldking, and you can call Gus to come get him."

"You're really in jail?"

"Yes."

"How could anyone think you're a terrorist?"

"I helped with that show," I sighed. "And I think someone in Homeland Security mistranslated it. My name was in the credits of the first few episodes. I'm sure that's why I'm here."

"What's your bond set at?" Steve asked.

"Seventy thousand," I said. "I might be in here a while. At least until my name can be cleared. I have to go. Will you pick up Gandhi and call the kids?"

"Sure," Steve said.

"Thanks," I said. "Tell the kids I'm okay. Tell them I said not to worry. I'll call you tomorrow."

As I hung up the phone, I had to close my eyes and take several deep breaths.

I remembered Carver was in L.A. tonight, to play the Dodgers, and I thought about calling him. But I worried I'd start crying. Not just cry—I worried I'd break down and sob—and I didn't want to stand here and bawl in front of these officers. I could call Carver and the kids tomorrow, when I felt calmer, and not sick with shock.

I told the police I was done with the phone, and an officer led me downstairs.

The basement held the inventory room of the jail, and I was told to remove my shoes and all of my clothes—even my underwear and my socks—and then I was given a hideous green shift to put on. It was sort of like a dress, but it didn't have any sleeves and stretched all the way to my ankles. I resembled a fat, misshapen worm with it on. It was brutally humiliating, but I managed not to cry. I sure wanted to though.

I kept thinking of the money I could have been making tonight, and how, no matter what I did, life seemed to keep sinking me in bills. I had paid down more than half of my MasterCard debt with that waitressing job, trying to make sure I could see Carver next month. And now I was in jail. Dressed like a worm.

Even being dressed like a Yeti was better than looking like a worm. I laughed, trying to cheer myself up, but when the officer glowered and snorted, my laughter broke off.

After leaving all of my clothing in the inventory room, I was handed a small mattress to carry, which had to be dragged on the floor behind me. Then I was given a blanket, a pillow, and told to follow another officer down the hall. We stopped at a white door, which buzzed before it opened, and I was ushered into my cell.

The room was the size of a broom closet, with white walls, a metal cot, and a metal toilet-and-sink contraption next to the bed. A camera was mounted on the ceiling.

I put down the mattress and asked, "Can I have a toothbrush?" before the officer shut the door.

"You're on suicide watch," the man said. "No toothbrush." The door buzzed closed behind him, and I was alone. I gazed around at the tiny room, wishing I'd simply answered *No* to the suicidal thoughts question, as that was obviously why I was here. I didn't feel suicidal, but looking around at this room sure made me want to kill myself. No wonder I couldn't be given a toothbrush. I'd probably try to stab myself with it.

I placed the mattress on the cot, dropped the pillow and the blanket on top of it, and walked back and forth beside the bed. Since I didn't have much room to pace in, I pinged back and forth like a stock market graph.

What would happen to me if these charges weren't dropped? I stared down at my feet and tried to think. If I was out in a week, I'd probably still lose my two remaining jobs, but at least I could get the kids back to school. They would miss the first few days of classes, but that could be fixed. If I was in jail for a month, I'd lose my apartment. When I called the kids tomorrow, I would have to warn them I might be evicted. My computer, my phone, my clothes, my diploma—they would have to collect my things and turn in my apartment key. I didn't know how to keep the kids in school if I lost my apartment though. How could I make sure they didn't drop out, if I was locked up in jail?

I sat down on the bed and hid my face in my hands.

Damn, did I have some bad luck.

I wriggled my toes. I didn't feel any better. I wondered where Mahmood and his friends were. I wondered if they were all sitting in jail cells like this. As frightened as I was.

I wished I could be with Carver. I wished he could hold me. I felt so alone. I promised myself I wouldn't cry when I called him tomorrow. I would tell him I was in jail, and I would keep my voice calm, and I would not break down and sob in front of those officers.

Hours passed, and the lights remained on. Sometimes I glanced up at the camera, wondering if anyone was really watching me or not.

I spent the night trying to come up with a fix: a way to keep the kids in school if I was in jail. I worried Richard would drop out and start working, so Ethan and Mia could finish—and I didn't want that to happen. I wanted Richard and Gus to graduate together. But I was so sad and discouraged to be locked up in jail—so scared I might be here for much more than a month—I couldn't think clearly.

I started to hear the way Mom would laugh when she found out I was in jail. I knew exactly what she would say, if she was here now. *I guess we don't need to worry about Riverdale High anymore! I told you getting that apartment was a stupid idea. And now you're in jail with the Taliban! You're an idiot, Mary Jane. A complete idiot.*

I covered my ears with my hands like that would help block her out. At least I knew Mom would never come visit me. If I could just banish her voice from my head, I'd be so much better off. I blinked around at the walls of my cell, and while I managed to silence Mom's voice, her words were replaced by the sound of Landon laughing at me, and then William and Jeff, and all of the horrible things they would say when they found out where I was. *Serves you right, you fucking high-minded bitch. Fucking cunt.* I buried my face in my pillow, struggling to stop hearing those evil things in my mind. It took me an hour before I could tune them all out.

A few months ago, being locked up in jail would have given me a panic attack. I didn't feel panic right now, but I did feel despair. There was no way of knowing how long I'd be in here. There was no way of knowing how big a mess I would have to clean up when I finally got out.

And then I started reciting this mantra: *No matter what happens, I can fix it… No matter what happens, I can fix it…*

Over and over, I chanted those words, especially if I started to think about Mom or Landon again. *No matter what happens, I can fix it…* and I thought about Carver, about how he would be there to hold me when this was all over… how he would hold me right now, if he could… and I pictured the kids graduating in their black caps and gowns, and how I would be there for each of them when they received their diplomas…. and that helped me make it through the night.

When the door of my cell buzzed the next morning and an officer walked in, I was sitting up on the mattress.

The officer said, "Here," and handed me a Nutri-Grain bar and a cup of cherry Kool-Aid. Breakfast. I poured the Kool-Aid in the sink and used the cup to drink water. I felt too stressed to even open the Nutri-Grain bar.

A few minutes later, my cell door buzzed and opened again, and another officer said, "Bring your things, and follow me." I stood, picked up the pillow and blanket, and dragged the mattress behind me. I followed the officer back to the inventory room.

I was instructed to remove the green shift, which I did, and a woman handed me a short-sleeved orange top and a pair of orange pants. I really wished I could have my underwear back, but that didn't happen. At least I was given rubber sandals this time, which was nice. Walking barefoot on concrete made me feel even more vulnerable than not having underwear.

I was allowed to brush my teeth, and then my hands were cuffed behind my back, my ankles where shackled together with a chain, and I was told to follow another officer into the hall.

We walked to the end of the corridor, through a couple of cinder block rooms, and into another wide hallway. I asked the man, "Where are we?" and he said we were in an underground tunnel, on our way to the courthouse.

"I'm already having court?"

The officer shrugged. "I don't know what's going on. The judge sent for you this morning."

The water in my belly sloshed around like choppy waves on the sea, and the chain at my ankles clanged against the floor with a sickening sound.

I didn't have a lawyer. I didn't have any money for counsel. And now I was about to stand in front of a judge, clad in an orange jumpsuit and handcuffs and shackles.

This day was competing with my most terrible nightmares for the title Worst Day of My Life.

I managed to keep pace with the officer, who led me up a flight of stairs and into another cinder block hallway. Then he opened a door, and ushered me into a courtroom.

48

SPECIAL AGENT GHORBANI

When I walked into the room, my peripheral vision darkened again, like I might pass out. I thought I heard Carver calling my name, and realized I was hallucinating. I stared at the floor and took several deep breaths. This courtroom had blue walls and brown carpet, rows of benches, and held several people. I had entered through a side door, near the back of the room. There were five police officers around me.

And then I saw Carver burst through the main door—not a hallucination—but really—*really*—*Carver*—and two officers tried to stop him, but he darted around them and grabbed me and hugged me.

"*Mary Jane!*" he cried, rocking me in his arms.

"I'm dreaming, I'm dreaming," I said. I was having a nightmare, and when I woke up, I would not be in a courtroom. I would not be wearing an orange jumpsuit. Carver would not be here hugging me.

There was so much commotion around me, so much noise. The police told Carver to release me and back away, the judge pounded his gavel, someone yelled at a woman to put her camera away—and then I closed my eyes and willed myself to wake up. *Wake up, wake up, wake up.* The police pulled at Carver until he released me. I stumbled a little, regaining my balance. *Wake up, wake up, wake up.*

I opened my eyes, but I was still wearing a jumpsuit. My hands were still cuffed. The police were still scowling at me. And Carver stood a few feet away, like a bright, fearsome angel descended into the hell of this courtroom.

He reached a hand toward me, and an officer snapped, "Back away, Mr. Greyson. Or we will have you removed."

Carver dropped his hand, and his face held so much anguish, so much worry and stress, I wanted to help him somehow, so I took a deep breath and sent him a smile.

"It's all right," I said. "I think someone mistranslated a show."

"Are you okay?" Carver asked. "Did anyone hurt you?"

I shook my head no. "I lost my job. But I'm okay." I could see how much bigger his body was now, so much thicker with muscle. He was supposed to be in L.A. for his game. "What are you doing here?"

Carver smiled and shook his head, like he couldn't believe I would ask. "Getting you out of here."

"You came to post bond?"

Carver searched my face. "Of course."

I was amazed that he had come all this way to post bond. My life had reached such a low level, that my boyfriend would be honor-bound to bail me out of jail. I was my father's daughter, all right.

The officer standing between us said, "Miss Logan, step forward," and I had to turn away from Carver and walk up to the judge. I stood in front of his elevated desk and waited.

This judge was an older man, with wrinkled skin and white hair. He peered down his glasses at me. A man in a black suit stood beside him. That man had shiny black hair, and he wore a pair of silver shades that hid his eyes. He was smiling at me. I felt a sudden rush of terror and looked back at the judge.

"Miss Logan," the judge said, gesturing to the man in the sunglasses, "this is CIA Special Agent Karim Ghorbani. He flew in this morning." The Special Agent smiled again, and his reflective sunglasses seemed more frightening than ever.

Oh my God. Maybe I *was* going to prison. Why else would a *CIA Special Agent* be in a dingy Riverdale courtroom??

I struggled to breathe. I struggled not to black out.

"It appears there has been a mistake, and the charges brought against you were false," the judge said. "Agent Ghorbani has cleared everything up, and you are hereby released. This case has been dropped."

I almost fell over.

Carver jumped to my side and said, "Can someone please take the handcuffs off?" and I sagged against him a moment, to keep myself upright. I didn't want to collapse on the floor again, like I had when the police had arrested me.

The Special Agent stepped around from the judge's bench and unlocked the handcuffs, and one of the officers removed the shackles on my ankles. As soon as I was free, I hugged Carver, who tossed me up in his arms like a small Lois Lane. His body felt so different to me. There was a reason he was a top contender on those silly "Hottest Man Alive" websites. He was *my* Hottest Man Alive though, for sure.

Carver held me and held me like he would never let go. We remained like that for a while, until Special Agent Ghorbani cleared his throat, and Carver reluctantly put me down.

Agent Ghorbani reached out and shook my hand. "Miss Logan, I apologize for your incarceration last night. I'm personally a fan of Mahmood Abbasi's *Daily Show*, so when I learned you had all been arrested last night, I flew out of D.C. to make sure you were freed."

"What about Mahmood and his friends?" I asked. "Are they all right?"

"They were released an hour ago," Agent Ghorbani said. "They tried waiting for you, but the police insisted they needed to be signed out first. So they are in a room at the jail, filling out paperwork."

Relieved to hear that everyone was okay, I peered at Agent Ghorbani's face and asked, "Why the sunglasses?"

"Oh, I recently had eye surgery," he said. "My eyes are light-sensitive," and he tapped on his sunglasses. "I have to wear these for another month."

I nodded, still so overwhelmed with emotion I couldn't speak for a moment. "Thank you for getting us out of here," I said. "Few things are as scary as being in jail."

"Miss Logan, it was truly my pleasure," he said. We shook hands again. Carver shook his hand, too. Agent Ghorbani smiled up at him. "I thought you had a game in Los Angeles tonight."

"I do," Carver said.

Agent Ghorbani caught my gaze again with a smile. Then he glanced back at Carver. "Good luck with your game, Mr. Greyson. I grew up in San Francisco. But I might watch the Dodgers tonight. Just to see if you hit another homerun."

Carver smiled and kissed the top of my head, like he wasn't prepared to discuss baseball, but I could tell he was touched that Agent Ghorbani had said this. "Thank you," Carver said.

Agent Ghorbani smiled and caught my gaze again. "Goodbye, Miss Logan. It was a pleasure to meet you." He nodded toward Carver, to include him in the farewell, and left the room.

Carver hugged me and kissed me—and wow—*wow*—did it feel good to kiss him. A wild and passionate kiss, a kiss that only propriety could force us to end. We held hands as we walked to the exit.

As soon as we passed through the main door, I spotted Steve in the hall—and then all of the kids—and I saw Carver's teammate, Matt Daughtry. The kids rushed me and grabbed me, and in the commotion, I realized how Carver had learned I was in jail—Steve had called him.

The kids were crying and frightened, hugging me so tightly it hurt, and I assured them I was fine, that a CIA Special Agent had flown to town just to make sure the police let me go. I dried Mia's face with my fingers. "See? I'm fine," I said, and she hugged me again and buried her head in my armpit. I gave Gus an extra hug, tousled Richard's hair, and kissed Ethan on the cheek.

Richard dried his eyes with the back of his hand. "Uh, Matt Daughtry is here," Richard said, and he nodded toward Matt. "He found Carver an airplane last night."

Matt wore a collared shirt and slacks, like Carver, but he also had one of those watches that cost more than a Range Rover. I reached out to shake his hand and said, "Hi, Matt. It's nice to meet you."

"Same," Matt said.

A court attendant approached me. "Miss Logan, you should go and sign out. The police need to take care of you."

So I had to leave everyone and return to the inventory room at the jail. I changed into my clothes and filled out my exit paperwork. Then I met up with Mahmood, Javad, Habib, and Bijan, and there were a lot of hugs and tears of relief.

Mahmood said, "There was suspicion in the FBI that our show was supporting anti-American policies. Apparently false charges like this are quite common, Miss Logan. Everyone is so scared about any more terrorism—but thank goodness Special Agent Ghorbani cleared everything up!"

The men shouted something triumphant in Persian, and then cheered. Mahmood invited me to join them for lunch, but I told them my family was here, and that I would see them all later.

When I finally left the Riverdale Jail, I found Carver and Matt and Steve and the kids waiting outside, throwing a Frisbee to Gandhi and playing around on the grass.

The kids ran and hugged me again, almost crying. Poor gremlins. I hated thinking about how scared they had been.

I gave Steve a big hug, and thanked him for helping me, and then I knelt to pet Gandhi. "You guys hungry?" I asked everyone. It was after one o'clock. I was starving.

At the mention of food, the kids perked up again, and a few minutes later, we were piling into the Navigator. Gus had picked up the keys in my apartment, and Steve had brought Gandhi in the Camry. Carver and Matt had taken a taxi to the courthouse, so they piled into the Navigator with us. We let Gus drive, and Steve followed.

A few minutes later, we were all gathered at Seth's Pubby Pub. We pushed four tables together, and Steve's girlfriend Emma joined us for lunch.

Before Carver sat down, he scooped me into his lap and held me against him, gazing at me like every star in the universe shone from my body. He would rock me or kiss my face on occasion, the way mothers coo over babies, and I could feel his heart pounding like he was out running. I kept my arms around him, and my cheek pressed to his chest, inhaling the sweet scent of his cologne and the softer scent of his skin.

"Mary Jane, Mary Jane," he murmured. "I'm so glad you're okay."

I made a high, squeaking sound, too happy for words.

I could hear the kids talking to Matt, and I could hear Steve and Emma talking and laughing as well—but I was with Carver right now. My Carver. My love. We kept our arms around each other, and the rest of the world seemed muted and distant, far away from the two of us.

"I was so worried about you," Carver said. "Are you really all right?"

"I think so," I said. "I hope I never have to do that again."

Carver hugged me tighter. "Me, too."

I pushed my hands through his hair and rubbed his jaw with my palms. I studied his bright silver eyes. I could barely believe he was real, that my Carver was really here with me now. I glanced at his lips and kissed him. A tremor ran through my body, and I felt Carver shiver. I knew he could not spend the night—but oh, how I wanted him to.

Matt said, "Carver tells me you're going to Africa? To film a documentary?"

It took me a moment to realize Matt was talking to me.

I turned so I could send him a smile. "Next summer, I hope. As long as the money comes through. I've applied for a grant."

"That's cool," Matt said. "You'll be like, another Ken Burns."

"Maybe," I said. "Ken Burns is in the major leagues of the documentary world."

That made Matt and Carver both chuckle.

I asked Matt, "Why did you fly out with Carver?"

"I had to make sure he came back," and Matt sent Carver a grin. "So we can beat the Dodgers, and I can have my revenge."

"We lost last night," Carver said to explain. Matt's comment made sense now: he didn't think the Cardinals could win the next two games in L.A. without Carver at bat in the lineup.

Carver sent Matt a smile, one of those wordless expressions that teammates developed, and whatever passed between them, it caused Matt to chuckle.

When it came time to leave the Pubby Pub, Matt called a taxi, and he laughed when a battered yellow Cherokee pulled up.

"Nice," Matt said with a smile, and he and Carver stood outside to say goodbye to the kids. Steve gave Carver a man-hug before he and Emma left. When the kids were finished with their farewells, I told them to drive the Navigator back to the apartment, to make sure Gandhi had food and water before they left, and then to head back to Goldking so they wouldn't miss their night shifts.

"Of course," Richard said, and he hugged me again.

Once the kids were off, I climbed into the backseat of the Jeep with Carver. Matt sat up front. The driver set off for the airport.

I rested my head on Carver's shoulder, and he kept his arm around me. "Will you come to St. Louis?" he asked.

He sounded so happy, and I felt so perfect, that I couldn't resist teasing him. "Sure, Carver. When the Cardinals make the World Series, I promise I'll come watch you play."

Matt roared with laughter. He slapped the dash of the Jeep and said, "I *told you* she'd say that!"

I quirked an eyebrow at Carver, who was laughing now, too. What the heck had he been saying about me?

I was about to make it clear that I had only been joking, but Carver shook his head, like that wasn't necessary. Then he glanced over at Matt and muttered, "I guess we better make the Series then," and Matt clapped his hands.

"Damn right, we make the Series!" he laughed. "Revenge, man. We're killing the Dodgers tonight." He checked his watch and added, "Flight leaves at three-thirty." It was 3:05.

When we arrived at the private airport, the driver pulled the Jeep onto the tarmac—and rather than finding a small plane on the runway—I saw a *corporate jet*. It was painted black with blue streaks down the sides, and it shimmered in the sunlight like a giant steel shark.

"Oh my *God!*" I said. "*That's* what you flew in?"

"Yeah," Matt sighed, grinning up at the jet. "It's a pretty sweet ride."

Carver squeezed my hand and said, "Come check it out."

"As long as you don't trap me," I said. "I can't fly to L.A. School is starting on Monday."

Carver laughed. "No kidnapping," he said, so I agreed to walk up the steps and gaze around at the plane. The interior was exquisite, like some glittering penthouse, with several couches, a full bar, and card tables.

"Wow," I grinned. "It's a flying hotel."

Carver asked, "Sure you don't want to come with?"

"I'm sure," I said. I turned to Matt and told him goodbye, and he shook my hand again and said what a pleasure it had been to finally meet me. When I heard him say the word *finally*, I wanted to blush. I wished I knew what Carver had said about me.

"Good luck tonight," I told Matt. Carver followed me off the plane and walked me back to the taxi. He opened the back passenger door, and we stood smiling at each other a moment. Behind Carver, the jet's engines turned on and began warming up. They were loud, but not deafening.

"Thanks, Carver," I said. "For coming today."

"You're welcome, Mary Jane." He held both my hands, and I almost couldn't bear the way he was looking at me. His expression was so broken open and raw. Happiness can about crush a person sometimes. When he embraced me to kiss me, I felt my knees go. It was a good thing I wasn't on that plane anymore, or I wouldn't have been able to walk to the Jeep.

Matt called from the airplane, "We can't *beat the Dodgers* unless we *get there!*"

So Carver waited until I'd taken a seat so he could shut the door of the Jeep, and then he jogged back to Matt and disappeared on the jet. The door closed, the plane eased away from the airport, and the taxi driver moved the Jeep off the runway while the jet cleared for takeoff.

I asked the driver to wait for a minute so I could watch them leave.

"Whose plane is that, anyway?" asked the driver.

"I think it belongs to a company," I said. "But the guy who's in charge of it must root for St. Louis."

49

WINS AND LOSSES

Since I'd lost my waitressing job at Serena's, I didn't have to worry about working a night shift that evening. So I went home to my apartment, took a long shower, and put on a dress. I'd found a blue sundress at the thrift store last weekend, and I felt so happy, I needed to wear something pretty. I opened all of my windows to let in a breeze, and then I dropped on the couch and put my feet up. Gandhi flopped down beside me and placed his head in my lap.

I watched the game in L.A. The Dodgers held a 2-0 lead throughout the first eight innings, and then scored another run at the top of the ninth. Dodgers ahead, 3-0.

Whenever Matt was on screen, I could tell he was upset. He kept removing his cap to wipe at his brow. The Cardinals came up to bat. Bottom of the ninth.

The pitcher struck the first batter out. The next batter walked. Third batter struck out. Two outs now, and a runner on first.

Things were not looking good for the Cardinals. They'd reached the last inning, down by three runs, and they already had two outs. This game was one out from over.

The fourth batter hit a line drive past third and made it on base. The runner on first made it to second.

Matt came up to bat.

Strike one, strike two—and then Matt hit the ball into center. The fielder didn't catch it, and Matt made it to first. All runners were safe. And now it was Carver's turn at bat.

It was like that horrible game I had played at my softball state tournament: final inning, bases loaded, two outs. The Cardinals needed 4 runs to win. If Carver was stressed by this situation, he sure didn't show it.

He chose to bat left. Carver had been hitting tonight, but he'd always been stranded on base before he could score. As he walked into the box, the catcher said something to him, and Carver laughed. Then he loosened his shoulders and adjusted his bat, all focus again as he prepared for his swing.

The first pitch was a slider that dropped. Ball one.

The second was a hit that went foul: strike one.

Carver stepped out of the box. He shook out his arms, returned to the plate and prepared for his swing.

He hit another pitch foul: strike two.

As long as Carver kept hitting pitches, he kept the battle alive. But the moment he missed one, the Cardinals lost.

Fourth pitch was a curveball. Carver struck it foul, and the ball disappeared in the crowd.

Fifth pitch was inside and almost pegged Carver's arm. I nearly cried out, I was so scared he'd be hit, but Carver moved back in time. Ball two.

I could hear the audience screaming full-boar on the screen. The fans knew anything could happen. It was anyone's game. Of all the people to land in that box, the Grizz induced the most panic. The Dodgers did not want to lose, and the Cardinals were down to the wire. If I was in the stadium, I would be on my feet. But at home, I sat huddled on my couch, barely breathing.

Carver stepped out of the box and stood flexing his shoulders. Then he smiled at the umpire and said something to him, and the umpire chuckled before he replied. I wished I could hear what they said. Carver seemed so relaxed. He'd seemed relaxed the whole game. Even the announcers were making comments about it.

Once again he returned to the plate, positioned his feet, and prepared for his swing.

Sixth pitch was a fastball.

Carver struck it foul, and the impact caused the bat to shatter apart and rain pieces on home. He left the box for a minute, removed his helmet and wiped his brow with his sleeve. I could see the grey in his hair. I could see his bright silver eyes.

The catcher walked to the mound and met with the pitcher. They covered their mouths as they spoke. They looked tense, uncertain. The catcher returned to the plate and snapped down his face guard. Carver chose a new bat, adjusted the straps on his gloves and stepped into the box.

Seventh pitch was another slider that dropped. The catcher pounced where it landed, lifting his face guard and glaring at the runner on third, who sprinted back to base. Ball three.

The crowd in the stadium continued to roar. People screamed, jumped, stood on their chairs. Men held up their children to see. A cluster of grizzlies waved their banners for Carver.

The sportscasters kept talking about his career, and how amazing this season had been. "I don't know if any player has had this kind of turnaround in one season," an announcer said. "The Cardinals are sitting at the top of their division—for good reason. The Grizz is the best clutch hitter in the league, and these guys are playing their hearts out this year."

Eighth pitch was a fastball: struck foul. The ball flew into the crowd behind home. The catcher leaped up to watch it leave. He regarded Carver a moment, and then glanced at the pitcher. The catcher leaned over to spit before he returned to position.

Ninth pitch was a changeup. Carver hit another foul, and this time, the catcher scooped it up behind home. All three runners walked back to base. Carver stepped out of the box with his bat, which had a split down the middle. It forked at the end like a tree struck by lightning. The announcers started talking about this second ruined bat, and what a prolonged ninth inning this was turning out to be.

The catcher pushed up his mask and walked to the mound. Carver chose another new bat. The men in the dugouts stared at the field. The grizzlies kept waving their banners. Matt stood beside first with his hands on his head, gazing toward Carver. Waiting for him to slam the ball, and bring them all home.

At the conference on the mound, the pitcher kicked the dirt, removed his cap and wiped his brow. The catcher was frowning, and his eyes were cold. The pitcher nodded though, agreeing to whatever they had determined to do. The meeting finished and the catcher returned to home plate.

Carver had a new bat, and his silver eyes watched the pitcher. He walked into the box. Set his feet. Prepared for his swing.

The pitcher tipped down his cap. Gripped the ball in his hand.

Only one man could win. Only one team would lose.

Everyone waited.

I remembered what Carver said he loved about baseball. *I love the speed. The speed of the ball. The speed of the game. The long minutes of waiting. The split second when lightning strikes.*

I studied Carver's body, poised and ready for the pitch. All that screaming around him. All that pressure. The threat of failure being pressed up against him. This was why Carver played. This was the part of the game he loved most.

The pitcher threw a fastball, down and away. Ninety-nine miles per hour.

Carver swung. He should not have swung at that ball.

That pitch was impossible. It was so far outside the strike zone, even the catcher had shifted to be able to catch it.

Carver stepped into his swing, and went to meet it regardless. If he'd only held back, it would have been called as ball four. He might have walked onto first, and forced in a run. He might have kept the game alive.

But Carver didn't hold back. He stepped out and swung, and hit the ball with such force, that pitch might as well have been in the strike zone.

The ball soared like a comet, trailing white heat. The left fielder sprinted toward the line, toward the wall, sprinted faster, and leapt with his glove, but the comet disappeared in the crowd.

Grand slam.

Matt jumped in the air and pumped his fists as he ran, and the runners gathered on home with the rest of the team. When Carver finished his trip around the bases and stepped on home plate, his teammates attacked him, with punches and man-hugs and a fierce round of butt-slapping. Matt leapt on top of him like a bear in a mauling. Carver was laughing and smiling with that grin like the devil.

The Cardinals had taken this game, 4-3.

I had been joking when I told Carver I would come see him in a World Series game. But now I realized the Cardinals might really get there—*they might be playing in the Series this year.*

The idea made me giddy. An announcer on the broadcast was still praising the Grizz. "This guy has turned himself around—and this whole team around with him. The Cardinals are on fire this year. What a game this has been—what a season!"

Gandhi wriggled against me, and I hugged him again. I couldn't stop giggling.

If Carver played in the World Series, I was definitely going. Whether it was four games or seven, I would be in the stadium to watch every one. I could pass up a trip to Tahiti, but I would lose both of the jobs I had left before I missed the World Series.

50

A PARADE OF PURE NOISE

That Sunday, I picked up the kids in Goldking, along with Gus in the Buick, and they moved back to Riverdale. Mom stayed in Goldking, which meant the apartment was quieter.

The kids started school the next morning, and we slipped into routine. I really hated that I'd lost my job at Serena's, and I tried to pick up another night shift somewhere, at a place where I would only have to work one or two nights a week—but I couldn't find anything that worked with my schedule. My MasterCard payments trickled down to fifty dollars a week.

At least I could watch Carver's games every night with the kids, as long as their homework was finished. But missing out on the money I needed to be able to visit him made me blue.

After the first two weeks of school, I started receiving rejection letters for *Nine Weeks in Nairobi*. I felt sad when I read them, and tried not to get discouraged. If I needed to create a new project, I would—because sooner or later, I would come up with something that would be accepted—as long as I didn't give up.

Richard and Gus decided to play basketball with Ethan this year, and Mia joined a gardening club for eighth graders. Richard started driver's ed classes, and I kept struggling to have enough money so I could miss work for a weekend and get away to see Carver. He was always sending me pictures of palm trees and white sand and blue water, he was so fixated on that vacation to Tahiti when his season was over. I worried what would happen if I couldn't go—but for the time being, I kept that to myself.

One Friday night near the end of September, he called me before his game started. We talked about his boys for a while, and how the kids were doing in school, and then Carver's voice changed. He sounded nervous.

"Mary Jane?"

"Yeah?"

"Do you ever think about being with me?"

I laughed. "Is this a serious question?"

"I mean… really being with me. Living with me. Do you ever think about that?"

"I have the kids, Carver. I'm not going to leave them."

"I know," he said. "I meant with your family. Do you think you could live with me that way?"

I pondered this for a moment. Anxiety crept into my voice. "You mean, move in with you, and bring the kids?"

"Yes," Carver said.

"In St. Louis?" I asked.

"Or wherever," he said.

I tried to picture myself living with Carver. In a house with his three boys, and his parents, and the kids, and Gandhi.

That was a hell of a lot of people to live in one house.

"I'm not sure you really want that," I said.

"Of course I do," Carver said. His voice was gentle and soft, reassuring. Like he'd been considering this for a while. But I certainly hadn't.

I had never even lived with a man on my own, much less with four teenagers in tow. Plus a dog. That seemed like a whole lot of pressure to put on a relationship... especially for a couple who had only seen each other *once* in nine *months*—and I had been getting out of jail at the time.

Combining our families meant I would have to uproot the kids from school, give up my apartment, and move everyone across country—and that was beyond my ability to comprehend at the moment. I would be... completely vulnerable if I did that. And so would the kids. It was a frightening thought.

I had failed to consider that Carver might want a future together, not simply to visit or go on vacation, but something like... something like what he had grown up with. A place where children were welcome and parents were committed to taking care of their offspring. I doubted Carver's father had ever screamed at his mother, *Get the fuck out of my house and take those filthy brats with you. I'm not footing the bill for you and those fucking kids.* From what I knew of Carver's dad, he probably would have died before he ever told his wife such a thing. But in my childhood, those were the words that inspired the most dread. It was hard to remember that not everyone saw the world on those terms.

I tried to put myself in Carver's place, and see this suggestion from his point of view—but I still felt so vulnerable. And scared. Trying to figure out how I might get vacation time to go to Tahiti—that was stressful enough. But merging my whole life with Carver's? How had I missed the jump in logic from finding time to visit each other to living together?

"I could sign with the Angels or the Dodgers next year," Carver said. He sounded upbeat but careful, like he understood how much he was taking me by surprise. "We could live in L.A., and you could find work in the film industry. I've been thinking about it for a while."

I almost fell over. Move to L.A.? With his family *and* mine? *So I could find a job?*

"Carver, that's—" I couldn't catch my breath. "That's a lot to take in."

"Will you think about it?" he asked. "And maybe when we go on vacation, you can let me know?"

I didn't know what to say. The idea of a vacation I couldn't get time off for made me anxious, but nowhere near as anxious as the thought of moving my family across country. There were so many questions—and details—and *fears*—I would have to work out—too many for one conversation. Too many to even begin to tackle right now. I took a deep breath and settled on, "Okay, Carver. We'll talk about it then."

He sounded relieved. "I hoped you'd say that."

I thought of how *crazy* this was—that Carver would consider moving his whole family to Los Angeles *with me and the kids*—and then I said as a joke, "You could have found another girlfriend, you know. You could have made this a lot easier."

"I don't want easy," he said. "I want you, Mary Jane. However I can have you, you're the one."

He was so incredibly sweet that I couldn't help smiling. And then I thought of all the things that had kept me from seeing him—losing two of my jobs, my rejection letters, my responsibilities—and my spirits plunged. I felt so incredibly sad for a moment. "I feel awful, Carver. That I haven't used those tickets you sent. That I told you I'd try to find a way to visit, and never have."

"Don't feel bad," Carver said. "I'd rather go on vacation and spend more than a weekend together, anyway. And my season will be over soon. We're almost to the end now, don't worry. I'm really proud of you, Mary Jane. No matter what happens, you always keep your head up and keep going. You're amazing. And the first night your documentary airs on PBS—we'll have a big party, with double-shots of wheatgrass and everything."

I felt tears in my eyes, and brushed them away. "Thanks, Carver. Hearing you say that… it means a lot."

"*You* mean a lot," Carver said. "You inspire me, Mary Jane. Everything that you do. And each day that goes by, I only wish I could wake up beside you."

I blushed, and then laughed. "I'm at work before you wake up."

"Details," he sighed. "I bet I could convince you to quit that job and start sleeping in."

I laughed again. What a sweet fantasy.

***

By the end of September, the Cardinals finished the regular season still ranked first in their division, which meant they would play in the postseason. Sportscasters were going wild over this, and Carver was interviewed constantly.

Mom remained in Goldking, and Landon and Janine moved back in with her. Mom said she missed living with Steve, since Landon and Janine refused to share their reefer with her. But she loved her basement grotto and her little herb garden, so as long as the propane held out, she would stay in Goldking. Landon actually had a job now, so my hopes were high.

Mom also started dating Dean Licks again, from the repair shop, since Dean had split with his girlfriend and was lonely. He bought Mom some new clothes and another hairdryer, since her old one had broken. I hoped he would buy her some propane when it started snowing again.

On the first Saturday in October, the Cowboy married Abigail Turner. The mountains were a brilliant yellow and green, showing off their vibrant fall colors, and the sky was deep blue. Abigail wore a huge puffy dress with long sleeves and a veil. The Cowboy wore his black cowboy hat with his suit, and a single red rose stuck through his lapel.

The ceremony was held in the Presbyterian Church, since Abigail wasn't joining the Latter-day Saints. The Cowboy paid for the reception at Town Hall, and while he stocked all the beer, he couldn't afford to buy everyone food. So the meal was a huge potluck that half of Goldking showed up for. The dancing took place on the Town Hall's back lawn. The Cowboy had rigged up the speakers, and I was in charge of the music. The kids ran around eating cupcakes. Richard and Gus flirted with girls. Mom told anyone who would listen that she wanted a donkey.

While everyone was still dancing, Mia wandered over to me. She watched the Cowboy spin Abigail, and asked, "Think you'll ever get married?"

Mia never made a fuss over anything related to weddings, and I knew kids often posed questions for other people to answer, when they were really trying to figure out an answer for themselves. "Why do you ask?"

Mia considered the dance floor and shrugged. "Kind of a big deal over nothing."

I smiled. "Since you are in eighth grade right now, I completely agree."

"What if I was your age?" she asked.

I turned thoughtful. "It's up to you, Mia. If you want a wedding, you can certainly have one. Finding true love is a pretty big deal. Even if wearing a big puffy dress seems kind of silly."

"You're prettier than Abigail," Mia said. "And don't say I'm biased. It's true."

I regarded Mia a moment, and tried to determine where this comment was coming from. I thought about the junior high drama she was facing: looks and hormones and popularity contests. "Are you having boy trouble?"

"Please," Mia scoffed. "I have enough of that at home. I don't need to deal with the brainless at school."

I laughed, and then sobered again. Mia had a crush, I was sure. Such a hard place to be. I said, "Eighth grade boys never hit on the prettiest girls. Or the smartest ones, or the sassiest. You've got character, Mia. And it takes boys a while to figure out what that means."

"You were my age when you met the Cowboy," she said.

"A year older," I said. "And the Cowboy already knew what he wanted. Not all guys are like that."

"Was Carver like that?" she asked.

I hadn't considered this before, but the answer was yes. "Carver had a crush on a girl in his class," I said. "He married her right after they graduated."

"Did he always love her?" Mia asked.

I tapped her nose to make her smile. "I think so."

"I bet he loves you more," Mia said. "No one is prettier than you."

"Oh, Mia," I sighed. "If you think a boy's love is all in your looks, then you better run away from that boy. You have

511

character, baby. And that means you want to hold out for a guy who's like you—honest and loyal, hard-working. And funny."

Mia laughed. "You think I'm funny?"

"I think you're a lot of things. Beautiful. Smart. And definitely funny."

"Will I look like you though, when I grow up?"

I smiled. "You'll look like *you*—only better." I gave her a nudge with my hip. "Now bring me a cupcake, please. A pink one."

"The blue ones are better," she said.

I nodded. "Blue it is." As Mia walked away, Bree Taylor strolled over. She wore an excessive amount of eye shadow, a pair of sparkling stilettos, and a purple dress with tulle bows that looked slightly ridiculous. She smirked when she looked at me.

"Hi, Bree."

"Hello, Mary Jane," she said, drawing the words out. Her voice was tinged with disdain. "I thought I might see you today." She glanced around at my little DJ table, taking pains to look bored. Then she cocked an eyebrow and gave me her iciest smile. "How's the dishwashing life? Oh, wait—you're changing diapers now, right? And flipping burgers?" She snickered. "Good thing you went to college. I guess you showed all of us."

I regarded Bree for a moment, and then glanced at the Cowboy, who was still dancing with Abigail. Bree's icy smile faltered.

"I'm not the reason he never wanted to date you," I said. "But if you want to stand here and act pathetic, by all means. Go ahead."

Bree snorted and placed a hand on her hip. "You're fucking some *pro athlete* for *money*, and you want to tell *me* I'm pathetic."

I set my jaw and stopped looking at her. "No one asked you to be at this wedding."

"*David* invited me," Bree spat.

The Cowboy would never have taken the time to invite her. Bree was here only because most of Goldking was here. But rather than argue, I said, "Get away from me, Bree. I have work to do." I waved a hand at my DJ station. "Putting my college degree to good use."

Mia returned with my cupcake, and Bree called me a few choice names under her breath before stalking away.

"What a winning attitude," I called after her. "It's no wonder all the guys want you. How could they resist?"

Mia watched Bree strut across the room. "What did she want?"

"A boyfriend," I said. "No one will dance with her."

Mia glanced toward Bree and rolled her eyes. "In that hideous dress? It's no wonder."

"It's not her clothes," I laughed. "Everyone else here is happy. And she came to act like a hag."

Mia stole some of my icing and grinned. "I know. Valerie Duomo's dress is ten times worse than Bree's—and she's over there dancing with Corman." I looked where Mia was pointing, saw this was true, and allowed Mia to eat the rest of my cupcake.

"You'll have to bring me another," I said.

Mia gave me a lopsided salute. "No prob."

***

Two weeks later, on October sixteenth, the Cardinals prepared for Game 6 of the National League Championship Series, and

I came home from work at the diner and checked the mail. I received a letter from the last agency I'd applied to.

I stood outside my building and turned the envelope in my hands. There was a slim piece of cardboard inside, so the paper couldn't be smashed. I walked beneath the shade of a tree and opened the flap. I usually skimmed these agency letters—and this letter looked equally brief, like any other rejection. But this one did not begin, *Dear Applicant, Thank you for your submission, but your documentary project does not meet our requirements.*

This letter was totally different.

> *Dear Ms. Logan,*
>
> *We are pleased to inform you that your documentary project,* I Want to Get into Stanford: Nine Weeks in Nairobi, *has been selected as our Social Sciences Project to be Funded in Full. Enclosed, you will find a check for five thousand dollars ($5,000.00) for your initial trip to Nairobi to procure dormitory arrangements for yourself and five high school students. You are requested to contact our office to receive the remaining funding ($30,000.00) for your camera equipment and living expenses in Kenya next summer.*
>
> *Congratulations and best wishes for success.*
>
> *Sincerely,*
> *Kendra P. Harley*
> *Vice President, Social Sciences*

I leaned against the tree as I read the letter again, and then I looked inside the envelope—and spotted the check. Made out in my name. For five thousand dollars.

I ran upstairs to show the kids, and then I called Carver. I was so happy I was crying, and as soon as he answered, I said, "My proposal was accepted. To be funded in full."

Carver cheered and *cheered*, he made such a huge racket. "I knew you would do it, Mary Jane!"

The kids were still running around with my letter, and waving the check in the air, jumping and shouting. Gandhi barked and barked and hid under the table.

***

During the game that night, Carver hit two homeruns—one in the second inning, and one in the ninth—and St. Louis won. The National League Championship Series was finished, and the Cardinals had taken the pennant.

Now they would play the World Series.

On TV, there were fireworks. A huge victory party. I knew the celebration wasn't really for me—but watching the Cardinals run around cheering, I still kind of felt like it was. Some things in life are so big and so happy, it all blends together in a huge bag of perfection.

The kids ran outside and banged pots and pans—and what they yelled was: *Mary Jane got accepted! Mary Jane got accepted! And the St. Louis Cardinals are going to play the World Series!* Mahmood and his friends came out and joined them. It was a parade of pure noise.

Later, when we were all in my apartment, toasting with apple juice, Richard told Mahmood and his friends that the American League was sending the Yankees, and that the Cardinals hadn't played the Yankees in a Series since 1964. Since the National League had won the All-Star Game in July, the Cardinals were given home field advantage. So Game 1 of the Series would be played in Busch Stadium on October 19th. Only three days away.

"And we're gonna go!" Richard added. "Aren't we, Mary Jane?"

"That's right," I said. "We're going."

The kids would miss a week of school, and I certainly didn't have any vacation time to use, but my grant proposal had just been accepted, and I was euphoric. I had promised myself I wouldn't miss the World Series, and now it was here, and I would see Carver soon.

When I talked to him that night, he laughed when I asked him to buy everyone tickets. "I knew you would come for the Series," he said. "I was counting on it, all this time."

"I'll need a hotel room," I said. "I bet St. Louis is already booked."

"I would never put you in a hotel," Carver said. "You're staying with me. I'll fly you all out."

I held my breath for a moment. "Are you serious?"

Carver laughed. "I wouldn't be in the Series without you, Mary Jane. Making sure you get to watch the show is the least I can do."

"I bought a new dress," I announced, out of nowhere.

"I'll try not to rip it then," Carver said, "when I get you alone and pull it off."

51

MADNESS

The next morning, Carver made the travel arrangements for me and my family, as well as Emma and Steve, who Carver invited along—and I helped the kids pack their bags. "We're taking carry-on only," I said. "If it doesn't fit in your backpack, it stays."

When I called Carver that night, I asked him to send me a link so I could print the boarding passes.

"You won't need them," he said. "I couldn't fly you commercial—there weren't enough seats—so I chartered a plane."

"You *chartered* a plane??"

Carver laughed. "You leave tomorrow at noon. Don't be late."

I tried to wrap my head around this. Tomorrow, I would not be going to work. I'd fly in a private plane. And see Carver. Crazy, *crazy*. My life was turning so crazy.

The next morning, I put on my new dress. With a pair of dark tights and tall boots and my jacket, I looked like a movie star. Even my hair was so much prettier now. It fell down past my shoulders, thick and glossy and perfect. Amazing what a difference a few months could make. Cut short, my hair had a mind of its own. But at this length, my mop had its magic.

When it was time to leave for the airport, I loaded the kids in the Navigator, and Mahmood came to take Gandhi.

"He will be safe with me," Mahmood promised. "No need to worry."

Gandhi licked my chin while I petted him, and I assured Mahmood we would be home in ten days. The first two games of the Series would be in St. Louis, and then we would fly to New York and watch the next three in Yankee Stadium. If there was a Game 6 or Game 7, we would return to St. Louis to see the finale, and then we'd fly home.

On our way to the airport, I picked up Emma and Steve. A half hour later, I parked the Lincoln at the private airport, and saw the plane Carver had chartered. Not a corporate jet—but it was still beautiful, and almost brand new. The kids kept asking me how much this had cost, and I had no idea. Two thousand dollars an hour? Three? And this flight took three hours or so? "Ten thousand, maybe twenty," I guessed, and Mia's eyes boggled.

"This is insane," she said, in a tone of voice that meant *This is awesome*. The kids grabbed their bags and raced each other to board. They had never been on an airplane before, and they kept jumping and shouting. I let it go, since I was too happy myself to try to make them calm down.

The plane had a lovely interior, with white leather seats and long polished tables. There was a snack bar that the kids could help themselves to.

"I want my own airplane one day," Mia said. "This is so rad."

We had two pilots and a flight attendant, and once our bags were stored and our seatbelts were fastened, we were up in the air, on our way to St. Louis.

Around four p.m. central time, we arrived at a large private airport full of corporate jets. The kids were star-struck by these planes, and they kept gasping and yelling, trying to determine which one was the biggest. They wanted me to weigh in, but I had a hard time trying to think about airplanes. As we stepped onto the tarmac, I spotted Carver strolling outside the airport, and even though the kids ran to him first, and bombarded him, I could tell by the way he smiled at me that he liked my new dress. I sure looked a lot nicer than the last time he'd seen me, after a long night in jail in that orange prison suit. The memory caused me to laugh, and when Carver finally broke away from the kids and hugged me, I laughed again.

He cupped my face in his hands, and when he leaned down to kiss me, I slipped my arms around his waist. "Thanks for getting us here," I said.

"Thanks for being here," Carver said. He kissed me again, and then he picked up my bag, and we joined the kids and Emma and Steve in the airport. Once we were outside again, Carver pointed to a black Hummer limo parked beside the main door, and told the kids to climb in.

Mia shrieked and shouted, "That's what we're riding in??"

"That's it," Carver said. The limo driver pulled open the door and held out his hand to help Mia in. She leaped up the steps, and the boys clambered in after her, more excited by the sight of this deluxe limo than they had even been by the plane.

Carver and I stood outside for a minute.

"You look beautiful," he said.

He wore his dark woolen trench coat, and I tugged on his scarf. "So do you."

Carver's expression changed—and he suddenly looked worried and concerned—and he embraced me again like I might disappear. "I want you to stay, Mary Jane. Please stay."

I felt his heart pounding, he held me so tightly. "I am going to stay," I said. "I came to watch the World Series."

"I mean, stay forever," Carver said.

I leaned back to peer at his face. "I thought we were going to… talk about this later. In Tahiti."

Carver blushed, a color that looked more pink than red with his tan. He tried to say something, but then he shook his head and held back the words. He gestured toward the open door of the limo. "Come on," he said, and the worry left his face when he grinned. "Everyone's waiting to meet you."

He meant his family, of course. They were still at the house, making dinner. So I climbed into the limo, and Carver sat down beside me. As we rode to his house, and Carver talked to the kids, the question of living with him weighed on my mind.

Did I want to move in with him—with the kids? Could Carver and I make it work? How could he be so certain he wanted to live with me? He might only love me because he couldn't have me. And he might come to resent me if he had to take care of my family.

Bringing us to St. Louis to watch the World Series—that was one thing. An extravagant gesture to celebrate his phenomenal year. It was like a vacation, like the big family cruise he wanted to take—it was outside of real life.

But living together—facing each day, rain or shine—that was different. That felt like… *marriage*… and I didn't want to get married. I wanted to stay me: Mary Jane Logan. Strong, independent, and free. I had worked so hard to be able to take care of myself. I didn't need a man to support me.

If I moved in with Carver, I couldn't live as an equal. I could never afford half the rent, or half the bills, or whatever the arrangement would be. I couldn't pay for cruise tickets, or meals in Tahiti, or anything that Carver was planning. We lived in two separate worlds, and no matter how much I struggled to make sense of combining them, our worlds did not mesh. Not unless I gave up the ability to take care of myself—to pay my own way. And that idea inspired… all my worst fears.

If I worked out a smaller percentage of the bills I could afford—probably a lot less than half, probably nowhere near the actual cost—and then moved in with Carver… that seemed even scarier. Because he might expect me to pay my dues in other ways… and do things for him. Like his laundry. Or cooking for him like a servant. I thought of Dole kicking the wall to wake up my mom, yelling *Get up, woman! I want breakfast!* The memory made me shudder, and I felt even more anxious. I couldn't imagine Carver ever acting like that. So why did it still frighten me so much?

I gazed out the window, and watched as the limo entered a gated community. Large homes, big lawns. Carver's neighborhood. He squeezed my hand and sent me a smile, and I smiled in return, despite how anxious I felt. Carver wanted me to be part of his life, to move into one of these mansions with the kids, and I knew we would have to discuss this before I flew home. It couldn't wait until later. The subject was a presence between us, heavy and ominous.

Carver pointed to a gorgeous brick house and said, "That's us," before the limo turned off the road and pulled into the drive.

The kids hopped out first, skipping and running, and the front door of the house flew open before they could reach it.

Carver's three boys spilled outside, and then his sister, Clarissa, and her four children and husband, and then Carver's parents.

We had a lively, funny greeting outside on the drive. The kids knew everyone's name, and everyone knew all the kids—even Emma and Steve didn't have any trouble remembering names—and it was a strange introduction because it felt more like a homecoming. Carver's family had been waiting for us all day, and as they ushered us inside, the house smelled like lasagna and fresh bread and olive oil. It was a beautiful home, with hardwood floors and antiques and framed photos of the children in the main hall.

Carver's mother hugged me a fourth time in the entryway. "I don't know how you ever got him to start hitting again, but we're so grateful you did."

I blushed and didn't know what to say. I hadn't made Carver start hitting again—he had done that himself. But his family kept saying these things and hugging me, like I had done something fantastic.

I glanced up at Carver, wondering if he was going to help me out here, but he only leaned down and kissed my cheek. "I hope you're hungry," he said.

We put our bags in the hall, and drifted into the kitchen. Clarissa poured glasses of juice for the kids. She asked me if I would like wine, but I said, "No thanks, just water, please," since I wasn't ready for wine. Clarissa ribbed Carver to tease him, since he couldn't drink alcohol on his diet.

I asked him, "Will you drink some champagne, if the Cardinals win the World Series?"

Carver laughed. "I hope so." Branch jumped for his dad to pick him up, so Carver scooped his youngest son into his arms. Jack and Christy came over to join us.

Branch tipped back his ball cap and grinned at me. "Dad says you ride horses and know how to shoot a gun. He says you're a real cowgirl!"

I almost burst into laughter. A *cowgirl?* Oh my. "Well, I do have a hideout," I said. "Maybe that qualifies."

"Can I see your hideout?" Branch asked. "Is it up in the mountains?" Jack and Christy looked at me expectantly, clearly wanting to be included in such an excursion.

"The next time you visit, I'll take you to see it," I said.

Jack and Christy high-fived, and Branch swung his legs to bounce on his dad.

Clarissa stepped over with my glass of water. "Carver told us you went to Swarthmore," she said. "And you're going to Nairobi next summer."

I nodded, astounded for a moment that this was really my life: I had attended a top rate university, and I was about to start using my degree.

"That's right," I said. "My grant proposal was just accepted. The same night the Cardinals won the pennant."

"Talk about fate," Clarissa said with a grin. She gave Carver a wink, and then tweaked Branch's nose. "You know about fate, mister?" she asked Branch.

"Meant to be," Branch replied.

"Meant to be," Jack repeated, and he glanced at his dad. "Cause everything that's here, it was all meant to be. Huh, Dad?"

Carver placed an arm around Jack's shoulders, and drew him into a hug. "Where'd you learn to get so smart?" he asked.

"From me," Branch said. "I taught him everything I know."

Clarissa and I burst into laughter, and Branch flushed with pleasure. Christy gave us all measured looks and said, "That's what Grandma says about Dad."

"You better believe it," Carver said.

***

We ate supper in the dining room, on a table large enough to seat everyone, even Clarissa's young children. With all eleven kids present and the mix of adults, there was no shortage of conversation around the dining room table. Steve asked everyone whether or not they liked to play chess, Carver's father asked Steve and the kids if they liked to go fishing, and as I sat listening, I realized that Carver's home made me feel warm and peaceful, the same way I felt when I was up in the mountains. I had never been under a roof and had that feeling before.

We lingered for an hour after the meal, before everyone ambled into the living room and found seats on the couches. The kids disappeared with Carver's boys to explore the rest of the house, and sometime later, while Carver's parents were talking to Emma about hairdressing, Carver and I slipped outside.

I buttoned my jacket against the cold, and then I took Carver's hand, and we walked into the darkness of his backyard.

"You're finally here," Carver said. He stopped and hugged me. His voice sounded rough with happiness. "I'm so glad you're here."

"Me, too," I said.

"Clarissa and her crew have the basement tonight," Carver said. "There's a big rec room down there, where she keeps all her stuff when she visits. Emma and Steve will have the guest room upstairs. Richard and Ethan and Gus are going to sleep in the loft, and Mia can stay in the office—Clarissa set up the pull-out bed in there today."

"Thank you for doing this," I said. "Between the plane and the limo and everything else, it's overwhelming what you've done to get us all here."

"Mary Jane, I… I told you… it was just some phone calls."

I stood on tiptoe to kiss him, and we stopped talking a while. Our kisses felt anxious and fleeting, like we were scared of each other. I could still feel the passion between us, but it was undercut with uncertainty.

I pulled away and said, "Let's walk the perimeter." So Carver took my hand and we walked around the edge of his yard.

Carver was quiet. More than quiet. He seemed nervous and tense. He kept glancing at me and looking away, and I could tell he wanted to say something to me, something he was struggling to hold back.

But I still wasn't ready to discuss moving in. I needed a few days, at least, to consider all this.

So I asked Carver about the batting lineup tomorrow, and how he felt playing the Yankees, and twenty other questions related to baseball and the World Series. Some of his tension eased, but not all of it. There was something bothering him that he couldn't let go. His apprehension rubbed off on me, and I began to suspect… that I knew what was on Carver's mind. My heartbeat sped up, and I hoped I was wrong. It was hard enough to contemplate moving in with him. If he asked me for more than that… what in the world would I say?

I kept the subject on baseball. I was afraid of what he would say if we talked about anything else.

A few minutes later, we returned inside, and it was time for the children to go to bed. There was a long commotion of teeth brushing and changing into pajamas and flipping on nightlights and reminders to lie down because we had a big day tomorrow. Mia disappeared in the office, Richard and Ethan and Gus climbed up to the loft, and it felt like a century before I was in Carver's bedroom with him, and we were alone.

Carver had a beautiful room, like the rest of his house. I gazed around at the furniture, and the lovely art on the walls, and then I met Carver's gaze. He stepped closer to me, and before I could stop myself, words tumbled out of my mouth. "I don't think I would make a good wife."

Carver took my hands and searched my face. His voice filled with tenderness. "Why do you say that?"

My breathing turned faint with nerves. "If I move in with you, we'd be like a husband and wife. And you might expect things from me. To wash your laundry. Or take care of your boys. And that's not what I want." I suddenly started to cry—tears that came out of nowhere—and I pulled away from Carver and crossed the room. I was so embarrassed I hid my face in my hands, and then dried my cheeks with my wrist.

Carver came to stand next to me, and his voice remained gentle. "I don't want anything like that, Mary Jane. I can wash my own laundry. And my parents take care of my boys when I'm not here. I just want to be with you, that's all. And I do want to… I do want to call you my wife."

I still couldn't look at him. "I thought you didn't want to get married again."

His words sounded so soft. "I don't feel that way anymore. Ever since I met you, I've felt… bigger, somehow."

"You *are* bigger," I said, trying to joke.

He laughed. "I'm happy again. And I'm not… scared about what could happen. I don't care what could happen. I want to marry you, Mary Jane."

I was crying again, trying to hide my face in my arm, but Carver turned me around and hugged me. I rubbed my cheek on his shirt, and leaned my head on his chest.

"I can't get married," I said. "I'm not ready."

"I know," he said softly. "I was trying so hard not to say anything. I didn't want you to feel like I had brought you here just to… just to put pressure on you. But when I saw you at the airport today, I could only think about how you would be leaving again—how I'd have to say another goodbye—and it upset me so much that I—" He broke off for a moment, and ran a hand through my hair. "I thought I could be satisfied just asking you to move in. But marrying you… it's always on my mind. I'm sorry, Mary Jane. I should have let it wait, like we planned."

I finished wiping my eyes and said, "You don't need to be sorry." I tried to smile in a way that let him know that I meant it. My tears still embarrassed me, so I added, "I need to wash up." Carver released me and I went into the bathroom.

I ran water in the sink for a minute, and then I cleaned my face and prepared for bed. I changed into my nightgown, which was a shirt long enough to reach my knees. Hanna had bought me this shirt because it resembled a jersey, and because she had wanted me to own something with *Swarthmore* printed across it. I only ever wore it on special occasions, and as I gazed at my reflection, I willed myself to pull it together. I was here in St. Louis. With Carver. I should be nothing but happy.

When I stepped out of the bathroom, I felt so incredibly tired. Carver was in the hall, talking to one of his boys—telling him to go back to bed. I heard the patter of small feet, and then Carver returned, closed the door, and sent me a smile. "Trying to sneak downstairs and play video games," he said, and I laughed.

I slipped into bed and lay down, waiting for Carver. He wasn't long. As he slid in beside me, I switched off the lamp. I rested my head on his chest, wishing I wasn't so drained. Carver wore boxers, and his bare skin smelled lovely. All those months of longing for him, all that aching—and now that I was in bed with him, I was already falling asleep. What a letdown.

Carver traced the sleeve of my nightgown, and then he hugged me against him.

"After Audrey Lynn died," he said, "I was so lost. I knew I was searching for something, but I didn't know what. Now I think I was just waiting for you. Waiting for you to walk into my life."

I placed my hand on his hip and considered these words. "Do you think something is wrong with me though?" I asked. "Because I don't want to get married?"

"Never," Carver said. "You're perfect, Mary Jane. Just as you are."

I smiled and closed my eyes, so relieved he had said this, and soon I was asleep.

I woke again in the night, and found Carver awake. I lifted my head to study him. "Why aren't you sleeping?"

He smiled. "I just can't."

I sat up for a minute, and realized I felt better. Like a gloom around me had lifted. And I was in bed with Carver. I knew why he was awake.

I ran a hand along his arm, up onto his shoulder, and gazed down at his body. Heat crept into my skin. How in the world had I lain here beside him and fallen asleep? Madness. I peeled off my nightgown, and in the shadowy light, Carver flashed me that grin like the devil.

He sat up in a heartbeat and swept me into his arms, and the warmth in my body flared into a fire. Carver's kisses left me gasping. He tasted wicked and smooth and as sweet as pure joy, and when I rolled into the sheets and pulled him on top of me, Carver made a sound like I'd burned him.

52

MY GREMLINS

Later, after Carver fell asleep, I remained curled up beside him. I listened to his soft, even breathing, and wondered if he was dreaming. I traced my thumb along his cheek, and ran my fingers through his hair. I didn't want to wake him, but I couldn't seem to stop touching him. Sometimes I leaned over and kissed his brow, or his shoulder, and then I would lie back on the pillow and clasp his hand to my chest.

I liked being awake while Carver was sleeping. Lying beside him, I felt radiant, incandescent, like I lit up the room with my happiness. I knew we would make love again as soon as Carver woke up, and this excited me more than even watching him play.

The room brightened with sunrise. I heard people in the hall, and the sound of children running, and then I heard Clarissa's voice, telling Carver's boys and the kids to come to the kitchen for breakfast. She was laughing at something, and I heard several people walk downstairs before the hallway fell silent.

I knew the kids would be fine in this house a few hours without me, and I felt no desire to get out of bed. I ran my fingertips along Carver's wrist, content to wait here until he woke up.

I kept thinking about what Carver had told me last night: that he thought I was perfect.

Even if I didn't want to get married.

So I lay there beside him and thought about living with him. Combining our families. How we might make it work.

My mother had always moved in with men because she was desperate, and because she needed someone to take care of her. But I wasn't desperate, and I didn't need Carver to take care of me. My life wasn't easy, but I could manage without him.

And I no longer worried Carver would come to resent me. If I ever thought that was happening, I could simply move out. And if Carver ever left me, or if I left with the kids—I knew I would survive. I wouldn't be penniless, sleeping in parks in a car. Nor would Carver curse and yell and throw me out the door if we ever broke up. All of those fears were completely irrational. I lived in a different world now, a world with manageable risk. I was only as vulnerable as my fear led me to be—and the truth was, I was not scared of Carver. I was scared of my ghosts.

The real question was whether I thought the good times would be worth any pain. Like lying in bed with him now, and all of the other mornings we might have together if we lived with each other.

If I moved in with Carver, I could spend entire days with him. Weeks, months. Even years. I could go on that trip to Tahiti with him. We could go anywhere that we wanted. Life with Carver would be full of joy. More joy than pain. More laughter than tears.

I leaned over to kiss his cheek, and touched his jaw. He seemed so much younger asleep—so much more vulnerable—than he ever appeared while he was awake. He looked like a boy, not a professional athlete. I held his hand and traced the lines of his fingers, felt the calluses in his palm from his long months of baseball.

Another hour passed, and around nine o'clock, Carver finally stirred. He pulled me closer against him before he even opened his eyes.

"Good morning," I giggled.

He smiled in response and peered over my face, before he rolled on his back and propped me up on his chest. "I've died and gone to heaven."

I tugged on his chin. "I hope not. You're supposed to bat third in the lineup tonight."

His gaze skimmed my body. "Maybe I'll just stay in bed."

"I'm sure your coach will love that."

"I'll lock the door," Carver said.

I laughed and sat up, and he put his hands my knees.

"I've been thinking," I said. I slid his hands from my knees and onto my hips.

He shifted his weight on the pillows to look at me better. "Want to stay here in bed with me?"

I grinned. "I think I do."

"All day and all night?" he asked.

"Even longer," I said.

He trailed a fingertip down my nose. "Forever?" he asked.

I took his hand and kissed his palm. I sent him a smile, and I could tell by the light in his eyes that my smile said it all. "Forever, Carver. That's exactly what I want."

***

Carver and I dressed around noon and walked downstairs to eat lunch. We strolled into the kitchen and discovered Carver's parents had made pizzas, which the children were devouring. I helped myself to a slice and took a seat beside Richard. Carver avoided the pizza, opened the fridge and removed a pitcher of green liquid. The kids watched with interest while he poured a glassful and drank it.

Christy said, "Dad usually makes those himself. But I guess he just wanted to sleep in today." Christy raised his eyebrows and shook his head a little, like he couldn't believe his father would be such a lazybones.

Carver laughed and poured another glass. "I like Pop-Pop's smoothies," he said, and he smiled at his father.

Carver's dad glanced up from the sink, where he stood rinsing dishes. "What time are you leaving?"

Carver glanced at the clock on the wall. "An hour," he said. "I'll ride over with Matt."

Clarissa was spoon-feeding her youngest, and she asked Carver, "Did you work out the deal with the seats?"

Carver nodded. To me, he said, "The original tickets weren't in the same section, but we were able to fix that, and keep everyone together."

At the mention of tickets, all eleven kids started bouncing—even the baby. They were really keyed up for this game.

"We'll head over at five," Clarissa said.

"So we can walk through the stadium and check everything out," Richard said. "Not even Mary Jane has ever been to Busch Stadium. Except she's been to a major league game before. Huh, Mary Jane?"

I smiled and nodded. "I saw the Braves play once, when I was in seventh grade."

Clarissa glanced at me quickly, curious, and then at Carver. "Were you playing that day?"

I blushed and smiled at Carver, and he stepped over with a grin and put his arm around me. The kitchen fell silent, with everyone intent on this answer.

"It was the year before he signed," I said, trying to keep my voice mild. My face still felt hot. "I think I would have remembered him, later… if I had ever seen the Grizz play." I smiled over at Gus. "Gus recognized the Grizz though. Thank goodness."

Gus beamed at me, and then Carver, while Richard and Ethan each gave him a pat on the back. In his soft, careful voice, Gus said, "I always knew the Grizz would start hitting again. That's why I kept his card all those years."

Carver laughed and tousled Gus's hair. "I'm glad someone knew I'd come back."

Clarissa was smiling, but she was also wiping tears from her eyes. "God, Carver," she sighed. "It sure took you long enough."

***

An hour later, after Carver left for Busch Stadium, I sat with the kids in the living room.

Clarissa was with her family in the basement, getting her children ready, and Carver's boys were with his parents upstairs. Emma and Steve had borrowed a vehicle and gone for a drive.

"It'll be cold tonight," I told the kids. "You'll need your hats and gloves." They nodded, not looking at me, and I realized they were glum. "What's the matter?"

"We were just wondering," Ethan said. "About Carver."

I waited, but no one spoke up. "What about Carver?"

Richard muttered, "If he wants to marry you."

Mia took my hand, and I saw she was frightened. "Will you move away, Mary Jane?"

I slid over and hugged her, unaware that the kids had been worried about this. I had never said anything about marrying Carver—but being here in his house, and seeing the two of us together—I could understand why they would be so upset. "I'm not going anywhere unless you guys come with me," I said. I glanced at Gus. "You too, Gus. We're a package deal now."

Ethan had tears in his eyes. "We thought it would be… like when you went to college… and we—"

I shook my head and put an arm around his shoulders. "No more dorm rooms," I said. "And Carver would never ask me to leave you. Never."

Richard started to cry. I left Mia and hugged him instead. "You guys are falling apart on me here. I thought you were excited to see the World Series."

"We are," Richard said. "It's just… we were worried."

"I don't blame you," I said. "Between the airplane and the limo ride and this house—this has been pretty shocking."

Gus tapped his hands on his knees, turning thoughtful. When he didn't feel shy around strangers, he liked being logical. Spock was his role model of late. "It makes sense that Carver would live like this. His last contract was more than twelve million dollars. And that was just for his past three years with the Cardinals, not even hitting homeruns. He made a lot more when he played for the Yankees. The first year he signed with the Yankees, he made twenty-one million. After that, his contracts kept going up. He was the highest-paid player in the majors, before he was dropped from the Yankees."

"And now he's gonna kick their ass tonight," Richard said. "Serves them right."

Ethan asked me, "How much money does Carver have?"

"I don't know," I said. "I think he was saving it all for his brother."

"What will he do with it now?" Ethan asked.

"He could buy his own airplane," Gus said. "If he wanted to."

"He could," I agreed. Though I couldn't picture Carver wanting to own his own plane.

"I wonder if it's invested," Richard said.

I laughed. "That much money? It better be."

"Does he really want us to live with him?" Mia asked. She waved a hand toward the room. "Like, here in this house?"

I nodded. "That's the plan."

"And you'll stay in Riverdale, if we don't want to go?"

I nodded again. "What do you think about living with Carver?"

"It's really nice here," Richard said.

"His kids are nice," Ethan added.

"His whole family is," Mia said. "I don't know why we'd want to stay in Riverdale. I'm sure there's a school in St. Louis with a gardening club."

"And basketball," Gus said. "And baseball."

"We'll go where you go," Richard said. "If you want to move in with Carver, that's okay with us."

"What about Mom?" Ethan asked. "What if she runs out of propane?"

The kids cast me anxious expressions. They obviously wanted Mom to be able to stay in Goldking.

"We'll make sure she doesn't run out of propane," I said. "Or lose the house for unpaid taxes. Or anything else."

Richard frowned and caught my gaze. "You wouldn't let her move here, would you?"

Mia and Ethan and Gus looked even more nervous, and I pondered this for a moment, glancing around at the living room.

"I think Mom's too destructive to be a part of this home," I said. "So no, I wouldn't let her move in with us. If she wants to be in St. Louis, she'll have to get her own place."

The kids sighed with relief.

"She won't want to leave Goldking, anyway," Mia said. "As long as her bills are paid, she'll stay there."

"She feels safe there," Ethan said. "I don't think she'd like to be in this house."

"I think you're right," I agreed. Being inside Carver's home would definitely wig Mom out. It was nothing at all like her little basement grotto, which was packed with her fairy collection and pot paraphernalia. Mom needed a certain amount of... confinement—and clutter—to truly feel peace.

Gus asked, "How long will it take us to move in with Carver?"

"That's up to you," I said, glancing at all of the kids. "Whenever you're ready to switch schools, Carver would like us to move in."

"Will you marry him?" Mia asked.

I gazed at the ceiling a moment, unsure how to answer. "Carver would like to get married," I said. "But I'm not sure I... I'm not sure about that."

Mia leaned back on the cushions and grinned at me. "Well, you know what they say, Mary Jane: finding true love is a pretty big deal."

"And you have to be brave to be happy," Richard added.

I laughed. "You guys are growing up to be some pretty smart gremlins."

"We'll all go to college one day—and then we'll be smarter than you, Mary Jane," Richard said.

I tugged on his sleeve. "I'm counting on it."

53

GETTING THERE

In the ballpark that night, Carver wore his white jersey, with a long-sleeved red shirt underneath. The uniform made him so different. He wasn't just Carver, when he dressed for a game. He was the Grizz. And he was magnificent.

Busch Stadium held such a beautiful ballpark. The air smelled like popcorn and hot dogs and beer and cut grass, and when I stood on the field, underneath the bright lights, I gazed over the distance a ball had to travel to land in the stands, and felt awed by the size of the park.

The kids begged me to let them see Carver before the game started. He had told me beforehand that this was okay, and as we made our way toward him, people were everywhere on the field. Taking pictures, asking questions. Reporters and cameramen, and lots of men in black suits, and other officials who were milling around. Carver broke away from all this to come say hello.

"Did you find your seats?" he asked the kids. They were laughing as they hugged him, as excited as I was to see him in uniform. Matt joined us and hugged the kids, and in the commotion, when Carver's gaze met mine, I felt such a jolt through my body. My heart slammed in my chest, and I suddenly couldn't focus on anyone but him.

Carver took my hands and kissed me—and dimly, I became aware that pandemonium had erupted around us. Within moments, those cameras, reporters, men in suits—all that chaos was suddenly focused on... *me.*

Miss! Miss! Do you live in St. Louis? What's your name? Have you known Greyson long? Where did you meet? Any comments about the season? The Cardinals? Is this your home team?

The questions sounded like gunfire, loud and threatening. I would have to yell to be heard, and I did not want to yell. What a circus.

Carver drew me against him, kissed my cheek and murmured, "Do you want me to answer? Or just walk you back?"

"Both," I said, and Carver turned to smile at the people around us. The volume of noise dropped considerably.

He told the crowd, "This is Mary Jane Logan. My girlfriend. She lives in Colorado. We met after New Year's, while I was in Colorado. We've been together since then."

The reporters kept yelling questions, but Carver walked me back toward the gate where the kids and I had come in. I was relieved to be getting away from those people.

"Did you kiss me on purpose?" I asked.

Carver laughed and shook his head no. "I forget to think, sometimes. It's a serious problem."

I grinned and hugged him, and then he swept me up—lifted me so high that my face was above him. I laughed and put my arms around his neck. His body felt hot as a woodstove, and made my skin tingle.

"Good luck tonight, Carver."

He kissed me before he put me down. "You're my good luck, Mary Jane."

***

When the game started, the Yankees did not let Carver bat. The catcher stepped away from home plate, and the pitcher threw balls until Carver walked.

The kids were let down, and every Cardinals fan in the stadium groaned in dismay—but once Carver was on base, he stole second, and then third—and the audience perked up and really started to scream. Ten minutes later, Carver stole home— *home*—in the *first inning*—and as his fans shrieked and went crazy, a round of fireworks lit the sky.

"This is so cool!" Mia shouted.

The rest of the game was exciting, even if the Yankees refused to let Carver hit. They walked him each time he arrived at the plate. But the Cardinals still took the win, 2-1.

Later, in Carver's bedroom that night, when he stripped off his clothes, I saw the marks of what his trip home had cost him. He had a bruise on his shoulder the size of a football, and another black and purple monstrosity on the back of his thigh.

"Oh, Carver," I said, worried to see such huge bruises. "Those look terrible."

Carver smiled. "They look worse than they feel." Then he slid his hands up my dress, and said, "I'll take a kiss to make it better though," as he scooped me onto the bed. I laughed and kissed him. "See?" he said, maneuvering me out of my clothes. "I feel better already."

***

The next night in the stadium, Game 2 of the Series followed the same routine as Game 1: Carver was walked every time he came up to bat, and the Cardinals still won the game, 1-0. It was widely agreed that the Yankees were struggling.

"They have tried to shut down the Grizz," an announcer said, "but the Yankees are failing to shut down the whole team. The Cardinals have surged ahead in this Series, and now we'll look to see how they do in New York."

Carver was quiet on the ride home that night. Before we fell asleep later, I asked him how he felt about being walked.

"Nothing I can do about it," he said, and he placed his hands on my waist and drew me closer.

I caught his gaze with a smile. "You're not sleepy yet?"

Carver nipped my shoulder and made a deep sound like a purr. He wasn't sleepy at all.

***

The following morning, we flew to New York for the next set of games. In Manhattan, we checked into a gorgeous suite of rooms in the Waldorf Astoria. I had never been inside such an extravagant hotel, and even the kids were stunned into silence. I joined them in the bedroom they would share for our stay, just to sit and talk with them alone a few minutes.

Richard informed me that I was all over the internet.

"Look," he said, and he used my phone to scroll through sports websites. Sure enough, I was in several pictures, with titles like THE GRIZZ FINDS TRUE LOVE and MYSTERIOUS GIRLFRIEND APPEARS.

"Oh, man," I laughed. I was happy that Carver's career had made him so famous, but it was still embarrassing to see my own personal life on the internet.

"At least you look great in the pictures," Mia said. She pointed to one article titled SORRY, LADIES: THE GRIZZ ISN'T SINGLE. "We should forward that one to Bree."

Ethan asked, "Why would you send a sports page to Bree?"

Mia chuckled. "Cause she's a witch."

I took the phone. "We don't need to send that to anyone. I think the whole town of Goldking knows we're here. She'll probably see it herself."

A few minutes later, the kids and I left the bedroom and joined everyone else in the sitting room.

Mia said, "This hotel is a freaking *palace*. It's like we flew to Versailles."

Steve plucked a few grapes from a fruit basket and gazed over the room. "You can say that again."

Carver was sitting near Christy, who was standing on his head on the couch. "I wanna go to Versailles," Christy said. His face was bright pink, and he was giggling.

Carver stood and grabbed Christy's ankles, and hauled him off the couch upside down. Christy squealed, and then chanted while Carver bounced him, "*I want to go to Versailles… I want to go to Versailles…*"

Carver tossed Christy in the air, caught him and tickled him, until Jack jumped on Carver's back and yelled, "Eat the giant!" which was the most popular roughhousing game the boys played with their dad. The goal of this game was to wrestle Carver to the floor and then pretend to bite his arms and neck.

Carver defended himself by tickling his attackers and tossing them around.

Clarissa said, "You make more noise than the baby, you know that? Good grief. Carver, why don't you take them outside, you want to horse around so much."

Carver laughed, but he didn't stop tickling Jack.

Branch asked Mia if she wanted to help hold Carver down.

"I think I'll pass on eating giant, thanks," Mia said. "I'd rather have pizza."

Branch said, "Suit yourself," and jumped on his dad.

Clarissa scooped up her toddler and pretended to scold Carver. "You're going to break one of these vases or something, and then we'll have to call for a vacuum."

Carver blew a raspberry on Branch's belly, which made him shriek. "We won't need a vacuum," Carver said. "We'll be good."

I laughed as I watched him play with his boys. Eat the Giant lasted until our limo arrived to take us to dinner. And Carver was right: we did not need a vacuum.

✳✳✳

The following night, by the end of Game 3, the Yankees lost again, 5-6. Everyone was wondering if the Cardinals would sweep them in four.

I could tell Carver was down though, not being able to hit. He was so good at hiding his feelings, but I noticed his smile wasn't as quick, and he seemed a bit distant. So I made sure we took the kids to a park the next morning, and played a game of baseball together.

As I watched Carver pitch to all of the kids—even Clarissa's youngest boy, who could barely hold onto a bat—I let my thoughts drift. And I wondered why Carver wanted to marry me, and why I was so determined not to get married. As I helped Clarissa's boy grip his bat and swing at the ball, I wondered if I was just running away from the babies. Three more boys meant three more children to raise. And I had sworn I didn't want to repeat that part of my life.

But hanging out with Carver's family, spending time with his boys, watching the kids play together—I enjoyed this too much to run away from it all. His three boys weren't the reason I didn't want to get married.

Carver knelt in the dirt to pitch softly enough for his nephew, and I wondered about the idea of belonging… how spouses belonged to each other. Did I want to belong to Carver, and let him belong to me?

Or was I only considering this because I wanted to make Carver happy?

And what if *not* getting married would actually keep us happier than tying the knot?

Later, when we finished our game, I let the kids race each other to the swings, and helped Carver pack up. He leaned over and kissed me—all tender and rough—and my whole body flushed. I pressed my face to his chest and took a deep breath, so delighted to be with him I was sure I was floating.

"Ready for lunch?" he asked.

"I'm getting there," I said. I gazed up at his face, and I could tell he was so much more contented now than he had been after the game… and I wondered if anything would really change, if we were married. Would I still be able to work on my own projects, and follow my dreams—if I was Carver's wife?

Could I still be myself if I belonged to this man?

Maybe. Maybe I could.

Watching him play in Game 4 that night, I kept thinking about the morning Carver had come to the courthouse. How he had grabbed me and held me and didn't want to let go.

After Hanna died, I had struggled so hard to tackle my grief. To be brave. To survive on my own. And maybe I was just scared to love Carver. To admit that I loved him as much as I did.

I didn't want to let him go.

And maybe that was all marriage was, in the end. Two people who didn't want to let go.

***

Game 4 tied in the ninth inning, but the Yankees hit a homerun in the tenth and won the game, 5-4. It was a sad night for redbird fans.

As we gathered our things to leave the stadium and return to our hotel, Mia was glum. "When are they gonna let Carver hit?" she asked. "I want to see him at bat!"

"He's too dangerous," I said. "The Yankees can't afford to pitch to him."

"Stupid Yankees," Mia grumbled. "I hate the Yankees."

The boys all muttered, *Me, too!*

That night in our suite, the kids were mopey, and clung to Carver like sea kelp. He wasn't upset by the loss—the Cardinals had too much of a lead for him to be worried—but his boys and the kids still decided to pile into bed with us. So we watched a movie and ate popcorn until three in the morning. Once the gremlins were snoring, Carver and I left the room, found an empty bed, and closed the door.

As I unbuttoned Carver's shirt and he nuzzled my neck, I touched his body and tried to think of him... not as my boyfriend, but my husband.

My husband.

Those words sounded so serious. So permanent.

Carver held me in his arms, and his words against my throat tickled my skin. "What are you thinking about?"

"You," I said. "Just you."

***

Later, I woke to find Carver sitting up on the bed, applying patches of Tiger Balm to his right knee, the one he'd needed surgery on three years ago. Sometimes that knee still bothered him, and his muscles would ache. I could smell the herbs as he opened the patches and placed them over his skin.

When he finished, he turned and found me awake. Carver smiled and I put my arm around his waist, to draw him back into the sheets with me.

As I lay with my head on his chest, and listened to his breathing change as he drifted to sleep, I thought again of how Carver was willing to sign with a team in L.A., just so I could find work in the film industry.

I thought about having a job that I loved—a job working with film—not only on a grant project, but an actual paying job that would let me take care of myself—and my heart beat faster.

I would never have thought about moving the kids to L.A. to follow my dreams. Moving everyone across country like that… when it was hard enough to pay the bills and keep the kids in school…? I had allowed the goal of making sure they graduated to eclipse everything else. Even writing my grant proposal, I had not allowed myself to dream quite that big.

Carver wanted to marry me, but he wanted more than just holding onto each other. He wanted to help me become the person I was meant to be, even if that meant changing his life. In becoming husband and wife, Carver wanted to be permanent teammates, and the goal of this game was not scoring runs. The game of life had only one goal to win, and that was to lead a life of significance. To find yourself, and to know how you wanted to spend the gift of each day you were given.

Carver had embraced his life's purpose: to be a son, a brother, a father, a ballplayer. And one day, he knew he would go back to college and coach.

And in the midst of all that he was, and the clamor around his career, Carver also believed in me and my destiny. He wanted to underwrite funding for my documentary projects. He wanted to throw me parties when my films found success. He wanted to love me forever. He wanted to be my best friend.

Maybe marriage was not just about holding onto each other. Maybe marriage was about finding that person who believed in your destiny, that person who would always be there to help you lead a life of significance.

That was a much deeper bond than a marriage license could ever put into words.

But that was why people held weddings, wasn't it? To vow to love each other, to believe in each other, forever.

I sat up and kissed Carver's chest, and then his jaw, and his lips. This was the man I wanted to love and believe in forever. This was the man I wanted to make those vows to.

Carver sent me a sleepy smile when I kissed him. "Are the kids awake?" he asked. He thought I was trying to tell him it was time to wake up.

My voice sounded light and whispery, full of joy. "I just wanted to kiss you."

He opened his eyes and ran a hand through my hair. "Can't sleep?"

I laughed and nestled my head on his shoulder. "Just happy, is all."

He kissed my brow. "Me, too."

I closed my eyes and thought about the decision I'd made—that I *did* want to marry Carver, that I *did* want to spend my forever with him—and I wanted to hold that inside me a while, hold onto my choice until it had settled and calmed, and banished the last of the fear from my heart.

But sometime soon, I knew I would tell him.

54

DREAMING AGAIN

The following night in Yankee Stadium, Game 5 was another nail-biter that went to ten innings. Carver still couldn't bat, though he did steal bases, and scored two runs. But the Cardinals lost, 7-8.

Gus said, "Well, at least this means more money for the Cardinals," since the next game would be played in Busch Stadium. "They'll make bank on the ticket sales."

We flew back to Carver's home in St. Louis the next morning, and the following night, we gathered in the stadium to watch Game 6.

The Yankees needed to win two more games to take the Series. But if the Cardinals won tonight, there wouldn't be a Game 7.

Game 6 was the most nerve-racking to watch. The Cardinals made several fielding mistakes—dropping balls, bad plays—and the Yankees surged ahead, 5-1. In the seventh inning, the Cardinals started hitting, and tied the game in the eighth, 7-7.

In the bottom of the ninth, the Cardinals loaded the bases.

And then it was Carver's turn to step up to bat.

The crowd in the stadium went *insane.*

"I'm going deaf!" Mia shrieked. But she was jumping up and down, like everyone else.

If the Yankees walked Carver now, they would force in a run and give up Game 6. They would lose the whole Series. So walking Carver to first was no longer an option.

I gazed around at the packed stadium—all of these people so ravenous to see Carver hit—but when he stepped up to bat, he wasn't smiling. He looked tense. He set his feet, prepared for his swing, and I held my breath. A hush fell over the crowd.

First pitch: struck foul. Strike one.

Second pitch: he missed. *Missed.* Strike two.

I bit my lip. *Come on, Carver. You can do this.*

Third pitch: he didn't swing. Ball one.

Fourth pitch was wide. Ball two.

The Grizz would have swung at those pitches. The fact that he didn't told me something was wrong.

Clarissa stepped around her children and handed me a half-sheet of poster board. "If you want to say something to him," she said, "now's the time." She waved a hand toward the video camera closest to us, and put a marker in my hand. "Send him a message, they'll put it up on the screen."

I glanced at the poster board, and returned my gaze to the field.

The pitcher stood on the mound with the catcher, conducting a conference. Carver was outside the box, flexing his shoulders and staring at the ground. He still wasn't smiling. I couldn't understand what was wrong.

Clarissa nudged my arm. "He might not come up to bat again," she said. "If you're going to write anything, do it now."

I took a seat, propped the poster board on my lap, and uncapped the marker. My hand shook. I couldn't think what to say.

Why was Carver so tense? This was his moment. This was what he'd been waiting for.

I glanced around at the kids and Clarissa, and then at Emma and Steve, and I remembered something Steve told me. *After the accident, Carver didn't even play ball again for a month—and this was in July, in the middle of the season. There's stuff online that says he cost the Yankees their bid for the postseason that year. Kind of unfair, don't you think, to blame something like that on one guy?*

And here he was five years later, playing in the World Series—with a chance to win the game against his old team—but he'd missed a pitch and he wasn't smiling at all. Something had unraveled inside him. He looked like he was fighting himself.

I gripped my right hand until it stopped shaking. Then I wrote my message for Carver, stood on my chair, and held up the poster.

Clarissa was right—as soon as I held up my sign, the cameras found me. A few seconds later, I went up on the screen.

I could read my print clearly: *They're here with you, Carver.*

As the crowd read those words, a ripple of energy pushed through the stadium. There wasn't a person here today who couldn't understand what my sign meant. Carver's story belonged to anyone who watched him play, or listened to the radio, or followed baseball in the papers. When Ben and Audrey had died, Carver had not been alone in his grief. His fans had all mourned, because people identify with their heroes. And when Carver stopped hitting, his fans felt his pain.

But they were all here with him now—all the people who loved him, even Audrey and Ben—and Carver needed to remember why he wanted to play.

He wasn't looking at the screen though. Not until Matt whistled and gestured with his chin, and then Carver glanced up.

I watched him read my sign, and then he turned and scanned the crowd. I knew the instant he spotted me in all that commotion and noise. I could tell he was smiling, though we were far enough apart that I could barely make out his features.

The cameras put him on the screen though—and then I could see his smile. He ducked his head for a moment, like he was suddenly shy. But as he strolled back to the box and called something out to his teammates, he grinned like the devil.

The catcher returned to home plate. Carver prepared for his swing.

Fifth pitch was a fastball: struck foul.

Sixth pitch was a changeup: another foul.

Seventh pitch hit the dirt at the plate. Ball three.

The fans were screaming so loud. The runners waited on base. The scoreboard still showed the tie game, 7-7. The pitcher kicked the dirt, gripped the ball. Held the fate of the game in his hand.

Eighth pitch was a curveball. The pitcher's best curveball.

The pitch Carver must have guessed would be coming, because his swing was perfection.

Crack. And this hit wasn't foul.

Carver sent the ball over right field, somewhere into the stands, and the scoreboard flashed a new tally: 11-7. The Cardinals had just won the World Series.

Fireworks lit the sky, and people grabbed me—grizzlies, fans—they hugged me and yelled, "God bless you, girl!" and kissed my cheeks. The attention shocked me, almost frightened me, and I struggled to break away. I wanted to run to the field to see Carver.

By the time I was free, and leaping down the steps, Carver had made it to home. The Cardinals were all grouped together on the field, jumping and cheering. As I dropped to the grass, so many people were rushing the diamond—too many for security to stop. Some of them were pushing and shoving, and I darted around them as I wove through the crowd.

The fireworks were still going off. I arrived near home plate, and the team was cheering so loudly, the sound made me breathless. Then Carver broke loose from the chaos.

He ran and grabbed me, so happy he had tears in his eyes.

"I love you," he said. "I love you so much."

I hugged him and kissed him. "I love you, Carver."

People were surging around us—teammates and fans and reporters and cameramen… and amidst the confusion, the kids arrived, and Carver's boys, and Clarissa with her family, and their parents, and Emma and Steve. The fireworks kept going off, and I stood on the diamond with Carver, laughing and so happy I felt breathless. Microphones were held up, cameras were flashing, and before Carver started answering questions, he caught my gaze and grinned like the devil.

***

Hours later—after our families went home, after the interviews finished, after the stadium emptied—Carver was still in his uniform, and we walked out to center field.

The overhead lights were still on. But the ballpark was silent.

I glanced up at the sky and said, "This is just like my dream."

Carver caught my gaze. "You had a dream about this?"

I giggled. "Sort of. You were wearing your uniform. But it was just you and me on the diamond. Waiting for something."

"What something?" he asked.

"I never found out," I sighed. "I woke up."

Carver glanced up at the huge TV monitor, which was black now, and sent me a smile.

"You know, Carver… I think I'm ready now."

"To fly to Tahiti?" he asked.

I laughed, and he hugged me. I searched his face and touched his lips. "Ready for us," I said softly.

He glanced down at his chest and put a hand in his jersey, reaching for something. He had to unfasten the clasp of his pocket before whatever it was would come loose.

Then he knelt in front of me, kissed both my hands, and asked, "Mary Jane, will you marry me?"

I dropped to my knees and embraced him. "I will, Carver. I will."

He opened his hand and held out a ring. It looked so tiny in the massive palm of his hand.

"You were carrying that with you?" I asked. "This whole time?"

"Since August," he said. "The day I flew back to see you— that was when I started keeping it with me."

He slipped the ring on, and I thought it was perfect. Not flashy or gaudy, but exquisitely lovely.

I wrapped my arms around Carver and kissed him again. "It's a beautiful ring, Carver," and I curled up against him.

We sat on the grass a long time, holding hands.

"I couldn't have done it without you," he said.

"You could have," I said, and I rubbed a hand on his jaw.

He stretched out on the grass, and I rested my head on his chest. We gazed up at the sky.

"You're my hero, Mary Jane. You saved me."

"You saved me, too," I said with a smile. "You helped me start dreaming again."

As I leaned over to kiss him, I remembered I used to call myself the Old Woman Who Lived in a Shoe.

Carver would have never called himself a Prince Charming… but I knew that he was. A prince who had wandered out of his own fairy tale, and walked straight into mine.

Only instead of a white horse and carriage and a big gleaming castle, Carver had shown up with a baseball stadium and World Series tickets.

No offense to Cinderella, but I'd rather have the World Series tickets. Any day.

ACKNOWLEDGMENTS

This book went through three separate drafts and many, many days of revision in order to find its final form and Essential Book Self. I'm very grateful to all of my readers who helped me discover what that Essential Book Self would be.

My Reading Angel, April Duclos, was the first person to read *Love and Loans* and offer her amazing advice to make the story stronger. From the first draft to the final, and all the revisions in between, I give my boundless gratitude to April for sharing her insights, opinions, and extreme reader savvy so that I could make my second novel the best it could be.

My Biggest Fan, Leslie McCabe-Holm, enjoyed the first and final drafts of *Love and Loans*, and I'm so grateful to have a reader who says, "Yay!! I love this!!" no matter what I send. Not every writer is lucky enough to have a cheerleader as smart and as awesome as Leslie. She has been a bright light in the darkest days of transforming this novel.

My BFF since fourth grade, Hilary Grimm, allowed herself to be interviewed while I gathered research for this book. Hilary provided crucial information to help with pivotal scenes in the story, and I'm so incredibly thankful for her candid thoughts and advice. She also read the first draft of this novel and provided excellent feedback.

My critique group was essential in helping this book grow and get better: Adriana Arbogast, Michael Carson, and Jeremy Hellman. I'm extremely thankful for all of their insights and questions. They endured reading multiple versions of the opening chapters, a main character who caused a lot of frustration, and a plotline that was confused and incoherent. Their feedback helped me turn a pile of jumble into a novel.

Adriana Arbogast took the time to read the entire final draft, and shared detailed feedback on the problems that still remained in the book. I am incredibly grateful to her for her extra time and assistance. Her comments are genius, and she spots everything from word repeats to character flaws and plot holes. *Love and Loans* would never have found its Essential Book Self without her.

Sandra Kern read my first draft and shared praise, grammatical corrections, and advice about baseball. She is a wizard with words and sentences, and I'm incredibly lucky to have her kindness, her support, and her belief in me and my stories.

Laurel Baldwin read the first draft of *Love and Loans* and shared so many positive comments that she helped give me the drive to keep making improvements.

My sister, Laura Gillon, read the opening chapters of the first draft, read the entire second draft, and then gave me the feedback I needed to start the book's final revision. Without her comments, I would never have realized the original story's single deepest flaw, and then been inspired to write the novel again. It's amazing how one or two sentences of feedback can be a wellspring for a whole new creation, which was what happened after my sister read my second draft. I am so incredibly grateful that Laura helped me see what I needed to in order to find a better story.

I entered the opening pages of the first draft of *Love and Loans* in the 2012 Rocky Mountain Fiction Writers Colorado Gold Writing Contest, and the feedback I received from the contest judges was amazing and generous and exactly what I needed to hear. Their comments inspired me in so many ways, and the advice they shared was crucial to helping me reshape my first two chapters. I thank everyone who participates in this contest, and especially the judges who share their advice.

My friend Lori Hallford read the beginning of *Love and Loans* and found herself hooked, and her opinions helped me retool my first chapters into sentences I could be proud of.

Brandi Bowker Stacy and Wesley Stacy offered important advice on the opening chapter of my first draft. Dale and Jessica Gillon also shared insights and opinions on those initial first pages.

My longtime friend Bonnie Jacobs read the final draft of this book and shared support and encouragement, and advice about how to fix the remaining glitches.

Bethany Bachmann volunteered to read the final-*final* draft, and answered my follow-up questions to help me determine if any more edits were needed.

My brother-in-law, Lonnie Stacy, also read my final-*final* draft, and provided wonderful feedback on my use of baseball facts and terminology, and my creation of Carver Greyson's career. I am so lucky that Lonnie coaches baseball and loves the game with such passion, as his comments were funny and delightful, and his expertise put a last coat of polish on this novel.

A big thank you to Beth McMacken for creating a beautiful cover for an ebook with a very long title.

And a huge thank you to my husband, Greg Stacy, who watched the 2011 World Series with me at home, and took me to see *Moneyball* in the theater. Those two events fueled my imagination and led to this book. Greg listened to me read aloud various chapters of *Love and Loans*, listened to me talk about my characters during dinners and car rides and any other time the mood struck, and answered my questions about explosives and guns. I am so fortunate I met Greg after I graduated from college. He helps me make sure I can follow my dreams.

ABOUT THE AUTHOR

Melissa Stacy lives in Durango, Colorado. She is the author of *The Etiquette of Wolves*, a mystery novel. *Love and Students Loans and Other Big Problems* is her second book.

You may contact the author at: **the_etiquette_of_wolves@yahoo.com** or visit her webpage at **www.melissastacy.com**.

Proof

Made in the USA
Charleston, SC
17 June 2014